CANYON OF CRYSTAL

KIERSTEN MICHELE
A.J. CERNA

MAGIA BOOKS

SOMBRIA
Calao
Plaja
Llodora
Ruinedlands
Frutífere Plains
River Recto
Royo Desert
River Muerto
Pesca
Lejon
River Festo
L'Lim
Cielo
River Mied
Lake Mied
Sémpere Sea
River Sol
Attalea
Hurozon
River Arrib
Arbol
Endes Mountains

*For anyone who's ever dreamed of being a badass bruja,
and for all the readers who supported City of Mages.*

Chapter 1

Alara

Alara woke with a start, her hand reaching for the dagger tucked in her belt. It was more reassurance than protection—the blade had remained dull over the last week as they trekked through the thick cloud forest. Still, she found herself checking for it every few hours, even in the middle of the day, as they took turns sleeping.

It was a moment before she recognized what had awoken her. Runeo leaned over her, dark eyes shining in the twilight. His long dark hair hung limp around his shoulders, forgotten over the past few days. Around them, the small clearing came to life in the growing shadows. Small purple flowers had opened up along the ground, giving off a faint glowing light. It would have been beautiful if Alara had the energy to appreciate them.

"We should head out soon." Runeo's voice was a clear and commanding whisper. He stepped away without waiting for an answer, shaking Quenti and Khuna, who curled together nearby. Mitteo was already sitting up, eyes cloudy with sleep. Suri gave Lili a small shake on her shoulder and the tierren batted her hand away with an annoyed movement. Alara knew things were bad when the even-tempered Lili was showing her irritation, her hazel eyes narrowed and pale skin flushed.

Alara was too tired to do more than roll over and take in the forest around them. The trees were thick, wide trunks with a tangle of vines and moss blotting out the sky above. A contradiction of silent, constant movement settled over the trees as animals moved through the branches, somehow quieter than a whisper.

Runeo drifted around the clearing in complete silence. Even while he was in his element, surrounded by the forest, his shoulders remained slumped.

It had been a few days since Alara had heard his voice crack with grief, and she wondered what he locked behind the grim look of determination. She learned not to mention his brother Micos's name after the third day, when the word sent Runeo into a spiral that ended with him not talking for hours.

Alara stood up, trying to shake the exhaustion and ache of hunger from her bones. It didn't work, but at least her brain had stopped spinning. She couldn't blame Runeo for how he felt. Her own gut clenched with grief whenever she dwelled too long on the events that had brought them here.

A botched escape from the Haven that led to an all-out battle, assisted by the bruyas who had hidden among the ranks of the mages for decades, and a brother who was lost to their mind-cleansing—now brainwashed like the very worst within the Haven. It had all seemed so simple at the time, but Alara knew that what they'd done at the Haven would have ramifications all across Sombria. She only hoped their strange ensemble of magites, bruyas, and even one mage could make it to Arbol before they were faced with the consequences.

"Alara." Suri's voice was close to her ear and she realized everyone else was up, eyes focused on her. "Are we clear?" The sole mage of the group's tone was patient, her brown eyes ringed with dark circles, easily visible under her pale skin. Her short hair stuck up in every direction, a result of her ongoing habit of running her fingers through it when she was thinking. Or tired. Or distracted.

Alara imagined her own knotted curls didn't look much better. She gave her a halfhearted smile before closing her eyes. She reached toward her core, fumbling with the familiar threads, trying to grasp her magia with any semblance of control. A wave of cold nausea rolled through her, but she grabbed a strand of power and sent it out around her.

She searched the surrounding trees, but nothing beyond the cold absence of magia greeted her. Not even a magiaful beast was within a mile of them. Over the past week of using her mind-stalking skills to scout out a path through the forest, grasping onto this power had become almost second nature. She'd even grown to notice the magia-filled cores of the animals that lived here—a few howlers and a fruit bear so far. The forest contained more magia than even the Council likely knew.

When Alara opened her eyes again, Lili, ever the caretaker, was at her side, hands hooked under her elbow. She leaned heavily on the tierren, another wave of nausea rolling through her.

"No one for at least a mile."

Alara tried to move her weight to her own legs, but instead she nearly collapsed, her knees shaking beneath her.

"We'll head south then," Runeo said.

"We should prioritize food. It's been two days of nothing," Lili noted.

"If we cross the river, we may find more game."

"Don't you think the councilguards have planned for that?" Quenti said. "There'll be just as many problems hunting on the south side of the river."

"So, what do you recommend?" Runeo said. "That we keep hiking in circles?"

"Those circles," Lili said, "have helped us avoid councilguard confrontations thanks to Alara."

Runeo's eyes bore into the ground with a fierce intensity Alara knew too well. Perhaps it was the hunger or the exhaustion, but everyone had been on edge over the past couple of days.

It had been a week since they had fled from Cielo, and they did so with only a meager amount of supplies. The morning after their escape, they woke up with plans to cross south over the river and head into the cloud forest toward Arbol. They hadn't even broken out of the trees before they'd heard yelling and the pounding of feet.

Runeo and Khuna had climbed a nearby tree to scout out the commotion without being seen. When they dropped down from the treetops, eyes distant and panicked, Alara knew her mind-stalking abilities hadn't lied to her. A platoon of councilguards were marching down the road, spreading out along the river, preventing their most direct route home.

They'd been running non-stop since, sleeping among the trees or in hidden clearings during the day and walking at night. But no matter how many directions they tried, they remained trapped by the councilguards staked out along the road and river. The borders within Sombria were officially closed, and they were stuck on the wrong side, far from the sanctuary of Arbol—their one beacon of hope, and the one place they couldn't get to.

It's something Runeo had never forgotten. Runeo, who had pushed them to keep going beyond exhaustion upon their escape.

His face reddened, and Alara was sure he was coming to the same conclusion. "This wouldn't have been a problem if we'd just kept moving that first day," he said in a sharp whisper.

Lili placed a hand on his shoulder. "Anger will take more energy than we have."

He jerked away from her hand, but didn't speak again.

The seven of them moved silently under the darkened sky, weaving between roots and low-hanging branches, heavy with moss and vines. Even Mitteo and Suri, both raised in the Haven for much of their lives, moved with relative grace across the soft ground. Alara could almost forget that the two of them had sacrificed everything to assist her and the other bruyas. That they'd given up everything... only to stumble through the dark alongside them, fugitives to the realm of Sombria. The occasional glowing flowers and glimpses of moonlight through the thick trees helped guide their way in the darkness, but they still moved slowly. Alara kept a light touch on her magia, sending out threads ahead of them to scout out the councilguards.

In a rare stroke of luck, each of the troops they had almost stumbled upon over the last week held at least one mage for Alara to sense.

Amid this, she noticed a strange pattern emerging. In some cases, she could have sworn she was able to sense the blameless guards alongside the mages. It was a skill that was proven unreliable in the days since, so she dared not speak of it to anyone. Not yet, at least. A part of her wondered if she was turning delusional with hunger. After all, she'd never read about mind-stalkers sensing a non-magia core.

Regardless, it was something she knew to keep an eye on. If there was anything she'd learned over the past few months, it was to never brush off any aspect of her abilities, no matter how unreliable or inconvenient.

Emaru would be proud, Alara thought with a sharp pang of guilt at the memory of her guardian-turned-enemy. She didn't even know if the councilwoman had survived the battle. Had she seen the last of the woman who'd cared for her like a mother? Would she even want to see her?

Alara placed a hand on the dull-bladed dagger at her hip. She thought, not for the first time, of the core she had sensed when she'd first found it. During her watch as the others slept, she'd taken to wrapping her threads around the trinket. A few times, she thought she had felt something, a sensation not unlike what she'd felt when detecting the blameless guards. But an instant later, it was gone, the dagger just as useless as it had *always* been— save for those few times when its dulled edge mysteriously sharpened.

Okay, maybe she *was* going crazy with hunger. She needed—

"Fish!"

For a moment, Alara thought she may have spoken her own thoughts out loud, but the group had stopped and was looking at Quenti. The aguen was smiling and pointing to a small clearing up ahead. In the silence that followed her exclamation, Alara could make out the trickle of water that signified a stream.

A stream... a pond...

"Fish." Khuna didn't wait for the others, but sprang forward, her hands already outstretched. Quenti darted after her and the rest trudged ahead with all the energy potential food could muster from them.

Khuna and Quenti were already bent over the pond by the time Alara made it through to the clearing. The water was black and still in the night, its surface reflecting the light of the moon that filtered through the thick forest in a perfect mirror.

Alara knew something was wrong before she could pinpoint the root of her unease. Khuna's hand held steady above the water, eyes shut. Quenti's brows furrowed.

"I can't sense anything," Khuna said, cracking her eyes open.

"That's because there's nothing left." Quenti pointed to the edge of the pool. The moonlight was dull, and Alara used the flint she had tucked in her sleeve to light a small floating fire.

In the sudden luminescence of the flames, the shore of the small pond was visible, along with the dozens of fish that laid still and unmoving in the mud.

Looking back at the pond, Alara took in the unbroken surface of the water. Not a single bubble or ripple interrupted the mirrored reflection. The pond was empty of any life.

"What happened?" Lili's small hand covered her mouth and nose as she looked down at the dead fish.

"Mages," Suri said grimly.

"I know they've been scaring the game away, but how could they... why would they?" Lili's voice quivered. Alara wasn't sure if it was from seeing life snuffed out so unceremoniously or from them losing their first meal in days.

"We were studying new ways of fighting bruyas." Suri paused, looking apologetically at the bruyas around her. In their travels over the past week, it had been easy for Alara to forget that Suri had spent most of her life undercover as a mage. Like Alara, she'd been one of them, and that included knowledge of some of their deadliest secrets. "The air and water mages worked together. They found a way to take the air out of water sources. Kill the lake, kill the fish, kill the people that rely on them for a source of food."

"That's disgusting." Mitteo spoke for the first time that night. His voice was rough and deep. "Humans are not the only ones who rely on water sources for food and survival."

"As long as the bruyas are dead, what do they care?" Runeo said, his voice cold.

No one spoke, but they all seemed of the same mind as they continued moving, leaving behind the dead pond.

Sweat dripped down Alara's back, the forest air laying thick and humid, even as the dry season was reaching its peak. It didn't rain as they walked through the darkness of night, but the air still clung wet to every leaf, tree, and piece of clothing. Her stomach sent a sharp wave of nausea to protest its emptiness.

When they'd left the Haven, she'd allowed herself to be naïve enough to expect the travels to Arbol would be quick—that it would only be a matter of time before she could settle into her new home. Now, they were on the verge of starvation.

She hoped the others who escaped Cielo were faring better than her group.

Guilt gnawed at her chest as she eyed her companions. She was the reason they were here—the reason the network of rebels outed itself within the city of mages. Her mind spiraled. If only she hadn't been caught by trying to sneak back to the Haven... If Khuna and—Alara's mind stuttered over the images of Zinita and Micos. One dead and one lost. So much death and grief and no time to process.

She forced herself to stop the moment her thoughts tried to skim over Adelmo's face. She'd already spent the first three days on the run crying into her arms, trying to drift off to sleep rather than feel that pain. It felt like she was drowning, the weight of it pulling her down by her chest, trying to suffocate her.

But she'd locked away that piece of her in a small wooden box at the corner of her mind. There would come a day when she would have the time and energy to examine it. But not now. Now, she needed to focus on moving forward, one step at a time.

"We can't keep walking forever." Alara startled herself with her own words.

"She's right," Runeo said. "We're going to starve before we make it across the river. And none of us is in any shape to face a council-guard in a fight, which is what this may come down to."

"What, then?" Suri asked, tone dry. "We march into the next town and ask nicely for some roasted cuy?" Alara tried not to think too hard about the fact that the lifelong spy in the group seemed as helpless as Alara felt.

"El'dyo, that doesn't sound half bad," Mitteo said. The week in the woods had thinned the boy's body, chiseling away at some of the roundness, but it left him looking gaunt rather than fit. The perpetual dark rings beneath his eyes and the lank dark hair didn't help the look.

"I was thinking more sneaking and thieving," Runeo said, ignoring Mitteo's comment.

Alara rubbed her fingers along the raised skin of her scar on the side of her neck. They had been heading west over the last few days, along the river and toward the sea. That meant that they were approaching the city that hugged the coast of Sombria.

"Hurazon isn't far from here," she said, almost absently.

Quenti flinched at the name of her home town, eyes finding Alara's in the darkness. "No."

"Your dad—"

"Is just as likely to give us supplies as he is to throw us at the councilguards himself."

Runeo watched the exchange, but seemed to ignore any subtext he might have heard. "It's settled. We're going to Hurazon to resupply."

Quenti opened her mouth to respond, but it was Alara that spoke first. "It's hardly settled. Give us a moment, will you?"

Runeo looked just as taken aback as Quenti did as Alara pulled the girl away from the others.

"I know it's not ideal, but Runeo has a point," Alara said in a whisper.

Quenti leaned against a tree. Her eyes were black spots in the darkness, but they bored into Alara all the same.

"It's a stupid plan. Papa was practically dancing as he packed my bags when you... when Emaru caught me."

Alara flinched at Quenti's correction. It wasn't a correction; it was a lie to make Alara feel less guilty for being the reason Quenti was ever dragged into any of this in the first place.

She was the one who had sensed Quenti's abilities in that early morning a million years ago. She was the one who blurted them out. She was the one who led Quenti into the Haven, kick-starting the series of events that resulted in them spearheading an escape from the very place Alara called home.

If it wasn't for Alara, none of this would have happened.

"His daughter had magia," Alara said. "He was thrilled, like most parents are." She met Quenti's lie with one of her own.

Quenti's look was deadpan. "Even if I believed that, he wouldn't be excited to see me begging at his door as a fugitive."

"Then maybe we don't knock," Alara said slowly.

"Okay..." Quenti narrowed her eyes.

"We need supplies. But Suri's right. We can't just march into town and buy what we need, but we can steal them. And you know Hurazon better than any of us. Besides, don't you want to shove it in his blameless face?"

"He's right, though, isn't he?"

"Who? Your dad?"

"No. Runeo," Quenti said. "This is the only way. And I can't be the reason why we die in the middle of the forest. I just... need a second."

Quenti closed her eyes and her shallow breaths grew deep. Alara wondered if, for a moment she'd fallen asleep when her soft voice broke the silence. "I hate this."

Alara fought her instinct to respond immediately, but let the comment linger in the air.

"I hate the way he makes me feel," Quenti said. "Even now. After all this."

"That's parents for you, eh?" Alara said, giving a sigh of empathy.

Alara recognized the shame the girl felt. It was the same shame Alara had whenever she put any thought into how small Emaru made her feel. She grasped Quenti's arm. "Cheers to shitty parents," Alara said.

Alara and Quenti returned to the clearing to see their five companions huddled and deep in conversation.

"Let's do it. Let's go to Hurazon," Quenti said. Khuna moved forward and wrapped her hand around the other girl's. "And I think... I think I know of something else we can steal to help."

Chapter 2

Quenti

It took three hundred and five steps for Quenti to regret agreeing to their plan. For the first time in days, the twisting in her stomach was not from hunger. Each passing moment, dread crept up her spine higher, like a vine ready to choke her.

This put her at odds with the rest of the group, who were brighter than they'd been for days. They were walking with purpose, finally having an end goal that didn't involve just *avoiding capture.* It was almost contagious.

Almost.

Khuna walked beside her—or more accurately, Quenti walked beside Khuna. She hadn't left her girlfriend's side since their near escape from the Haven. She still had nightmares of Khuna stuck on the other side of the prison bars, pallid and weak. Every time, Quenti was unable to reach her. She'd wake up, heart pounding, arms reaching for Khuna lying beside her. Khuna was a good few inches shorter than Quenti, but she found herself leaning into the bruya, as if she might be able to support the weight of the world on her shoulders.

For her part, Khuna accepted Quenti's newfound clinginess and gave in without question. She'd curl her smaller body around Quenti when they slept on the ground, hand running through her tangled curls. Quenti couldn't tell if it was out of a sense of obligation, but she didn't question it.

She'd spent years dreaming of such things when she was still living in Hurazon under her father's thumb. Even before her mother had died, she'd hoped to run away to find the magiaful place Khuna called home. After—when it was just her and her father—the dream of leaving was the only thing that had kept her sane.

"You okay?" Khuna's soft voice brought Quenti out of her reverie. It took her a moment to realize Khuna had slowed her pace, leaving them several yards behind the rest of the group.

A curl of hair had fallen loose in her face and Quenti reached to tuck it back behind her ear without thinking. Despite the weeks without a shower, Khuna's hair managed to look perfectly disheveled, the few longer strands almost curling in the humidity. She felt like a grimy mess standing next to her.

"Quenti?"

"Yeah. Yes. Just lost in thought, I guess," she answered, moving once more, not wanting to lose the others. As they walked, Khuna took Quenti's hand in her own and ran her thumb along the sensitive skin.

"We don't have to seek him out, you know?" she said.

Quenti only nodded, not trusting her voice. Khuna had seen her cry before. In fact, she'd seen her cry when her mother died, but now wasn't the time to show weakness. That's all emotions were. She had learned that at an early age.

Her father had never tolerated sadness or anger—unless it was his own. Even her mother just brushed her tears away and whispered for her to be strong.

"Or, if you want, I could send an arrow through the old man's throat," Khuna continued.

Quenti laughed at this with only the slightest twinge of guilt. "I'd just be happy if I never saw him again."

They fell into an uneasy silence, slinking through the night. The moon had set, leaving behind only shadow, and day was still hours away, but they needed to execute the first step of their plan—which was perhaps the craziest one: find a group of councilguards.

Quenti was still coping with the fact that they'd spent a week avoiding the people they now needed to hunt down. It had to be the hunger and exhaustion. Why else would they think this was a good idea?

It was Alara who first raised her arm and stopped their quiet march an hour later. Her eyes remained closed for several long seconds before she turned to the rest of them.

"Seven at least," she said. "Just under a mile away. Most of them are still. Probably sleeping. At least two are pacing—probably guarding the camp."

"We'll need to move quieter from here on out," Runeo said. "No sounds."

Alara shot him a deadpan look, which brought a smirk to Quenti's face.

"How do we know there isn't a mind-stalker among them?" Lili said, voice edged with apprehension.

Alara shook her head, but it was Suri who answered. "Even if there is, mind-stalkers powerful enough to sense others past a half mile are rare, even in the Haven." She gave a pointed look at Alara. "As long as we stay out of range until we want them to sense us, we should be okay."

"We'll be in the trees. If they approach, we'll need to be ready to move," Runeo noted.

"Okay," Quenti said. "But not all of us can just walk along the tree line without breaking our necks."

"Then we hope for the best," Lili said with a genuine optimism that only she could manage without coming off as sarcastic.

Quenti awoke in the pink light of dawn and a soft nudge against her thigh. She didn't even jerk as she came to, legs straddling the large branch she perched on. Her body had adjusted to waking up a hundred feet from the ground over the last week. At least the thick moss that covered the trees cushioned the precarious bed. With a nod to Runeo, who had woken her up, she loosened the knot of rope that secured her to the tree trunk and passed it to Khuna, who tucked the rope into the rucksack she carried.

Runeo and Lili stood a few feet away, balanced on a thick branch. In stark contrast, Suri and Mitteo huddled around the trunk, knuckles white and shoulders tense as they sat wide-eyed and anxious among the foliage.

Alara was awake now too and had slipped over to where Runeo and Lili stood. She didn't move with the grace of the bruyas, but Quenti was envious of her confidence. It had only been a few weeks ago that Quenti was the one teaching Alara how to survive the cloud forest, but now, with her memories returned, the former magite had gained a sense of herself Quenti hadn't seen before.

Everyone looked exhausted, dark circles stark against sallow skin, having only had a couple hours rest after they located the council-guard camp. While they'd already discussed the plan the night before, Quenti still ran through the steps in her mind, using it as a mantra to calm her stammering heart.

They tied their supplies to the tree, leaving Suri and Khuna behind as they maneuvered their way down closer to the forest floor.

It was Mitteo and Quenti who finished the journey to the ground, landing on shaky legs.

Quenti could just make out narrow streams of color darting through the branches above them as Alara, Runeo, and Lili slinked through the trees. She and Mitteo were no longer tasked with staying silent—that wasn't the point at all.

Yet, while their entire purpose was to be distracting and loud—obnoxious, even—neither of them could find a topic to talk about. It's not like they had a lot in common to begin with. So, instead of speaking, they both took every opportunity to snap the dried out branches scattered along the forest floor.

They were the bait—a fact Khuna was not happy about. Quenti wasn't thrilled about it either, but they were the only two with decent-looking enough magite clothing. At least with them, any councilguard they stumbled into wouldn't shoot them on sight. Hopefully.

Once Runeo and Lili had gone over their plan, even Khuna couldn't argue the logic. It had still taken a lot of convincing to get Khuna to stay behind with Suri to guard their supplies. The fewer people they had trampling along the forest floor, the better.

It was ten long minutes before Alara let out two short hoots. Quenti's heart flew into her throat. That meant two councilguards were on their way toward them. The plan was working.

"Second step in this stupid plan—don't die," Mitteo whispered under his breath beside her.

"My favorite step," Quenti agreed.

She heard the first snap of a branch in the distance when five strangled hoots echoed above them.

Five councilguards.

"Oh, for Sol's sake," Quenti cursed, fighting the urge to grab at her empty belt.

If they see weapons, they'll shoot before you can even draw them,

Alara had said with a shrug the night before as she took Quenti's dagger and bolas.

All they could do was wait.

Twenty hours later, by Quenti's estimate, five councilguards came into view a few yards away, two spears and three arrows pointed at the duo.

"Hi," Mitteo said with an awkward wave.

The lead councilguard's eyebrows furrowed together in almost comical confusion. But no one had time to reply. With a rustling from above, Lili descended from the trees, slamming onto the shoulders of one of the guards. To his credit, the guard didn't hit the forest floor immediately. Lili scrambled to take off his helmet, pressing her fingers to his temples until he keeled over into the soft earth. Chaos erupted as Alara and Runeo jumped down to join the fray.

Quenti dodged a flying arrow, still weaponless, and reached for the thread inside, summoning her powers. Thousands of dewdrops rose from the surrounding vegetation and coalesced into a thick cloud around a guard's face.

He was quick to pull his head from the cloud, but it distracted him long enough for Alara to sink a dagger into the flesh of his thigh. He cursed as he went down and roots sprung up to wrap over his chest.

Mitteo may have been standing back from the fray, but his hands blurred in a series of complex motions as roots shot up from the ground and snagged at the enemy's legs. With another whip of his wrist, a root lashed at a female councilguard's knees at the same moment a vine flew down and twisted around her neck. She grabbed at her throat as it pulled tighter.

Quenti watched, officially impressed.

Runeo and Lili dealt with two councilguards of their own, one of which was an earth mage, himself. Every time Lili attempted to trip up the guards, the earth mage would push the roots back in the bruya's direction. Runeo did what he did best, sparring with the blameless guard with a spear he had stolen from another fallen enemy, accenting each blow with a rush of air. Alara grabbed a spear of her own and jumped into the brawl.

Quenti noted a fallen bow on the ground by her feet and snatched it up, searching the ground for an arrow before one appeared in front of her face. She gave Mitteo a smile and plucked it from his hand, notching it and aiming before she had a moment to question herself.

The arrow rooted itself in the neck of the earth mage, and he collapsed with a gurgled gasp.

"El'dyo, that was amazing!" Mitteo said next to her.

"I was aiming for his legs," Quenti said between clenched teeth. She wasn't sure what to make of the numb indifference at the realization she'd killed someone.

The last councilguard's eyes widened as he noticed the odds shift. With a loud shout, he turned away toward the camp. Quenti looked around, holding the useless bow in her hands, having half a mind to throw it at the soldier's head. But it was Mitteo who acted first. The large branch of a tree gave a sharp creak as it swiped toward them, hitting the man in the chest and sending him sprawling.

Lili leaped forward and placed a hand on his temples, his muscles loosening as he fell unconscious.

The five of them stood panting, surveying the damage. One councilguard was dead, two unconscious, and two still struggling, which Lili rectified with a touch of her hand.

And then there was silence.

Alara had her eyes closed, shoulders tense. They all watched as she crouched, unmoving. It was several long moments before her shoulders dropped and she took a deep breath.

"No one heard," she said. "No one's headed our way."

They all sighed and went to work, removing the uniforms and

weapons from the fallen guards. Much to Quenti's chagrin, the black tunic of the councilguard she had killed was stained with his blood, but she stole his bolas and leather vest all the same.

No time for weakness now.

When all said and done, they came out with four uniforms—two more than they had planned for—and a new store of weapons. Alara found a small pouch of coca leaves and stiff bread on one of the councilguard's belts. The team devoured the bread in moments and passed the leaves between them to chew.

Quenti relished the moment of respite the leaves gave her. The inside of her mouth grew numb, and the nausea that had been eating away at her insides fell away. She knew the feeling wouldn't last, but she promised herself that she'd enjoy it while it did.

Now, their plan depended on speed and stealth, though they intentionally left behind a smear of footprints along the way. When they neared Khuna and Suri, they found a dry patch of ground, and Runeo helped the rest of the team back into the trees. To the councilguards, it would be as though their quarry had evaporated into thin air.

The sky was lit by the bright light of sunrise as they made it back to Khuna and Suri. The two looked pale, but relieved.

"Onward?" Quenti asked, flourishing the spear she used as a balance.

Alara smirked, looking all too smug in the councilguard uniform she'd probably been wanting to wear since she was seven. "To Hurazon."

CHAPTER 3

QUENTI

The group split up in the forest outside of town, not wanting to be seen together—councilguards and magites. They shuffled outfits as best they could, leaving Khuna, Quenti, and Suri dressed in haphazard tunics and trousers, and the other four in complete stolen councilguard garb.

Runeo looked especially uncomfortable in the tight vest and leather boots as he pulled at the neck of his black tunic. "How do they even fight in these tight clothes?"

"Based on my experience, perfectly fine," Alara said, voice peevish. "So, keep your head down and stop looking so uncomfortable."

"The dock is the second from the last one on the bay, toward the river," Quenti told the group, ignoring Alara's back-and-forth with Runeo. "Look for a blue boat with white sails. Khuna, Suri, and I will have it ready when you all get there."

Mittco, Lili, Runeo and Alara gave hesitant acknowledgements, buzzing with anxiety and exhaustion in equal measures. They were too wan and lackluster in their appearances to be playing councilguards. Quenti hoped no one would notice. Out here near the edge of Sombria, the Council and their guards were more feared than honored, avoided rather than fawned over. They could use that to their advantage.

Following a series of nods, they all went their separate ways, footsteps silent.

Quenti let out an anxious sigh. Her resolve diminished with each passing moment. She was almost to the point where she didn't want to do this at all, let alone in the daytime.

Her chest thrummed as she had felt the familiarity of the forest around Hurazon creep under her skin. Khuna read the change in her body and placed a calming hand on Quenti's arm as they hiked. She knew more about Quenti's family than anyone. She'd been the shoulder Quenti cried on for years before all of this. But Quenti couldn't help but feel that Khuna would never truly understand her —not when she had two loving parents waiting for her back in Arbol.

"Blue boat, white sails," Suri repeated under her breath as they circled the edge of the town toward the docks. They broke through the thinning forest and onto a small path. The houses here were worn down—eaten away by the salty air. No one lived here. Instead, the buildings stored fishing supplies for men who owned boats. The poorer villagers in town didn't have that kind of money, so many rented from the men who owned these buildings, paying them with their earnings at sea. More often than not, the arrangement led to generations of servitude that one could never escape.

It had been a point of pride to Quenti's father that he'd scraped enough together to purchase a vessel of his own—a move that brought him freedom. It would make it feel that much better when she took it away from him.

As Quenti looked out at the horizon, she could just make out the small ridge of land that encompassed the bay. Past that was open sea. When she was younger, before she knew Khuna, she dreamed of stealing his boat and running away. Just her and Mama. The thought brought a sharp pain to her throat, and she focused back on the docks.

"There," she said. The fishing boat rocked gently as the breeze sent ripples across the bay. The sails were folded up, but the distinct bright blue of its hull was unmistakable against the murky water. It looked as orderly as ever. He always had loved that boat more than anything else.

Quenti scanned the dock. There was only one man preparing his own vessel, and a few lonely boats rocking in place. The others were likely already gone, engaging in longer fishing expeditions out on the Sempere Sea. Her father was never one of those men. His boat was small, only large enough to handle the smoother waters of the bay. She supposed she was lucky. Every vessel not prepping for a long haul was already out, reaping the benefits of an early morning. Nothing could convince Papa to get out of bed before late morning—not even a better fishing day.

Then again, Quenti had never known her father very well.

"El'dyo, bless me. It's really you." The voice sent a shock through her. They were just a few yards from the boat, the wood of the docks swaying under their feet.

"Hi, Papa," Quenti said, voice steady. That's all she could choke out as she saw him, standing on the dock, eyes shining with an emotion she couldn't wholly read. Her body tensed and she could feel the apprehension of Suri and Khuna on either side of her.

Before her brain had time to react, her father's arms were wrapped around her, fingers tangling in her curls as he pressed her to his chest.

"There were rumors of a fight and magites dying up there in the

Haven," he said, voice shaky. Who was this man? "And I thought to myself: that's it, my Quenti is gone. It would've been all my fault. I knew I had done it, sending you off like that." His voice was thick and deep. Out of habit, she smelled his breath with a deep inhale; it smelled of tea and spices—not ferment.

This wasn't the father she left behind. She thought if she saw him again, she'd scream at him. Hit him. Instead, she wrapped her arms around his broad shoulders. She held them for only a brief moment before she pulled back.

He gave her a warm smile, eyes shining and nose red. He suddenly seemed to register the other two women she was standing with.

"What are you doing here?" His eyes didn't narrow, but she heard the sudden confusion in his voice.

"We're on a mission with the councilguards," Suri said. "Inspecting the security of the coast, so we can't stay long." Her words were clear, without even a pause to suggest she was lying.

"You'll have to stay for a bit."

"We really can't go off mission," Khuna cut in, her voice a bit sharper than Suri's.

"Nonsense, even mages need to eat!" Her father turned. "Xavier!"

A young boy was running toward them before Quenti could say anything else. His skin was dark from the sun, hair cropped close along his ears. A red birthmark stood out on his face, covering nearly half its length. His eyes were large and wide as they flickered toward Quenti and her companions.

She could see it. The familiar spark of fear all villagers had when faced with a magia user. The same fear that Quenti had spent her life dreading.

Quenti clenched her teeth.

Her father leaned down and spoke to the young boy. His voice was low, and she couldn't make out their words from where she stood. A small shiver of dread creeped up her spine as she watched the exchange. Then the boy ran back the way he came, small legs moving fast.

"And don't you dare leave the fire unattended or I'll have your hide," her father called after the boy—a flash of the papa she knew.

"We truly can't stay," Quenti said.

The man shook his head. "I won't have that. Who knows when I'll see you next. Besides, you look like you can use some more meat on your bones. What do they even feed you up there?" He reached for her and ran a calloused hand across her cheek. "Please stay, miya."

Chapter 4

Alara

All eyes turned to Alara, Runeo, Mitteo, and Lili as they walked into the small tienda at the town's center. A hush settled into the room. Then, just as quickly, most of the villagers looked away, gazes skirting the dirt floor or returning to their respective companions. Only a small child gripping the hand of her mother remained wide-eyed and staring as Alara walked forward.

"We need supplies for travel." Her voice was sharp, and she didn't meet the seller's eye behind the small counter.

"We have options," the shop owner said, his voice clipped and reserved. "Do you have coin?"

Alara tossed down the few coppers they'd nicked from the councilguards.

"We need two pounds of quinoa, two dozen tortillas, three pounds of dried beans, and some jerky, if you have any." She tried to sound the right mixture of bored and angry—something every councilguard she knew had mastered.

The man's eyes narrowed, and she saw a suppressed sneer twitch the corner of his lips. But he said nothing as he turned and started scooping the supplies into small burlap bags. Alara suppressed her own sigh of relief. She knew the villagers wouldn't go against a group of councilguards, but she also wasn't sure how far they could press their luck.

"You with the others who were just in?"

"What others?" Alara asked, distracted. She was watching Lili, whose wide-eyed stares were a bit too suspicious for her liking. Runeo noticed her gaze and gave Lili a sharp jab in the side.

"The other councilguards that passed through earlier today."

Alara turned back just in time to see him place their food on the counter.

"There are a lot of us spread out." She gave a half-hearted shrug, trying not to let her tension show. "Not sure if you've heard, but we're looking for a band of wanted bruyas and traitors. Must be another group already passed by."

The seller shook his head. "Not passed by. They're staying in town just down the way. At a small inn."

"Eating poor Pilar out of house and home over there," one of the other patrons said with a disapproving grunt, "and barely paying her nothing." His partner's eyes widened at the comment and pulled him out of the doorway without a backward glance. They'd expected her to be offended by the comment as a fellow councilguard, but she couldn't help but have a twinge of pity for them. Pity for them, and shame for herself. Ever since her own run-in with the councilguards outside of Arbol, where she saw their treatment of others firsthand, her reverence for them had plummeted.

"We didn't know anyone was stationed here," Mitteo cut in. "Perhaps we should move on, then. Keep heading south."

"Yeah, well, one of the traitors from the Haven used to live here, see?" The seller leaned over the counter, voicing a whisper so loud Alara knew everyone else could hear it too. In his excitement at spreading some gossip, he'd forgotten who he was talking to. "The witch's dad still lives here, just across town. He packed her up just this year. Sent her up to the Haven with the rest of the freaks. Though she made a right awful mess of things pretty quickly, it seems."

"That's what magia does for you," someone piped in from the corner. "We'd be better off without 'em."

Alara felt Runeo tense up beside her. Her own throat tightened. There had always been distrust among the blameless for those with magia—but to hear it spoken out loud so casually... and in front of someone wearing the garb of a mage councilguard. There was a confidence in it that didn't bode well. Even as recently as a few months back, she couldn't imagine hearing villagers speaking this way, though whether or not it had to do with Emaru's presence, she didn't know.

"Thank you for the food," Lili spoke first, grabbing what she could from the counter. "Looks like we should go check in with the rest of our crew." Mitteo took the rest and sidled to the exit.

When the faded curtain that covered the tienda doorway swung closed behind them, Alara finally took a breath.

"That was enlightening," Runeo ground out beside her.

She was about to comment when a flash of movement caught her eye. A small boy with a large red mark across his face slipped into the building a few doors down, only to emerge a few seconds later with an entourage of councilguards.

Mitteo moved first, grabbing Lili's arm and pulling her into the shadows between the tienda and another stone building. Runeo and Alara followed suit, eyes following the guards as they rushed by, completely oblivious to the group in the shadows.

Alara's heart stuttered, and she tasted copper on her tongue. They were headed directly to the docks—toward Quenti and the others.

CHAPTER 5

QUENTI

Quenti pulled away from the touch of her father's hand against her cheek. His eyes were bright, his face cleanly shaved. Studying him up close, he looked better now than he had in years. Better even than when her mother had been alive.

This was the man she'd always wanted. The father she'd prayed to Sol and El'dyo for every time her abilities had been accidentally revealed. On five separate occasions, she had let slip her secret. Once to the neighbor, once to another young boy in the village, and three times to her father. Each time, her mother made the problem disappear with a simple cleansing of their minds.

Three times she had watched her father's face twist into a seething hatred as he cursed her, denouncing magia as a disgusting scourge on Sombria. Three times he had told her she was no daughter to him. Three times, Mama had erased any trace of those words from his memory.

After each incident, it became harder for Quenti to see the man as her father. Mama'd offered to cleanse her own memories of incidents, but Quenti always refused. As painful as it was, she refused to live in ignorance of who her father truly was.

And this man who stood in front of her? No, this was a lie. An illusion. A deliberate deception.

Quenti took another step back, heart tight in her chest. "Where did you send that boy?"

"He's preparing the cooking fire and table," the man said. "You'll stay for a meal. You must."

Her stomach turned to lead. Her father had never hosted a guest in his life. He never even managed to cook dinner after Mama had died, leaving such trivialities to his daughter.

Quenti scanned the docks. There was only one older man down the way, distracted with readying his own boat. Khuna and Suri still stood behind her, waiting for a sign of what to do.

She let out a curse, looking toward where the rest of the town sat, where Alara and the others had headed. *Why were they taking so long*?

"This plan sucks," Quenti said. Without thinking, she pulled at the bay behind her with the threads of her magia, bringing an enormous bubble of water between them. Three times she had hoped for something better from her father, and every time he'd disappointed her. She was smarter now.

The greasy-haired man stumbled back with a small yelp, his face draining of color. Any pretense dropped, and she saw the familiar flicker of disgust there. But that wasn't all.

"You're afraid of me, aren't you?" she said. "Your own blood is standing in front of you, and you're scared."

"Quenti, what're you doing?" Khuna's voice was strained behind her, and a soft hand landed on her shoulder.

"They'll know we're here by now," Quenti said. "He sent that boy to tell someone."

"Then we need to leave quickly." Khuna's voice was infuriatingly calm and soft in her ear. "Hurting him won't help us."

"But it'll help me."

"It won't make you feel any better."

"Won't it?"

Quenti turned back to her father, whose eyes followed the bubble hovering between them, hardly a glance spared in her direction. His stance was crouched, hands thrown up in submission. But the disgust was still written clear in his features.

Her lip curled in a sneer. "You have no idea what you've done to me over the years," she said. "That's the sickening part. You've known before what I could do. Did you know that? You caught me when I was little. You found out again just last year."

Her father's eyes narrowed.

"You don't believe me," Quenti smiled, happy to shatter his world. "You don't remember. Mama made sure of that."

"You've gone magia crazy," her father said. "You aren't making sense. I'd hoped the Council could help you, but they've only further stoked your curse."

"Curse?" Quenti's laugh was sharp and cold. "You didn't even know your own wife had magia. All that hatred spewed, and you were living under a roof with two magia users. Two *bruyas*."

Something seemed to strike him then. Perhaps clarity.

"Exactly. Every time you caught me, *Mama* cleansed it from your mind. But never mine. I remember every curse and kick and beating. I remember every time you called my abilities a curse. Well, at least you're consistent."

"You deserve whatever the councilguards have coming for you." His voice was acid, and it washed over Quenti. "Your mother's lucky she's dead already. If what you're saying is true, she deserves worse than what she got for her part in all of this. That lying—"

Something snapped inside of Quenti. Her hands twitched, and

the bubble of water covered her father's face, choking off his sentence before he could finish. Her magia, usually a cool rush, felt like ice in her veins. It poured through her, blood singing with power. She directed every ounce of hatred and fear and anger at him, flowing out in threads.

Khuna yelled something beside her, but her roaring blood shut out her voice. All she could hear were her father's gurgling chokes.

In that moment, she knew. *She could do this.* She could kill him. So easily, and without remorse. It felt... good.

And then a sharp jab to her ribs and a spin of her body wrenched her back to reality. Khuna held her shoulders, eyes two inches from her face.

"Why—" Quenti pulled herself away from the other girl. But then she saw the movement a few yards away and registered that Khuna was pointing and motioning. There was a group in black running toward them. A group of councilguards.

It took Quenti's hatred-addled mind a moment to realize that it wasn't Alara or the others. She didn't recognize any of the faces, but she knew the black uniform and the lack of markings indicating there wasn't a single mage among them.

A growl erupted from Quenti's throat, and she launched herself forward, water whipping around her.

She left the prone body of her father on the dirt behind, chest rising and falling in uneasy gasps.

CHAPTER 6

ALARA

Alara and the rest followed behind the true councilguards at a safe distance, not wanting to engage the group unless they needed to. By the time they turned the corner toward the docks, Alara was met with the sight of Quenti, who was wild-eyed, foolishly taking on two councilguards alone.

Behind her, Khuna and Suri fought off another two. While Khuna was a trained fighter and more than holding her own against the male councilguard, Suri was clearly undertrained and over-whelmed. She'd been a researcher at the Haven, not a warrior. She blocked blow after blow without returning a single attack, face draining of color as she fumbled back a few steps.

It was Runeo who jumped into action first, sending a blast of wind at her opponent's back and throwing him to the ground.

"Get the supplies to the boat!" Alara snapped at Mitteo and Lili as she darted toward Quenti, who danced around, hair wild and water swirling in quick strikes at the guards.

She wasn't defending herself. She was attacking. There was a look in her eyes that Alara was sure she had herself just a week ago when she was ready to kill Emaru.

She sent a small flame to catch on the sleeve of the closest councilguard to her. The man stumbled back, eyes catching on Alara. She smirked as he turned his attention to her.

He swung his spear down toward her shoulder, but she dodged to the right at the last moment, snatching the club from her belt and catching his side and knees in two quick blows. He went down and she struck his temple—just hard enough to disorient him for a few minutes.

Quenti had the other guard on his knees, water wrapped tightly around his throat and face, following every movement as he tried to bat it away or shake his head free. She wasn't just trying to kill him— she was making sure it hurt.

"Quenti, stop! It's over," Alara said, voice high.

The other girl didn't move or even give any indication that she had heard her. It was Khuna, in the end, with a soft hand on Quenti's shoulder and a whisper in her ear, that got her to back down. Water splashed onto the stone path as she released her powers, shoulders slumping forward in exhaustion. The councilguard lay on the ground, unmoving. None of them bothered to check his pulse.

"The boat," Alara said. Just as much to remind herself of what this all was for. "We need to get to the boat."

"It's just down—" Quenti started, voice scratchy with use, but she didn't get to finish her thought.

The vessel at the end of the dock was engulfed in flames. The man Alara recognized as Quenti's dad stood nearby, a look of glee on his pasty face. She saw the torch in his hand as he stepped away from the flames that now threatened to spread to the docks. Mitteo and Lili stood, supplies tossed at their feet. Mitteo had his hands raised in a clear threat, but on the small dock, there was little the two tierrens could do.

Alara caught a weak thread of magia and pulled at the flames, only managing to put out a single sail. A second later, it was quickly engulfed again. Her heart lurched in frustration and the thread of magia still connected to the boat sent the fire dancing higher. She let go of her magia with a start. After all this time, she still couldn't control it fully.

The others had gathered around Alara, standing in a semi-circle, all eyes on Quenti's father where he stood on the docks.

"I would rather destroy my entire life than let you escape," he said, staring straight at his daughter. His lips were curled in distaste. "More councilguards will come and you'll be captured. I heard they weren't even taking rebel prisoners back to the Haven these days."

"Why do you even care?" Quenti asked, throat tight. "The Haven is full of mages and magia-users like me."

"For now," he sneered. "But times are changing. One day, the blameless will realize that cowering down to your kind will only lead to Sombria's ruin."

Without so much as a twitch of her face, Quenti flicked her wrist, sending a wave of water that threw her father onto the docks a few feet away. Another column of water ascended from the bay and onto the boat, the fire quenched with a hiss of steam and smoke.

The rest of them just watched as Quenti drifted over to where her father laid coughing. She looked down at him, a sneer on her face to match his own.

"I could kill you, you know. I *should* kill you."

"Quenti," Alara said in warning.

"He was always scared of magia. With good reason." Quenti's voice was soft and distant.

"We have other boats we can steal. Let's go." Alara was pleading now.

"That's what makes it all the more stupid and senseless," Quenti said. "You destroyed your own livelihood out of pure spite and it won't even stop us."

Her father didn't say anything. His eyes were narrowed, but Alara could see the flicker of fear under the surface whenever Quenti moved her hand or twitched a finger.

"I know no one wants to admit it, but Quenti's right," Runeo said. All eyes swiveled to him. He shrugged. "We should kill him and the rest of the councilguards before anyone else comes."

"Runeo." Lili's voice was sharp.

"What's the other option? Leave them here to go running into town the second we sail off? We'll be safer if he's dead. We'll be safer if they were all dead." Runeo looked to Alara. "You know I'm right."

"We can't become what the Council thinks we are. We're not murderers."

"Except we are, or have you forgotten the lives we've taken already?"

"We don't kill needlessly."

"It's what they think we do anyway. Maybe the only way to win this is to just give in."

Alara shook her head. "No. Not that," she said, though a part of her knew he was right. She'd spent most of her life thinking just that.

Runeo turned to face the others, eyes imploring, but no one else stood with him. Even Quenti shied away, eyes still focused on her father.

"They'll follow us," Runeo said. "They'll *kill* us."

"They don't know where we're going," Alara answered. "Let's just leave."

Alara moved to put a hand on Runeo's arm, but he quickly pulled away.

"We won't win this war being merciful."

Silence descended on the group as they chose a boat a few docks down that was big enough to hold the seven of them, but still small enough to move swiftly.

As they cut through the water, sails open wide with Suri's wind abilities, they watched the shore. Quenti's father had finally scrambled up and was running back into town. They couldn't hear him over the wind, but Alara imagined he was yelling.

Quenti made a small sound beside her and Alara turned to see a twinkle of mischief in her eyes again.

"Let's make it a little more difficult for them to follow."

Alara looked at the girl and then back at the docks, eyes widening with realization. "I think I can handle that," she said with a smirk.

She raised her arms, snapping the flints together and sending a column of fire toward the docks. She felt a wave of warm pride as they caught fire. She twisted the threads of her powers a few more times and then sat back with a satisfied smile, for once happy to indulge in the more destructive side of her abilities.

"I think that will do."

Quenti nodded her assent and the two of them watched as the entire dock of Hurazon and each of its boats were rapidly eaten by flames.

CHAPTER 7

ALARA

Alara's body was numb with pain and exhaustion as they crested their second mountain for the day, pausing briefly to look over the land stretched out before them. To the southeast, the jagged peaks of the Endes Mountains traced along the horizon, snow blending into clouds. They looked so close from here, so much so she had the urge to reach out and touch them. But she knew Arbol was still days away and the snowy mountains even farther.

Behind her, the bay had disappeared behind the horizon and the layers of hills. For the first day of walking, they had been able to look back and see the bay stretched out behind them. She had watched it, waiting to see the movement of ships coming toward where they had landed. But the waters remained empty and flat as they hiked.

They had been careful. With Quenti's help navigating and Suri and Runeo taking turns providing the wind, they had managed to cross the bay, heading west toward the open ocean. Only after any trace of the town and coast behind them had vanished did they turn back toward the east end of the bay.

At some point during the journey, the wind had picked up and the water turned choppy, moving as if it had a life of its own. Mitteo and Quenti had jumped to Suri's rescue as she lost control of the wind and sails. In that moment, Alara learned that Mitteo had grown up along the coast by Pesca. She had known the boy for nearly ten years and had never thought to ask where he was from. She tried not to let the guilt settle in her stomach.

It was Khuna, in the end, who saved them. Leaning precariously over the edge of the boat near the bow, she stretched her hands out. Alara could feel the pull of the girl's powers from where she sat. The water in front of them calmed, and seconds later, they were gliding along the smooth surface again.

When they made it safely to shore, they'd disembarked on shaky legs. Suri pushed the boat back into the bay with a sharp gust of wind and they watched it shrink slowly on the horizon.

The group didn't make it far inland that afternoon. It was Khuna who collapsed first, but Quenti and Suri weren't far behind. Even Runeo didn't argue when they started passing out tortillas and dried meat. They were too close to the outskirt cities still to build a fire, but after days of near starvation, the food felt like a feast.

That was two days ago.

"Keep up, bruyita," Runeo said with a smirk. Alara shook away her thoughts and realized she was still standing, staring out at the horizon.

The rest of the group had continued on, but Runeo looked back at her expectantly. She gave the mountains one last glance as she caught up with the airen, shouldering him playfully.

"Be careful who you call bruyita. I might need to challenge you to a duel to protect my honor."

"Even without your cuffs, it wouldn't be a fair fight."

"You're right," Alara conceded. "Perhaps, if I tie one hand behind my back, you'd have a chance."

Runeo gave a huff, but his lips quirked up in the hint of a smile. Alara felt a swell of pride and something more. It was the closest thing to happiness she had seen in him since they had left the Haven.

They walked in companionable silence, the rest of the group some yards ahead, scouting their path. They hadn't run up against councilguards since leaving the bay, and the return of the wildlife and fish spoke to the fact that the guards hadn't made it out this far. It seemed they were finally home free, so long as they didn't give into exhaustion before reaching Arbol. Runeo had guessed they were only a day's walk from the river crossing and then two days to home from there. *Home.*

Alara had spent days avoiding the emotions and thoughts that surrounded that word for her. But then again, that's what Arbol was. It was the closest thing she would have from now on, at least.

She threw a glance behind her, unsure of what she was expecting. They were back in the densely packed forest again and any trace of the sky or horizon was obscured.

She heard a soft chuckle beside her.

"What?" she said, irritably.

"You're worried." Runeo was looking at her, eyes reading her expression.

"It's fine."

"You've been looking behind us a few times every hour since we left the coast."

"Just being careful." Alara shrugged.

"You're worried we're being followed."

"We aren't though."

"You're not wrong."

"See?"

"I mean, you're not wrong for what you're feeling."

Alara gave Runeo a sideways glare. "And what am I feeling?"

Runeo gave a soft hum. "You know, we should have killed them."

"Who?" Alara said, knowing the answer.

"All of them. The councilguards, Quenti's dad, and anyone else we could get our hands on. We should have killed them and you worry you'll live to regret it."

Alara began to shake her head, but Runeo's face was suddenly serious, his eyes penetrating.

"I know the look," he continued. "I know that feeling all too well."

She tried to brush off his words, her voice light. "Your tone suggests that you've never let a councilguard live, willingly." She was smiling, but she caught the look of pain on Runeo's face as her words touched on something. She didn't push it and he didn't explain.

"I don't want to turn into the Council—treating humans like sacrifices for the greater good," Alara said. "I spent too much of my life thinking that way."

"But sometimes that's what we are though. Sometimes we have to be. Especially in war," Runeo breathed.

"I don't want to start a war."

"I think we already have."

He placed a warm hand on hers, a reassurance she wasn't expecting. The touch was brief, but left her skin tingling, even long after he caught up with the rest of the group.

She hated him for being right. She *was* worried about the guards they had left behind. With every step she took, a small voice whispered in the back of her head that she had been weak. That letting them go had been a mistake.

Her eyes followed Quenti as she walked, fingertips brushing against Khuna's with each swing of her arm. Just days earlier, Alara had also seen Quenti almost kill her own father. Something had broken in her in that moment, watching the other girl's eyes, pupils blown black with hate. She recognized a piece of herself in Quenti in that moment. The same piece that wanted to see Emaru burn. And it scared Alara more than she would ever admit.

If they had started a war, Alara wanted to know that she had ended up on the right side. The good side. But what did that mean?

"You're thinking too loudly. It's making my head hurt." Suri's voice was loud, breaking through Alara's thoughts. She looked up to see the rest of the group staring back at her, waiting for her to catch up.

Alara's laugh surprised even herself, and a few minutes later, they spoke animatedly about the food they would eat when they made it back to Arbol. They talked about introducing Suri and Mitteo to their families and their friends, about showing Suri the old abandoned outlook and Mitteo the farmlands. And for a moment, Alara felt like she knew what it was like to have a family.

Everything will be okay when we make it back to Arbol. She held on to that thought like a mantra as they walked. She refused to think further on the subject. She didn't ponder on what the next steps would be or what it would truly mean to make Arbol home. She just kept moving forward, refusing to let herself look back.

Everything will be okay when we make it back to Arbol.

Chapter 8

Alara

Alara was still holding on to that thought days later as the group slowed to a stop in front of an enormous tree. A sense of familiarity and utter foreignness settled over her as she recognized the forest floor that served as the entrance to Arbol. Or rather, the forest floor from which they would ascend to her new home.

Lili was the first to collapse, legs crumpling beneath her and eyes watering with more emotions than Alara could read. It was Suri who ended up next to the woman, an arm wrapped around her shoulders.

Mitteo's head swiveled around, eyes alight with confusion, and Alara couldn't help but smile at the irony of how recently she had had that same look on her face.

But her sense of ease was immediately erased and her stomach clenched as she raked her eyes over the ragged group of rebels and bruyas around her. Micos and Zinita, the ones who hadn't made it back from the Haven, held a presence in the group and weighed heavily on her heart.

The forest was quiet after Runeo's verbal signal to the guards in the distant treetops above. The wildlife seemed to have disappeared and even the wind held its breath.

Each heartbeat rallied against Alara's chest as they waited. She had a sudden image of the councilguards laying siege to Arbol. After all, amid the concern of being followed, it had taken them weeks to make it here. If the Council knew where it was, it wouldn't have taken but a week for someone to show up. But the Council *didn't* know. Alara reminded herself of that fact. They *couldn't* know. Against all odds, Arbol had remained hidden and safe for decades.

"What are we waiting for?" Suri asked, breaking the unspoken rule of silence.

Runeo jumped at her comment, giving away the nerves that were plaguing him, just like the rest of them.

"The lift," Khuna answered, her comment clipped.

"The what?" Mitteo's question went unanswered as a tree branch creaked above them and all eyes turned upward. Alara could feel the sigh of relief from the group as the small platform came into view, a single familiar face looking down from above.

"So, you've finally come back to us." Quil'la's voice was soft, her face a mask of deliberate composure. Her eyes darted around the group, counting, no doubt taking stock as the platform came to rest on the ground.

Alara twitched as the woman's eyes stayed on her for a beat longer than the rest, but she met her stare with her own. The leader of the Arborelis gave a small fleeting smile before turning away again.

"Come on, then." Quil'la said after far too long. "Let's get you all home."

The words seemed to break something and then the entire group was moving, shuffling onto the platform as Quil'la and two of her Arboreli guards stepped out of the way. Khuna and Quenti's hands were clasped tight at their sides, and now Lili was the one holding on to Suri, who stared at the platform with an air of barely suppressed terror. For his part, Mitteo stepped onto the platform without hesitation, eyes taking in the mechanism that moved it with blatant curiosity. His shoulders were relaxed and confident, and Alara was struck again by how little she knew about the magite—the *rebel*—in front of her.

Alara and Runeo were the last onto the platform. Quil'la placed a hand on Runeo's shoulder, and Alara saw them slump under the unspoken weight of that gesture. She wanted to take his hand in that moment. Squeeze it and tell him it would be okay. But she didn't dare move her hands in comfort, though even she couldn't understand why. Was it the sheer weight of Runeo's sorrow, the presence of the Arboreli leader, or something else?

"You didn't need to come meet us yourself," Khuna's words were part comment, part question.

Quil'la smiled. "Believe it or not, I've been worried about you. All of you. And when the scouts told me you were coming, I was curious." Her eyes rested on Alara again for another moment before shifting back toward Mitteo and Suri. "I have a lot of questions, but I'd be cruel to make you answer them now. A meal and tea will do you all good."

No one argued the point, and the platform finished its prolonged ascent in silence.

A strange sense of nostalgia washed over Alara as Quil'la led the group off the platform and into Arbol, its wooden platforms and rope bridges as visually arresting as ever. Suri remained glued to Lili's side, but the rest walked with easy strides. Much to Alara's surprise, the city felt halfway abandoned, with only a scattering of tree dwellers wandering about, looking as though they had somewhere to be.

The group was escorted into a building near the same Council hut Alara had been interrogated in during her initial stay in Arbol. There was a small fire crackling and a pot of water already boiling when they arrived. The group jumped at the food like starved animals. Despite the meager rations taken from Hurazon, they hadn't eaten particularly well over their journey, and the spread of roasted corn, fruit, and fresh powdery tortillas was gone in a few short minutes.

Quil'la waited patiently as they settled in, passing mugs of tea among themselves. Mitteo and Suri looked only slightly unsure as they gazed around the room, sipping from their mugs only after the others did. In the ravenous silence, Alara noted the room that made up the majority of the building was one that had been shaped from tree branches by a tierren. The walls were an intricate weaving of vines and branches twisting among themselves to create beautiful patterns. Leaves and moss grew from these branches, painting the walls green.

The group settled, but still no one spoke. Alara's mind raced through her thoughts. Where did they even start?

"Perhaps I should start by asking—where are Micos and Zinita?" Quil'la's voice was soft, but her eyes were deep and knowing as they bore into Runeo. The silence was heavy. "So, of all our captured, you only managed to rescue Khuna?" Quil'la guessed.

"It's more complicated than that," Lili finally interjected when no one else spoke up. "We found them. Well, Zinita and Khuna and others. We found them all. And we did break them out, just as planned."

"And then everything went to shit," Quenti finished, splattering the delicate picture Lili was trying to paint.

Quil'la's eyebrow raised sharply at the curse, but Quenti didn't so much as flinch.

Her voice was flat and emotionless as she explained what happened after they left the dungeons, though she left out the part Micos had played in the chaos, as if not speaking, it would change what had happened. When she finally revealed Zinita's fate, Quil'la pressed her lips together and whispered a short prayer under her breath.

Finally finding her voice, Alara spoke. "And I think... I think we may have started a war," Alara said bluntly, recalling Runeo's words some days earlier.

Quil'la tilted her head, glaring at Alara as if she herself were a mind-walker seeking the validity of the bold statement. "Oh, is that all? And whose side are you on, young Alara Ayar?"

Alara let the question linger in the air for too long. "The Council killed my family and stole my mind," she finally said. It wasn't an answer and she knew it, but she didn't much feel like being on any side of a war right now.

Quil'la only nodded and turned to the rest of the group. "So, then. Others escaped?"

It was only then that Alara revealed the existence of the Network of agents that had permeated the entirety of the Haven. Whether or not the revelation surprised Quil'la, Alara couldn't tell.

"And when the entire Network revealed themselves to the Council," Lili said, "they had no choice but to flee once the barrier came down. We don't know how many made it out though. We spent weeks dodging the councilguards on the southern road. It's hard to imagine no one was caught."

"And Micos—is he with the others?" In a rare expression of emotion, Quil'la's voice was filled with hope, though her creased forehead and downturned eyes spoke a different story.

"He's gone." Runeo finally said. "He was..." The unfinished thought lingered in the air for no less than twenty seconds.

"His mind was cleansed by the time we got there," Alara finished.

Quil'la closed her eyes, and Alara saw her breaths deepen. "You've all had a long journey. I'd say you should all rest, but perhaps you'll want to join the festivities that are happening."

"The..." Alara started. "I'm sorry, the festivities?"

"It's already the solstice?" Lili said. Her face lit up at her own words. "I didn't even realize what day it was."

"Everyone is already celebrating, but you are all welcome to join." All of a sudden, the half-empty walkways made sense. "We can finish talking politics in two days' time."

"Wait," Alara cut in. "We have a message from Cruz." It had already been weeks since they had left the Haven, and Alara suddenly felt a sense of being too late.

Quil'la looked at the girl expectantly.

"Now that the Network has been revealed, she says they can't expect bruyas to continue living on the outskirts."

"Oh, really?" Quil'la's tone was dark, almost challenging.

"She says she'll bring others to meet where the River Muerta meets the River Mied."

And then, the challenging look evaporated from Quil'la's gaze, and her eyes went wide for a brief moment before she shrouded her expression back behind her pallid mask. It was enough for Alara to infer one thing: Quil'la understood the importance of Cruz's call.

"I know the place." Quil'la didn't elaborate, brows furrowing in thought. "Thank you for the message. You've given me a lot to think about. When the holy days are done, we will meet with the rest of the Arborelis to discuss what this means."

Alara opened her mouth to argue, but it was Runeo who cut in. "This isn't something to sit on and talk about. The Network is gathering an army. Our time to hide is behind us. A war is coming, and we need to help them."

Quil'la's eyes were admonishing as she turned to Runeo. "The impending war will still be here in a few days' time. Better that we take it to rest and think."

Runeo opened his mouth to argue, but was cut off by a wave from Quil'la.

"These are some of the most sacred days to our people," she said.

"The lives of all the bruyas in Arbol and across Sombria will change because of the actions you took. Today, let them celebrate and be merry. The time to mourn will come."

With this, she swept out of the room and didn't look back.

"And what about the time to fight?" Runeo said to no one in particular, his shoulders slumped, the anger seeming to drain from him. Alara wanted to empathize, to feel the same fire he had. But right now, all she wanted was a bit of normalcy. They had fought the first battle; they deserved to take time to forget the pain. They deserved a single night to ignore the horrible things in the outside world.

A cry from behind them had Alara turning, hand on her dagger. But she quickly released her grip as Khuna's parents burst through the door, eyes searching desperately before landing on the small bruya. The three of them collided in soft sobs and murmured words.

After only a moment, Khuna's mother opened her arms to add Quenti into the huddle, pulling her in and placing kisses across her brow and cheeks.

Alara watched the display from a distance, trying to ignore the heaviness in her chest. She heard someone shift beside her and felt Runeo's warm hand squeeze hers briefly. Lili moved to her other side, arm wrapping around her shoulders. Alara swallowed her grief and bitterness, pushing it down somewhere it wouldn't bother her. Not tonight.

For the first time, Alara thought she understood why the Arborelis chose to live here in the cloud forests, cut off from the country they resided in, but never truly belonging to. Hiding and forgetting is so much simpler.

She deserved simple tonight.

CHAPTER 9

QUENTI

Despite the tension, everyone took Quil'la's words to heart. In fact, they seemed relieved at the promise of a release, even at the expense of rest. An hour later, they found themselves on the main platform of Arbol, surrounded by bruyas dressed in a riot of colors, dancing and singing and yelling into the darkness.

Drums beat and pipes sung from seemingly all around them. Quenti was baffled by the silence of the forest floor given the cacophony among the trees. It was a wonder the group had been concerned about the civilization's wellbeing in the first place.

The smell of smoke and roasted guinea pig wafted through the air and she found herself craving the savory meal, despite having just eaten. The night was illuminated with fuegen fire dancing above them in small globes, colorful bursts of flames.

They seemed to have missed the main performances, but those who had danced earlier were still wearing their costumes as they swayed with the rest. Underneath the heady scent of smoke, Quenti could just make out the sweet fragrance of chicha and ferment. The

Arborelis around them were red-faced, and their eyes shone with more than just joy. She knew the signs of intoxication, and it was clear almost everyone here had long since lost themselves. Maybe Quil'la had a point. It's not like anyone would be able to get much done in their current state, let alone mount an army.

Lili grabbed Suri's hand, leading her into the dancing crowds, laughing as though they hadn't spent the past two weeks running for their lives. And then, Alara, of all people, followed Mitteo, a smile stretched across her face. It was the most content she'd seen the former magite since they had left the Haven. She wanted to be happy for her, but a gnawing sense of envy clawed through her stomach, mixing with the rage that had settled there. Alara had lost more than even Quenti, yet here she was laughing as Mitteo swung her around in his arms. She willed the rage to leave her as she had done every morning since they had left Hurazon, but it only coiled tighter inside.

Beside her, Khuna ran a hand along the small of her back and she felt the bruya lean in, breath warm on her neck. "Do you want to dance?"

Quenti couldn't answer for what felt like forever. She was choking on her own emotions, and for the first time she could remember, it was something she didn't want Khuna to see. She answered eventually with a short "No." Her partner gave her arm a reassuring squeeze before sliding into the crowd and joining the others as they danced.

"Amazing how they can look so carefree," Runeo said beside her. His voice was deep and rough and Quenti could tell he was in the same mental place as her.

"They want to celebrate," Quenti said, trying to connect with the sentiment, but feeling nothing.

"There's nothing *to* celebrate."

"I know."

"You're seeing common sense," Runeo said.

"Oh?"

"I saw you back in Hurazon. You know what has to be done if we're going to win this war."

Quenti shook her head. "That's not what happened."

"Stop lying to yourself."

"I just got angry. It was a mistake," Quenti said, though the words rang false on her lips. She could sense the conviction—the conviction in her trying to convince herself. She had spent the days since Hurazon going over the moments with her father and the councilguards in her head. She wanted to feel guilty about what she had done. What she had almost done. If anything, she found herself regretting she didn't take things farther. Regretful that she let the others stop her.

That's not normal, is it? Though she kept these thoughts to herself.

"The mistake is trying to win the war through mercy and weakness."

"You're angry," Quenti said. "I get it. I'm angry too. But anger has never helped us make good decisions."

"You and I have very different experiences, then," he said, locking eyes with Quenti. "Anger is what motivates us to keep moving forward despite everything."

The words wriggled into Quenti's brain and she bit the inside of her cheek. She walked away without answering him, disappearing into the crowd as though sinking under a wave. She let the dancing mass move her until she found Khuna and she grabbed the other girl's arms, pulling them together. Bodies pressed tightly, she closed her eyes and let herself move with the music. Khuna's skin was damp and warm against hers, and she traced her fingertips against her arm, feeling the goosebumps. The desire. Her lips found Khuna's and she lost herself in the softness.

The night was chilly, but within the crowd the air was warm and wet and the cloying smell of chicha overwhelmed her. At some point, someone—Alara, she thought—had placed a cup of chicha in her hand and she downed it quickly, letting the warmness seep under her skin. Khuna pressed another kiss against her lips and she tasted the drink there as well. Her girlfriend's body was soft and warm under her hands as they swayed and moved as one. She could feel her breath graze her lips, smell the salt and sweat of her skin, and she let her eyes close at the familiarity of the scent.

And then the night took her, music singing in her blood. She alternated between kisses and chicha until the taste of it all blended together, allowing herself to forget just a moment about the rage still thrumming in her body.

The next morning, Quenti woke up to a pounding in her temples. Her tongue was fuzzy and her throat burned as she let out a groan.

She opened her eyes to find Lili standing above her, a cup of water in one hand and bitter smelling cafi in the other. She reached for the water first and gulped it down in one swallow, ignoring the wave of nausea that threatened to sink her as she sat up. She then traded it for the cafi and took a careful sip of the hot liquid. She winced. It was as bitter as it smelled.

"Trust me, it will help," Lili said with a smile.

"How are you so chipper this morning?"

"I hate the taste of chicha. Besides it's not morning anymore." She failed to hide the laughter in her voice.

Quenti took another sip and looked around the room. The group was strewn about the floor of Lili's living room, all looking as bad as Quenti felt. Hair and clothes disheveled, faces pale. Everyone else was still asleep, though she noticed Runeo was absent. She didn't remember seeing him last night after she'd ended their conversation so abruptly. He had probably gone home, alone. Something she didn't want to dwell on now. As for the rest of them, she had the vague memory of them stumbling back to Lili's house when the first rays of dawn had hit. She remembered more clearly falling asleep wrapped around Khuna, who still laid beside her, a damp spot forming on the blanket below her mouth.

She slunk from the room, tiptoeing into the kitchen where Lili was puttering away, boiling beans and quinoa. She thanked Sol it only smelled of steam. She didn't think she could take the smell of actual food.

"I have nothing fresh for us," Lili said, "but my dried goods were still stocked. It'll be a few days before the market is up and running to buy produce or game."

"It'll be a week before I can stomach food again," Quenti huffed out, sinking into a chair at the table.

"The whole of Arbol will be feeling that pain with you. This happens every holy day. There is a day of celebration and another day of recovery."

Lili sat across from Quenti, a mug of cafi clasped in her own small hands.

"Can't you use your magia to make this go away?" Quenti gestured vaguely to her head.

"Sorry to say, but I think that's a pain you're going to have to feel."

"So, can you or can't you?"

Lili only smiled in response.

"You're cruel."

"So, you and Khuna had fun last night," Lili said, eyes dancing over the rim of her mug as she took a sip of cafi.

Quenti let out another groan and let the heat rise in her cheeks, though she couldn't tell if it was from embarrassment or the hangover. "Not talking about this right now."

It was another hour before the rest of the group finally stirred, each waking to a mug of cafi and a cup of water from Lili. By the time Suri finally crawled off the floor, Quenti was starting to feel a bit better, and was the one to offer the young woman a cup of the piping hot brew.

They moved the chairs and pillows to the small porch outside as Lili filled serving bowls with quinoa and mashed beans mixed with Arbol spices. The air was warm, but the sweet breeze cutting through the trees seemed to do everyone some good.

Yet even as the headache Quenti had been nursing finally drifted away on the wind, the gnawing sense of impatience rushed back in. Why were they all just sitting around and waiting? As much as she disliked Runeo's smugness, she couldn't shake the feeling that he was right.

A war was coming, and they needed to take their place in it.

"When will the meeting be?" she asked, shoveling a spoonful of beans into her mouth, taking in the spicy paprika and chili flavor with each bite. She had worried her stomach would revolt at the food, but every spoonful seemed to only make her hungrier. "There *will* be a meeting, right? She wasn't just trying to shut us up?"

"Tomorrow morning I should think," Lili said. "Quil'la seems to understand the urgency."

"How is tomorrow urgent?" Quenti bit out the words.

"This coming from someone who's just spent half the day sprawled out on the floor," Lili said. "Quick decisions aren't our forte here. We meditate on them, knowing the importance they carry. Humans are rash and fickle, and one mistake can mean the difference between survival and eradication. If we're too shortsighted, it could mean the end of Arbol as we know it. You didn't see the weeks of debate that went into Khuna finally inviting you to come here."

Quenti bit her lip. All she'd known was that Khuna had disappeared for nearly a month after Mama's funeral, and when the bruya had returned, it was to beg Quenti to return to Arbol with her. She had asked for time to think. Though maybe that was a mistake. Maybe if she had simply made the decision in that moment and left Hurazon, none of the last few months would have happened. Would that have been better or worse?

She shook off these thoughts, her mind reverting back to her conversation with Runeo. "Sitting around twiddling our thumbs is going to get us killed," she said. "We saw the mages and council-guards. They aren't just looking to rein us in and bring peace again. They're looking for a war."

"Be careful, Quenti, you're taking my lines." Runeo came up behind them across the small bridge that connected Lili's home to the rest of Arbol, a lopsided smirk on his lips as he swiped the bowl of mashed beans from Lili's hands and took a giant bite.

She slapped him lightly and stole her bowl back. "Get your own, you thief."

With a chuckle, Runeo did just that, sitting down heavily beside Lili. No one mentioned his swollen, red eyes, despite how starkly they stood out against his dark skin.

The room fell silent and the air around the room grew heavier with each passing moment. Quenti studied Alara where she sat, a look of ease and contentment on her face. It twisted something in her stomach, and she couldn't quite understand the other girl's newly found peace.

"And you're okay with this, too?" Quenti asked Alara, barely suppressing the anger rising up in her cheeks. "Waiting around for decisions to be made?"

Alara looked at her, the barest hint of guilt in her eyes and the rigid set of her shoulders. "It's been weeks since all of this started." A long pause. Quenti could sense the hesitation in what Alara said next.

"Another day is hardly going to make a difference. I think we all deserve a moment to take a breath."

Quenti heard the desperation in Alara's voice. And why wouldn't she be? After everything that happened, Alara wanted nothing more than to settle into a new status quo. Quenti had seen Alara act stupid before, but she'd never seen her act so...

Weak... Is that what this new side of Alara was? Weakness?

Quenti hugged her knees to her chest and leaned into the body to her right, feeling Khuna's warm arm brushing against her own.

Khuna and the Arborelis were the reason Quenti was here, free and away from her father, Hurazon, and the Haven. She took a deep breath and tried to channel the peace that Alara seemed to be begging of her. She could do this. She was here, surrounded by friends and fellow magia-users. Fellow *bruyas*. They were safe.

Perhaps the Arboreli way of making decisions was for the best. They had survived for centuries this way. Despite what the Council and the Haven tried to throw at them, they *survived*.

And Quenti was one of them now. Like them, she would survive.

Chapter 10

Alara

Alara relished the lazy day ahead. She knew she should feel more pressure, more anxiety, more *something*. She saw the fire raging behind Quenti's eyes and the pain that Runeo carried everywhere, but she couldn't quite find it in herself to feel more than an exhausted numbness. The box in the corner of her mind that held Adelmo's face, the comfort of Emaru's hand on her shoulder, and Micos's laugh was still locked tight, and she didn't have the energy or strength to look at it now.

Her body ached from the weeks of walking, and her stomach hurt with both hunger and fullness as it adjusted to eating a full meal for the first time in weeks. All she could truly think about was that she felt at home for the first time since she had left the Haven's gates on the mission to find Quenti. There was a strangeness to it, finding herself at home in the same place she once was held captive. But when she had fallen asleep, head spinning on Lili's floor the evening before, she had felt settled and warm—and not just from the alcohol thrumming in her veins.

"I'm going for a walk," Alara announced after breakfast had

finished and an uncomfortable lull had fallen over the group. She wanted time away from the sadness and grief. She needed time to just *be*.

"How about giving us a tour?" Mitteo asked, nudging Suri beside him. For her part, the mage was suddenly surprised at being addressed. She looked around, eyes meeting Alara with the look of someone who hadn't quite processed where she was.

"I don't know if I really know enough. Maybe Lili—" Alara looked at the bruya, but the woman was already shaking her head.

"I need to settle some things now that we're home. I need to find someone selling sleeping pads since it looks like we're going to be having a giant sleepover until other arrangements are found." Lili turned to Mitteo. "If you all do plan on staying, I would love to discuss creating a new house with you. If we worked together and did it all organically, I would die. When I did my wall in there, I always wanted to experiment with creating an entire building," Lili paused, seeming to realize she hadn't taken a breath in her excitement. Mitteo's cheeks were tinged pink as Lili's bright eyes focused on him. She didn't seem to notice his reaction to her attention. "Anyway, with the way Micos and I dragged you around, I'm sure you'll be a good enough guide," she finished.

And so Alara found herself leading Mitteo and Suri across the bridge from Lili's house twenty minutes later. They walked in silence for a while, with Alara wandering toward the center of the city—where Lili had once taken her to the market. It was quiet, with only a small scattering of Arborelis meandering, most looking as pained to be moving around as she felt earlier that morning. Suri was starting to look less pale after a full breakfast, and Mitteo's face was characteristically bright as they walked.

In the end, he was the one to break the silence as he started noting the intricate tierren work of the platforms and buildings. He even pointed to a few of the bridges that had been grown from the trees, rather than built with rope and chopped wood.

Alara and Suri listened, the former with only somewhat feigned interest.

"It's amazing what they've managed to build here," Suri cut in during a brief pause in Mitteo's ramblings.

Alara agreed, remembering her reluctant fascination with the city during her first visit in captivity.

"If you aren't afraid of heights, Micos showed me an amazing spot on the outskirts," Alara said, ignoring the twinge in her gut at the name.

"Were you close with him?" Mitteo asked, seeming to read the shift in Alara's features. "That was Runeo's brother, wasn't it?"

She shrugged, not wanting to encourage the conversation, though it was strange that, despite how much time she spent thinking about Micos, that there were some in their group who didn't even know who he was.

Who he is, she reminded herself. He was still out there some-where, even with a cleansed mind.

"It must have been difficult," Mitteo continued, "to see him after..."

"After the councilguards ripped out his thoughts and memories and mind?" Alara said. "Yes, a bit."

Suri sneered. "I always suspected what was going on with the bruyas, but we never had any proof. The Network had spent a decade trying to understand what was happening, but Cruz had to have known. She was covering it up just as much as that hag Wila."

"I'm sure she had her reasons," Mitteo said. "She had to protect the Network just as much as the bruyas, if not more so. Everyone was depending on the Network staying secret."

"Well, that's blown up in all our faces," Suri noted with a pointed look at Alara.

The conversation had taken another turn that Alara didn't dare follow. She didn't want to think about wars or battles or networks. She didn't want to remember the last month of running and hiding. She didn't want to remember the smell of burnt flesh and blood.

Alara's stomach lurched at her thoughts and she focused on her nails biting into the palms of her hands until her mind silenced itself again.

As they stepped onto another bridge, she realized that she was no longer walking toward Micos's platform, having drifted to the left and toward the other side of Arbol. But she said nothing and kept walking, without thinking of where she was going or how long Mitteo and Suri would follow her without question. The two of them were still locked in debate over spies and rebellions. Alara almost missed the stuttering, bumbling mess that Mitteo had once pretended to be.

She was still locked in her own thoughts and ignoring the debate behind her when Quenti called out.

"Come to help, then?"

Only then did Alara notice they had wandered onto the main platform where the party had taken place the night before. Quenti and Runeo were helping clean with a few other older bruyas Alara didn't recognize.

"How did you get roped into this?" Alara asked.

"Lili seemed to think staying busy might help us," Quenti said.

"Or she just wanted us out of her hair," Runeo grumbled.

Alara noted that cleaning had in no way helped Runeo's dark mood and seemed to have only given him more time to ruminate on his own thoughts. A conundrum Alara knew well. She crouched down next to Runeo who was washing a never-ending stack of cups in a large basin of water. Without thinking, she started manually drying them with a nearby llama-fur rag, setting them aside into a neat pile.

"I can do that easier," Runeo noted. Alara ignored him and continued her work, focusing her mind on the task.

"The meeting's been moved up to tonight," Quenti said after some time working in silence. Her tone was casual, and she didn't look up from where she wrung out the wool tablecloths. Mitteo and Suri had joined her and were helping to dry and fold the cleaned fabric.

Alara's heart gave a small jump. She knew the meeting was important and they had already waited long enough, but it didn't stop the unease that had settled in her gut. She wasn't ready. She wanted more time to recover—*to avoid*, a voice whispered in the back of her mind.

Runeo grunted beside her.

"What?" She turned to him, the tone of her voice snappier than she intended. A small twinge of guilt tickled at her conscience, but she pushed it away with annoyance.

"You've lost your thunder," he answered finally after a few beats. "After all you did at the Haven, after everything we saw, you're just like any other Arboreli, ready to tuck tail and hide."

"I never had any thunder," Alara snapped.

"That's a lie. You were full of fire and thunder when you convinced Quil'la to let us go on a rescue mission. Now you have the chance to fight for something bigger, and you've already given up."

"I was just doing what was right."

"And now? What's right now?"

"I don't know," Alara admitted. Maybe that was part of the problem.

Runeo shook his head and turned back to the washing basin with a grim look. "Don't worry, you won't be alone when you stay behind to hide. But I won't be the only one ready to fight, either. Things are changing, and there are plenty of bruyas and rebels who know it."

His eyes were on Mitteo, Suri, and Quenti now. "We'll fight so you can enjoy your peaceful life hiding among the trees."

Alara bit her lip at the snide comments. She knew Runeo was insulting her, trying to goad her. Yet, she couldn't help the relief and warmth that pooled in her stomach at the idea of just settling down here. She could find peace among the trees. Would that be so bad? To just let others fight their battles without her for once?

The question drifted unanswered in the breeze as they worked in silence.

CHAPTER 11

ALARA

The sun had set hours ago and the sky shone an inky black through the gaps in the canopy high above the city of Arbol. A few stars could be seen twinkling in the distance, but the moon was either still hiding behind the horizon or too thin to light the night. Instead, torches danced along the walkways, sending shadows scattering as their light fought the darkness.

Their entire group had walked together to the large wooden hut that sat at the heart of the tree city. Runeo hadn't said more than two words to Alara since that afternoon. Still, she stood by what she had said: she was tired of fighting. But the grim look he gave her every time their eyes met made her stomach twist with something more than discomfort. She hated that his judgment bothered her.

The calloused pads of her fingers grazed the hilt of the dull dagger at her belt. She didn't know why she carried it with her everywhere, but despite its uselessness, it still gave her a sense of comfort. There was a warmth its hilt lent her, even in these trying times.

The room was already full when they walked in, the three main leaders of the bruyas sitting at the opposite end of the hall, Quil'la in the center, in front of a fire that seemed to crackle in perpetuity. The two men who helped Quil'la maintain order and peace within Arbol —one elderly with deep creases, and the other closer to middle-age— were positioned on either side of the younger woman, although Alara admittedly didn't remember their names. Others who Alara assumed held some important role in Arbol sat in small clumps around the room.

Quil'la motioned them forward with a small gesture of her hand and the chamber immediately filled with whispers. Alara kept her head down and eyes trained on the floor. She wondered if she would ever feel welcome sitting among these people.

It was Khuna who stepped forward, acting as spokesperson for the group. Runeo had tried to volunteer, but eventually even he admitted he wasn't ready to tell the story of what had happened to Micos. For her part, Alara wasn't even sure if it was smart having Runeo in the room as they recounted the story, though she kept that thought to herself.

"I know you are all restless to know what has happened," Quil'la started.

"We want to know why we're suddenly collecting mages from the Haven," one man said, hand waving toward them.

"They could be spies and we're just letting them wander around free!" A woman in the back stood up to yell. Alara could feel Mitteo and Suri shifting uncomfortably beside her.

Quil'la raised her arms, but remained silent. The din in the room immediately ceased. Despite only being an inch or so taller than Alara, the woman managed to hold the room with ease.

"All will be known, but I fear this may be a long story. Perhaps we should listen now and ask questions after?" Quil'la's voice was soft, but her sharp eyes scanned the crowd, daring argument.

A few shifted in their seats, but there was finally silence.

Khuna's voice was soft as she spoke, but it didn't waver as she described her capture and the events at the Haven. There was rapt silence until she chronicled Senye Cruz and the Network's rescue. Suddenly, even Quil'la's sharp gaze couldn't keep the room quiet.

"Shut up!" Runeo waved his hand next to Alara. A violent gust of wind blew past her, skirting the edges of the chamber, blowing out the torches and dropping it into darkness.

Finally, a hush fell over the room. Alara could feel Runeo shaking beside her. She felt a nudge against her arm. "Can you...?" he muttered.

Alara didn't answer, only flicking her wrists in response. The threads of magia from her core connected with the embers of the torches, and the room was flooded with light again.

No one spoke as Runeo stepped forward. From a distance, Alara could no longer see the quiver in his shoulders, but his lips were pale as he spoke.

"We have been hiding in these trees for generations, praying to Sol that the Council won't find us. Perhaps they never will. Maybe they'll allow us to forever stay in our hidden fortress," Runeo said. "Or maybe, one morning we'll wake up to the Council knocking down our door."

"They've never found us before," one of the men next to Quil'la said—Rom—the name of the elderly man suddenly came to Alara.

"No, they haven't," Runeo agreed. "But I'm no longer content waiting around, dreading the day it comes. What happened at the Haven is something our allies within the Network also hoped would never happen. Like it or not, we've forced their hand. Now, the Network is gathering to discuss next steps. Change is here. If there was ever a time to stand up and fight, it's now. It's happening whether we join them or not. I say we need to join them."

"We *need* to do nothing," Rom said sharply.

Quil'la didn't look at the man, her sympathetic eyes focused on Runeo. "We have some important decisions to make," she said softly.

"So important we had to wait a full day to talk about them," Runeo said.

"You've lost your brother," she said. "No one can fault you for your pain."

"He's not lost. He's still out there. And every second we just sit around and wait is another second he—"

"—loses himself more?" Quil'la finished. "Don't mistake us for a naïve set of bruyitas. This isn't the first time we have lost one of our own to the Council. The only solace we have is that they have never been able to use our brethren's memories to find us before."

"I wish they had. Then we wouldn't be up here, wrapped safely in our own ignorance."

"Runeo." Quil'la's voice was sharp in warning.

Alara startled as Quenti jumped up beside her. "He's right, though! And this isn't just about one or two bruyas anymore. The entire Network is meeting. Senyc Cruz *asked* us to meet her."

"I know the place, and I know the request," Quil'la said. "She's calling upon the First Pact."

The two men on either side of Quil'la jerked as one at this declaration, and the room again burst into a cacophony of voices vying for attention.

"The First Pact?" Alara asked, turning to Runeo. He glanced down at her, but didn't answer.

"The First Pact was put in place generations before even us, but it is an agreement, not a contract." Rom's voice was low, but it cut through the noise like a gust of wind.

"We can't just leave them all—" Runeo started.

"What we cannot do is force our people to risk their lives," Quil'la said. "This is a time of great upheaval, but these times have come before, and they will come again. The decision we make today may very well affect whether or not we will be here to see them." She turned back to the audience in the chamber. "I suggest a vote of all those in favor of passing on the call and remaining in Arbol."

Alara looked around the chamber as nearly everyone raised three fingers to their brows. As confused as she was, she didn't miss the dark look in Runeo's eyes.

"You're all cowards," he said.

"We're done here," Quil'la said. The others took this as permission to leave and many filed out without a second glance back.

Runeo and Quenti stared daggers at Quil'la, while the others sat by, dumb looks on their faces. Even Alara, who had been wanting more than anything to stay behind in Arbol, felt empty. She expected them to do something—to send *someone*.

"We're just leaving them to fight alone?" Alara asked after a beat.

Quil'la, who had been speaking softly to a man next to Rom, turned to Alara with a small sigh. "They will not be alone. There are other bruyas, other enclaves that may join, and our own blameless may heed the call."

"Your blameless?" Alara felt her thoughts tripping over themselves. She had never thought of the fact that there were blameless bruyas. She knew, of course, that those with magia sometimes gave birth to those without, but she hadn't thought—she hadn't seen any blameless in Arbol.

"Those who were born without magia who have left us still know the pact."

"Blameless bruyas?"

"A blameless can never be a bruya," Quil'la said. "But yes, the blameless who are born here."

"What happens to them?"

"They leave, of course, when they turn sixteen. Where they go after is up to them."

"You kick them out?" Alara said, more statement than question.

"They want to leave. They could never truly fit in here as a blameless. They know that. If there is one thing that history has taught us, it is that bruya and blameless will never live together in balance."

"What about the Haven?" Alara said. "The entire kingdom of Sombria."

"You mean the very kingdom on the verge of war?"

Something in Alara's chest coiled around her heart and tightened, leaving her breathless. Now thinking back, she felt ignorant for not having noticed the absence of blameless among the treetops.

Quil'la sighed, as though noticing the panic on Alara's face. "The point is that we are not the only ones who will hear the call and know the pact. Your people will not be alone."

Your people. Were they still her people? She thought she could find her people here among the bruyas, but the pressure on her chest built and the corner of her eyes stung as she thought of Adelmo. His warm laughter and rough hands as he taught her how to throw a spear; his sandpaper fingertips as he wrapped her bruised knee when she was seven and fell off the roof of his house trying to chase a hummingbird. He had promised not to tell Emaru. It was a promise he kept until he...

Blameless and bruya will never live together in balance. She didn't believe that. She couldn't.

Alara heard a scream. It took her a few seconds to pull herself from her thoughts. Had that been in her own head? But then, almost as one, everyone moved toward the doorway. Quil'la was a few steps from the entrance when the curtains flew aside and a man stumbled in. He fell to the ground with a groan, an arrow protruding from his back. And despite the raspy whisper and the commotion outside, everyone in the room heard his words.

"Councilguards."

CHAPTER 12

ALARA

The world was on fire.

Alara ran outside before anyone else even moved, but she felt them on her heels. Across the walkway, the roof of one building was engulfed in flames as a mage threw balls of fire at the dry wood and thatch, the heat eating up what little humidity there was in an instant. Screams erupted from inside as the roof collapsed, and for a moment Alara felt like she was a child, reliving her false memory yet again—the memory of the inadvertent murder of her family. It wasn't true. She knew it wasn't, but that didn't stop its impact.

Bruyas fled around them as dozens of councilguards spread out through the city. Bodies fell and fire spread indiscriminately.

She needed to breathe. Why couldn't she breathe?

It was a hand on her shoulder that snapped her from her panic, and a vague sense of peace hummed just beneath her skin.

"We need to run," Lili whispered in her ear. "You can do this." She felt the bruya's hand under her elbow and she stumbled to her feet. When had she fallen down?

The air was still thick with smoke and screams, but somehow, Alara could breathe again. She nodded without looking at Lili, but the bruya took the cue and then they were running.

Ahead of them, she could see the others—Runeo threw blasts of air at councilguards as he ran, knocking one from the platforms and into the unyielding air below. Quenti and Khuna threw small bubbles of water at the growing fires, but the air was too dry and the flames too strong for their powers to do much of anything.

Alara tripped over something and went down hard on her knees, her skin peeling away against the splintering platforms. She still felt Lili's hands on her shoulders, even as she faltered beside her. Ignoring the sting on her knees, she stood back up, trying to reorient herself in the chaos. The group was ahead, crossing a bridge to another platform. Lili and Alara moved to follow when a burst of flames hit the rope bridge. It took only an instant for it to blacken and the ropes to turn to ash.

Alara couldn't see past the smoke and flames to check if the others had made it to the other side before the bridge tumbled into the darkness. But Lili was already pulling her in another direction, and she followed as best she could, feet stumbling after her with a mind of their own.

"We need to get to the east side of Arbol. There is an escape ladder that leads out." Lili's voice came out in pants.

Without breaking stride, Alara nodded, feeling a sense of direction settle over her. East. Head east. They crossed two more bridges, Lili navigating them. They passed a councilguard throwing fire and Alara shot her hand out, grabbing ahold of the flames and twisting them back at the guard. He screamed and fell back, feet slipping off the platform as his black uniform caught fire. Alara looked on with a small amount of satisfaction, but didn't have much time to celebrate as a building collapsed nearby. Without another word between them, the pair was running again. Her eyes stung with smoke as she watched the city around her burn. Something dark and twisted was settling in her stomach as they ran, the heat of the flames only fueling her anger more.

A high cry split the air around them as they crossed a large platform. Alara turned sharply to see two councilguards bearing down on a small bruyita, curled in on himself, brown curls dusted with ash. They were a few yards away. She turned to tell Lili, but found her already moving toward the boy and guards, hands outstretched.

A small branch from the tree beneath the platform shot up and wrapped around one of the councilguard's ankles. It took only a second for him to slash the tree away with his spear, but now Lili and Alara had their attention.

Feeling the solid absence of her spear, Alara shot forward and landed a swift kick at the blameless guard's knees. He grunted and stumbled, but didn't fall. Instead, he swung around, a spear arcing toward her, tip already bloody. She dodged and jammed her elbow into his side.

He twisted around, faster than Alara expected and the spear sliced through her shirt, drawing blood and a sharp sting of pain. But the wound was shallow.

"Lili, duck!" She screamed over the crackle of fire.

She threw her hands up, calling the inferno around them and sending them swirling at both councilguards, a wall of chaotic flames. Lili dodged out of the way, but just as quickly the fire veered off to the side and crashed into a building, blown off course by a burst of air from one of the guards.

"Lili, grab the kid and go! I'll be behind you," Alara said, throwing another attack at the councilguards, blocking them from view as a wall of fire sprung up between them. She could see by the color of his aguayo that one of them was a wind mage, but the other's uniform had been blameless. She just needed to kill the mage first.

Lili didn't respond, but after a beat, Alara saw her grab the child, scooping him up in her arms.

"East side, to the left of the u-bent branch," Lili said, breathless. "That's where the ladder is."

"Got it," Alara said, trying to breathe as more fire flashed around them. "Now, go!"

Lili ran, but Alara was focused on the two councilguards before her. One mage, one blameless. Two spears and leather armor. Alara had a dull dagger and was wearing a woven skirt. Not exactly an equal fight.

She lunged forward, magia first, sending fire skittering around the two councilguards. The mage raised his hands to attack and she quickly twisted around him, kicking the back of his knees. She grabbed at his spear and twisted the shaft as he tried to aim at her, pulling him down. The other councilguard's spear came toward her and she rolled to the side, bringing the other guard's body with her. The spear slashed into his chest and she felt more than heard the groan of pain above her.

Stumbling backward, she let the mage councilguard's body fall to the ground. He was no longer moving, and Alara stood to face the blameless guard, spear pointed at her chest.

She was weaponless. Alara felt a shudder move through her as Emaru's voice whispered in her mind. *You're never weaponless.*

Throwing up her hands, she pulled at the threads of magia burning in her chest. It was easy connecting with the fire around them. The air itself sizzled with magia, heated by the burning wood around them. A funnel of fire flew at the councilguard, aimed directly for his chest.

He twisted his wrist and the fire veered to the left and hit the tree behind him. Alara's teeth clenched and her eyes found the single bronze band on his arm—the mark of a blameless councilguard.

The bastard was wearing the wrong uniform.

He lunged the spear toward her. She rolled to the side and scrambled for something—anything. Her fingers found the dagger at her belt and wrenched it out, slashing it in front of her to block the second jab of the spear.

She jumped to her feet, dodging again and twisting around to jam the dagger into his side. Even a dull blade would pierce if she stabbed hard enough. A burst of air threw her off her feet before the blade could connect.

"You're supposed to be blameless," Alara growled, indignant, as if they were obligated to play by fair rules. She twisted around him again, trying to use her speed and size to her advantage. He didn't turn fast enough and Alara brought her dagger to his side, hoping the hit would send him off balance. Instead the blade sank into his flesh, sending a splatter of bright red blood sizzling across the heated wooden platform.

She pulled the blade back and looked down at the sharp edge of metal stained red.

Sharp?

There wasn't time to ponder the dagger or its apparent ability to turn sharp when she needed. The wind mage was coming toward her again, one hand clenched to his bloody side, but the other outstretched. She braced herself for the attack, but it didn't come.

Black eyes widened as they met her own and she saw him twist his arm again and again, but to no avail. Alara didn't hesitate. Pulling her threads of magia toward her, she threw a column of fire at him and lunged for his legs with her dagger. He took a sharp step back, dodging the sharp tip of her blade, but the fire pelted him in the chest. He didn't even yell as he toppled from the platform and into the abyss below.

Alara felt her knees give out and let herself crumple to the ground. Her heart beat hard and fast in her chest and her hair stuck to her sweat-soaked face. The air around her was thick with smoke, searing her lungs. She couldn't get a deep breath. Fumbling for her magia, Alara stretched out the threads and tried to pull at the fires around her. She didn't know what she was doing—how to put the flames out—but she had to do something. She tugged and twisted her magia, trying to dampen the power of the fire, but the flames only danced. She felt helpless with her powers for the first time since she had faced Emaru.

She didn't know how long she tried to fight the roaring inferno that circled her, but she felt her magia growing weak. Her head spun, whether from lack of oxygen or exhaustion, she wasn't sure.

And then a hand landed on her arm, tugging her.

"What are you doing?" Runeo's voice was loud in her ears. "We need to go!"

He was pulling her forward, but she resisted. "Lili said to go east."

"It's too late for that. We need to go down *now*."

Alara's heart stuttered as he pulled her to the edge of the platform. She looked down into the leaves and branches where the councilguard had fallen to his death. She shook her head. "Are you crazy?"

"Probably. Trust me?" He was smiling. He was actually smiling as their city was burning around them and they were about to jump to their very probable deaths.

"No," Alara said a split second before he pulled her down with him.

His arms wrapped around her waist and she could feel the air rush by her ears. In a small corner of her mind, she remembered a very similar moment mere weeks ago when Quenti had pulled her over the edge of a cliff and started them down this path. Then they hit a branch, cracking it under their weight. Then another. And another.

Seconds or perhaps hours later, Alara felt them slam into the ground. Air rushed from her lungs. Beside her, Runeo lay gasping for breath, blood trickling from a fresh cut on his cheek.

"Can you get off me?" He groaned, tugging at the arm that Alara realized was trapped under her weight. She didn't answer, still trying to let the air return to her body, but she rolled over and released him.

"If you wanted to kill me, there are easier ways," she finally bit out.

"You're welcome for saving you."

"I still might be dead."

"Stop being dramatic. I slowed us down and we missed the bigger branches." He stood up slowly, muscles moving under his skin as he assessed the damage to his arm.

"Barely," she muttered and stood, at last able to breathe. Looking around the forest where they landed, she felt a wave of confusion at the white snow that blanketed the ground. But then her stomach turned and she looked up at the trees above her. White ash was falling from above.

Arbol rained down on them.

A few yards away a large charred branch crashed down, sending embers flying, one hitting her cheek with a sharp zip of pain. The forest was lush and green from the wet season, but the heat in the air was starting to dry the wood. This was a forest fire waiting to happen.

"It's too dangerous to stay here," Alara's voice was hoarse.

Runeo stared back at her, eyes sharp with purpose. This was the man that she hadn't seen since the Haven. The warrior prepared for battle instead of the boy with the broken heart. He nodded as another chunk of smoldering wood fell nearby. It was a piece of a building or platform. Or something... not that it mattered. Anger seared through Alara as the blackened lumber was eaten away. The place she thought she could call home. Her chance at peace.

The Council had taken everything from her again.

Her eyes scanned the forest around them. She could hear people running—other bruyas fleeing, likely… but also…

She saw a flash of bronze to her left and followed without hesitation. Her dagger was back in her hand, still bloodstained and sharp as she ran, following the snapping of branches. She moved like a pumisi, jumping over roots, hunting the councilguard as he bolted through the forest. It was almost impressive how he moved, natural in the trees like few councilguards were, but it took only a single stumble for her to catch him.

Her elbow made contact with his side as he turned to meet her. He was darker skinned than her—uncommon for a councilguard— eyes black under thick brows, lips pulled back in a sneer over crooked teeth.

Blade first, she lunged for him, slashing at his chest and hitting only leather armor. Her abilities were exhausted, but she threw a punch at his side and heard the grunt that followed with satisfaction. She felt the earth under her shudder. He was an earth mage, despite the bronze blameless signifier on his arm. She refused to find out what he could do. The blade was slashing wildly again and she felt it sink into skin, warm blood flooding onto her hands. His fist made contact with her a few times, but she felt nothing. Nothing would interrupt her focus.

She didn't stop slashing until he was falling, knees crumpling beneath him. He was groaning—crying out.

"Stop!" His voice cracked.

Alara listened, her breath ragged as her arms dropped to her side. She heard Runeo behind her and realized he had caught up to her at some point. The man before her looked pathetic, blood leaking from the corner of his mouth.

"Please," he pleaded. She knew what she needed to do. What she should do. Yet, her dagger was still hanging by her side, loose in her grasp.

Runeo's warm hand was on her own, and he gently took the dagger from her bloody fingers. With a single slash, he brought the sharp blade across the councilguard's neck.

CHAPTER 13

QUENTI

Anumbness settled over Quenti as she watched the councilguard in front of Runeo collapse to the ground, blood spilling from his neck. She wanted to experience pity or disgust for the execution she had just witnessed, but instead, there was only a disturbingly cool disregard for the fallen mage.

She witnessed dozens—*hundreds*—of bruyas stumbling and screaming through Arbol. How many of them would come out alive? Why should she regard this man with any more thought than she gave them?

She didn't dwell on the lives lost for long, though. She couldn't. Khuna was alive and well, searching for Lili and the other survivors. Quenti had found who she was looking for.

"You made it." Her voice was too loud to her ears as she came into the clearing. Runeo and Alara looked up, drawn faces streaked with mud, ash, and blood.

"Alive and well," Runeo said, trying to smile but settling for a grimace.

"I wouldn't be so sure. Khuna may still kill you for running back into the fires."

Alara's eyes were wide and distant. She blinked a few times before she came back to herself. "Well, I'll defend his decision."

Quenti bit her lip and flung herself toward Alara before she could question it. She wrapped her arms around the girl's trembling form and held her for a moment.

"I'm glad you're not dead."

"Me too," Alara said with a harsh laugh that turned into a mix between a ragged cough and sob.

Quenti's throat was raw from smoke too.

"We should get moving," Runeo said. "It's going to continue to rain fire until…" His words seem to stick in his throat, but it didn't matter. They didn't need him to finish the sentence.

Until Arbol is completely gone.

Quenti took a deep breath, ignoring the sting of smoke in her nostrils. "This way. I left Khuna with some others."

"We should look for other survivors," Runeo said. No one answered, but they all moved forward in agreement.

The ground was scattered with ash, smoldering embers, and bodies. Some were councilguards, their dark uniforms splattered with blood, limbs and heads twisted in unnatural ways from the falls. Many more were bruyas. The trees were broad and clumped close together, blocking their view of the forest as a whole. Each time they moved around a trunk or through a particularly thick underbrush, they stumbled upon yet another macabre tableau just beyond.

As they picked up a few injured bruyas, who now trailed behind them in stunned silence, Quenti felt her numbness giving way to anger and hatred. This is what the Council wanted. The death and destruction of anyone who opposed them. No, to anyone who dared try to live outside of them. She had known this. She'd been told the story of the early Bruya Wars by her mother, and the horrors the blameless had inflicted on those *cursed* with magia. But those had always just been stories. They never felt real.

Hidden away in the trees with Khuna and the others, she'd hoped to forget. A part of her had wanted to believe in Alara's fantasy of living in peace, and of Quil'la's belief that they could simply hide here until the war was done and everyone was safe. Nothing was safe anymore. Would those who held magia ever be safe when the blameless still held power?

But she knew it hadn't only been blameless who attacked here today. Many of the councilguards were mages—brainwashed and controlled by the Council to turn on their own kind. This was what Quenti and Alara could have become. This is what Micos *had* become.

Those with magia would never be safe in Sombria, not as long as the Council held power.

Quenti chanced a glance at Runeo. He limped as they walked, his arm wrapped around another bruya's waist as he half carried her. One of her arms was wrapped around Runeo, but the other hung at an unnatural angle at her side.

They found Quil'la at last, dazed and wide-eyed, but still ushering people east, away from the falling ash. The small band of Arborelis they had collected on their way moved past them and followed the rest of the group. Runeo passed the injured woman he was helping to another man.

Quenti's eyes scanned the crowd until she saw Suri and Mitteo helping sort through the injured. They were pale and shaking, but unharmed.

"What's the plan?" Runeo looked to Quil'la expectantly.

Quil'la didn't answer right away. Her eyes were still wide and unblinking.

"This doesn't make sense." Her voice was soft when she finally spoke, ignoring the question. "None of this makes sense."

"The Haven is full of murderers. We already knew that long before this happened," Runeo said.

"But this was just chaos." Her eyes were focused above her now. "They should have surrounded the perimeter, stopped us from fleeing. Instead they just burned us down and ran."

Quenti felt the words settle like a stone in her stomach. It wasn't murder they were after. They had left enough bruyas alive to, what— spread the word of what they were willing to do now? This was just the opening message.

How did they find us? The thought hit Quenti like an icy wave, and she wasn't the only one thinking it. Quil'la's black eyes were focused on Alara in something akin to pain.

"We were safe until you came." Her voice was half accusation and half plea.

"I'm... I didn't..." Alara's face was losing color fast and her eyes moved between them with shock and fear. Before she could say more a cry filled the forest around them.

"Help!"

Heads swiveled to find Khuna running out of the forest, blood staining the once pale dress she was wearing.

Quenti's heart froze in her chest at the panicked look in Khuna's eyes.

"It's Lili."

CHAPTER 14

ALARA

Khuna guided them, running through the trees, each second stretching out as Alara's heart thundered in her chest.

She had left Lili. *She* had told her to run.

Lili was supposed to be safe. Alara had made sure of that.

Thoughts battered her mind with every step.

Minutes, or perhaps hours later, Khuna finally slowed. Lili lay prone in a small clearing. The first thing that Alara noticed was the dead councilguard sprawled nearby, a knife in his neck, and behind him the little boy she and Lili had saved, eyes and mouth wide open. His skin was pale, the stillness of death settled over his small body. Alara's stomach churned with acid, throat still burning with smoke. She took in the scene with a sense of cold dread.

Lili's dress was ripped open at her side, blood and something more spilling from a deep wound beneath. Burns ran up the side of her chest and face, disfiguring the tattooed vines that spiraled up and into her hairline.

The acrid sent of burnt skin assaulted Alara's senses and made her stomach churn. She pushed away the nausea as she fell to her knees next to Lili.

"Hey, we're here," Alara said, grasping her unburnt hand in her own. "It looks like you need a healer."

She tried to smile, give something reassuring, but her face wouldn't cooperate. Her head whipped around, looking at those who had followed them. Mitteo and Suri were there—off to the side. She made eye contact with the earth magite, but he only shook his head, shoulders slumped. Suri stood beside him, eyes stricken, a hand clasped hard over her mouth.

"Come on, Mitteo. You have to be able to do something," Alara said.

He shook his head again. Alara looked at the others one by one. "Someone. She needs help."

No one moved. The clearing seemed to hold its breath as Lili groaned.

Her chest rose and fell in erratic, shallow gasps. It wasn't the sound of someone needing to heal. It was the wheezing breaths of approaching death.

No.

Alara tore at her tunic, pressing the dirty fabric into the wound on Lili's side. She had healed Quenti once with her magia. She could do it again. But even as she plucked at the threads and called it to her, she took in the gaping wound.

"I need someone to hold it closed!" she snapped. Her own fingers were slick with blood as she tried to grasp the skin, pulling it together. No one moved and as her fingertips burned with heat, Lili convulsed beside her. She let go of her fire immediately, sick with guilt. Three new fingerprint-shaped burns marred the bruya's skin, but the wound still gaped.

"I was the one that was supposed to sacrifice myself in some heroic way up there," Alara said, tears burning her eyes.

Lili let out a trembling laugh, and Alara felt her hand squeeze in her own. "You can't steal all the fun."

Runeo kneeled on Lili's other side, running his fingers through her hair. She kept gasping, small tremors going through her body.

"Can someone take away her pain?" Alara asked, eyes scanning the others in desperation. "A mind-walker or..."

"I'm okay." Lili's words were only a whisper, her eyes distant, unable to focus. "I can't feel anything."

A sob clawed up from Alara's throat and she slumped over Lili, tears falling heavy and unchecked. She'd been the first bruya to truly accept Alara—the only one to trust her. And this is what had happened. This is where her trust had gotten her.

Without quite knowing why, she reached out with the threads of her magia and felt for Lili's earthen core, pulsing weakly beside her. The tierren's powers smelled of petrichor and moss. And then they were fading, magia dimming even as Alara scrambled to keep hold of it in her mind.

It went out like a candle and Lili's hand went limp in Alara's.

Alara didn't let go right away, her hand still grasping as if she could pull her back. Her mind searched for the core that had just been there, pulsing and alive one brief moment ago, but she felt nothing but Runeo beside her.

He breathed heavy, but his eyes were dry. Alara could see the muscles twitching in his jaw as he continued to run his fingers through Lili's tangled hair. Alara moved her hand to place it on his, but stopped herself before she touched him. Instead, she stumbled back, getting to her feet and just making it to the edge of the clearing before she emptied her stomach.

She felt a hand on her back a moment later, Quenti's presence cool and soft beside her.

It wasn't fair. Lili was the best of them. The one who taught

Alara what freedom could feel like. She was a healer, not a soldier. She shouldn't be the one lying dead after all of this.

Quil'la was right. This was Alara's fault. They had gone decades without the Council finding them, but now...

We had *been followed*.

It was the only thing that made sense. The councilguards they had left alive in Hurazon had tracked them.

Her jaw clenched as she pulled herself upright, her mouth sour. Quenti was silent and let Alara stagger away, back to where they had come from.

As she walked, the cries and soft whispered prayers faded behind her and the sounds of the forest hummed.

There could be no more half-measures. No hiding and hoping for the best. If they wanted peace—if Alara wanted a home and a life —the Council needed to be destroyed.

CHAPTER 15

ALARA

They left what remained of Arbol behind a few hours after dawn. In total, a few hundred had survived—out of the thousands that had lived there. Most were on the road with them, but a few dozen had stayed behind. Some stayed because they couldn't bear to leave their loved ones behind, and others because they knew that some would still come looking for Arbol—new arrivals or recruits, bruyas from other hidden villages, or the twins who so many months ago Alara had been waiting on to cleanse her mind. They had been due back over a month ago now and still hadn't been heard from. It seemed likely now that they never would. They would be grieved along with the rest of those who had simply disappeared into the ashes.

When Alara last saw the Arborelis staying behind, they'd been combing through the rubble, looking for bodies to bury. Khuna's parents had been among them, refusing to leave until her cousin was found.

Alara knew that those that followed Sol and the Many—the old religion—never burned their dead. Without a body, their souls would be lost, unable to move on to the next world. Or so they believed. In extreme circumstances, the Council had purposefully ordered bodies of bruyas to be burned in outright defiance of this back in Cielo and even the outskirts, although many still ignored this law. She didn't know if they had burned Arbol with this in mind, but the consequences had been the same.

By the time they had left, only a few dozen bodies had actually been recovered and buried. Those of the councilguards were left where they had fallen.

Alara had tried not to search the faces of the dead for Ardo, her lifelong councilguard friend she'd betrayed back in the Haven, but her eyes hadn't obeyed her commands. Thankfully, she never saw him. She hoped he hadn't been here at all—murdering defenseless families.

Lili had been laid to rest with the other bruyas that had been found, a line of graves in the middle of the cloud forest. A small root marker was placed above each, carved with a name—though only if someone was able to identify the person encased in the soil below.

Would she ever see these graves again? When would she get the chance to hike back here and pay her respects to the bruya who had been filled with so much love and light?

Adelmo wouldn't have a grave—his body would have been burned. There'd be nowhere she could go to honor him.

A roster of the dead ran through Alara's head as they marched through the forest in a line two or three people wide. A name for each step. Her parents. Tony, the prisoner who had helped in the battle at the Haven. Adelmo. Zinita. Lili. Hundreds of bruyas she didn't even know the names of.

She didn't know if her thoughts were written plainly on her face, but Quenti reached over and clasped her hand. On Quenti's other side, her fingers were intertwined with Khuna's. The three of them walked in silence, holding each other until they stopped for mid-day meal—a meager ration of corn and potatoes that had survived the attack. There had been food stored by the farming terraces, away from the main part of Arbol. The councilguards either hadn't found the buildings or hadn't cared to destroy the food stores.

The food needed to get them all to the meeting location—Cueva —which was still a week's walk away at the pace they could move with bruyitas and curve-backed welos leaning on walking sticks. There were a few alpacas and l'lamas holding the food they could, with the stronger bruyas taking their own burden of supplies. It was a sad and disheveled caravan.

"Well, at least we're used to being hungry," Quenti said, poking at her last bites of corn.

Alara finished her own meal and tried to ignore the gnawing in her gut.

The decision to leave Arbol had been uncharacteristically quick for Quil'la and the other leaders. But then again, what other choice did they have? They couldn't simply wait around for another attack from the Council now that their location was known. There was no reason to stay, especially if survival was the goal.

"Do you think we'll pass by a river we can fish in?" Mitteo asked. He and Suri were sitting close together, looking a bit more relaxed, as they were finally headed toward familiar allies.

Khuna groaned at this comment. "I would rather survive off bark than eat more fish."

"I second that," Alara said.

Suddenly, she heard a curse and felt something wet land on her cheek.

"Murderers." The word was whispered, but everyone heard it. She wasn't sure who had spoken, but as she looked around, she noticed a gathering of bruyas staring at them with a mixture of disgust and hatred painted on their faces.

"How can we let them walk free?" A woman spoke this time, her voice coming out in a sharp hiss.

Alara's heart thrummed heavy in her chest as she searched the faces around them for any sign of pity or trust. She wiped the spit from her face, peering into their soot-stained faces. Drained of hope and exhausted, she couldn't blame them for how they were feeling.

Quil'la walked through the crowd that had gathered, a look of consternation on her face. Beside her was Rom, the eldest of the leaders, face looking worn and tired. Tocco, she now knew as the younger of the male Elders, had remained behind in Arbol to help with the search and clean-up. Quil'la lifted her hand, and the bruyas around her fell silent.

"My people have a point," she said, eyebrow raised and eyes directed at Alara. "I have allowed you all freedom in Arbol, but my trust is finite. And it is broken now, burnt to ash with our sisters and brothers."

Alara took a sharp breath and opened her mouth. She didn't have anything to offer except denials and promises. Perhaps she deserved this derision if the councilguards had indeed tracked them from Hurazon.

Before she could think of anything to say, though, another voice spoke from behind her.

"Lili trusted her. I trust her." Runeo came from somewhere in the crowd to stand behind her, close enough that she could feel the heat from his body. "I trust them all." His words were directed now to the gathered crowd. "They helped save Khuna, betraying their own people to aid us. If they led the councilguards to us, it wasn't intentionally. And as I was also in the group, I'm as much to blame."

Quil'la's eyes were inscrutable and her face impassive as she listened. The crowd around them appeared disquieted by his words.

"Enough blood has been spilled," Quil'la said, voice soft and thunderous at the same time. "No harm will come to them. Now is not the time for an arrest or trial."

Alara felt her shoulders slump in something akin to relief, but Quil'la stepped toward her, voice low so that only their small group could hear.

"But I will be watching you all. And if Mena and Beno return, they will read your intentions and find the truth."

Alara stiffened, tilting her chin up in defiance. "They won't find anything I haven't already said."

"Good," Quil'la said, turning on her heels and disappearing back into the crowd.

A few hours after lunch, the small dirt path they had been following since Arbol suddenly turned into a stone walkway, moss clumped thick between cracks. It was old—older than anything Alara had seen in Sombria, and she commented as much to Khuna.

"There are paths like this throughout the cloud forests," she said. "They were built by the bruyas before the invasion and the war."

"Invasion?"

"The invasion that led to the Bruya Wars. When the outsiders came and tried to suppress magia." Khuna spoke slowly, looking at Alara as if she was stupid.

Alara shook her head. "The Bruya Wars were started by the bruyas, not an invasion."

"Of course that's what they told you," Runeo's voice came from behind them. "But that's not what we grew up learning. Before the outsiders came, this land was full of magia. There were no blameless, only bruyas."

"That sounds like a wonderful place," Quenti said, voice wistful.

Alara didn't respond to this and silence fell among the group again. She wasn't so sure it sounded wonderful, and she definitely wasn't sure she believed the bruya's stories of the times before.

Then again, a world where she wasn't constantly fighting just to have a home, didn't sound half bad. Arbol had almost been that safe haven, but then the councilguards had destroyed that. They had killed thousands. Killed Lili. Almost killed Alara. If it hadn't been for her dagger...

Alara gave a start and tugged the dagger from her belt, fingers running along the edge of the bronze blade.

"Why do you still have that, after all this time?" Quenti asked. "Did you try stabbing the councilguards with it back in Arbol?" The girl's voice was light, but there was a tightness in her face that made the tone feel forced. Alara still appreciated it.

"I... I did."

"You're kidding."

"No, I really did stab someone with it—cut them."

Quenti raised an eyebrow, giving her a look somewhere between condescension and concern.

"The blade was sharp."

"I feel like we've been through this before," Quenti said, grabbing the dagger from Alara and slashing it across her arm. "Yup. Still dull as a spoon."

Alara let out a growl of frustration as she wrestled the dagger back from Quenti and looked at the blade carefully. "I killed someone with it."

"I have no doubt you'd be deadly with a spoon, as well."

She rolled her eyes at the declaration, but couldn't help the smile that tugged at her lips. The banter felt familiar and lifted a weight off her chest.

"I'm not crazy," she said. "It drew blood and afterward the councilguard..."

Her words faded and her footsteps slowed as she pictured the scene again in her head. The blood trickling from the wound in his side as he flung his hands out, desperate to grab his magia.

"I think it took his magia." Her voice was barely above a whisper. Now she knew she sounded crazy.

It was Mitteo who spoke next, coming up beside her, eyes lit with the same brightness she used to see back in classes with him.

"I've heard of experiments to imbue weapons with magia. The Council made the practice illegal, stating it was too dangerous."

"It doesn't have a receptive," Alara said twisting the dagger around to show him. "That's the only way to store magia."

Mitteo shrugged. "I think there's a lot that we don't know about magia. Things the Council didn't want us to know."

"Including Cruz," Suri muttered from behind Alara.

Mitteo ignored the comment. "Where'd you get it?"

"I found it outside Attalea, wedged between some rocks," Alara said, thinking back to the outcrop of rocks she had stumbled on and the glint of metal in the shadows. She thought of the familiarity of the clearing she hadn't understood in the moment. Now she remembered. She had been the one to hide the dagger there the day her parents died. "I was the one..." She hesitated, unsure of why she didn't want to tell them the truth. "I don't think it's just a dagger."

It was important, and it needed to stay secret, although she couldn't quite remember why. Her memories felt hazy as she tried to focus on them, even now, slipping from her grasp like the memories of a dream upon waking. She may have unlocked the piece of her that Luis, the Council's mind-walker, had hidden when he cleansed her mind, but she still couldn't seem to grasp them readily. There were two histories in her mind vying for attention when she thought of that time.

"Perhaps you should put your weapon away while you remain under suspicion." Quil'la's voice was sharp but quiet as she fell into step beside them.

Alara started, but didn't comply immediately. "I think the dagger has magia—"

"I will ask again that you put it away and stop talking about it," Quil'la said. "Now is a time of mourning, not the time to speculate about trivial weapons."

"It's not trivial."

"I'll decide what is and isn't trivial, child."

"Your decisions are what got us here," Alara said, unable to help herself. "Maybe if the Arborelis spent more time thinking about weapons, Arbol wouldn't have been destroyed so easily."

"If you don't drop this subject now, I'll be forced to take the dagger for myself."

She knew she had crossed a line as the woman's eyes narrowed and the lines around her lips pulled taut. Alara's jaw clenched, but she slipped the bronze blade back into her belt without another word.

Quil'la gave her an impassive stare that she couldn't read and then walked forward and back into the crowd without looking back.

"Someone had to say it," Runeo said, taking Quil'la's spot beside her. "I'm just glad it wasn't me speaking the truth for once."

"Even if the Elders had decided to head for the gorge sooner, Arbol would still have been attacked," Quenti noted.

"Perhaps, yes," Runeo said, voice hard and cold. "But our complacency was decades in the making. The Elders kept us in hiding and made us vulnerable with their fear of taking the offensive."

No one spoke to argue the point.

"None of you can deny it," he continued. "Arbol needed to act a long time ago. I can only hope that this attack acts as a wake-up call. The world is changing and women like Quil'la are going to die if they don't change. Worse still, if they don't allow those around them to change, we're all going to die alongside them."

Alara bit the inside of her cheek, trying to push away the burning pain behind her eyes as she thought of Lili and all the others they had left behind. The group fell quiet and kept walking, eyes focused ahead.

CHAPTER 16

QUENTI

Quenti was beginning to think the rest of her life would just be walking. Her feet and legs no longer ached, which was something to be grateful for, but she still longed for a place to rest that wasn't a wool blanket on the hard ground. Each morning she woke up feeling a bit more drained than the morning before.

She had lost track of how long ago they'd left the remains of Arbol behind. The days blended together as their sad, quiet processional followed an old stone path across mountains and valleys, only broken up by the occasional rope bridge that had to be tested and crossed with care, a few bruyas at a time. They passed ruins of old settlements as they walked, low stone walls that formed mazes, the thatched roofs of the buildings having years ago disappeared or decayed. Some nights, they slept within these dead cities, pressed against the crumbling walls to hide from the sharp winds. Despite the increased warmth on those evenings though, Quenti tossed and turned uneasily during these stays. She preferred the openness of the woods, without the press of lurking ghosts.

The group moved in surprising stealth given its size, their silence a mixture of mourning, exhaustion, and the fear of councilguards hidden and ready to pounce. Nowhere felt safe, but they didn't run across another living soul. Even the animals seemed to steer clear of their path.

The steady march gave Quenti too much time to think, and she was pulled into the spiral of grief and anger. At times, it was Lili's face that haunted her, drained of blood and wailing in agony. Other times, it was her father's face twisted in hatred as he glared at her. And then there was the older, but still sharp ache that came at night when her mother's warm voice rang in her mind and she woke only to remember she was long dead.

The only time words were exchanged was at night as they negotiated guard duty and rolled out their sparse wool blankets. Khuna and Quenti shared one between them, curled on their sides and pressed together for warmth more than affection. The tension in just their small group was heavy as Runeo continued to stew in his anger and Alara spent hours on end staring at her dagger as if it might start speaking to her.

A part of Quenti understood the restless energy seething beneath the surface, but another side of her just wanted to forget everything —let Senye Cruz and Quil'la deal with whatever came next.

The final part of her was mad beyond all belief.

The warm sun streamed through the trees that had been thinning out over the past day. The land had started to flatten a few days before as well. The rolling mountains of southwest Sombria were now behind them. Sweat trickled down Quenti's back and she closed her eyes as a cooling breeze swept over her.

The pleasant sensation was short-lived, though, and her deep breath was quickly followed by a gag as she threw her hand over her mouth in horror.

"What is that Sol-forsaken smell?" she asked.

The breeze brought with it the bitter odor of metal and—rotten meat. She wasn't the only one looking queasy as the group slowed, whispers escalating.

"Welcome to the River Mied," Runeo said. He'd wrapped a bit of cloth over his mouth and nose and Quenti considered ripping a piece of her own shirt hem to follow his lead.

"I've been to the River Mied before," Alara said, "and it's never smelled like...this."

"You've never been past the point where it merges with the River Muerta, then," Runeo said with a shrug. "The River Muerta, which comes down from the eastern mountains and—"

"Runs directly through the Ruinedlands," Alara finished, a realization in her voice.

"I always thought the Ruinedlands were a myth or an exaggeration," Quenti said.

Alara shook her head, eyes peering into the distance at where Quenti assumed the lands lay. "Every new mage at some point takes a trek to the Ruinedlands, as a lesson—a lesson of what happens when magia is allowed to be unleashed without control or consequence."

Beside her, Khuna snorted.

Alara didn't look at her, but her voice was sharp. "No matter whose side you're on now, what happened to the Ruinedlands was horrid. Nothing lives or grows there—the mountains were turned into a landscape of black, endless sand. Not even magia can be wielded there. The land rips it from you and unleashes it in chaotic and unnatural storms."

"I don't argue the consequences of the battle that happened there," Quenti said, "but I'm not going to pretend that it was bruyas that caused the tear in the magia. It was the blameless who tried to steal the magia from the people, and instead stole it from the land itself."

"That's a convenient story," Alara said.

"No more convenient than what the Council teaches you," Runeo retorted.

"It doesn't matter what version of the history you want to believe." It was Mitteo's soft voice that interrupted the brewing argument, speaking directly to Quenti. "The results are the same. The waters from the River Muerta run tainted by the Ruinedlands, merging with the River Mied and straight into Lake Mied. And the lake is cursed."

Quenti shuddered at this, looking out at where she heard the river churning in the distance.

Khuna rested a hand on her shoulder, giving her a small reassuring squeeze. "Just don't drink the water and you'll be fine."

It took them longer than Quenti expected to make it to the river's banks. They truly had come to the exact spot the two rivers met, the River Mied from the west and the River Muerta from the east. The waters of River Mied flowed murky and brown, dirtier than the River Sura, but it was the River Muerta that drew her attention. It ran the color of blood, despite being nearly translucent. She could see the rocks and mud beneath the flowing currents, and thought perhaps those were what was giving the water the colors. Yet, as the river clashed and waters roiled, she could see red water meeting brown and turning the whole river a dark, opaque crimson.

They followed the river as it ran south until they came to the narrowest part, still at least twenty feet across. Even without the color of death staining the river, the waters would have looked deadly.

The smell was nearly unbearable and more Arborelis had ripped up tunics and skirts to tie around their noses. Others simply breathed through open mouths, faces pinched in discomfort. Quenti tried this, opening her mouth in a deep gasp only to gag at the taste of copper and death on her tongue. Perhaps the smell was better.

The mass of bruyas started to move, and Quenti could hear the orders rippling through the group.

"All tierren, move toward the front to help build a bridge," one said.

Mitteo followed orders, marching through the crowd as bruyas split, some following and others stepping aside. As a path parted, Quenti could see where the banks sloped sharply into the river. A few feet on either side, the grass stopped abruptly. All signs of life ended before the waters.

Quil'la directed the other tierrens, her own magia flowing as the ground beneath Quenti shifted. The trees were at least sixty feet from the river's edge, but suddenly four roots burst from the ground a few yards from the banks and began weaving around each other. She watched the lines of concentration and near pain that painted each tierren's face as the roots twisted and undulated to span across the waters. There was nothing beautiful or flowing about the display. Not like she had seen in Arbol as tierrens built or repaired bridges there. It was almost violent. The water fought back at every bit of magia that pushed toward it.

By the time the bridge stretched across the waters, three of the tierrens had collapsed. No one spoke as they were set gently on the backs of the l'lamas that danced nervously on the river banks.

The mass of bruyas crossed the twisted bridge of roots with silent unease. As Quenti stepped off the land and above the red waters, a sickening dread sank into her stomach, weighing her body down, and each step felt like walking through waist-deep mud. The thickness immediately disappeared once she was on the other side of the river, past the dead patch of land that flanked each side of the river.

"That was... unnatural," Khuna said, face green. The rest of the group didn't comment, even as Mitteo stumbled over to them looking pale and shaken. Only Alara seemed unperturbed by the crossing, and Quenti wondered again what it had been like for the girl to spend her life with her magia suppressed. What did it feel like now to suddenly be unleashed?

Quil'la ordered the bridge to be destroyed, which somehow seemed to take just as much energy from the tierren as creating it had done. But after a few long minutes, the roots split apart and fell into the waters below, swept away by the current in a matter of seconds. Any trace of the roots on either side of the river sank back into the ground, leaving the shores unmarked.

And with that, they started walking again, this time south along the eastern bank of the river as it descended into a small gorge. Despite each passing minute, Quenti never seemed to get used to the bitter smell in the air. If anything, as the gorge deepened and the walls clawed up on either side of them, stretching above their heads now, it only seemed to grow all the more pungent. It was as though the gorge was *trapping* the smell.

The ground they were on turned to dirt and stone.

"Why does nothing grow against the river?" It was Alara who asked the question that Quenti had been mulling over for the past half hour. Not so much as a strip of weeds present between the shadow of the walls and the deadly waters on their other side.

"This land is built on magia—the grass, the trees—it's all born from magia. Like the Ruinedlands, this river suppresses it, taking life from everything in the process." Khuna's voice was soft, careful of the echoes that easily climbed the canyon walls.

A shiver ran up Quenti's spine as she gaped at the red waters flowing just a few feet away. They were far enough away that she could feel her cool magia flowing through her chest, though it was sluggish and she felt the unnatural sense of dread sitting not too far from her consciousness, as though standing on the edge of a cliff, teetering between life and death.

Alara ran her fingers along the wrinkled burn that curved along her cheek and chin. It was the scar that Alara had gotten the day her parents died. They had only briefly spoken about it since fleeing the Haven—just enough for Quenti to know that the Council had been responsible, though Alara spent an entire lifetime blaming herself.

Quenti still didn't know how Alara had managed to pull the memory back from the mind-walker, but she had never pressed the subject. She wasn't even sure Alara had wanted to share any of the information with her. Quenti just happened to have been on guard while the others slept when Alara woke up from the nightmare, hands clawing at her throat. She'd told the story to Quenti in sharp whispers, staring out into the trees as she did. And then they had sat in silence until the sun began to set and the others started to wake.

Alara never spoke about the conversation again or the day her parents died. There were some things that didn't need to be relived.

Their small group fell into silence again as they followed along behind the other bruyas. The canyon itself seemed to quiet most conversations, and the only sound was the water rushing beside them.

An indeterminable amount of time later, they finally stopped and murmurs quickly passed through the crowd as Quenti realized they had arrived... somewhere.

The canyon walls looked exactly the same as they had before, pale brown and lifeless, stretching toward the darkening sky high above.

"What's going on?" Alara whispered, peeking around the mob of bruyas in front of them, a comical endeavor given that most of them had at least four inches on her. Even with Quenti's height, she couldn't quite see where Quil'la stood against the gorge wall.

"Come on," she whispered, grabbing Alara by the arm and pushing them through the crowd, moving toward the gorge wall. They managed to maneuver through, popping out a few yards from the front of the group. She felt movement behind them and saw that

Khuna and Runeo had followed suit. Alara opened her mouth to speak, but Quenti lightly shoved her elbow into the girl's stomach, not wanting to draw attention. She wasn't sure if the bruyas would think this information classified from the likes of their magite and rebel group.

Quil'la was running her fingers along the stone walls. From where they stood, Quenti could just make out the small etchings, long lines with notches along the spine.

"She's reading it." Khuna's breath whispered into Quenti's ear, voice barely even a whisper.

"Reading what?" She tried to keep her voice just as quiet.

"The old language of the bruyas—before the invasion. It was used as a code during the wars, sent on ropes and string."

Quenti bit her lip, nose wrinkled in concentration. "I think Mama—she had an art piece hanging on our wall when I was little. She always told me it represented her favorite verse from the scriptures. It was a series of knots and colored string. Almost like the weaves merchants use for record keeping, only... different."

Khuna's warm hand settled on her waist, squeezing lightly. "I always knew your mama was secretly a rebel."

Quenti let out a small huff of air. "Maybe, but she never managed to leave Sombria. She never managed to leave..."

Papa.

Me.

Would it have been that simple? To run into the cloud forest with her baby and never look back?

Another squeeze on her waist, this time sharper, brought Quenti out of her thoughts. Thoughts that would only lead her down bad places anyway.

Quil'la spoke to a few nearby bruyas, and they took their places along the wall.

Those around them watched in transfixed silence as the scattering of bruyas along the walls connected with their magia, and the wall started to glow and shudder. And then, where nothing but smooth wall had stood a second before, a crevice appeared, just wide enough for two bodies to slip through.

The group surged forward, but the momentum came to a sudden halt as a tall woman stepped through the newly formed doorway and surveyed the crowd. Quenti recognized the figure as Senye Cruz—one of their allies back in the Haven. The one who called this meeting to begin with.

Senye Cruz's voice rang out and echoed briefly against the gorge's steep walls. Although Quil'la stood in front of her, the ex-councilwoman's eyes landed on Alara and Quenti. A small smile lifted her lips.

"Welcome to Death's Throat. We have much to discuss."

Chapter 17

Alara

No one moved forward as Senye Cruz and Quil'la stepped aside, speaking too quietly for Alara to hear. It took a few moments for either of them to notice no one had moved forward.

"Everyone, please come in," Senye Cruz said, eyes sweeping the crowd. "If you follow the corridor straight, you'll find the main hall has food waiting," She turned her eyes back to Quil'la. "Our lookouts saw your group approaching, so we've been preparing."

Still, no one moved until Quil'la waved her hands impatiently. "You heard her. Go on."

The spell was broken as families, l'lamas, and alpacas surged forward like a wave.

Without having to speak, Alara and the others sidestepped and fell in line against the stone walls, letting the rest of the Arborelis pass. No one else lingered, perhaps because of the promise of food or the urge to get farther from the pulsing waters of the river.

Alara had seen the unease it caused and had felt it herself. But rather than a sickening nausea in her throat, as Quenti felt, Alara was only left with a slight hollowness, as though a tiny hole had been punched in the very corner of her mind. Perhaps it was because she was already used to feeling like her magia was jutting up against an impenetrable wall. This sense of foreboding had defined her entire existence until recently, as she had spent most of her life wearing a magia-suppressing bracelet.

It took nearly twenty minutes for the whole of Arbol to slip through the narrow doorway, but eventually it was only their small group, Quil'la, and Senye Cruz left.

While Quil'la seemed annoyed by the intrusion, Senye Cruz smiled broadly. It was a smile Alara had never once seen on the woman's face before, even having grown up around the council-woman. Then again, she and Senye Cruz had never had the strongest relationship. Not for the first time since their narrow escape from Cielo, Alara wondered if Senye Cruz hadn't hated her growing up, but rather only disliked her guardian, Linda Emaru.

"I'm glad you made it here," Senye Cruz said. "I was beginning to worry you hadn't escaped."

"For a while," Alara said, "I was worried we wouldn't make it either."

Senye Cruz's eyes drifted back to Quil'la.

"I am happy to see you came as well," she said, "but I admit, I expected fighters, not families."

Quil'la gave the woman a pinched expression. "As you said, we have much to discuss. Perhaps after the children have been shown their rooms."

Alara didn't bother to hide her annoyance at the tone of the bruya's voice or the use of the word *children*. Senye Cruz's eyes shone with amusement, but she agreed and motioned for them to follow her and the rest of the group, the door of the cavern closing with a groan behind them.

The hallway was thrown into darkness, causing Alara to stumble as she tried to get her bearings. It took a few seconds for her eyes to adjust. A wan light emanated from small torches lighting the walls at inconsistent intervals. They burned with natural fire, the smoke leaking out above them through ventilation holes. The system was similar to the Haven's own, but older and running without magia or receptors.

The corridor itself was narrow, with rock ceilings pressing down low—though still well above Alara's head. The Haven had some areas like this as well, but they were often tucked away in the deepest and least traveled parts of the underground city.

Despite its clear disuse, the darkness and the cobwebs in the corners, Alara felt something like contentment settle in her bones. The smell of stale air and earth was familiar.

They walked for a few minutes before the corridor opened to a wide cavern. It was large—though not nearly as large as the marketplace back home. The word *home* twisted something in Alara's gut, and she felt a burning behind her eyes she quickly swallowed down.

The Arborelis split up and disappeared into separate corridors. Senye Cruz led their own small cohort down a narrow hall to the left and into a large chamber stocked with dusty bedrolls and carved rock jutting out from the walls that acted as seats. A door to the right led into a small water closet. After weeks of mostly camping in the woods, even the small room felt like a luxury.

Quil'la had stayed back in the main cavern, helping direct traffic, so it was only Senye Cruz that stood in the doorway, watching as they shuffled into the room.

"It seems that I have a meeting to attend now," she said. "But I look forward to speaking with you all about what's happened since we left the Haven. I have a feeling it will be an interesting conversation."

Her eyes took them in with a warm curiosity that Alara had never seen in them before. And then her lips turned down in a frown, brows knit tightly together.

"There was another one—a bruya with you," she said. More statement than question, but the intention was clear.

Alara felt the blood drain from her face and Runeo clenched his fists beside her.

It was Mitteo who answered, voice soft. "She died in the attack that sent us all here. Councilguards."

Senye Cruz pressed her lips together. "A lot to be discussed indeed. I'm sorry for your loss, though I know the words mean nothing."

With that, she turned on her heels and gently closed the door as she left.

And then they were alone, and the silence was heavy and painful. Alara numbly sat on the ground, back against the stone wall, seats and bedrolls forgotten. The others followed, Mitteo and Runeo taking their seats along the indentations while Suri, Khuna, and Quenti fell onto the dusty bedrolls, sending thick clouds of dirt into the air.

Silence descended on the group, each of them seemingly lost in their own thoughts and emotions. Alara couldn't stop her own from drifting back to the feel of Lili's magia going dark within her. When Adelmo had passed, as painful as it was, she didn't have to feel his light dissipate. It was a sensation she'd never felt before and she hoped she never would again, though Alara knew Lili wouldn't be the last to die in this impending war. That thought alone sent a sharp wave of pain through Alara, her fingers finding the ridges of her scar and skating across her face.

She didn't want this. There had to be a way to stop it before it started.

"We should be in that meeting," she said. A few of them startled at the declaration.

"There's a lot to this—more than we probably know about," Mitteo said after a beat.

"Which is even more reason we should be there," Alara said.

"I'm sure Senye Cruz will let us know when they need us."

"So, never," Suri cut in. "Senye Cruz acts as her own council."

"I trust her," Mitteo said, eyes looking between them all.

"We know," Alara said.

He flinched at her tone and didn't respond. The group fell into silence again, but after a few minutes, they began shuffling around. Quenti and Suri set about cleaning off the bedrolls and arranging them along one side of the room. Khuna went to investigate the water closet, coming out a few minutes later looking horrified.

Alara tuned out the hushed voices and drew her dull dagger, no longer surprised by the capricious nature of the blade. It turned sharp when she needed it—or at least when it *wanted* to. Was there a difference between those two things? A small voice whispered in her mind that she was thinking about the dagger as if it was alive.

This is what going insane feels like.

But then again... Alara thought of the times she had sworn she had felt a core of magia, small but distinct, radiating from the dagger. Mitteo had said some objects could be infused with power. Is that what it would feel like?

She reached out toward it with her mind, blocking out the magia of the others around her, flickering with different shades of restlessness and grief. For a second, she felt nothing.

Insanity, the voice whispered again.

But then—there was a spark of magia, warm and shimmering in the corner of her awareness, the dagger warming in her hands.

El'dyo, what are you?

"That's it," Runeo said, eyes bright and jaw clenched. "I'm crashing their little meeting."

"They made it clear they don't want us there," Mitteo said, flinching under the glare that Runeo sent his way.

"They think they can just push us aside and we'll wait here nice and quiet with our hands folded. That might be the magite way. It may even be the Arboreli way, but it's not my way." Runeo left without a second glance at the group.

Alara was on her feet before she could even think. "I'm going too," she said to no one in particular as she rushed out after Runeo, dagger still clenched in her hand.

"No." Runeo didn't spare her a passing glance as he walked. "Go back."

"Don't tell me what to do," Alara said peevishly. "I have questions for them, too, you know."

His eyes fell to the weapon in her hands. "About magiaful daggers?"

She bit back any response. That's exactly what she wanted to talk about.

"Just don't get in my way." His voice was rough. She wanted to be angry at him, to smack the snarl off his face. But under the simmering rage, she could sense the bitter hint of grief.

She had only known Lili for less than a season. Runeo had known her since they were bruyitas. He had lost her, Zinita, Micos.

So instead, she opened her mouth to say something comforting or soft. "Runeo—"

Before she could think what to say next, a man turned the corner, eyes tightening as he saw Runeo and her coming toward him.

"Alara?" the newcomer said. It was half question, half statement.

She nodded.

"Quil'la is looking for you. Follow me." The man turned without even looking at Runeo, who grunted in confusion as they followed the man.

He ushered Alara and Runeo through a door at the end of one of the many halls in the hidden caverns. The room was filled with a table nearly the same size as the floor, with chairs tucked neatly along the edges, mostly full with an assortment of bruyas and magites. A few familiar faces like Senye Cruz and Quil'la stood out, but the vast majority were strangers.

As she stepped in, she was aware of the small commotion behind her. Runeo was in the doorway, the staff of a magite blocking him from entering.

"Only her," the man that had fetched them said. Runeo's eyes burned into the back of Alara's head as she turned.

A part of her savored the smugness of being let in without him. Another part of her felt very alone standing in front of the room.

"Thank you, Bruno," Senye Cruz said before motioning for Alara to sit in the empty seat beside her.

The bruyas and mages around the table had gone back to the argument they had been having when Alara entered. No one was looking at her. She recognized a few of the faces, and her heart gave a small jump to see Elna—one of the mages who had assisted in their escape from the Haven—and her familiar spiked hair.

"They can't be trusted," Quil'la's voice was sharp. "Extra bodies do us no good if they turn on us."

"This isn't the time for petty—"

"Petty?" Quil'la snapped. "They are willing to murder anyone who gets in the way of their agenda. Even us."

"I'm inclined to believe the bruya on this matter," Elna said.

Senye Cruz watched the discussion with lips pulled down and brows furrowed. "Perhaps this argument should be continued at a different time." Her voice was soft, but sharp.

Quil'la's nostrils flared as she scowled at the other woman, but she was silent as she turned to Alara.

"Did you bring it?"

Alara gave a look of confusion. "I…"

"The dagger, child."

Her cheeks flushed at the bruya's use of child, but set the dagger on the table.

A man in the back corner sneered as he spoke. "I know I don't understand bruyas well, but why should I care about a dagger?"

No one replied, but Elna shifted in her seat as if biting her tongue to not agree out loud.

"It's not just a dagger," Alara said, chin tilted up. "I… at least I don't think."

Quil'la gave a nod of assent and motioned for her to continue. So she did, the words spilling from her mouth like a waterfall. She tried to ignore the looks of incredulity as she spoke, knowing she sounded insane as she explained that the blade could turn sharp at random intervals, and seemed to have the ability to take away powers.

She did not mention the spark of magia that she felt from the dagger, as if it were alive, or the fact that she remembered hiding the dagger herself on her mama's command. There were some things she still needed to understand herself before she shared something like that.

When she was done talking, the room was quiet, as if no one wanted to be the first to question or accept what Alara had just said. It was Senye Cruz who stepped forward first, motioning for Alara to hand her the dagger. She did so, pleasantly surprised at the gentleness and reverence the mage held the knife with.

"Thank you, Alara," she said, nodding her head toward the guard at the door.

Before Alara could piece together what was happening, she was being led none-too-gently from the room. The heavy wooden door shut in her face with a soft thud, her mouth left open as if to argue or respond or... anything.

"Told you that you didn't have the guts to stand up to them," Runeo said, standing beside her in the claustrophobic hall.

She bit her tongue to stop the automatic response. She knew he was right.

CHAPTER 18

ALARA

Four days passed without word from Cruz, Quil'la, or anyone else in the chamber. Often, Alara found herself reaching for her belt and the dagger hilt that had become so familiar only for her fingers to brush air.

Restlessness and simmering rage crawled under her skin, worsened by Runeo's brooding stares of accusation. No one said a thing, but it was impossible not to feel the weight of guilt settling on her shoulders. She should have done more—said more.

They had breakfast in the dining hall with everyone else, made up of overly bitter cafi and plain tortillas—supplied by a storeroom that was older than Alara wanted to dwell on. No one spoke to them and they stayed huddled in the corner, keeping their own company. They spent the rest of their day wandering the narrow and dusty halls, finding nothing much of interest. Midday and evening meals consisted of the same unseasoned quinoa and dried meats. It seemed that no one managed to make it to the hideout with fresh produce, and it would take hours of walking to make it far enough out of the gorge to find anything growing or alive. She almost—*almost* missed fish.

Overall, the entire situation left Alara chafing and stewing in her thoughts.

"Want to find the old training rooms?" Suri said, lying upside-down with her back on the seat carved into the wall, hair brushing the ground.

"I could definitely use more practice with the spears," Quenti agreed, looking at Khuna. "I'd love to get to the point of not dropping it the second I get hit."

Runeo spoke from his spot in the corner, not even bothering to look over at the rest of them. "I don't know if we have enough time for that."

"He made a joke," Quenti said, perking up from where she slumped against the wall. "I didn't think he could do that."

Alara smirked at Runeo's eye roll. While she loathed to admit it, seeing him in just as horrible a mood as herself was making her feel a little better.

"You coming?" It took longer than it should have for her to realize Quenti was speaking to her. The others—all except Runeo—had stood up and moved toward the dormitory door.

The offer was tempting, and Alara almost followed. It would feel nice to get some of her anger out in the form of aggressive training. But the pit in her stomach sat like a stone, dragging her down.

"No." The word was bitter on her tongue, and no one commented as they shuffled out the door. The dorm was suddenly quiet, and she could almost hear Runeo's scowl. She itched to run after the others and join the group. While no one had been in high spirits since they had left Arbol, the others had been able to find some semblance of normalcy in the mundane days of waiting. She craved that.

Instead, she stood, hands clenched into fists. *I'm going to the meeting chamber.*

"Do you plan on breaking down the door?"

"I haven't knocked since the second day. If they have news—"

"They wouldn't share it with you," Runeo cut her off.

"I'll make them." She said the words with a bravado she knew she didn't have. But it pulled a small smirk from Runeo, and she couldn't help the flush that crept up her cheeks.

"Well, in that case, I definitely have to see this." He stood and brushed dust from the back of his trousers—as if it did any good when they hadn't even washed their clothes since the fire.

They didn't speak as they navigated the halls, both of them focused on their task. Alara noted a few familiar faces as they walked —magites and mages from the Haven that she had once known in what felt like a different life. Each time she saw someone she recognized, it sent a small jolt of anxiety through her. A small and *stupid* voice in the back of her mind still saw them and labeled them as the enemy. She wondered how long it would take for her to consider herself one of them. What was she now—a bruya? A rebel? A traitor...?

It was another emotion for Alara to swallow down and lock in that box she kept deep inside her chest.

It wasn't just familiar faces that they passed—news of the rebellion in the Haven had spread, inspiring other bruya outcrops and villages to rise up. Only a few dozen, but it still was a strange realization of how many people scattered across Sombria opposed the Council.

By the time they made it to the meeting chamber, Alara's courage was flagging. Two guards stood outside the door, as they had for the past four days since she had been unceremoniously thrown from the room. She recognized the pair as two mages—or *former* mages, she guessed—but couldn't place their names. Unsure of protocol, and frankly not giving a copper about it, she stepped forward, raising her hand to knock on the door between the two women.

Their expressions didn't change as their spears came down and crossed in front of the door.

"I need to see them," she snapped.

"No one may enter."

"I planned on knocking. If you could just—"

"They are not to be disturbed," the same guard spoke again, eyes still not even flickering to Alara. Her blood boiled and her fist clenched—no longer aimed at knocking on the door.

The second guard who hadn't spoken moved before Alara could, wrapping a cool hand around her thin wrist. She let out an undignified snarl and looked up at the woman. She was at least a foot taller than Alara—likely Runeo's height.

"Anyone who defies the rules of the pact leaders will find themselves in the cells looking at charges of treason."

"I—" Alara started, face now red with anger, but it was Runeo who cut her off with a warm hand on her shoulder.

"Clearly, we should be going, then. I would hate to imply any disloyalty to the leaders." Alara wondered if the guards heard the saccharine bite of the last sentence, but they seemed to relax. The guard dropped Alara's arm, and Runeo pulled her back and down the hall the way they'd come.

"You just gave up!" she said.

"I stopped you from getting yourself thrown into a cell over a hopeless fight. You're welcome."

She frowned, refusing to acknowledge the logic in his statement. "So, what? You're just resigned to waiting around like the rest of them?"

"For once, I'm thinking about strategy over blunt force."

Alara's eyebrows raised at the comment. "Clearly a mind-walker's got a hold of your brain." The sentence was said in jest, but the shadow that passed over Runeo's face had her breathing hitch. Perhaps this wasn't the time to joke about mind-walkers stealing bruyas's personalities.

Micos's eyes burning with disgust and hate as he fought Runeo in the Haven. Another memory for the lockbox.

"So, are you going to let me in on your plan?"

He shrugged, not looking at her. "We wait until evening meal—they have to leave the room eventually."

"That's a terrible plan."

While Alara stood by the fact that his plan was terrible, in the hours that followed, she couldn't come up with a better one—a fact which Runeo was happy to rub in when she muttered as much.

Which is why, when the bells echoed through the halls, calling for evening meal to begin, she found herself down the hall from the chamber door again, trying not to look overly eager as it swung open with no resistance or interference.

"Senye Quil'la," Runeo said first, rushing forward. "I was hoping to have a word with you."

Alara stood beside him, their bodies combined taking up two-thirds of the narrow corridor. Not that it mattered. The mixed group of mages and bruyas alike made to move past them without so much as a glance.

"Perhaps tomorrow, Runeo," Quil'la said with a nod. "It's been a long day."

"But—"

The old bruya swept by him.

"Senye Cruz!" Alara rushed after the mage as she passed by on Quil'la's heels.

The former councilwoman paused with a heavy sigh. "Yes, Alara?"

"It's been days since I gave you the dagger. We should know what's happening." She stomped her foot in frustration, only slightly ashamed at how childish the gesture felt.

"We will tell you when there's something you need to know," Senye Cruz said with a strained voice.

"That's not good enough."

"You don't give commands here." It was Quil'la who spoke, voice sharp and eyes cold from where she stood down the hall.

Alara frowned. When had she *ever* given commands? Neither the Haven nor Arbol allowed her such luxuries.

"We are *requesting* information," Runeo said.

"And we are declining it." With that, Quil'la turned on her heels and followed the rest of the group. Senye Cruz gave Alara's shoulder a reassuring squeeze before she too turned and left.

The guards who stood watch by the doors all day were the last to leave, giving Alara and Runeo smug looks as they passed.

"That plan sucked. Next time you should just hit someone like we both know you want to."

He gave her a look of pure exhaustion, shrugging off her words. "We should go eat."

She was tempted to reach out—to touch the hand that was clenched so tightly in a fist at his side—but she gripped her own trousers instead, feeling the coarse material beneath her fingers, and breathed.

The next day, Alara had planned to wake up early and head to the chamber room before their meetings started. It may have worked out had she not overslept. She was only woken when Quenti nudged her shoulder and told her it was time for morning meal. She'd spent the remainder of the day stewing in her own disappointment and annoyance, Runeo always out of the corner of her eye feeding off her bad mood. It took two more days for Alara to wake up before the morning bells in the darkness of their dorm room. She hadn't explained the plan to Runeo, but he was awake the moment she rose from her bedroll.

The plan ended up no better than Runeo's, with the two of them sitting inside the meeting chamber when the pact leaders arrived after morning meal. She wasn't shy about expressing her frustration as the guards dragged her and Runeo away.

This was how Alara ended up tucked in a small cabinet two evenings later, neck and arms bent at awkward angles. A part of her recognized the ridiculousness of her situation. They could have continued to wait until the leaders deigned to respond to any of their questions. But where was the fun in that? And as far as she was concerned, she had been patient enough.

Runeo had begrudgingly agreed that the petite magite was the only one of them who could fit in the small wood cabinet that sat in the back of the chamber. After, of course, she had promised to pass on *everything* she heard that day. He emphasized that point multiple times as he helped her slip into the small space, closing the door behind her. She was pretty sure she saw a flicker of amusement in his eye at her grunts of discomfort.

"We need to make a decision soon or the stores of stale maize and quinoa are going to run out, and we'll be doing the Council's job for them."

Alara's heart jumped in her chest at the sound of voices entering the room. They were muffled by the thick wood between her and them, but she heard the words clear enough.

"Shush, Elna," Senye Cruz's voice cut in. "This is a decision that shouldn't be rushed."

"Although, Lena, she has a point." A male voice cut in. "Perhaps if we make a decision before the next holy day."

"By all means, let's make the choice, then," Quil'la spoke sharply, "Let's throw the Sol-forsaken blade into Lake Mied where it belongs."

"That would be a foolish move," Senye Cruz said. "This dagger has the ability to turn the tide of the upcoming war in our favor."

"That dagger—if it is what you claim—will destroy us all," a deep female voice responded.

"Ah, yes. Now I'm remembering why we haven't come to a decision." Elna said with a not-so-amused laugh.

"Even if we were to agree to use the dagger," Quil'la said, "none of us know how to. It remains as useless as it is dangerous to keep it."

"Alara used it." It was a male voice she vaguely recognized—Rom—one of the leaders of Arbol.

"By accident," another male voice replied, "Much like she does everything, it seems."

"Dante," Senye Cruz admonished. His voice was young and Alara remembered the black-haired mage she had seen in group during their meetings. She had never seen him before in the Haven, but his pale brown eyes had pierced her with malice.

"He isn't wrong," Quil'la said. "Using it accidentally in the heat of battle and wielding it against the Council are quite different tasks."

"There are *places* where these secrets are still known." Rom's voice was soft, not bothering to speak over the others. But they fell silent, nonetheless.

"You know that would be dangerous. And the last two we sent there haven't even returned yet," Quil'la said.

"They've been sidetracked before," Rom said. "It means nothing that the twins aren't back yet."

"Yes, well, until they are, discussing crossing the Ruinedlands is a moot point," a female said. "We can't do so without them."

"If you send me," Alara recognized the voice as Dante's, "I could find them before crossing. Perhaps the two of them need to be fetched anyway."

Alara let out a small huff of air. Who was this man to be talking about taking *her* dagger?

"There is still the matter of how Alara used the weapon," Senye Cruz said, one of Alara's few defenders, it seemed. "She is the only one with any idea how to get the powers to work."

"If she speaks the truth."

"I trust her," Senye Cruz said.

"I don't."

Alara was starting to tire of this argument between the unseen voices.

"We need to speak with the child again," Rom said, cutting between the two arguing again. "She may know more than she understands. If we talk to her further."

"After what she's been pulling with the attempted spying," Dante said, "should we trust her discretion?"

"She's curious and the dagger belongs to her," the older male said.

"She's a nuisance."

"I believe she can be trusted, despite her youth, *Dante*," Senye Cruz spoke, his name being spoken like a jab.

"It's time she knows what she possesses," Rom spoke.

No one argued the point, although she thought she heard a snort of air from someone.

"Agreed, then," Senye Cruz said. "I will go get her myself," Alara suddenly felt the blood draining from her face.

Son of a bruya.

There was shuffling around the room and time slowed as her

brain spun in circles. There had to be a way out of this. If she could...
if Runeo would...

She heard the door click open before she came to her senses. Nothing good would come of this, but then again she didn't have a choice.

The door of the cupboard creaked loudly in the chamber as she tumbled out onto the floor in a disheveled heap. All eyes turned to her and the room—finally—fell silent.

CHAPTER 19

QUENTI

Quenti heard Alara and Runeo sneaking out of the dorm that morning, before the morning bells had even rung. It was nothing new for the pair over the past few days, and she rolled over in her bedroll, moving toward the edge that was set close to Khuna's own. Her arm was slung across the blankets, and Quenti ran her fingers along the warm skin, appreciating the few silent minutes in the dark and the soft wave of contentment she knew would wash away at daybreak.

Not that they had seen daybreak in over a week.

No one had been allowed outside of the shadowed cave since they had arrived and the dark halls felt more suffocating than the Haven even had. But she tried not to think of such things, because inevitably her thoughts came back to the cool breeze through the trees of Arbol and the mingled smells of forest and spice in Lili's home.

She swallowed hard at the emotions that threatened to rise within her, contentment replaced with feelings she couldn't quite name. Beside her, Khuna let out a slow breath, her arm moving beneath Quenti's fingers.

"Why are you awake?" Her voice was raspy and heavy with sleep.

"Alara and Runeo ran off early again."

Khuna didn't reply, but instead wrapped her arms around the other girl's waist and pulled her tight against her body. Their heat mingled under the wool blankets and Quenti closed her eyes again, letting the musty scent of her partner lull her back to sleep.

Alara wasn't at breakfast that morning, but Runeo was, looking annoyed and anxious, though Quenti couldn't tell if it was any more than usual. He barely grunted in response to any of their comments or inquiries, and left shortly after finishing his bowl of plain quinoa, leaving the rest of them with only a brief nod and vague grumble.

As had become their routine over the past few days, directly after morning meal, the group found themselves in one of the back storage rooms training. They paired up, Suri against Mitteo and Quenti versus Khuna, as Khuna led them through a group of exercises with a set of dulled and rusting spears.

Following two days of sitting around waiting for nothing, Quenti had pushed for the group to start training officially, working on their skills with the blameless weapons. Suri was about as hopeless as she was, but Mitteo seemed to know his way around a spear, and Khuna was teaching them the finer points of using a club. The bow and arrows laid untouched in the corner of the room—there wasn't enough space to make a proper target range.

"Hand forward a little bit," Khuna said with a nod toward her right hand. "That far back and you'll lose your spear the second someone hits it."

Quenti bit her lip and her hand slipped forward a few inches, trying to mimic her partner's grip. She braced her toes in her sandals, gripping the ground as Khuna had taught her and swung the spear. A loud snap echoed in the room as she knocked away the other girl's spear.

"Nice! Again."

Quenti gritted her teeth and stepped back into position, trying to ignore the ache in her forearms. It had been a few hours at this point, which was a record for her. The first time they trained, her arms had given out twenty minutes into holding the spear. After that, they had spent the first part of each day doing drills of various movements to push their bodies. She hadn't realized quite how weak she was until now.

For all the work that she had put into training her magia skills when she was growing up, she had never expected that it wouldn't be enough. That she wouldn't be enough. She had also never seen herself ending up in battle, let alone two battles in less than a few weeks.

If history was any indication, it wouldn't be the last, and she never again wanted to feel as powerless as she had felt back in Arbol. Amid the flames and chaos, she did manage to send some spirals of water at a few of the fires, but with the air being as dry as it was, her attempts ultimately amounted to nothing.

Even if she couldn't use her magia, she wouldn't allow herself to be that helpless again.

By afternoon meal, Quenti was struggling to grip a spoon, let alone a spear. She barely listened to Khuna as she spoke, too busy shoveling the under-spiced beans in her mouth as fast as she could manage.

The girl chatted animatedly with two bruyas sitting across from them who had just arrived the day before from Uodora in the north.

Like everyone else who had arrived since they did, they were haggard and worn. But their arrival had confirmed one key fact: that word had gotten out about the rebellion in Cielo, and the unrest was starting to spread.

"Quietly, though," one of the bruyas, Paz, clarified. "It's not out in the open as much as it is just in the air."

The female bruya—Isa—leaned over, eyes narrowed. "That's because the Council is arresting anyone who dares speak about what happened in the Haven." She gripped her knife with a white-knuckled fist. "When we passed the fork to Lejon, there were more guards and prisoners than I'd ever seen before. They're trying to hide it, but something is changing."

"More guards and prisoners?" Khuna said, brows furrowed.

"The receptive mine is outside of Lejon," Quenti clarified. "They've always used indentured prisoners for the hardest labor there."

"They send them there to die," Isa said. "It's a convenient way to make troublemakers disappear."

Quenti felt her stomach clench. These were the conversations her partner had been having all week.

Khuna had picked up gossip and news from cities as far as L'lim and Uodora over the past few days, all from making friends with the various newcomers. While Alara and Runeo had been trying to bully information out of the leaders, Khuna had managed to smooth talk herself into more information than anyone else in their group.

For her part, Quenti had sat back, watching the exchange with a queasy stomach. Talk of arrests and public executions, setting examples across Sombria. A part of her recognized that she—that *they*—had started this.

"Now they have more people than ever ready to disappear," Paz said, pushing their bowl away from them. "It was a parade of council-guards going toward Lejon—to the point that we lost count."

Isa shrugged. "They all look the same in that ridiculous drab garb."

"Except for the one with the patterned skin. You don't see that very often," Paz said as Isa nodded.

"What did you say?" Khuna's tone was suddenly sharp.

"The guard with the patterned skin?" Paz said slowly.

"What did they look like?"

"They... they had brown and pink patterned skin?"

"*Other* than the patterned skin." Khuna's voice was raised, uncharacteristic of her.

Isa and Paz exchanged a look before Isa answered. "Cropped hair. A woman I think, but taller than any I had seen before."

"When was this?" Khuna asked impatiently.

"Just about a week ago now, probably," Paz said.

Her eyebrows were furrowed, a look of concentration on her face that Quenti couldn't quite understand.

And then she was standing, wrapping a hand around Paz's arm. "Come with me."

"I—"

Khuna didn't let Paz finish before sweeping them out of the room and into the hall. Quenti and Isa took only a second to jump up and follow behind, curious at what had just happened.

CHAPTER 20

ALARA

Six pairs of wide, unblinking eyes stared back at Alara. Rom looked almost amused, his wrinkled skin folding tight at the corners of his eyes. The others' expressions ranged from slightly perplexed—Elna—to downright enraged—the young man Alara assumed was Dante.

The silence was finally broken by Senye Cruz as she snapped the door shut again with a small scowl. "Well, at least you saved me the effort."

Alara stood, straightening her shoulders with a slight twinge and looked back at the others, still silent.

"Let me go on the mission."

"Absolutely not," Quil'la said.

"You need me."

"We *need* you shipped off to another country where you can't cause trouble," Dante said.

"Who even are you, anyway?" Alara said, surprised by her own brazenness.

Dante's mouth hung open, as though unsure of how to process the question.

"Besides," Alara continued, "I'm the only one who's been there when the dagger did—anything." She stood up a little taller, which did very little with her small stature, even with most of the others sitting. They were unmoved. She took a deep breath and switched tactics. "Look, I can do this. I'm the one that broke into the Haven."

"You made a bit of a mess of that." Elna gave a small shrug.

"And broke out!"

"Again, still a mess," Elna said. "One that we're still unraveling right now, in case you haven't noticed."

"Let's talk more about this dagger," Senye Cruz interrupted. "And then we can decide on the next steps."

Alara bit her lip. "I won't say anything until you promise I'll be involved in whatever the next step is."

Quil'la practically growled at this, nails digging into the table. "This is not a game, you fool."

"The girl is right, though," Rom said softly. He didn't bother to raise his voice to be heard over the others' grumblings, but he drew their attention, all the same. "It is her dagger. As far as we know, it's been hers for as long as we can trace back. She has every right to be a part of this. Plus, if she is somehow connected to its powers, we'd be fools to remove her as a variable. I, for one, would love to know as much as we can."

There were a few more sharp words tossed back and forth, but it was clear that Alara had won. When finally prompted by a begrudging Quil'la, she crossed the room and sat down in an empty seat.

"Before I start," Alara said, careful not to sound too demanding. "I want to know what you know. What you all *think* this dagger is."

The group exchanged furtive glances, unspoken communication

passing between them. Alara watched them silently, and for once, patiently.

"Fine," Quil'la said sharply. She grabbed the dagger from the center of the table where it sat and pushed it closer to where Alara sat. "If what you've told us so far is true, then this dagger may have belonged to the first bruya."

"The first..." Alara was starting to think they were just screwing with her.

"Bruya. The first of this place who was gifted with magia from the gods."

"You mean like the myth? That's just a tale told by—"

"Bruyas?" Quil'la noted with a small sneer.

Alara's mouth snapped shut at this.

"The myth, as you call it, states that the dagger was gifted by the god of water themself, to allow the first of the blessed to grant the power to all others. It has the power to both grant and revoke magia."

Alara's chest tightened at the words. It made sense—but to suggest that the gods were anything but lies made up by bruyas to excuse their misuse of power was blasphemy. It would take her longer still to adapt to this new lifestyle as a rebel.

"The dagger is named in Dyoism, as well." Senye Cruz spoke softly, clearly aware of Alara's spinning thoughts. "For those who follow El'dyo, it is believed that his shadow helped humans create the dagger so they could control the powers of El'dyo for themselves."

"Then it's a curse," Alara said.

"If you believe in the words of El'dyo," Senye Cruz said.

"Whichever legend you believe, this dagger is dangerous," Quil'la said, voice hard. "And if it falls into the wrong hands, this war will be over before it begins."

"So we make sure it doesn't," Dante said.

"Here we go again." Elna let out a groan, running a hand through her hair.

"You're saying this dagger could stop this war, and you want to throw it in the ocean?" Alara asked. "We need to learn how to use it." She surprised herself with the words. Cursed or not, if the dagger would ensure the safety of her country—her friends—she wanted to use it.

"Easier said than done," Dante said.

"Well then, let's begin," she said.

This time, she told them everything. Well, most everything she could remember. She noted each thought she had and every word she recalled that was spoken between her and the mages she fought over the past several weeks. She described the feeling of Luis's magia flowing between them as she had pulled her own memory from his mind.

Admittedly, she still didn't mention the spark of living magia she felt inside the dagger at times. She saw Dante's raised eyebrow of incredulity when she mentioned the idea that the dagger seemed to *know things* and stopped there.

This time when she was done speaking, there was silence.

Dante was the first to speak. "It does exactly as we predicted," he said, voice almost reverent. "The question is if it only answers to her."

He reached for the dagger that still laid at the middle of the table. Alara quickly slid it toward her and out of his reach, though ignoring eye contact. She couldn't tell if the others had noticed the awkward exchange between the two of them.

"We should test what we know," Senye Cruz said. She laid a hand on Alara's shoulder, the command unspoken. With a small huff, Alara picked up the dagger, handing it handle first to the ex-councilwoman.

"You can try it," Alara said.

"Exactly how do we plan on testing it?" Elna responded. "Grabbing a random bruya and stabbing them to see if they keep their magia?"

The room went quiet again.

"Bruno!" Quil'la's voice was sharp.

A second later, the guard popped his head into the room. He made eye contact with Alara and a puzzled look crossed his face.

"Come here."

Alara clenched her fists under the table as the guard complied without question. Senye Cruz hesitated for a moment before grabbing his arm and swiping the blade across it as she spoke the words, "Make him blameless!"

There was a collective breath in the room. The guard looked down at this arm—unmarked.

"Can you use your magia?"

He shifted uncomfortably where he stood, but finally gave a sweep of his hand, sending a few papers scattering across the room in a gust of wind.

"Perhaps it does only follow the girl," Elna said.

"Or perhaps we don't know how to harness it properly yet." Dante's voice was tinged with annoyance. "Why would it only follow her?"

Alara's hands played with the edges of her tunic, mind abuzz. A part of her was disappointed that the others hadn't seen the power she had. Another part of her was happy that the dagger hadn't worked in the hands of someone else, though she couldn't explain why.

"There is something else you should know," Alara said softly, barely above the sound of her own pounding heart. Only Senye Cruz picked up her words and turned to look at her.

"Out with it," she said.

"Where I found the dagger—outside of Attalea—I was the one that hid it there." No one spoke. She cleared her throat, pulling up her shoulders. "When I pulled the memory from Luis's mind, I saw myself hiding the dagger as a child. From the councilguards. My mama was the one who had it before that."

"What was your mother's name, child?" Quil'la's voice was hoarse.

"Camila... Ayar," she said, looking at the bruya's wide eyes.

"And her family name before she married?"

"Quizpe."

Quil'la bit her lip, pulling away from Alara's stare.

"I assume that name means something?" Alara said.

"So it's possible this dagger is somehow connected to your family line," Rom said, answering the question without actually answering the question.

"It looks like you do need me, after all," Alara said, leaning back in her chair.

"None of this changes the fact that the best chance we have at learning about the dagger is across the Ruinedlands," the female bruya that Alara didn't know said.

"Valaria is right," Rom said, voice soft. "Perhaps it's time to discuss sending a group over the dunes, after all."

"Without the viajera, that's suicide." Quil'la's fist landed on the table with a thud. "And the twins still have our only one."

Dante stood, ready to speak when a commotion just outside the door sent everyone's attention to the front of the room where Bruno still stood in the closed doorway.

"I have important information!" Khuna's voice was breathless on the other side.

"Sol take me," Quil'la snapped, striding across the room to yank open the door. "What do you need, Khuna?"

The girl stumbled into the room as the guard let her arms go at the sight of the older bruya.

"Mena!" Khuna said. "I think Mena is in Lejon—or heading there. She was seen dressed as a councilguard." Her words were broken between gasps for air, but the room still seemed to understand the implications.

For her part, Alara remembered the name perfectly well. The mind-walker. The twins that they were so keen on finding, originally for no other reason than to cleanse her mind of all memories of Arbol.

"Mena was seen?" The girl had gotten Quil'la's attention now.

"Or... a woman—with patterned skin," Khuna amended.

"Who...?"

"Paz." Khuna's voice rang with authority. "Tell her what you saw."

Alara noticed a young, unfamiliar bruya standing halfway in the door. Paz's eyes went wide, darting around the room full of strangers, and behind them she could see Quenti and another girl peering into the room. Paz's words were stuttered and soft as they came out.

"You want to know about the councilguard I saw?"

"Yes, yes," Quil'la said impatiently.

The small bruya spoke quickly, answering Quil'la's peevish questions without hesitation. *What were the colors of her skin? What did the pattern look like? Where was she headed? Are you sure there wasn't another with her—with patterned skin?*

"It sounds like Mena," the female bruya, Valaria, said, "Though we can't be sure. Besides, why would she be heading to Lejon? And alone?"

"Benicio and her were due back in Arbol months ago now," Quil'la said. "We have no idea what may have happened."

"But it sounds like we may now know where your viajera is." Rom was sitting back with a mild look of satisfaction.

Quil'la's lips were pressed tight and eyes narrowed. "It is still an extremely dangerous proposition."

"So is anything we do at this rate," Senye Cruz cut in. "We are on the verge of war, after all. We are going to be dragged in whether we want to or not. We should do so prepared with every weapon at our disposal."

The silence that followed was heavy and left Alara's chest tight.

"If we do this," Quil'la said, "I want assurances that if we can't discover how to control the dagger, we are still willing to destroy it, rather than risk it falling into the hands of the Council."

"I couldn't agree more," Senye Cruz said.

The rest of the group gave murmurs of agreement, seemingly uneasy in the sudden truce.

"To Lejon, then?" Alara said, chin raising slightly as the others in the room turned to her.

"She can't go," Dante said, face turning red.

"Without me, you have a useless hunk of bronze," Alara snapped back.

"You and your entire *posse* are a liability."

"It's my dagger. Besides, who invited *you* along?" She was yelling now, which probably wasn't the best argument toward being mature enough to come on this mission.

Dante opened his mouth to respond, eyes sparking with anger. She took a bit of satisfaction at being able to ruffle the man's feathers.

"She's right, Dante," Quil'la said, voice rising above their squabble and cutting off his next words. "The dagger has so far only answered to her. Until we know otherwise, she'll have to be there."

Alara gave Dante a biting smirk.

"But Dante will also go along, I think. Someone to ensure the dagger doesn't fall into the wrong hands if things go wrong."

"I will go as well," Senye Cruz added, her eyes falling on Dante with what seemed like uncertainty.

"If Dante's coming, then I'm bringing my *posse*," Alara said, narrowed eyes focused on the red-faced man still standing across the table.

"You don't get to make demands," he said.

"Seeing as you need me, I believe that's exactly what I'm doing."

Senye Cruz raised a hand, ending the argument before it began. "If they wish to accompany us when the risks are explained, then I am happy to have them join. Crossing the Ruinedlands is an arduous journey, and perhaps it will do us good to have some young fighters with energy."

No one argued this point and Alara wondered briefly what she had just volunteered her friends for. She glanced up at the doorway where Khuna and Quenti were still standing. The latter's eyes were bright and her smile wide, not a hint of fear to mar the excitement.

"You should leave as soon as possible," Rom spoke, a wrinkled hand pushing the dagger back toward Alara. "We don't know how long Mena will stay in one place, particularly if Beno is missing."

Quil'la nodded, the skin tight at the edges of her lips.

"It looks like we have packing to do," Senye Cruz said, standing up from the table and effectively ending the week's long meeting. "We leave tonight."

CHAPTER 21

QUENTI

"Are you sure you're okay with this?" Alara asked for the fifth time since leaving the meeting chamber.

Quenti rolled her eyes, throwing a bag over her shoulder. "Stop asking. You're not going to talk me out of this."

"I didn't mean to force you—"

Quenti turned to Alara, eyes bright. "If you think I'm going to pass up a chance to cross the Ruinedlands, you're more of an idiot than I knew. And if it helps us defeat the Council, then who am I to complain?"

The girl glared at her, brow furrowed and lip between her teeth. "Believe it or not, you and Runeo are not the only ones who just want to do *something*."

Khuna popped up behind Alara, holding a handful of staffs and a bag of her own. "Is she still trying to convince herself she doesn't need us?" She smirked.

Alara groaned and threw a look over her shoulder. "That's not what I'm saying."

"That's exactly what she's saying." Quenti spoke over Alara's protests.

Instead of arguing, she motioned to Khuna's arms. "Are those for us?"

"We can't carry conspicuous weapons once we get to the road. They'll stand out if we cross any councilguards. But walking sticks won't."

After she had handed the two girls their own staffs, she was still left holding an extra one. "Where's Runeo?"

"I think he's still complaining to Quil'la that we were invited," Quenti said.

Alara scowled at this and knocked the end of her staff onto the packed dirt floor. "If it wasn't for me, *he* wouldn't have even been invited. He thinks he's so special."

Quenti and her partner exchanged a knowing glance. Alara spent a lot of time complaining about Runeo these days.

"Are Mitteo and Suri still sure they aren't coming?" Alara said, apparently eager to change the subject.

Khuna shook her head. "Mitteo is getting scarily excited about finding a way to grow food and craft medical supplies down here, and Suri is still off flirting with Dominica."

"You mean practicing her airen skills," Quenti corrected with a wink.

"Ah, yes," she said. "I've noticed they've been practicing all night for the last few days."

Quenti smiled. She was happy to see Suri enjoying herself, but she couldn't help but feel the sadness of leaving the two mages behind. After weeks alone in the forest with them, she had grown fond of the pair and their bickering.

Runeo's gruff voice rang out from the open doorway. "Are you all ready to leave?" His lips were pulled tight, but it was the only sign of his annoyance. After all, this was what he wanted.

Quenti grabbed the small bag she had claimed as her own and gave a nod.

It took them a couple of hours to make it to the main road that stretched between Cielo and Lejon. As discomforting as it was to walk along the well-worn path, pretending not to be a group of fugitives, the landscape in this part of Sombria left little choice. The land here was empty, with only the occasional tree breaking up the horizon. Even the hills were flattened here, as if the gods themselves had given up in shaping this side of the realm.

Their group was dressed in practical, unadorned clothes. The drab look of poor villagers looking for new work. At least that was what Dante had insisted. They were half a day into the trip, and Quenti was already picturing the man accidentally falling off a cliff. So far, he had pointed out every tree and plant he knew the name of, discussed his wide repertoire of fighting skills, and insisted that he had found the key to fighting off the annoying mosquitoes that pestered the low-lying lands of Sombria. She assumed it had to do with talking them to death.

"Who has the tortillas?" Alara asked, speaking over Dante's ongoing ramblings. "My stomach is about to start eating itself."

Khuna reached into her bag and tossed one into her waiting hands. Quenti took the one offered to her, biting into the salty dough.

Dante didn't even look over his shoulder as he spoke. "Make sure you ration the food. The closer we get to Lejon, the less likely we are to find anything edible out here. Did you know that the land here was permanently scarred by the Bruya Wars? Legends around the dagger state that one side or the other tried to use the blade to control all the magia, but in doing so they broke its ties to the land

and left it going wild. In theory, that dagger could destroy our realm if it falls into the wrong hands. Over the past ten years in Lejon..."

Quenti groaned softly and rolled her eyes at Khuna, who was holding back a laugh. "He's not going to stop any time soon, is he?"

"I didn't know this trip came with history lectures," Khuna responded.

"Did you know that the Ruinedlands are a deadly desert where nothing grows but *ruin*?" Quenti said.

Khuna opened her eyes in mock surprise. "Oh, Sol. I did not know that. You're *so* smart."

Silence fell for a few minutes—or at least silence among the four young rebels. Dante was still ahead of them rambling about all the lovely adventures that awaited them in the Ruinedlands. Deadly tornadoes, walking skeletons, fire raining from the sky. Quenti was confident at least a few of those were just lore born from fear of the blameless. Nonetheless, Lena Cruz nodded along with his lecture as if it was the most fascinating thing in the world.

It was Alara who broke the silence among the rest of the group, her voice low to avoid interrupting Dante's ongoing tirade.

"Do you think we're making the right choice?"

"By not throwing him into the river?" Khuna asked. "It's debatable."

Alara shot her an annoyed look. "By choosing to leave over a possible magiaful dagger versus staying behind and fighting the Council head-on?"

Runeo let out a snort of derision from beside them. "Do you think they would have invited you into battle? After everything it took just to be invited into a meeting? Not that there is going to be any battle. If I know Quil'la, they'll spend the next three years debating the next move. Maybe she only agreed to get us out of her hair."

"Do you think they'll be safe in the caverns?" Alara asked. Quenti could see the fear in the girl's eyes as she spoke.

"I don't even think the Council knows those caverns exist, let alone how to get into them," Runeo said.

"Arbol was supposed to be safe."

Quenti's stomach lurched. No one spoke, but she knew they were all thinking the same thing. Arbol *had* been safe. Until *they* had come back from the Haven. As many times as she had tried over the last weeks, she couldn't convince herself that it was a coincidence.

"If you four are done chatting back there," Dante's voice cut in, "then we need to hurry. There are some travel huts along the road we can stop in for the night."

Quenti bit her tongue to stop from commenting that the man hadn't stopped talking since they left. Then again, she had to admit, with his long strides, he had managed to stay ahead of everyone with an easy pace. Perhaps she could accidentally smack him on the knee with her staff. That might slow him down.

In the end, it was Alara who broke the man's stride. They had passed a few other parties on the road, but they only exchanged weary nods before moving to the edges to allow each other room. And thanks to a few whispered words from Alara, they knew none of the travelers had been mages.

The sun was near its peak on the third day when Alara stopped in her tracks, inhaling sharply. She stuttered as she spoke.

"There's a mage ahead." A hand came up, pointing at the small black dots on the horizon. They were still a fair distance off, but growing larger by the minute.

"Keep moving," Dante said. "It's more suspicious to stop."

Despite the look of trepidation, Alara heeded Dante's words and started moving again. But as they grew closer, they were able to make them out more clearly, including their familiar garb.

"Those are councilguards." Quenti glanced along the horizon. "We should pull off the road somewhere."

"And hide where?" Dante said. "Do you plan on lying down in the grass and hoping for the best?"

Loath as she was to admit it, he was right. There was nowhere to hide. No other paths to take. They were headed directly toward a squad of councilguards, including a mage who very well could have Alara's same mind-stalking abilities. For all they knew, they'd know right away who they were dealing with.

"Just don't look suspicious." Cruz's face was unwavering.

"Oh, is that all?" Quenti said. "You and Alara are from the Haven. What if they recognize you?"

"As long as they aren't Cielo guards, they shouldn't recognize us any more than they'd recognize you. They'll expect us hiding, not wandering down the main road."

The woman's words did nothing to stop the flutter of nausea in Quenti's stomach.

The next minutes seemed to stretch into hours as the two parties drew closer together. Quenti tried to keep her stride steady, but she felt like she might crumple at any moment. Beside her, Khuna kept a warm hand resting on her arm, knowing the emotions that roiled under the surface of her skin without Quenti needing to say.

As the dots on the horizon turned into people, it was obvious that Alara was right. It was a squad of six councilguards, draped in blacks and greens. They walked calmly, but each of them was burdened with an assortment of spears, bows, and daggers. Most of them had scarves wrapped around their heads and faces, protection from the sun and dirt. Even with the training she had been doing, Quenti was sure she would last approximately five seconds against any one of the guards.

Beside her Alara's eyes scanned the group as they approached, eyebrows furrowed. At the front, Dante and Cruz's heads were held high—what Quenti assumed was their version of acting casual.

"If you don't want to draw attention, put your heads down," Quenti said through gritted teeth. Voice low in hopes it wouldn't carry. "Don't make eye contact unless commanded to."

While Haven residents may have been used to looking directly at the guards of Sombria, Quenti knew that no outskirt villager dared tempt fate with the capricious guards. They seemed to understand her earnest words and their chins lowered as the guards slowed down in front of them, a line of bodies blocking the road.

"What business do you have?" A male councilguard stepped forward, spear gripped loosely in his hand, casual, but ready.

"We're heading to Lejon for work," Dante responded.

Quenti's lips twitched as she noticed he continued to follow her advice, not looking the councilguard directly in the eyes as he spoke.

"This is a dangerous time to be traveling."

She could feel his gaze lingering on each of them as he spoke. A ripple of unease moved through her.

"There have been bruya killings along the border recently," he continued. "The Council has been advising against movement along the roads."

Runeo took in a sharp breath behind her and she somehow felt anger rolling off him. How often did they use made-up bruya violence to defend their ever tightening control over the people?

"We're coming from Hurazon," Quenti chimed in. "We must have left before any missives had come."

Dante's shoulders stiffened at her interruption, but she didn't regret it, as she saw the councilguard's hand loosen on his spear. A woman near the back, face wrapped in a scarf stepped forward and whispered in the man's ear. Their group shifted uneasily as the unheard words were exchanged, Quenti's eyes lingering at the swaying of the simple bronze earring dangling from the woman's right ear.

Quenti was so focused on the pair, that she didn't notice that a councilguard in the back had ambled closer until he was right on top of them.

"You." His voice was high and his face young, but he had the same air of authority as any other guard, and his spear wasn't gripped gently as he moved in front of Senye Cruz. "Let me see your face."

CHAPTER 22

ALARA

The air left Alara's lungs like she had been punched. She felt the others around her shifting, her magia churning uneasily beneath her skin. Senye Cruz paused, not following the order immediately. But his tone brokered no argument and there was no talking their way out of this.

She slowly raised her face, hands already stiffened at her sides. Alara plucked at a thread of her own magia, readying herself as she scanned the group before her. She knew at least one of them had magia—she could feel it. But the rest were blameless. A part of her wondered if she should strike now before the inevitable even happened.

But something stopped her. Perhaps leftover guilt at betraying her once-home. Or perhaps the sight of the boy in his black and green uniform who looked like Ardo at a glance. Either way, she didn't act. She just let the scene play out, helpless.

As Senye Cruz made eye contact with the guard, his green eyes widened in surprise and his face flushed red. He opened his mouth to speak. "This is the—"

"—friend we were talking about earlier," a soft voice said, "How wonderful to see you again."

The tall female guard who had been speaking to the leader stepped over to the boy and rested a hand on his as it clenched around his spear, knuckles white. He blinked, still looking at Cruz with a mixture of anger and disgust. But after another few seconds, the emotions melted from his face into understanding. He nodded slowly, taking a step back, a hand coming up to run through his tight, dark curls.

"Yeah, a friend," he said, still looking confused. "I don't know why I…"

"It's the sun out here, making us all a little tired," the woman said, her voice light and airy.

The other guards chuckled at this, heads nodding in agreement.

Alara stood completely dumbfounded. Cruz's hands were still clenched at her side, a tight smile plastered on her face that came off more like a grimace.

"I can escort my friend here and her companions to Lejon," the woman continued. "To keep them safe from the bruyas, of course."

"That won't be necessary," Runeo said, his tone biting. He stepped forward and the lead councilguard's hands tightened around his spear again.

"Not so fast." The woman's hand came up to unwrap the scarf tied around her head, letting the material drop away from her face. "I wouldn't want you all falling into the wrong hands."

Beneath the black folds of cloth, her face was young, her lips twisted in a small smirk, and her pale brown eyes dancing in amusement. But it was the woman's skin that drew Alara's attention first. It was a deep brown, darker than most she had seen, but pale pink skin lined her eyes and mouth, like splotches of paint. Another strip went down her neck and disappeared beneath the shoulder of her tunic.

Mena.

Without thinking, Alara reached out to the woman and felt the light coolness of air magia churning beneath her skin. The woman's eyes flashed up toward her and Alara stepped back, as though the councilguard had stepped into her personal space. Except she hadn't. Alara couldn't tell why, but she could tell the woman had *felt* Alara's mind-stalking abilities. Alara pulled her magia back quickly and bit the inside of her cheek, trying to slow her heart.

They were still surrounded by the councilguards who looked somewhere between confused and suspicious.

Mena—or, at least Alara assumed—turned with a flourish and squeezed the captain's hands briefly.

"They need an escort if they are to make it to Lejon safely, and I'm not needed here."

"But wasn't she—" Another female councilguard started, but was cut off by the captain's gruff voice.

"No, she's right. She's the only one who can stay behind." He gave her a brief handshake before motioning at Alara and the others. "Now, move aside. We've wasted enough time here."

Alara and the others shuffled to the edge of the road, not questioning the order. A few of the guards stared them down as they passed, but they too didn't question the order as they marched forward.

The group stood like that until the councilguards were small smudges on the horizon, breaths held as if they may turn back at any moment. Runeo's shoulders relaxed first, and he turned toward the woman, still draped with councilguard green.

"Mena, what in Sol are you doing here?"

"You're welcome, Runeo," she said, eyebrows raised. "And great job at not ruining things for once by lashing out before you understood what was going on. You've grown so much!" She placed a patronizing hand on his shoulder.

"Shut up," he said, though he didn't brush the hand off his shoulder.

Khuna wrapped an arm around the taller woman, pulling her away from Runeo and embracing her tightly.

"How did you... what just happened?" Dante asked, sounding more offended by the last few minutes than thankful. "Did you just mind-walk them?"

The woman barely glanced at the man as she returned Khuna's embrace. "Just a few memories placed in here and there. It's amazing how far just implanting a familiar face will go."

"That's... terrifying."

"I for one am very thankful," Khuna said. She turned and motioned for Quenti to move forward. "This is Quenti."

The woman broke into a wide smile. "I've heard so much about you. I'm sorry I wasn't there to greet you when you finally made it to Arbol." She turned then, eyes roaming over the last three, Dante, Senye Cruz, and Alara.

"Is it true, then?" she asked. "Did the Network really reveal themselves?"

"Something like that," Senye Cruz said with a tight smile.

"And Quil'la agreed for you to work together—to leave Arbol?" She turned to look back at Khuna and Runeo.

The entire group shifted in discomfort, no one willing to speak first. It was Alara who lost patience with the silence first, though the words burned in her throat.

"Arbol's gone."

Mena's eyes flashed, face turning from red to gray in quick succession. "How... I didn't—"

"There's a lot you need to catch up on," Runeo said, waving the group forward. As they finally began to walk, Mena's face retained its gray color, her eyes distant.

The events of the last couple of weeks were laid out for the woman. They tried to keep the details vague, but it almost felt worse purposefully avoiding the details. For nearly ten minutes, they went back and forth between Mena and the bruyas, listing off who she had known and who had survived—or not. It was a horrific reminder of just how few Arborelis had made it out.

Although the woman mourned for many of those that had disappeared after the fire, she didn't ask after family. It seemed she wasn't the only one without those ties.

"Your brother," Alara said suddenly, breaking the uneasy lull that had followed the list of the dead. "Where's your brother?"

Mena's pale eyes scanned over to her, making her feel suddenly naked under the mind-walker's gaze. For a second, she was flashed back to the feel of Luis's hands on her head, the feel of the mind-walker back at the Haven sucking the memories from her mind.

"Who are you?" Mena said. "And what do you know of my brother?"

"She," Khuna said brightly, "is a long story. But it was Beno and you we came for. Well, you and the viajera."

Although Alara hadn't known it possible, the woman's face seemed to gray further. Long, fine fingers reached up, thoughtlessly playing with the small blue gem in her ear.

"That's why I was coming this way. I was headed back to Arbol for help."

It was Dante's turn to look worried now, his eyes scanning over the woman's council garb as it if might answer his unasked questions.

"I don't have the viajera," Mena said.

"Who does, then?"

"Beno does."

Dante's lips pressed tight. "And where is Beno?"

She took a deep breath before speaking, her voice coming out distant and cool.

"We made it across the Ruinedlands and back safely, but once we were back here... I'm assuming it had to do with whatever you pulled up at the Haven, but it was chaos in Lejon. They were rounding up anyone and everyone they suspected to have magia who wasn't working for the councilguards. We didn't realize..." She broke off. Her hands may not have been shaking, but she gripped the spear she carried tightly and she refused to meet anyone's eye. "All he did was brush up against a Council mind-stalker. I wasn't close enough to do anything but watch."

"He's a mind-walker, too. He wasn't able to...?" Runeo gave a general wave.

"He's always been more of a fighter than a walker, but even then, there were too many. Even if I had been closer, I'm not sure I could have done anything."

"So, once again, I must ask," Dante said, his voice taut. "Where is Beno now?"

The two-toned woman tilted her chin up and gave the man a look of cold contempt.

"He was taken prisoner. He's within the Chuya Mines."

CHAPTER 23

ALARA

"So, you're telling us there's no hope." Dante's words were sharp.

Mena's eyes narrowed. "There's always hope. Look, I've already managed to get into the base that runs the mines. With some help, I can figure out exactly where he is. That's where you all come in."

"So we can, what, break into the mines?" Dante said.

"That's the easy part," Mena said, as if that was the part anyone was worried about. "It's the breaking out that's going to be complicated."

"There is no way," Dante said, his face somehow more pinched than usual. "There is no way in Sol we are getting anywhere near the mines and breaking out a prisoner. The Chuya Mines are the best-guarded prison in the country."

"Well, if you want the viajera, then that's exactly what we're doing," Mena said, voice icy.

"This was not a part of our mission."

"That *is* the mission," Alara cut in, feeling more than defensive for the woman she had just met. In the thirty seconds she'd known her, she brought something Alara hadn't felt since Arbol burned down. Hope. "We get the viajera, we can cross the Ruinedlands. Finding the viajera has always been our step one. Step one just became more complicated, is all."

"Step one became a suicide mission."

"Enough, Dante," Senye Cruz said, her voice pointed.

Dante almost recoiled at the voice, looking down at the ground.

"The mines may be well-guarded," Mena said, "but the anxiety brought on by the Haven situation is making the city more chaotic. Besides, the guards out here are either stupid, lazy, or both. I've been sneaking in and out of the base for weeks now without any problem.

"Except for your brother being captured."

"I know where the records of prisoners are kept," Mena said, her tone insistent. "We find Beno, and the viajera is within our grasp. All I need is some more hands. And maybe a bit more magia."

Dante's silence was louder than his complaints, but the others ignored him. All eyes fell on Senye Cruz, whose face was placid and pensive.

"Tell us more," she finally said, speaking for the group.

Under normal circumstances, sneaking into a military base—even one in far-flung Lejon—would have been an impossible endeavor. Being a lowly magite, even Alara hadn't ventured far into council-guard territory within Cielo when seeking out Ardo.

Yet, with Mena in the lead, slipping through the gates was uncomfortably easy. One of the guards on duty even tipped his hand to the group before Mena even touched him.

"Back so soon, Maria?"

"I just missed your face too much," she said with a wink.

The young guard flushed as he laughed, barely glancing at the small group in tow that consisted of Alara and Runeo.

They'd left Dante, Senye Cruz, Khuna, and Quenti behind camping outside the city, trying not to look conspicuous.

While the mind-walker only had one extra outfit, which annoyingly enough fit Runeo much better than Alara, they hoped the two uniforms would be enough to distract from the magite's haphazard disguise. She wore her brown tunic and pants with Mena's black scarf draped around her head.

While the headwear might have stood out in any other city, the wrap appeared to be common attire this far east in Sombria. Alara started to understand why as they approached the councilguard encampment that stood a mile or so outside the city proper. The grass and dirt of the road had quickly turned into sand and stone. Each small gust of wind sent dust and sand spinning through the air and into their unprotected faces. While it was a pain to walk in, Alara couldn't deny the beauty of this place. The stone was a rainbow of colorful striations twisting along the rocky landscape. The sand itself was made of plain shades of brown and yellow, infused with patches of bright red and blue in the soil. Despite the lack of foliage, the landscape managed to be just as colorful as the rolling green hills and cloud forests to the west.

Or perhaps her infatuation with the landscape was simply a distraction from the fact that they were marching into a military base and she was most definitely a fugitive.

Mena walked with purpose across the grounds, chin raised and lips tilted up in a perpetual smile. By the time they made it to the main office building at the center of the camp, she had flirted her way past at least five guards—two of them female. Alara noted that Mena only needed to walk into one man's mind, and that was when he started to look at Alara with too keen an eye.

The mind-walker seemed confident in her abilities, although she acknowledged that she could only change one at a time, and only if she was touching them. Plus, after the manipulations on the road, she was already looking a bit tired.

"The small memories I implant may only be temporary since we're moving so fast, but as long as we don't run into them again anytime soon, it should be fine. So long as they encounter minimal conflicting information, they're less likely to dwell on any strange actions they performed while under my control."

Alara wasn't sure the mind-walker's reassurance was as comforting as she seemed to think, so she used her own powers to keep an awareness of all the mages she could as they walked through the base, even though most of their enemies seemed to be blameless, with mages being outnumbered five to one. She tried to focus her threads of magia on the blameless as they passed, pulling at that sense she had begun to feel in their time in the cloud forest. A few times, as they turned a corner, she found herself simply *knowing* that there were blameless there. Then again, there were blameless around nearly every corner, so perhaps she was just fooling herself.

Outside the main building, the camp had been bustling with activity. The outcrop was a town of its own with barracks, offices, and supply stores. The central building took up one entire side of the main plaza, stretching three stories into the air and, as they found out once they entered, even more stories into the ground. And there were hundreds of guards roaming the halls in just the one building. It all made Alara's stomach twist and roil. More than once, she found herself holding her breath, trying to calm her stuttering heart.

Then again, now that they had made it inside, no one seemed to spare them a second glance. It was an ignorant confidence that no intruder would ever make it this far.

Alara commented as such, voice barely above a whisper, as they passed through an empty hall.

"That may be," Mena said, just as softly, "but don't get too cocky. We still need to make it into the Weave and Tapestry Library without drawing suspicion."

At least they wouldn't be starting from absolute zero when searching for Beno. Mena knew her brother was in the mines, and she knew he was in one of the lower levels, based on rumor of how prisoners were assigned work. But the mines themselves were a sprawling enterprise with layers and sections hidden underground. Plus, while they could find out where Beno was being kept, there was no guarantee it would lead them to their personal effects, which could be kept anywhere. So that, as it turned out, was an added wrinkle, despite Mena's optimism. Alara tried not to think of what they'd do if the viajera wasn't with Beno.

Still, she wasn't as scared as she'd expected when they'd first discussed the plan. And if breaking into the mines was as easy as breaking into the base had been, maybe there'd be no reason to.

I hope.

Just as the words ran through her mind, Alara's magia snagged onto something familiar. It wasn't magia, but it was smoky and warm and oh-so-familiar. The moment her brain caught up with her, a group of blameless councilguards rounded the corner and Alara's heart plummeted as she saw the man at the center, his eyes as bright as ever.

Ardo.

CHAPTER 24

ALARA

Alara froze in her tracks as the two groups came face to face. Beside her, Runeo seemed to recognize Ardo and his hand went to his belt, brushing where a weapon would normally rest.

She elbowed him sharply in the side as a soft breeze stirred beside her. They were too deep into the base to start a fight and escape with their lives. Her mind raced to come up with a better solution as Ardo approached her from down the hall, his pale gray eyes wide and focused solely on her.

The last time she'd seen him, he'd been standing over Zinita's dead body, spear in hand. Yet the emotions that tumbled through her stomach were more than just fear and hatred, and the knowledge of that made her hate herself.

It took her only a moment to register the bronze bands along his arm, indicating his higher status. He had been promoted after the battle at the Haven. The thought of what he had done to earn the promotion turned Alara's stomach. Yet he wasn't working as Emaru's guard any longer…

"Runner Gomes," Alara said, still not processing what she was saying.

"What are you doing down here, soldiers?" Ardo's voice was cold, but his eyes still held Alara's with an intensity she couldn't read. It took her a few seconds to understand the question.

"We..." Her brain had stopped working.

"We're headed to the Weave and Tapestry Library," Mena said, only the slightest bit of uncertainty coating her voice as she pushed Alara aside. "We were sent by Senye Baldo in strategy."

"Why would he need three of you?" one of the other guards asked, eyes narrowed.

Heart racing, Alara open her mouth to defend them, but it was Ardo that spoke first.

"It takes at least five people to find anything in that mess of a place." He looked over the group, eyes finally leaving Alara's. "Perhaps you should come back at another time. Major Francisco needs the Library today and doesn't want to be bothered."

What's going on?

Alara's head spun. Nothing made sense, and Ardo only stared back at her, eyes communicating something she couldn't process.

"We just need—"

"I said to abandon your orders, soldiers." Ardo's voice was rough and left little room to argue. He spoke as a superior officer to his subordinates and the other guards looked on, just waiting for disobedience.

Mena moved first, stepping forward and giving a small salute, her hand coming down to brush against Ardo's arm. His eyes narrowed on her as she stepped back.

The bruya looked back at Alara and Runeo and gave a barely perceived shake of her head.

"He's right," she said, looking at the others, "If the major is storming around in there, I don't want to be anywhere near the records library. Senye Baldo can wait."

She backed away, pushing the other two along with her. Alara's jaw clenched, but she moved back down the hall, eyes flashing back to Ardo's, trying to understand.

He hadn't turned them in. He *should* have turned them in.

The squad followed them down two more passages before splitting off in a different direction, but not before Ardo ensured they were headed up the stairs toward the exit.

"Send Senye Baldo my regards and tell him to stay out of trouble," he said as he turned away. Alara didn't feel her jaw relax until they were leaving the base. She almost expected the guards to come running around the next corner calling for them to be arrested, but they never did.

"We should have killed him," Runeo growled out.

Mena gave him a sharp look that quickly shut his rant down.

They walked in silence until they exited the base, Mena giving the guard at the gate a quick hug before they left.

"Hopefully he doesn't remember we were ever here," she said.

"Hopefully?" Alara asked.

"I'm exhausted. That affects my abilities. We'll see how that goes."

"Did... you mind-walk Ard—Runner Gomes—back there?" Alara said, trying to sound casual.

Mena's lips twitched. "I'm assuming that was tall, bronze, and gruff back there?" She didn't wait for an answer. "I couldn't do anything of use. You were so intertwined in his memories. So, either of you want to tell me how we know a high-ranked councilguard?"

"He was... a friend." Alara stumbled over the words.

"He murdered Zinita," Runeo said at the same time.

The mind-walker's eyebrows quirked up, eyes gliding between the two of them. "Well, there is definitely a story there for later. For now, we should get food and rest. I *need* a burrito the size of a small child to refuel my magia. I won't be of any use until then."

Neither of them smiled or laughed at the joke.

"Come on. I know somewhere we can go after we collect the others."

By the time they made it to the outskirts of Lejon, Runeo and Mena had retold the story of being caught by Ardo three times over. Senye Cruz and Dante both appeared insistent on reading some hidden meaning in the interaction.

Quenti, on the other hand, walked next to Alara, giving her hand a reassuring squeeze a few times as they walked. She didn't want to think about the reasons her friend thought she might need comfort.

"So, where are we headed?" Khuna asked. "I'm excited for the food I was promised."

"To the inn," Mena said simply, leading them down a narrow street. The town was a vibrant burst of color to rival the rainbow sands of the surrounding landscape just beyond its borders. The smooth sidings of the buildings were painted in a multitude of bright blues, greens, and yellows. There wasn't a stripe of white or brown to be seen among the designs. Most of the buildings were single story, but a few rose up two or even three stories, each level boasting a new set of colors and designs.

The streets themselves were much the same as they were in Cielo and Hurazon, but the interlaced stone paths were completely covered in a layer of drifting sand, which colored them as brightly as the buildings. It was nothing like the gray towns in the west or even the bright blue cities of the north that Alara had seen before.

"Can we trust an inn?" Dante's jaw was tight as he spoke.

"We can trust this one," she said, not bothering to look back as she turned down another street. She stopped a few blocks later on the edge of a small plaza.

The open area was relatively empty, with only a few people strolling through and another handful sitting on benches, eating and chatting. At the center of it all stood a worn stone carving, faded and chipped from lack of care over the years. But she recognized the symbols and faded figures at the center. It was a carving of the first Council—the first blameless and mages to come together after the Bruya Wars.

Alara tasted blood as she bit the inside of her cheek. The first Council had wanted peace. It was what they claimed they wanted, even now. Yet they murdered to retain it. Would death always be the price of peace?

"Stay here for a minute," Mena said. "I need to talk to Tiago first."

Before any of them could ask who Tiago was, she had taken off across the plaza toward a tall structure painted in yellows and greens, mountainous murals framing the main doors.

The rest of them slunk back into the shadows and away from the open air of the plaza. The street they were on was wide, but a narrow alley sat off to one side, behind a small row of buildings that bordered the plaza. Senye Cruz led them back toward the alley, heads and hats low. Their first mission tomorrow would be buying some headscarves to cover some of their more... conspicuous faces. Such as the ex-councilwoman traitor they had in their midst.

The slamming of a door had them all turning to look down the alley.

"El'dyo curse you, child!" A man's deep voice rang out. "I needed that water boiling ten minutes ago."

There was a small squeak and the sound of flesh on flesh.

Beside her, Quenti flinched, hands drawing into fists at her side as she gazed down the alley. Tucked in the shadow, a small girl huddled over a large pot, a stocky man hovering over her, fist still raised in the air. The cook fire beneath the pot was weak and dying as the pale-haired girl tried again and again to light the flint in her hands.

"Absolutely worthless! Get that fire going or I'll send you to the mines, where you might be of use to someone."

Chapter 25

Quenti

Magia ran through Quenti's veins like ice as she stepped forward, eyes focused on the man's sun-worn face as he glared down at the trembling child. Any logical thoughts left her brain the second she had laid eyes on him with his greasy hair and untrimmed beard. The physical resemblance he bore to her father was passing at best, but there was something in his mannerisms that set her off, taking control of her body.

A hand tightened around her wrist and its sharp warmth brought her back. She looked over her shoulder to where Alara stood, eyes wide. She shook her head and pressed a finger to her lips.

Quenti wanted to curse Alara. Instead, she swallowed down her magia, letting the warmth of the other girl's hand settle her icy blood.

Without another word, the man walked back inside, the slam of the door rattling through her chest.

"He deserves to be sent to the mines," Quenti's voice came out rough and low.

"If you attack him," Khuna said softly, "he won't be the one ending up there." She laid a hand on Quenti's shoulder. Quenti tried not to bristle at her touch. She knew it was for the best, but that didn't make the ordeal any easier. A few deep breaths later, she turned to face Alara, whose eyes were still cast toward the little girl. She was still struggling with the fire.

"Keep them distracted." Alara motioned to the others, before stepping forward.

It was Quenti's turn to reach out instinctively to grab Alara, but she moved quickly, making it down to the girl in a few seconds, and Quenti didn't want to cause an entire scene.

They were too far to hear the words whispered between them, but the girl placed the flint in Alara's outstretched hand. Alara flicked the flint a few times, allowing the stone to spark above the wood a couple times before fire roared up from the kindling. She winked and pressed a finger to her lips before rushing back down the alley, just as quietly as she had left.

"Are you crazy?" Khuna said.

"It's fine," she said, face flushed. "I just told her I was good at using flints."

"If she reports you—"

"All she saw was me light a fire. It doesn't take a fuegen to do that."

Quenti knew she should side with Khuna on the argument, but she was saved from taking sides by a sharp whistle behind them. Mena poked her head out from an alley a few yards back on the other side of the street, giving a wave before disappearing around the corner.

The group followed without question. Leaving the girl with her newly started cooking fire behind. The new alley they moved down was even narrower than the previous one and the buildings too tall to let any sun in. Mena wordlessly waved them along until they arrived at the back of the inn.

An older man waited, a small door propped open, eyes sweeping up and down the alley. He ushered them in and shut the door before speaking.

"Come," he said moving toward the crooked staircase in the corner. The door had opened into a hot, cramped kitchen. A fire roared in the center hearth and pots boiled above—two filled with beans and quinoa and one with what looked like laundry.

"You were supposed to be gone by now." The man spoke in sharp whispers as they filed up the stairs. "It's only getting more dangerous here."

"I was coming back no matter what," Mena said. "I'm not leaving Beno behind."

"Your brother can take care of himself, you know."

"He's always seemed to think so."

The man laughed. "Right, right." Quenti didn't know what to make of that comment, but she could sense a fondness in the man's voice.

They climbed two flights of stairs before coming out onto a long balcony that centered around an open area below, where a series of doors with animals painted across them lined the walls. The man unlocked, then opened, the door with a capybara painted in profile that sat along the left wall.

The group filed into the room, though it was too small for the seven of them. There were three beds pressed against the walls and a small rug in the center.

"This is the best I can do for now. The rest of the rooms are filled. The washroom is on the northwest corner, but be careful running into people."

"We'll make it work," Mena said.

"There are more councilguards swarming the streets than usual. I suggest wearing headscarves around if you need to go out in public."

"We'll need some extra, if you can manage." Mena placed a few bronze pieces in the man's hand and he gave a nod.

"I can try and buy some today. The market is going to be shut down tomorrow morning." The man's eyebrows cut thick lines across his face as he looked across the group. "It's gotten worse since you left. They're buckling down on anyone suspected of holding magia or being sympathetic to the cause."

"When haven't they?" Mena said, face grim.

The man shook his head. "I'm serious. It's never been like this. Tomorrow morning, there's a mandatory meeting in the main plaza. A couple of traitors were caught, and they plan to make an example of them. From what I hear, it's been happening all across Sombria. They're parading prisoners through the cities before bringing them to the mines."

Senye Cruz's face went red. "The Council has never made a public spectacle of punishment."

"Goes to show what you know," he said, and Quenti could see the war in Senye Cruz's eyes before she tightened her jaw shut. "Besides. You have to forget what you know. Times are changing." The man gave a final squeeze of Mena's shoulder before leaving them, shutting the door tight behind him.

"Are we sure we can trust him?" Dante said.

"I trust him with my life," Mena said.

Quenti hated agreeing with Dante, but she too stared at the closed door, thinking of how long it would take for the innkeeper to return with guards. If he'd really wanted, what would stop him?

"He's a blameless," Quenti said. It was more accusation than question.

"He is," Mena said, looking at her through narrowed eyes. "And he's a better man than many I've known." She looked over at Runeo. "He's one of the men who helped smuggle Beno and me out of Sombria when we were younger. I owe him my life. There is no one I trust more."

After several long seconds, Runeo nodded, his shoulders loosening in relief. Khuna took this as her cue to settle in, and she moved over to one of the small beds, flopping onto it with a sigh.

"Does he do food deliveries?"

The tension released in the room as the others followed suit, dropping bags and sitting down along the beds. Only Dante and Quenti remained standing as the others removed their sandals and boots and stretched their legs.

Quenti wanted to trust Mena—wanted to believe the woman. But the man was a blameless, and after what had happened in the Haven, there was surely a price on their heads. Was his history with Mena enough to stop him from seeking a small fortune for just a bit of information? Quenti ambled over, taking a seat next to Khuna, thoughts still churning in her mind.

Get Beno, get the viajera, and get out. They just needed to hold that man's trust long enough to complete the plan.

Chapter 26

Quenti

Despite the warmth and softness of the blankets, Quenti struggled to fall asleep that night.

Dante, Cruz, and Mena had taken the three small beds, while the other four of them were given extra blankets and rolls to lay in the middle of the floor. It was cramped, but still nicer than any of the camping they had done over the past few months.

Still, in the silence of the night, she could almost hear the pounding of boots clambering up the stairs, councilguards ready to knock their door down and drag them into the streets with the other traitors.

But another hotter emotion burned bright under her fear: a crippling desire. She wanted to run down to the town jail herself and break out the captured bruyas. She wanted to set this entire town on fire and watch it burn as Arbol had. Let the blameless sit by, helpless as their lives turned to ash around them. Put them in as much constant fear as her father had her entire life.

She gritted her teeth, trying to swallow the anger that threatened to consume her, but that had never been her. Mama had always been the one to speak of forgiveness and love. No matter how many times her father had left bruises on her skin, she would whisper to Quenti in the night of how anger and revenge would only leave the world burning.

So, what could she do? Run?

She could do that.

Perhaps Alara hadn't been so wrong to crave peace back in Arbol. This viajera, whatever it was, could be her way out—her path to freedom.

And perhaps, once she and Khuna crossed the Ruinedlands, they wouldn't need to return.

The next morning, drums beat through the streets and the bells of the worship hall chimed incessantly starting at dawn.

The entirety of the town shambled toward the main plaza, many ushered by the surprising presence of councilguards scattered throughout the town. Many looked as reluctant as Quenti and Alara to see what was in store for the prisoners. But the spark of excitement in some of their faces turned Quenti's stomach. They swarmed like flies to a carcass, pushing their way to the center of the plaza for the best view.

The air was hot and dry, the sun beating down heavy, accented by the mustiness of the crowd. For all the discomfort, Quenti's multi-colored headscarf helped protect her dark hair from the sun's heat. She'd initially been concerned that its flamboyance would make her and the others stand out, but as she shuffled into the town square, it was hard to pick out any one individual in the sea of scarves, let alone them.

That didn't make the experience any less unnerving, standing along the edge of the plaza, backs pressed to the cold buildings, looking out at the mob of blameless who would turn on them at their first opportunity. Cruz, Dante, and Mena pushed forward into the crowd, navigating toward the center where a stage of sorts had been raised. From where she huddled, Quenti could just make out a deep voice projecting from the platform into the crowd. She couldn't understand every word, but a few stood out, injecting ice into her veins: *"traitor..." "El'dyo's shadow..." "Punishment to achieve forgiveness...."*

It was the same brainwashing garbage she'd heard for much of her life from her father.

"Should we move closer?" Runeo asked.

"I'd rather not see what's in store for us if we're ever caught," Alara said, voice tight.

"We should see who it is—if it's someone we..." Khuna's lips pinched.

"I can't," Quenti said, shaking her head.

Khuna gave her hand a tight squeeze before she and Runeo ducked into the crowd after the others, leaving Quenti alongside Alara.

"This is disgusting." Alara's teeth were clenched and her face pale.

"Did you see how happy some of the townspeople looked? They act like it's a holiday."

"Or a celebration."

They both fell silent, letting the hum of the crowd and the distant voice wash over them. It was odd being on the same side of an issue with Alara. A couple of short months ago, this exchange would have turned into a heated debate, likely resulting in the former magite going silent, seething in anger at the complete lapse of logic in her own position.

At some point, the energy in the plaza shifted, and everyone around them held their breath, as if waiting for something. And then she heard the whistle and crack of a whip, forcing her to look up. Beside her, Alara's entire body went rigid.

"How can people watch this?" Alara said.

Quenti had no answer for her, but it didn't matter, because Khuna was breaking through the crowd and scrambling back toward them. Her eyes were wide and focused on Alara.

"You need to see... come with me." Khuna's words were a rush, and she was grabbing Alara's arm before she had a moment to answer.

Something in her tone left neither of them room to argue. Quenti followed, both reluctant and curious, hand gripping at Alara's as they pushed and twisted through the mass of people. It took a few minutes for them to shove their way to the central platform, the man's words becoming clearer by the second.

"This," he said, "is what happens to those who commit treason against the Council. It is our duty to ensure you understand that nothing will protect you if you act against the realm's interest—especially if, like the traitor before us, you seek to destroy the peace we've kept for centuries. No longer will the Council go easy on the bruyas and rebel mages that plague Sombria."

A cheer rose up from the surrounding crowd as another crack of the whip echoed through the air. They were close enough now that Quenti could hear the slap against skin and the breathless cry from the stage—from the woman they were whipping.

Quenti ran into Alara's back as she stopped short in front of her. They were almost on the edge of the crowd, but had a clear view of the platform a few yards away. A line of councilguards stood sentry around the wood structure, facing outward. On the platform, a large councilguard stood, his leather armor splattered with blood, glistening in the sunlight. And in front of him, a woman was slumped, her tunic ripped open and blood streaking down her battered back.

For the briefest of moments, Quenti almost thought she recognized the middle-aged woman.

Beside her, Alara made a sound in the back of her throat that reminded Quenti of a dying animal, and her voice came out rough and choked.

"Senye Emaru."

Chapter 27

Alara

Alara's stomach churned with acid as she looked at the woman who had raised her. The woman who had betrayed her. Lied to her. The woman who read her bedtime stories when she was too afraid of the dark tunnels of the Haven to fall asleep. The one who had convinced her that it was her own magia abilities that had killed her family.

And now she was on her knees, bleeding and broken in front of her.

She didn't know what she'd expected when Khuna had grabbed her and pulled her into the crowd, but it wasn't this. Anything but this.

The man on the platform began to speak again and Alara reluctantly shifted her gaze to him. Her jaw clenched as she saw the stout, red-faced man—a face she recognized from her time in the Haven. The power-hungry Major Francisco, still preening from his recent promotion.

The man's hair was oiled back, his face was freshly shaven. Were it not for the blood, one would have expected him to be in attendance at some promotion ceremony. Between the ragged breaths, Alara could swear she saw a smile tugging at the edges of his mouth. It was as though he was happy that the blood of his once friend and colleague dripped down his chest.

"For crimes of treason and conspiracy against the Council, Linda Emaru is sentenced to life in the mines. Rest assured, everyone she helped and all those who helped her will be found and punished."

His whip came down again and again, Alara's entire body flinching with every crack, as if it were breaking the skin on her own back. But she couldn't look away. She couldn't close her eyes or shut out the sound of Senye Emaru's pained grunts. Pained, but still strong. Still defiant.

Eventually, it stopped.

Francisco took the small dagger from his belt and cut the ropes that were holding Councilwoman Emaru—*No.* Just *Emaru*, Alara reminded herself—up. Without them, she slumped onto the wooden planks of the platform. As she fell, Alara almost felt the woman's gaze fall over her, and the sensation sent another wave of nausea through her stomach. She looked broken. But then again, wasn't this what Alara had wanted back in the Haven? She'd wanted all of the pain and anger she felt toward Emaru to be turned back on her ten times over—this woman who had killed her family and conditioned her to her own purposes.

This was her dream come to fruition. So why didn't she feel any better?

"Come on. We should go find the others," Quenti tugged Alara's sleeve, pulling her back from the platform.

How had Emaru gotten here? When they'd left her, she was fighting *against* Alara, the bruyas, and the rebels.

Very much *not* committing treason.

And then, something else nagged at her mind, making her stop and pull back at Quenti.

"Ardo," she said, looking around the crowd uselessly—a crowd made up of individuals at least three inches taller than her.

"What?" Quenti said, looking around with her, "Where?"

"No!" she said more forcefully, annoyed they weren't reading her mind.

Khuna and Quenti both looked at her like she was crazy.

"Just... hold on. Please," Alara said with a huff as she closed her eyes. She could almost feel the other two staring back at her, frustrated and anxious, but she didn't care.

Back in the guard camp, she had sensed him coming around the corner, known him in her mind. Taking a deep breath and trying to ignore the jostling crowd, Alara retreated into her mind, stoking the magia that churned warm in her chest. She let it connect with the sense that always sat in the back of her mind and stretched out her awareness.

She pushed past the cool magia of Khuna and Quenti, farther until she met the four others, their magia swirling together across the plaza from them. She gave a small lurch of surprise to find her mind sensed the presence of a few other magia users in the crowd, though not a single councilguard standing in the center was a mage.

Questions crowded her mind and she pushed them away. There wasn't time for that right now. She brought her awareness back to the crowd. He had to be here somewhere.

There.

She felt the subtle smoky warmth of him behind her, moving among the crowd and turned, trying to scan the mass of heads around her.

"Quenti, can you see if Ardo is over that way?" Alara said.

Quenti's eyes narrowed suspiciously, but rather than argue, she turned and swept her gaze over the crowd for a few seconds before her hand shot out. To her credit, she only paused for the briefest of moments before saying, "That way—near the corner street."

Alara didn't wait for the others to follow as she slipped through the crowd, ignoring Quenti's annoyed protests, her small stature finally coming in handy. By the time she made it to the edge of the plaza, the crowd was starting to disperse, and she still couldn't see him. She closed her eyes again, smiling as she felt him around the corner moving away.

She sensed Quenti and Khuna following not far behind her, so she moved again, not slowing down, for fear of losing her quarry. As she strode down the street, the crowd thinned, moving in all directions, back to their homes and store fronts. Finally, she caught a glimpse of his bronze curls. He was out of uniform and had a hat pulled down low on his face, but as he glanced around, he caught her staring.

Most of her face was still covered by her headscarf, but his eyes went wide with recognition all the same. For an instant, Alara expected him to run or call out for councilguard backup. Instead, he held her gaze for a long moment and then purposefully turned to stride down an alley to his left.

She waited only a second before following, her own gait quick and short to keep up with his long one. The alley was narrow, but still churning with people, and as she passed by, the doorways of small stores and public dining rooms already filling with customers for their morning meals. How anyone could eat after the display in the plaza, she didn't know. The thick smell of roasted meat and bitter cafi turned her stomach.

Ardo turned right down another alley, this one wider than the first. The sun angled perfectly to shine onto the cobbled streets, highlighting the brightly painted buildings on either side. The space was wide enough here that small groups of villagers stood huddled in doorways, speaking in sharp whispers that Alara couldn't quite pick up as she moved by.

And then he started to run. Gritting her teeth, and sparing a glance back at Quenti and Khuna, she launched into a sprint. Her steps may have been shorter than Ardo's, but a footrace between the two of them would still be close. He turned one corner, and then another.

The farther they ran, the emptier the streets became. There were no longer store fronts and dining halls, but rather gates into small courtyards locked tightly. The buildings were painted less brightly here, or the paint was just more chipped and faded. They had moved into a residential area and only a few stragglers moved in and out of houses, carrying out their daily chores. There was plenty of room for her and Ardo to weave in and out without causing a big scene.

At last, Alara turned a corner into a small alley that was made up of the back of two lanes of houses, nearly pressed together, but with enough room for a single person to move.

She hesitated, breath heavy, realizing that all of this could be a trap. What if he'd purposely dragged her away from the main plaza? He could still arrest her or—worse. And now, he'd managed to isolate her friends, who hadn't been able to keep up.

She shook that feeling off. Who was she kidding? Why drag her out here if all he wanted to do was turn her in? Besides, there wasn't a version of this that played out without her following him. He had information she needed. Whatever had happened with Emaru, he knew. He had to.

She ducked quickly into the alley, where she found him stopped, back toward her, shoulders heaving from exhaustion. She too stopped in her tracks, widening her stance.

"Glad to see you're still keeping up with your training," he said. "I don't think I could lose you if I tried." When he finally turned around, she was surprised to see a smile spread across his face. "It's great to see you, Alara."

CHAPTER 28

QUENTI

They made it several blocks before they started to lose Alara. Or rather when Alara started to run.

Quenti immediately made to follow. She had the advantage of only being one small, surprisingly fast, person. As Quenti and Khuna pushed through the crowd, more people started to take notice, even as they kept their faces covered.

After turning the third corner, even Quenti had to admit they'd all but lost her. Quenti clenched her jaw and growled. "That little... I'm going to kill her, if he doesn't first," she bit out, turning another corner.

"She can handle herself," Khuna said, though her tone was less sure. "Right?"

"In a fight, sure," Quenti said. "But with him..." She trailed off. Even she had to admit, she didn't know the true depth of their relationship. Could they trust Ardo? Could they even trust Alara when it came to Ardo? "I don't know." It was a more honest answer than she'd expected to give, and she hated the anxiety it brought with her. She hated how it made her hate Alara, even if just a little.

Something soft grazed her hand and she recoiled at the touch, only to notice it had been Khuna trying to get her attention.

"Are you okay?" Khuna said.

"That boy's dangerous," Quenti said. "And now, if Alara's in trouble, we won't even know."

"She'll be fine," Khuna said, tone still unsure. "She'll be fine," she repeated, this time in a sterner voice, though Quenti didn't know if it was any more confident.

She didn't say anything. She *couldn't* say anything.

No. Alara would be fine. She had to be fine. But as Quenti dwelled on this idea, she had to admit to herself that it wasn't just Alara's safety she was worried about.

CHAPTER 29

ALARA

"What in El'dyo's name are you playing at?" Alara said.

They were still in the thin, windowless alley. The angle of the morning sun left much of the space in shadows, granting a sense of safety, which was good considering the scene they were making.

She was straddled across his chest, the flat end of a waqtana she'd snagged from the side of the road pressed against his neck. Yes, she had attacked first and no, he hadn't put up much of a fight before she'd flipped him onto the dusty road, but she was angry. If she really meant to threaten him, she would have pressed the serrated edge against his throat. She was playing nice.

"I already told you," he said between breaths. "I had nothing to do with what happened today. There are things happening that you don't understand." His words were hoarse, and she could feel the tension in his muscles. But he didn't fight to push her off, even though he could have done so without breaking a sweat. He may not have been able to beat her in a fight every single time, but even she could tell he was holding back.

It only made her more angry.

"Then tell me," Alara said. "What is it I don't understand?" She punctuated the sentence with an extra nudge of the farming club. It was a power move on her part, though she wasn't sure why she did it. Maybe it was some childish way to find some semblance of power—something she hadn't felt much of since Arbol had burned. No. Since Adelmo had been killed trying to protect her.

The gesture didn't so much as make him flinch. His gray eyes were boring into her own so intensely she almost flinched back from *him*.

"So much," he said. "There's so much you don't understand. Didn't you wonder why I didn't turn you in?"

"It's the only reason I haven't flattened your thorax, Ardo," Alara responded. She had no idea why, but she felt mean—like she *wanted* to take it all out on him.

Then, without warning, he grabbed the serrated edge of the waqtana, catching it in a vise-like grip. He knocked it to the side, using his bodyweight to overpower Alara and roll on top of her. Before she could so much as react, he had her pinned beneath him, wrists restrained over her head in his strong hands. The ground was cool beneath her and she felt the grit of sand on the cobblestone. His body weight easily kept her from moving.

Her face heated as she glared up at him, trying not to show him how much she hated how easily he had overpowered her. She was also trying hard to ignore the heat of his body against hers and the familiar musty scent she had spent years associating with safety. He was no longer a safe place for her.

"I haven't turned you in because I may need your help," he said between ragged breaths. "*We* may need your help."

Alara's eyes narrowed and she let out an undignified growl. "You must be crazy if you think I'll ever work for that monster. He's always been a pig, but now he has the will of the Council behind him."

"Not Major Francisco," Ardo said, leaning deeper into her personal space and speaking quietly. "I could never be loyal to someone like him."

"Then who are you loyal to?" Alara tried to ignore the heavy breaths that grazed her cheeks, making her flush.

"I'm loyal to Sombria," he said after too long a moment.

Alara scoffed. "That's not an answer."

"I would never betray you."

"Still not an answer," Alara said, her voice level. Silence reigned once again, and she could see the battle in his eyes—the conflict between their last meeting and the years before that.

He loosened his grip around Alara's wrists and stood up, avoiding her gaze as she followed him to her feet. She suddenly felt colder.

"Ardo, what happened after we left the Haven?"

And then, of all things, Ardo started to laugh. It wasn't malicious or angry, but rather humorless and somber. It was a laugh that was never intended by the gods. He covered his face with one hand, pressing down on his eyes in clear frustration. "You know, even just a couple of months ago, I would have died for the Council. Without so much as an explanation. Because I believed more than anything that my death would've meant something. It would've preserved the peace of an empire that's lasted hundreds of years. I didn't realize how fragile it was."

He finally met Alara's gaze, and she saw pain. "To think that it could be dismantled so easily by a teenage girl on a justice streak..."

"That was never my intention," Alara said. "I just wanted to save —they didn't deserve what the Council was doing."

"Even more evidence of the delicate balance of our realm," he said. His tone wasn't accusatory. Alara imagined he'd spent the last several weeks thinking about this. "Senye Emaru..." he said after a long pause. "Senye Emaru never committed treason against Sombria. After you left, the Council changed fast. Both her and Senye Cruz made up two-thirds of the mage representatives, and when you broke out from the Haven and Senye Cruz left, who do you think the blame fell on? The others said she'd lost control over the magites and mages—that the balance was tipping and the blameless needed to take back control to stop it."

Alara bit her lip at the thought. How had things gotten even worse?

"There's only one mage left on the Council now. It's unclear how much power he even has left. Some call him the puppet of the Council—at least they do in secret. Wila and the other blameless say the rebels that showed themselves during the battle were just the beginning. That more would come if they sat back and did nothing. Now, they're rounding up mages throughout Sombria whose loyalties are in doubt, all in the name of peace and safety."

"So, this is all our fault," Alara said in a whisper, barely believing. Barely breathing.

"You disturbed an already fragile system," Ardo said. "We just didn't know how fragile it was. Things were already unstable between the blameless and mage members of the Council. As Senye Emaru told me, this was nothing more than an excuse to take action. With Senye Cruz gone, the scales were already tipped in favor of the blameless councilmembers."

Alara crossed her arms, eyes raking the ground, her mind lost in thought. "So, what does this have to do with you?"

"Not all blameless agree with the Council," he said. He moved closer again, hands coming down to rest on her arms which were crossed tightly against her chest. "I can't do this alone."

"Do what alone?"

"Free Senye Emaru," he said. "Free her and give Sombria some chance of survival."

Alara's mouth opened in some parody of confusion, and she pushed back from him again. She didn't know what to feel in that moment. Red started to creep in on all sides of her vision and she took a deep breath, looking around the thin alley for anything to distract herself and slow her thoughts. There wasn't much to look at: a few crates, a pile of sand where the wind had formed a dune against the alley wall. The red grains stood out vibrant even in the dark shadows.

A part of her wanted to beat Ardo to a pulp, but the sad little girl inside of her wanted to believe him. She wanted to believe that she'd misunderstood everything that had happened at the Haven, and that the woman who raised her wasn't some horrific monster.

The two warring sides of her wouldn't let up, and a ringing started to sound off in her eyes, her breath threatening to overwhelm her.

Then she felt it, a warm, heavy hand on her shoulder. She looked up to see Ardo's kind eyes, the grey speckled with black and the long eyelashes that always made her envious. And just as he'd done countless times before, he brought her back from the edge of panic, allowing her an escape from the brutal world, even if just for a few moments.

And then a smirk crossed his face.

"I know that look," he said. "You need to hit something."

Hundreds of shaky breaths later, Alara found herself standing in a copse of trees with Ardo. They were in a clearing of sorts. Though the vegetation was so sparse here, there was room to move freely throughout the small clump of trees that grew outside of Lejon. It seemed to be an attempt at an orchard despite the dry, sandy earth, but it was empty and private, no workers wandering the area in the heat of the afternoon sun.

Alara stood silent, watching as Ardo tied his hair back and rolled his sleeves up to the elbow, revealing the muscles of his forearms. His skin was tanner than she remembered, no longer pale from long hours spent underground in the Haven, though his curls had seemed to almost brighten from the increased sunlight. It had grown longer, brushing along his shoulders in haphazard waves. He really had been through a lot over the past several weeks, hadn't he? He looked completely different and yet the same as he always had, the familiarity of years spent growing up together.

"Catch!"

She startled out of her thoughts as a staff of wood flew at her. She caught it on pure instinct, pulling herself back into the moment. Ardo's lips were quirked in a crooked smile and he was spinning his own staff casually in one hand.

"Have you fallen out of practice, running around with those bruyas?"

She couldn't help but smile. "You tell me." She lunged at him, bringing the edge of her staff toward his face. She saw him flinch, moving his own staff to meet hers. At the last moment, before contact, she twisted and moved the bottom end of her weapon toward his knees, where he'd left himself unprotected. She barely caught the fabric of his pants before he stepped to the side, elbowing her back and pushing her forward into a stumble.

"Is that a yes, then?" he asked, laughing as she balanced herself.

Alara didn't answer, her eyes narrowing as they circled each other, thin sandals scraping lightly on the sandy soil. She stepped forward on her left foot before quickly moving back to her right and spinning around him. Her staff caught him in the right calf and she let out a satisfied breath. But before she could celebrate more, he had struck out with his other leg, tripping her and giving him time to twist around and lay a sharp, yet harmless, smack against her shoulder. She didn't think as the pain welled up, using the sensation to fuel her movement as she whipped around. In spite of the growing annoyance in her chest, there was a familiar calm that came with it. The calm that came whenever she'd faced off against Ardo.

She could almost pretend they were outside of Adelmo's stable, living their simple, ignorant lives. The very thought sent a spike of pain through her heart.

It was as if Ardo could read her thoughts, and he immediately dropped his staff, shoulders sagging as she took a sharp breath in.

"I missed you." His voice was low and rough.

She didn't answer him right away, trying to calm the staccato of her heart.

"I missed you, too," she said, still unsure if she could trust him like she used to. The world they now lived in was so different. "I didn't think I'd ever see you again. And I worried that if I ever did, you'd be coming at me with a spear."

His thick eyebrows tensed low and his mouth pulled thin. "I'm sorry for what happened in the Haven. I... well, I don't agree with what you did, but I understand it. I think."

Her shoulders slumped and she found herself leaning against a tree, all the fight leaving her. He still didn't know the full extent of what he'd done. That girl he'd murdered wasn't just some random bruya. She was a beloved Arboreli. Then again, there were a lot of dead and beloved Arborelis these days, and each one of their deaths could be traced squarely back to Alara.

"I don't even know if I understand what I did," she said.

"You were doing what you thought was right."

"Just because something feels right, that doesn't mean it is."

"That's true."

"If I'm being honest, I don't even know what feels right anymore."

He walked toward her, his staff loose in his grip. "It's 'right' to do everything you can to save your people. It's what you always wanted."

"And I'm failing miserably." She paused, eyes studying his face. "Arbol is gone."

She spotted surprise in his eyes, the honesty of it loosening her chest. She didn't know what she would have done if he'd been involved in that mess.

"The bruya city?" he said. "It's real?"

She'd almost forgotten that its existence and location had escaped detection for so long that many doubted it was ever real. Example number eight thousand and six of how the world had completely transformed over the past few months. The tightness returned to her chest. "Not anymore," she said.

"How?"

"How do you think? Councilguards."

"And you think I heard something about it?"

"Did you?"

Ardo's shoulders slumped, but he stared back at her, challenging.

She stared into those gray eyes once again, wanting more than anything to believe him.

"Did anyone survive?" he asked.

Alara furrowed her brows. "I don't... I don't know," she said.

"That's a lie."

"No it isn't."

"Yes, it is," he said, eyes narrowed. "I've known you for years. I know when you're lying."

"Stop looking at me like that," she said, voice growing louder as her heartbeat thudded heavily in her chest. "What do you want from me?"

"The truth."

"I can't tell you the truth."

"Why not?" he pressed closer to her, invading her space and making the blood rushing through her body heat.

"Because I can't trust you anymore." She realized how loud the words came out and took a deep breath, biting her tongue and focusing on the pain for a moment. "I don't know who I can trust."

She didn't know what to do with herself. With this anger. With this energy. She leaned up against a tree. They were tiny saplings compared to the towering trees of the cloud forest and Arbol, but the wood was sturdy against her back, grounding her. Her shoulders slumped against her will and she buried her face in her hands, the staff left leaning against the tree, forgotten. Strangely, the part of her that would have normally been embarrassed to show weakness was absent. She never had to worry about any of those things around Ardo, even if she was mad at him. It seemed there was some part of the trust still there.

A bird chirped in the distance, as if to fill the silence between them.

"I'm sorry," he finally said. "I'm sorry for the loss of your friends. And I'm sorry we were caught on opposite sides of the conflict last time."

Alara scoffed. "Please," she said. "*You* were caught on the *wrong* side." She looked up, not bothering to wipe her eyes.

He smiled back, filling her stomach with a warmth she didn't expect. "We have a chance to be on the right one this time. Together."

"Okay, so, are you going to explain to me how exactly you plan on 'freeing Emaru'?"

"I'm going to break her out of the mines."

"You're insane." Alara ignored the small voice in her brain that reminded her that was their plan, too, only with Beno. "She doesn't deserve your suicide mission."

"She's fighting for the same things as you—peace, balance."

Her laugh was harsh. "She fights for mage dominance over bruya. That is *not* peace."

"You used to think otherwise."

"I've learned a lot since then. Do you know what she did to me? What she did to my entire family—my past?"

She watched his reaction and saw the truth in his confused expression. Something unfurled in her chest that she hadn't been aware of—another sense of relief. Apparently, the list of things she worried Ardo was involved in was longer than she thought.

"You didn't." It was a statement. Not a question. "You really didn't."

"What did she do?"

"She killed them, Ardo. And then she stole those memories from me, letting me spend my whole life thinking it had been all my fault."

He cursed, looking down at the ground, where his staff dug into the hard soil. "She wouldn't..." He drew back his automatic denial and bit his lip, sitting with her words. The silence was heavy between them, but he finally looked up, eyes meeting hers. "I had no idea."

"I know."

"But still," he said, "if there's a chance to bring peace back, I know it's with her."

"I hate her."

"She's trying her best."

"She always does."

"What she did to you wasn't okay, but I know what she's trying to do now. Sombria is built on balance. If we lose that..." he trailed off, the threat unspoken.

"What she wants isn't balance, it's oppression."

"But the bruyas—"

"The bruyas don't want the chaos you think they do," Alara said, standing back up. "They just want to be left alone. They want their freedom. Like we all do."

"Is that what you're doing here with all of them?"

"That's a secret." She smirked, putting her finger to her lips.

He shook his head, but his eyes were bright as he looked back at her. "I think we are all fighting for the same thing."

"That's hard to argue when the Council has spent centuries suppressing those with magia."

"So, we're back to this again?"

"It's always been in the name of power."

"Not with Senye Emaru."

"*Especially* with Emaru."

"She's always wanted equality. Just like you. And the only way to ensure equality between the blameless and magia users was to—"

"Oppress bruyas?" Alara said, now standing.

"To help them see a different way."

Alara narrowed her eyes. How was it that the same arguments she once used sounded so foreign to her ears?

"Maybe I don't want equality anymore," she said, the words shocking even herself. "Maybe we should just be free from the blameless."

"*All* blameless?" His eyes seemed to darken as they met hers.

Something had changed in the air between them, and she saw him step forward, closer to where she still stood, pressed against the tree. There was barely a foot between them now, his face tilted down to meet her wide eyes. The fire magia danced in her chest, connecting to the heat that radiated from his body. She could see the beads of sweat dripping down his temple and along his jawline from their earlier duel and the hot sun.

"And what would you do without me?" he asked.

"You're the one who claimed to miss me."

"And so I did. The sun didn't shine as bright and the wind blew in silence without you." The last of these words came out in a whisper of heat against her lips.

"Ardo…"

"Yes?" His voice was soft and low. She could only hear him because of how close he was to her. She couldn't help the tilt of her chin as she looked up at him, his own face leaning down, closer and closer to where she was. His eyes were bright and his lips were pink, cracked in places. She wondered if they would feel soft or chapped…

She took a deep breath. "You shouldn't let your guard down."

His eyes flared wide, but he didn't react quickly enough as she brought the staff around to smack against the back of his legs. He stumbled backward in surprise.

"I think that's cheating." He had his own staff held up before him, the heat not gone from his eyes.

"No such thing in battle, soldier," she said, smirking.

For the next thirty minutes, the only sound in the small clearing was the smack of wood on wood and heavy breaths. All talk of ethics and politics were lost in the clash. By the time Alara lowered her staff, sweat was dripping salty down her face and back. Ardo's face was red and shone, a match for her own. Most of his hair had broken from his tie and curled around his face and neck, frizzy in the heat.

"I know you don't trust Emaru and I can't blame you for that," he said, "but we can help each other."

"And how is that?" she asked, twirling the staff between her callused palms. He walked toward her, nonetheless, and moved to stand in front of her again.

"I wasn't a part of Emaru's personal guards when she was arrested. They were sentenced to the outskirts after the rebellion, but I was missed in the suspicion."

"So you mentioned. And I'm sure your murdering bruyas in the battle helped in your favor." She regretted it as soon as the words left her mouth, but that didn't make it false.

His mouth tightened and his lips went pale at the accusation. "Yes, I think it did. It also helped that I volunteered to join the base out here, making myself all but invisible to the Haven after the battle, leaving Senye Emaru to her fate." He looked sick at his own words.

"And what's changed now?"

"This can't be a coincidence, Alara," he said. "I couldn't make a difference in the Haven. But this is El'dyo giving me a second chance. I don't know who I can trust here, but maybe with your help, we can break her out from the mines."

"And why would I do that?" Alara said. "Why would I help Emaru?"

"Am I wrong in assuming you're also looking for someone in the mines?"

Alara didn't speak.

"Whatever information you were looking for when we first met, I can get it for you. And I can do it without you risking getting caught."

"What makes you think we would have gotten caught?"

"Major Francisco really was in the Weaver and Tapestry Library when you were on your way. And he'd recognize you, Alara."

Alara let out an involuntary curse as her heart rose into her throat.

"So, do we have a deal? I get the information you need, and we help each other get Emaru and whoever else you need out of the mines."

"You really think you can do that without getting caught?"

"I've been promoted since we last saw each other. I can go where I need to."

Alara reached out and placed her hand over his, where it still gripped her staff. His skin was warm and damp. "And should I trust you?"

"You already know the answer to that." His voice was husky and low. He covered her hand with his other and squeezed it lightly.

Her heart was in her throat again and the heat of the day seemed to grow between them.

"Then prove it."

CHAPTER 30

QUENTI

"We should head back," Khuna said, touching Quenti's arm gently to gain her attention. Her tone suggested it wasn't the first time she'd said the words and Quenti flinched internally, realizing how focused on following Alara she'd been. She'd been turning down every alley and street, trying to read the air, as if it might show her the path the other girl had taken.

"We can't leave her out here," she said as she turned down another street—one that, for some reason or another, *felt* right. "What if we miss her?"

"If we keep wandering around, we'll miss her."

"Fine," Quenti said, not looking at Khuna. "Then you go back to the main street and I'll keep looking."

"I am not leaving *you* alone out here," Khuna said. "You've already garnered enough attention as it is. It's like you're hunting a wild rabbit through the streets that only you can see."

Quenti threw up her hands. "Then you're following me on my invisible wild rabbit chase." She stopped at the next corner, baffled at where to go next, the slow creeping realization that she had no idea what she was doing tickling the back of her brain. She wasn't a mind-stalker; she couldn't do this. That was a talent wasted on Alara, who hadn't even acknowledged her magia until recently. "She's going to get us all killed," she said, throwing herself against the nearest building and crossing her arms. "She's going to get herself and then the rest of us killed!"

Any concern she had for Alara was replaced by anger and mistrust.

What had that boy wanted with Alara, and even more concerning, would she listen to him? How could she so much as listen to him after everything he'd done?

Khuna came to stand in front of her, not quite blocking her view of the street. She grasped Quenti's face in her hands, directing her gaze down to her own bright eyes.

"Alara isn't an idiot—"

"—yes she—"

"—*all* the time," she said, voice soft. "She can take care of herself. What I want to know is why you are acting so crazy. You've been off ever since we got here."

Quenti let out a hiss of breath.

"You have to talk to me."

Quenti's jaw clenched. She really didn't. What good would it do? "It's just that... we're in a city full of blameless."

"That's nothing new."

"But here, they are *literally* trying to hunt us down. I'm sorry, but I can't be as casual as you and the others."

Khuna grimaced and Quenti couldn't help feeling the smallest bit satisfied. Despite all the horrible things that had happened to them over the past month, Khuna always managed to seem too put together and calm. She didn't have the cheery optimism of Lili, but an unaffected coolness that made Quenti feel crazy for feeling anything.

"See that," she said, still cognizant of keeping her voice low, "That's the first genuine emotion I've seen from you since Arbol burned to the ground. Since Lili's death. All of this is not okay. *I'm* not okay!"

Khuna let out a hollow laugh that made Quenti's lips pull into a frown.

"You think I'm okay?" she said. "I'm a mess. I'm lucky if I sleep through the night without having a panic attack if I don't feel you next to me. Every time I hear someone moving at night, I think it's some councilguard come to kill us all. I'm just trying to keep it together for you because I know *you're* struggling."

Quenti felt something unclench in her chest. "I don't need you to always be the one to protect me."

"It's not just you," Khuna said. "It's Runeo. You and him both. After everything he's been through, that boy's on the brink of a complete meltdown."

"And who made it your responsibility to take care of us?"

"If I don't, who else will?"

Silence stretched between the two of them, and a light breeze sent a smattering of sand across the street.

And then Quenti laughed. "I can't believe you lump me in with Runeo."

Khuna smiled in response. "Don't worry. He's on a completely different level than you."

Quenti leaned down, pressing her forehead against Khuna's, only thinking briefly of the people milling about around them.

"I don't need you to be strong or protect me. Not from your emotions. Not from yourself."

Khuna's eyes were piercing and bright. "From the moment I saw you, I knew I needed to protect you. I wanted to be your strength."

"And I want the honor of holding your pain and sadness beside my own. We're strong together, and we'll face the world and all its pain *together*."

She grasped Khuna's face and pulled it to her own, letting the kiss linger. She'd never been one for public displays of affection, but somehow she didn't have the energy to care. Khuna tasted of rain and wood, and her morning cafi, her lips warm from the morning sun and their hike through the city. She didn't seem inclined to stop the kiss either, pushing back into Quenti with a fervor that made her magia churn like waves crashing against the pier, cool and heated at the same time.

"You're right," Quenti finally said, her rationality finally catching up with her brain.

"I am?" Her breath was warm against Quenti's lips, her eyes still closed.

"We should head back."

Khuna gave a nod after a moment of silence, pulling away with clear reluctance.

They were quiet on the walk back, both stewing in their own contemplations. Quenti's chest stilled churned with unease and anger at Alara's reckless behavior, but she also thought about Khuna's admission. It made her face warm to think that she cared enough to protect her, but she couldn't help but feel sad at the same time. She didn't want to be the reason Khuna was shutting her emotions away.

"Should we tell the others?" Khuna said.

"Not yet," Quenti responded. "Let's at least give her until nightfall."

"I should tell Runeo," she said.

"Sol, no," Quenti said, shaking her head vehemently. "He'll run off and murder Ardo in *front* of Alara. We do not need that drama."

"He's going to find out eventually, and he's going to kill us for hiding it from him."

"We'll cross that bridge when we come to it." She grabbed Khuna's hand. "We're in this together. Us against the world—or a crazed Runeo."

"Sol, he's going to get himself killed."

"They both are."

That bridge came sooner than expected as Alara stepped over the threshold of the inn another hour later, cheeks red, lines of dried salt framing her face. She looked as though she'd seen the lost soul of a deceased.

"Where have you been?" Quenti's tone was harsher than she'd intended, but if Alara noticed, she didn't show it. Instead, her eyes remained cast downward, as though the answers to her questions would be found in the lining of the limestone tiles.

"I need to talk to Senye Cruz." Alara's voice was vacant.

"You left us," Quenti said. "You could have been hurt and we wouldn't have been able to do anything about it."

"I'm fine," she said, finally looking up.

Quenti was shocked to see the resolve in her, so dangerously at odds with her voice.

"Do you know where Senye Cruz is?"

"What happened?" Quenti tried to lighten her tone, but could tell it didn't do her any good.

"Not now," Alara said, not sparing her a glance.

"We waited for you. We looked for you."

"Not now."

"What *happened*?" Quenti all but shouted, still doing her best to keep from making a scene.

Another guest walked through the front door, passing between them and toward the front desk, and the two of them stood in silence for several long seconds.

"Back in our rooms," Alara whispered. And then the smallest of smiles crossed her lips. "I think I may have found a solution to our problem."

CHAPTER 31

ALARA

"And you trust him?" Dante said, eyebrows furrowed at the revelation of where Alara had spent the last couple of hours.

"He hasn't turned us in yet," Alara answered.

"And I doubt he will." Unexpectedly, it was Senye Cruz who came to Alara's defense.

Alara wasn't sure she'd ever get used to that woman not having it out for her. It was odd living in a world where she was the ally and Emaru was the villain.

"Ardo is an honorable young man," Senye Cruz continued, "and would never turn on his word."

Dante's face scrunched up in annoyance and turned away with a bitter expression. Alara knew he would have liked nothing more than to discredit what she was about to say, but even he had to draw the line at Senye Cruz's word.

The thought gave Alara an extra boost of confidence, but it was quickly undercut by the sight of Quenti at the other end of the room, sitting on the bed, arms crossed. The thought that she, of all people, didn't trust her hurt more than she wanted to admit.

"But we can't ignore that *she* can still be compromised," Dante said.

"I'm not," Alara said. "He's a friend, yes, but I wouldn't jeopardize the mission."

"Are we going to talk about the fact that your friend killed mine?" Runeo's voice was cold and low. He glanced around the room. "We can't forget about Zinita. And what about the others we lost in the Haven? How can we trust someone who bore arms against us? What's changed since then?"

She hadn't seen that look of contempt in his eyes since they had first met in Arbol. It made her chest tighten. "A lot," Alara said, turning to Senye Cruz. "Senye, do you even know what happened when you left the Haven?"

"I have eyes and ears everywhere," she said. "Of course I know what happened. And indeed, even if it weren't Ardo, the tide would have shifted enough to warrant a discussion."

Runeo growled and clenched his fists, but Cruz held up a hand that sent a burst of heat through the room as the fire in the small hearth flared.

"There are many important things for us to discuss, but I would first like to hear the rest of what Alara discussed with the boy." Her words were sharp, and Alara flinched to see the sharp eyes boring into her.

"He wants to break out Emaru," she said, ignoring the sharp breeze that swirled around Runeo as she spoke.

Alara expected the room to erupt into chaos, but instead, her statement was followed by silence, and even the breeze swirling around Runeo stilled.

"We help him break out Emaru, and he gets us the information we need to retrieve Beno and the viajera. Those are his terms," Alara said, glancing over at Mena, whose face remained stoic in one of the soft chairs by the door. "And that's what we need, right? We find Beno, we find the viajera, and we find the secrets of my dagger."

The eyes on Senye Cruz's calculating face wrinkled at the corners. "And what did you tell him?"

Alara paused for the briefest of moments. For the first time, she realized the consequences of what she'd shared with Ardo. "I told him who we were looking for."

"El'dyo," Dante said with a groan. "It's bad enough that we're trusting him with the knowledge of any of us being here. Now we're trusting him as we actively work to undermine the entirety of the Council?"

"Not the entirety of the Council," Senye Cruz reminded him.

"You know what I mean," Dante said. "As much as even I'd hate to admit it, any influence on the Council you once had is all but gone." To Alara's surprise, the comment truly did seem to pain Dante to say.

The discussions went round and round, and at the end of it all, Alara found no support in the rest of the room. Quenti wouldn't so much as look at her. Khuna was too preoccupied trying to calm Quenti and Runeo in turn, and Mena's eyes were stuck to the floor. Though, knowing Mena, she likely only kept silent so as not to influence the group with her own bias.

This wasn't going well at all. She knew it would be tough to convince the others, but she hadn't expected each word to be as difficult as pulling an arrow from a rock.

She'd spent the entirety of the walk to the inn dreading what was coming next, but she knew it had to be done.

She just hoped she wasn't risking Ardo's life in the process. Taking a deep breath, she cleared her throat, barely cutting through the quiet animosity in the room, with each person angrily trying to make their own point through hushed whispers. To her surprise, the group went silent, attention focused on her. Now that she had it, she almost didn't know what to say, but she pushed away her fear.

"I haven't told him what we're planning," Alara said, taking a deep breath before diving into the next thing she said—the thing that would change everything. "But I did tell him where we're staying. He's going to come once he's done with his shift, which should be soon."

A quiet intensity passed over Runeo's eyes, and while no one else looked quite as livid as him, they didn't exactly look thrilled themselves. Alara spared a glance in Quenti's direction, and her position was exactly the same: sat on the bed, legs and arms both crossed, and an impassive expression on her face.

"And I trust him," Alara said. "Like Senye Cruz said, he's a man of honor."

"He's also a man of the Council," Senye Cruz said.

"And so are you. Or at least you were."

Senye Cruz's lips pulled tight, and Alara could see the remnants of the Cruz she knew from the Haven—the one who punished her for so much as setting one toe out of line. Though, it said a lot that the woman didn't berate her then and there. Alara knew in that moment that she'd made the right decision. Were it up to this group, they never would have followed through with her plan willingly. Not unless it was a last resort.

After all, she was in the company of Arborelis and Rebels from the Haven, neither of which had a history of making decisions without having their hands forced.

The room remained silent as everyone exchanged looks, the seconds stretching into what felt like hours.

"And you told him where we are?" Senye Cruz said.

Alara nodded.

"Then we have to adapt."

Runeo's face dropped at the unexpected declaration. "You can't be serious."

"We're in the middle of a city surrounded by our enemies," Senye Cruz said. "We cannot afford to turn on each other now."

"So, what?" Dante said, eyes somehow almost as piercing as Runeo's. "We do nothing?"

"Like I said—we adapt," Senye Cruz said. "We have few allies within this city's borders. Now, we have one more. Or so I hope."

"And what about Alara?" Dante said.

"What would you have me do?" she said. "Tie her up and whip her in front of the entire group as an example?"

"And what if her friend brings a platoon of soldiers with him?"

A knock on the door sent the group back into silence. Alara's own heart skipped several beats.

Ardo said he would come alone, she thought. *He said he would.* But what if he'd been deceiving her all along?

No. He never would, she knew. But what if he did? And what if the others were the ones to pay the price for it? Even the most good-hearted people in the world can become victims of war. Lili had been proof of that. Ardo's honor would have been the smallest of casualties. Hardly noticeable in the grand scheme of it all.

Runeo was the first one to move, hand resting on his dagger. Senye Cruz pulled the flame from the fire, throwing the room into shadows, except for the slightest sliver among the drapes and the flicker she held in her palm.

The knock came again. Hesitant.

The maneuver made Alara feel the slightest bit better. If Ardo had run off to collect his fellow councilguards, they would have just knocked down the door. Wouldn't they?

Dante was the one to actually move to open the door, acting in what was either pure bravery or arrogance. Alara couldn't see his expression in the dark, but she was almost certain it was the latter.

He twisted the doorknob, and with a pull, a thin stream of light poured into their quarters, only to be instantly smothered again by Dante's body.

"Who is it?" he said in a raspy voice.

Alara wasn't sure if he was trying to be intimidating, but if she'd been on the other side, it would have been. Despite his thin frame, the man could still cut a threatening figure, especially from the shadows.

"I'm here to see Alara," came Ardo's familiar voice.

A few seconds passed, during which time, Alara could see Dante's head tilt side to side, looking to see if there were any surprise visitors accompanying the already unwelcome guest. Then, with a swift movement, Dante opened the door just wide enough for Ardo to enter, blanketing the entrance in the light from the hallway. A deep frown of suspicion was visible on Dante's face in spite of the darkness.

Alara's heart settled back into its normal rate. He wouldn't have betrayed her. She *knew* it. But that hadn't stopped her from doubting. She wondered if she'd ever stopped doubting herself after everything that had happened over the past couple of months. Her world had been torn down around her. How could she not doubt?

She moved forward, not knowing if she planned on hugging him or simply acknowledging him, but before she could make it more than a few steps, a figure threw itself at Ardo.

Alara could tell from the sharp wind kicking up in the room that it belonged to Runeo.

His fist connected with Ardo's cheek at the same time that his wind powers slammed into him from behind, throwing his body forward. The smack of bone on skin cracked through the room and rattled Alara's teeth. Ardo's own arms came up, fists flying up in defense. He connected briefly with Runeo's jaw before he was thrown against the wall by another gust of raging wind.

Cruz had let go of the flame in her fist, returning it to the hearth and letting light fill the room, showing the scene in all its glory. Ardo's blood smeared across his face, dripping from his nose, and Runeo's lip bled profusely. Neither man seemed to notice their injuries as they continued to brawl, fists connecting and magia forgotten.

Alara wanted to throw herself between the two of them or scream, but neither seemed like a solution. If they weren't quiet, their attempts at staying hidden wouldn't last long.

It was Khuna who finally acted, pulling water from the wash basin and surrounding air and shooting a stream at the two bleeding men. As Runeo stumbled back, Ardo leaned against the wooden door and lifted his hands in surrender.

"I didn't come here to fight," he said, ignoring the blood dribbling down his chin, unchecked.

A growl escaped Runeo's throat, even as Khuna had an arm across his chest, holding him back. "That was for Zinita," he said. "If it were up to me, your head would be on a stake."

Alara had no doubt that Zinita would have preferred that course of action herself. "That's enough," she finally said, stepping between them.

"I'm sorry," Ardo said.

"No," Alara said. "You didn't do anything wrong."

"No," Ardo repeated. "I'm sorry."

Alara turned around and could tell the apology wasn't directed at her, or even the group. It was squarely aimed at Runeo.

Alara felt a warmth rise from her stomach. Ardo didn't have the slightest idea who Zinita was, but he apologized nonetheless. Whether it was in dedication to his duty or genuine remorse, though, Alara couldn't quite tell.

And then she saw it. The smallest glimmer of regret in the wrinkles at the corners of his eyes.

"We killed a lot of people that day ourselves, Runeo," Khuna said, voice soft.

Runeo didn't seem to hear the words, but he didn't lunge again. He only clenched his fists at his sides as Ardo remained frozen.

Senye Cruz stepped up to Ardo, eyes sharp and focused on his face, and then she motioned for him to step away from the door. Ardo obeyed, eyes widening as he recognized her face in the light.

"S-Senye Cruz," he said.

"Everardo Gomes," Senye Cruz said. It was hard not to hear the amusement she coated Ardo's name in. "Glad to see my presence here hasn't made its way into your circles." And then, her face hardened. "Dante. Make sure he wasn't followed."

Dante nodded and ducked from the room without question, throwing a last look of suspicion at Ardo as he did.

"Sit," she said in a stern tone that Alara recognized all too well.

He looked uncomfortable at the idea, but didn't argue as he slipped into a small wooden chair.

Senye Cruz crossed her arms and planted her feet to the floor. She glared at him with an uncomfortable intensity. "Well," she finally said. "Go ahead. Convince me we should trust you."

He pushed his shoulders back, trying to look brave in the face of the ex-councilwoman, but Alara could see the small twitch in his eye as he looked around. Nonetheless, his voice didn't quiver as he spoke, sharing the same conversation that he and Alara had already had.

"She's already explained that much to us," Cruz said. "I understand why you need us. Tell me why we need you," Cruz said, voice cold.

"You came to the base." He looked at the faces around the room, eyes settling on Mena and Runeo, the latter of who looked away. "Did you find what you were looking for?"

Again, more silence.

"Well, then," he said. "That's why you need me. You're looking for information? You need to get into the mines? I won't need to carelessly try to mind-walk everyone on base to make it happen. I can help. But only if you promise to help me."

Senye Cruz leaned over Ardo, studying his face. "You want us to break Senye Emaru out, yes? The same Senye Emaru who declared us traitors to the Council and tried to kill us?"

"I want to break out Senye Emaru, the same woman who helped keep the Council in check for years as your colleague and friend."

"Through oppression and control," a voice from the corner of the room said, and Alara was surprised to see Quenti finally speak up.

"Through compromise," Ardo said. He turned back to face Senye Cruz, somehow not looking intimidated despite his seated position in front of her. "You know the complexities of the politics. If she didn't enforce the system, the blameless on the Council would force it. She had no choice. *You* had no choice."

Alara's jaw tightened. These were conversations she was never allowed to have with her former guardian. Nuance wasn't something Emaru had ever allowed Alara when it came to the Council and its role in controlling mages. A part of her was... envious of Ardo. What conversations had the two had in the time since the breakout at the Haven? What conversations had they had before that?

Though she already knew it, it still felt like a stab to the heart to realize how little she truly knew the woman who had raised her.

"All Senye Emaru has ever wanted was peace."

Runeo and Quenti both scoffed.

"It's true," Ardo continued. "Why else would she fight so hard to keep the status quo?"

"And now that the status quo has been broken?"

Surprisingly, it was that question that gave him pause, and he thought for a long moment. "I trust her to make the right decision."

"Mena," Senye Cruz said after an extended silence, turning to the mind-walker standing next to the hearth. "What can you gather from the boy?"

"I can feel out his intentions," she said. "But I'll only do it with his permission. Sifting through someone's mind and cognizance is much more invasive than just adding or adjusting a memory."

Ardo's eyes widened at the turn in conversation and sought out Alara's own. She could only return his look with a small smile of reassurance that she tried to believe. She could see the muscle in his jaw tense as he nodded slowly.

"Well, boy?" Senye Cruz said, the unasked question in the air.

"I'll agree," he said.

With that, Mena stepped forward, sitting on the floor in front of Ardo's chair, laying her hand on his and closing her eyes.

Alara felt something twist in her stomach as Ardo looked back at the woman with curiosity. It only took a minute, but it felt like an hour before she opened her eyes once more. She gave Ardo's hand a squeeze before letting go.

"His intentions are genuine."

"So," Senye Cruz said, "you believe everything you just said." It wasn't exactly a question, but it may as well have been. "That Linda Emaru fought to maintain peace. I suppose we can't all be blessed with superior judgment." She sighed deeply, turning to face the hearth. "While I don't agree with the methods Emaru has used in the past, the threads have already spilled in Sombria. If she were to go free, it's not as though she could just snap her fingers and revert everything to how it was. With war all but imminent, she wouldn't be the worst person to have on our side."

All the air seemed to leave the room.

No one spoke, exchanging looks as they all seemed to debate the next steps in silence. It was Ardo who broke the silence, apparently too exhausted to care about everyone's discomfort.

"So does that mean you agree to help Senye Emaru escape?"

"That all depends on what you have to offer us," Senye Cruz said. "Alara has told us you know who and what we seek. The real question is if you can give us what we need."

"Your target is in the lowest sections of the mines. Level Five."

Senye Cruz looked from Alara to Ardo and back. "There's a reason I didn't come straight here with Alara," he said. "I needed to find something worth your trust."

Senye Cruz frowned all the same. "There is no fifth level," she said.

"Not on the public record, no," Ardo said, "but yes, there is. It's where they keep the most dangerous of bruyas and enemies of the state."

"Mena?" Senye Cruz said.

Ardo and Mena exchanged a look with one another, and Ardo nodded with a sigh as she placed her hand on his and closed her eyes.

"He shares this information with honesty," she said.

Senye Cruz nodded, her face stoic. Alara couldn't tell if she was pleased or not that they'd stumbled into this wealth of information before enacting some insane plan. If she was, she didn't show it. The former councilwoman displayed the same withholding personality that had made her so difficult to be around back at the Haven. Apparently, not everything about the woman had been an act.

"So, then," she finally said. "Beno is on this mysterious fifth level. That's... a challenge."

Mena laughed at this, a humorless and bitter sound. "So, what then? We sneak in and break out my brother in hopes that he still has the..." She glanced up at Ardo. "...our target on him?"

"You didn't tell me he had something on him," Ardo said.

"It's the entire reason we're taking this risk in the first place," Senye Cruz said.

"Not the *entire* reason," Mena said, her eyes boring into Senye Cruz. "But yes."

Ardo sat back in his seat, looking almost comfortable for the first time.

"The prisoners' possessions are usually taken when they're brought into the mines. Unless he hid it extremely well, it will be with the other personal effects. Unless it's been sold off. And, I'll be honest. I don't know if Level Fivers have a different location for their belongings. But it's something I can look into. Either way, it's highly doubtful he still has it. Does it look valuable?"

"Only if you know what it is," Mena said.

"So this could all be for nothing if the compass has been sold or taken," Alara said slowly, guilt filling her stomach.

"Yes," Ardo said with a frown.

No one responded, but Alara was sure it didn't change a thing. At this point, no one else had a better plan.

CHAPTER 32

QUENTI

Quenti watched as the others made plans, her hostility and suspicion clear in her expression. She wanted to trust Alara, but she knew the girl's heart made her stupid around this blameless guard, as much as she'd argue otherwise. She had seen it in her eyes when they had first broken into the Haven, and she saw it when she'd lost them in the city earlier that day.

Even as he was explaining how they could break *Emaru* out of the mines alongside Beno, Alara trusted him. Quenti would have been happy to see the woman rot in chains for what she had done. Instead, Alara had convinced the others to go along with her insane plan.

And as much as she hated what was happening in front of her, Quenti didn't know if there was anything she could do to stop it.

"I can get us into the upper level of the mines," Ardo said. "But once we pass the third level, even councilguards are screened and only essential soldiers are allowed down."

"That's not a problem if I'm there," Mena said, voice smooth and lacking any ego, despite the confidence of her words. "I can convince them we work down there."

"That doesn't solve trying to move two prisoners back out of the mines without being noticed," Cruz said, not sounding nearly as confident as the other two.

"Can't she," Ardo said, motioning at Mena with a wave of his hand, "just convince them they aren't prisoners?"

Mena sat back on the bed, crossing her arms and shaking her head. "Sure, I can convince a few guards of specific information, but escorting two prisoners out of an entire mine system... I wouldn't have the strength for that. Planting a memory of a guard being in a certain position in the lower levels is small compared to convincing them that two prisoners—who will probably *look* like prisoners—are guards. And that's assuming we only run into one or two of them at a time."

"We can only assume that the security in the lower levels will be tight?" Cruz said.

"Good assumption," Ardo said. "Based on the logs, I'd say there are about three times as many councilguards on the fifth level as in the others.

Cruz nodded. "This likely won't be a simple in-and-out mission, then. It will take at least a few days of reconnaissance before we act. We don't even know if they would have kept the viajera in the mines or not. Any information we can find on that will be crucial. Once we work to break out our two targets, we won't want to waste any time on side missions. Is that something you can help with, Ardo?"

Ardo rubbed his chin. "Hard to say. Based on what little I've already looked into, it's clear there's a lot of information that goes unwoven. I don't know if they'd log mysterious artifacts—especially if they're being held in secret locations."

"But there's a chance," Dante said.

"No, the boy is right," Cruz said, voice heavy. "If they truly wanted to keep this a secret, logging something like this within the weaves and tapestries would be foolish."

"What, then?"

"Ideally," Cruz said, voice hesitant, "we would already have someone down in the mines who could take the time to search before we enact the rescue."

Quenti almost had to stop herself from snorting. The idea was so idiotic in nature that there was no way anyone in the room would actually entertain it.

Wasn't it?

A swirl of anxiety rose up inside her when she noticed no one else in the room laughing, or so much as contesting the thought. On the contrary, they all seemed to be entertaining it.

"Wait, you're not serious," Quenti said. "We're trying to get two prisoners *out*. What good would it be to have another one of our people in?"

"It's just a thought," Cruz said, "and I agree, it's a risky one. But to have someone who can do our lower-level recon prior to the breakout would be valuable."

"Senye," Dante—who had returned after ensuring no one was lying in wait behind Ardo—said. "I agree with the girl. This isn't the wisest course of action."

"Then tell me what course of action you would take."

Dante opened and closed his mouth as if to say something, but nothing came out. Finally, after a few false starts, something did. "It's too dangerous. Give us some time and we'll find a better plan."

"Great, more waiting," Alara said with a sigh.

Dante scoffed at her comment. "Thinking and planning are what make us soldiers and not children playing war."

"I've spent my entire life being trained as a soldier," Alara said, "but I've already seen too many people die thanks to the inaction of those in power."

Khuna, reading the room and shifting uncomfortably, stood up. "I think we should get food. It's well past midday and none of us have eaten since morning, if at all."

"We don't have time for that," Dante said, not even looking at Khuna where she stood.

Cruz didn't brush the suggestion off so quickly. "Why don't you pick up something from the market and bring it back for all of us?"

Khuna turned to Quenti expectantly. "I'll need a hand. Can you come too?"

It was tempting to get out of the stifling room and away from the bickering, but she also didn't like leaving them to make decisions without her. Not when she seemed to be the only one with any amount of hesitance in trusting this blameless councilguard in their presence—even if that resistance was admittedly pathetic and passive.

She shook her head, trying to say as much to Khuna with her eyes, but she only raised an eyebrow and frowned before leaving. Quenti watched her go, feeling guilty, but as she turned back and saw Alara's eyes narrowed on her, she was glad she had stayed.

The two of them hadn't exchanged so much as a word in private since Alara had returned, and now there was an undercurrent of tension that Quenti knew couldn't be one-sided, even if everyone else seemed content to ignore it.

"Is Beno as powerful as you?" Alara asked, focused back on Mena.

The woman gave a smirk. "Not nearly, and that's assuming he'll be in good health and in possession of his powers."

"They'll be cuffed, no matter how much security is down there. So, at the very least, his abilities will be suppressed. But maybe I can find a set of keys," Ardo said.

"So, we'll have Beno and Mena with their mind-walking skills," Alara cut in, "and I can help us avoid as many guards as possible."

Ardo shook his head at this. "I checked the logs. Every guard that works below the third floor is blameless. You won't be able to sense them coming."

Alara's lip twitched at the comment. "I've been meaning to tell everyone," she said slowly. "That... may not be a problem."

The entire room went still, the only sound the crackling fire in the hearth.

"What?" Dante asked.

"It means that I lately—I *think* at least—I've been feeling blameless, too."

Cruz stared down at the girl. "*Feeling* blameless?"

"Just like I can sense mages and bruyas. Sort of. It's actually how I chased him down," she said nodding to Ardo. "But it's not just people I know. In the weeks we spent running, I noticed almost a blankness around some councilguards where there should be something. Like I can feel the absence of magia when I focus on them."

"You're sure?" Senye Cruz said, and Alara once again responded with a nod. "then we use the powers we have. And with them, this adds to our odds in making it through the mines safely."

"If everything goes perfectly, of course," Mena said.

Quenti's stomach twisted as she listened. Somehow, amid all this, no one had stated the obvious. "Does anyone else think something is seriously wrong? If it was as easy as using magia, wouldn't people have escaped already?"

"Not everyone has a councilguard on their side," Alara said. "Plus two powerful mind-walkers and a mind-stalker."

"No," Senye Cruz said with a sigh. "Quenti is right. We are likely missing something. There is a reason we can't just go in blindly." She gave Ardo a pointed look.

He raised his hands. "I've told you everything I know so far."

"You're assuming we believe you at all," Quenti said. Her voice was low, but in the quiet room, it was easily heard.

"It's possible there are things you don't even know are helpful,"

Cruz said to the councilguard, ignoring Quenti's comment. "But time is on our side. Perhaps we can use you to further infiltrate their ranks. If we can somehow get you down there, deep into the mines, maybe you can help us. Maybe you can get us something—"

Before she could finish the sentence, the door to the room crashed open and Khuna burst through, a look of terror in her eyes.

"We have a problem," she said.

CHAPTER 33

ALARA

In the moment it took Alara to register Khuna's words, a crashing of wood sounded from downstairs, followed by the echoing of yells up through the main plaza.

"What—" Cruz started.

"—The councilguards are knocking down doors all around the city," Khuna said, cutting off the former councilwoman. Her eyes swiveled and focused on Alara with a measure of cold in them. "They're looking for a female fuegen who's been spotted around town."

Everyone spoke all at once, but all Alara could hear was the sound of blood rushing through her ears, her eyes still focused on Khuna, who looked back accusingly—as though Alara had gone running through the streets of Lejon announcing herself.

"How could they know? I didn't..." But she couldn't even finish her own defense because *she had*. Her eyes found Quenti's and she saw the dawning awareness and a rage building, in time with her own shame. But Quenti had wanted to help the little girl too.

"We will have to deal with whatever this is later," Senye Cruz said, looking between them. "For now, we need to get out."

If it weren't for having grown up around the woman, Alara may have assumed her as calm and calculating as ever, but there was a shiver in her voice that she had never heard before—not even during the battle at the Haven.

Senye Cruz was afraid. That, more than anything, sent a cold wave of terror through Alara.

"If that prick Francisco thinks there is a bruya here," Dante said, "he won't rest until he finds them."

"He doesn't know for sure if she's here," Senye Cruz said. "For all he knows, she already escaped from town."

There was another crash from downstairs and a wave of screams as the soldiers made their way into the inn. It would only take a few moments for them to get upstairs.

"Either way, we have to leave *now*," Cruz said. "Grab what you can and let's make a plan to get out."

"You can use the window—go to the roof," Ardo said, wearing his guard-mode as a second skin.

"And just hope no one looks up?" Dante said.

Alara watched the exchange helplessly, adrenaline pumping through her veins, though somehow leaving her frozen. *Francisco wouldn't stop until he found them. No. Her.* She knew helping that girl would have consequences. And she did it anyway. Once again, she'd been too foolish to see the bigger picture.

"Stop!" she said with all the authority she could muster. "None of you need to run. He isn't looking for you. He's looking for a fuegen, right? He's looking for me."

"You act as though he won't recognize Senye Cruz the moment he comes sweeping in here," Dante said.

"He's not going to come in here," Alara said. "I'm going to him."

"Are you—"

"Alara, I will—"

"That's—"

Everyone spoke at once, but she only held her hand up. "If he doesn't arrest someone, he'll tear this whole town apart," she said. She hadn't had a lot of firsthand experience with Major Francisco, but his stubborn persistence was infamous, even in the Haven. "We need someone he can arrest to make him happy, and we need someone to get into the mines for information, right? I call this a win-win."

Her voice didn't waver and she held her face straight, but it didn't stop the fear from turning her stomach and making her lungs ache as she spoke. Even she knew the plan was crazy as she spoke it.

"Are you stupid?" Quenti, of all people, spoke first. "That's the dumbest thing I've ever heard. We all agreed that this was a dumb plan."

"No," Alara said. "You agreed. But when we break out Beno and... *Emaru*..." The name felt like vomit leaving her throat "...we'll need to know where to find the viajera. We won't have time to waste. We need someone down there to know where to look, otherwise it'll be a waste."

"There is no guarantee he'll take you to the mines," Senye Cruz said.

"But they *will* take her to the mines," Ardo said. "It's a direct order since the Haven battle to take any bruyas straight to the Lejon and into the mines. All precepts of trials have been halted."

"It's too risky," Senye Cruz said.

Another crash from the first floor.

"And it's too risky to try and escape," Alara said. "We don't have a choice."

"There's always a choice."

"Then we don't have *many* choices." *Crash*. Their options dwindled by the second.

"No." Alara was surprised to hear Runeo's voice—even more that he was disagreeing with her. He had been watching silently from his corner since Ardo had arrived, looking disgruntled at even having to share air with the councilguard. "We're not sending you into a prison alone. Everyone else is right. It's a stupid plan. And you're stupid for having it."

"They're not going to stop looking for me. We need to give them what they want." Alara looked around. "Ardo, how would you like to get in Francisco's good graces?"

She stepped toward him, hands outstretched, exposing her wrists to him.

"I can do this," she said. She was speaking to everyone, but her eyes were focused on Ardo. "Once I'm in, I can work on finding Beno *and* Emaru. And I'll find out where they're keeping the viajera."

He looked back at her, expression grim. She watched the muscle in his jaw twitch, but then he reached behind his back and pulled at the cuffs hanging from his belt as another crash rang out from downstairs.

"Lovely," Quenti drawled, "the councilguard we're supposed to be trusting has a pair of magia-suppressing cuffs in his back pocket."

"You know just as much as I do that these barely do anything to her," Ardo said, throwing Quenti a glare.

Alara wished this were true. Yes, she'd spent the better part of her life wearing bracelets with the same effect as these cuffs, but she'd gone weeks without them, and wearing them now had her feeling claustrophobic. It was as though a lid she had forgotten about had been placed over her head. She could still function, but it was somehow more difficult than she'd expected.

With a flick of her wrist, she pulled a thread from the fire at the hearth. Relief filled her as she saw the flames twitch at her will.

It's okay. It's still there. It's still in me. Ironic that the abilities she'd spent most of her life trying to avoid now brought her comfort in the most troubling of times.

"You're sure you want to go through with this?" Senye Cruz said.

Alara nodded. "I'll do my job down there. You get us out."

She turned to face Quenti, but the other girl only turned away. Still upset. Still untrusting.

No one else said a word as she and Ardo left through the door. Alara thrashed in Ardo's arms, twisting against the cuffs and his hold as they made their way across the balcony and toward the stairs.

"Ease up, will you," he said, whisper against her ear.

"Wimp," she said, unable to stop her smile.

Ardo huffed in amusement, but the moment was short-lived. The very next, they rounded the corner and descended the stairs toward the courtyard where a handful of guards were knocking down doors.

"I've got her!" Ardo shouted over the cacophony. "At ease," he said, louder this time to grab their attention. The guards stopped where they were, faces contorted in confusion as the stranger hauled Alara past them and through the front room of the inn.

Ardo didn't bother to look back as the guards trailed after him, and it made sense. Councilguards were too used to following orders to question his command as a superior officer.

When they passed back out into the sunlight and the plaza beyond, Alara had to squint against the brightness. The sky was cloudless and the painted city shone brightly.

Francisco was easy enough to spot among the gathered crowds and guards rushing about. He was dressed in all black, ignorant of the unrelenting sun's heat, standing at the center of the plaza, shouting orders.

Ardo marched forward, but there was a sudden reluctance in his strides. Even as she struggled, his hand rested gently on her arm.

"You'd better know what you're doing," he said as they broke through the final group of soldiers, coming to a stop in front of Francisco. "I believe she's the one you're looking for."

The man turned. He was just as Alara remembered. Jaw chiseled, a permanent salt-and-pepper stubble covering his harsh, slate-brown skin, and lips twisted in a permanent sneer. His eyes grazed over Ardo before landing on Alara with a sharp intensity.

"You," he said. "I don't think we ever formally met."

"We have," Alara said. "Twice. It wasn't a pleasure."

Francisco smiled. "I should have known it was *you* causing trouble. First the Haven, and now you grace us with your presence?"

"I was on vacation," Alara said. She had no idea where this false confidence was coming from, but she worried it was all that was stopping her from collapsing in fear. "Lejon is quite beautiful this time of year. The dust, the heat, the self-serving councilguards."

"You're just like your mentor," he said. "And like her, you're a traitor to your people and the cause. Though, I suppose I should thank you. Without your actions, who knows how long she would have escaped detection."

"What cause is she a traitor to exactly?"

"The very integrity of this country of ours, and the peace we have fostered for hundreds of years," he said, stepping closer to her. Ardo's grip on her tightened, as if he was holding himself from stepping back.

"If only that were true," she said, her voice softer than intended. Still, the message seemed to reach Francisco, as he tilted his head in curiosity.

"Oh?" he said. "So, you deny the claims of your traitorous acts?"

"I deny—"

She didn't see the slap coming. One moment, she was facing the man's grizzled face, and the next, a sharp pain pelted and rocked her head to the side. Ardo grunted in shock as the back of Francisco's hand cracked across her temple.

"We don't give traitors a voice here in Lejon." Alara heard Francisco say through ringing ears. "Congratulations on your arrest, soldier."

"My only thanks is to serve the Council, Major," Ardo said, voice vacant of any insecurity or concern.

Alara looked back up in time to see Francisco give Ardo a sharp nod. "Glad to know I can trust your loyalties." It was a statement, but it sounded like a threat.

"My loyalty will always be to those who keep Sombria safe from the threat of magia and madness."

Francisco grinned coldly. Alara had seen the expression countless times before, more often with pathetic councilguard trainees given too much power. It wasn't lost on Alara that Ardo never explicitly supported the Council in his statement. She hoped Francisco was too stupid to notice.

She was still chewing on her lip when a lumbering force sent her sideways, body skidding across the ground as Ardo was thrown off his feet behind her. Her eyes popped at the change in air pressure around them and she turned with a groan to look back at where the burst had come from.

Her groan only soured to see Runeo standing in the doorway of the inn, hands outstretched. He looked particularly proud of himself, wearing a smirk that somehow rivaled Francisco's in its smugness.

"I hear you were looking for a fight," he said, directing his gaze at Francisco, who was still on his feet, stance wide and low. Though the gust had only blown him back a few feet, from the expression on his face, it had caught him off guard.

"I should have known there'd be more than one of you. Rodents always travel in packs." With that, he swept his arm down in a cutting motion and his soldiers sent a flood of arrows at Runeo, without much regard for the civilians on the other side of the threshold.

Runeo brushed them aside easily with his magia, but he only

barely dodged the club that came from behind in the next moment. He fell to the ground, spinning away from the swing and pushing back the guard that had tried to surprise him. Alara couldn't help the scream that tore from her as an axe flew through the air toward Runeo's back.

CHAPTER 34

QUENTI

Khuna looked at Quenti with the same conviction she had only seen once before.

"No," Quenti said.

"He's going to get himself killed," Khuna said, a hand wrapping around Quenti's shoulder.

"Then Runeo can die like the idiot he is." Her words came out as a growl.

"I'm sorry," Khuna said, ignoring any argument. "You can yell at me when I get out."

Before Quenti could grab her and hold her back, Khuna had already shoved Quenti back and flung her arm out, calling up her magia. A bubble of water materialized in the air, wrapping around a flying axe as it careened toward Runeo, slowing its trajectory and throwing it off course.

The fighting and chaos stopped for the briefest of moments, and Quenti could almost hear the confusion coming from both inside and outside of the inn.

"How many of there are you?" the head guard's harsh voice called out.

Quenti wanted to step forward, to throw herself into danger as easily as Khuna had, but she was frozen in place, as though by magia. The nightmares that had haunted her dreams for the past several weeks of Khuna disappearing into the night behind Runeo—the day she was captured by the Haven, and the event that forever changed Sombria. The next time Quenti had seen her, she had been dirt-stained and thin behind bars in the dungeons of the Haven.

She couldn't let it happen again.

Yet, even as she moved forward, legs numb and head buzzing with adrenaline, an arm wrapped around her waist and a hand clamped over her mouth.

"Don't you dare," Senye Cruz hissed into her ear, pulling her back.

Quenti was in such a daze that she somehow let Cruz pull her away from the main plaza and up to the second floor.

"What the hell are they thinking?" Dante whispered from beside her, rage clear in his voice. Quenti couldn't help notice how empty their quarters had suddenly gotten, their party now reduced to four —A stern Cruz on one side, an angry Dante on the other, and a somehow-calm Mena, even-breathing and mellow. a different kind of collected from Cruz.

"Away from the door," Cruz said as she would to a child, guiding Quenti toward the window that overlooked the plaza. A small curtain was draped across it, but they could still see onto the street beyond.

Cruz's grip on Quenti loosened, her hand dropping from her face, but she didn't quite let go as they watched. Quenti's arms twitched at her side, her senses returning, and all of them now asking *"Why? Why didn't you try to help Khuna?"*

Not that Khuna needed her help. From their window, Quenti

could see her girlfriend holding bubbles of water over two guards as they struggled for air, only for Runeo to knock them down. They moved in unison, a grace brought on by years spent fighting and working together. A history and a loyalty that Quenti envied, despite knowing where Khuna's eyes actually fell.

Quenti finally tore her eyes away from the powerful moves of Khuna to watch the guards. None of them were fighting back with magia. Despite the large group of black clad guards in the plaza, they were all blameless. It shouldn't have surprised her, but it only reinforced one thing: that this new leader of Lejon—this Francisco—knew exactly who he did and didn't trust.

How deep did this go in all of Sombria?

A pit formed in Quenti's stomach as she saw the guards easily holding their own against the two bruyas. And of course they would be. They were vastly outnumbered and out-trained.

That was the whole point, wasn't it? This wasn't a fight they were supposed to win. Alara *wanted* to get captured, and while he said nothing, Quenti was sure Runeo had planned on joining her in the same plan. Which meant that Khuna was fighting a losing battle to protect her friend from his own stupidity.

Damn you, Khuna.

A shout from across the plaza caught Quenti's attention, and she looked to see Alara struggling as Francisco dragged her to her feet. Ardo, a few yards away, stood by as a dagger was pressed against Alara's throat.

Francisco said something that Quenti couldn't quite make out, but it was probably a threat. This was confirmed when Khuna dropped her hands, sending spheres of water plummeting to the ground.

Runeo looked to be debating whether or not to listen; she doubted it was easy for the bruya to surrender even as a part of the plan. But after several too-long seconds, he finally dropped his arms, shoulders slumping. In the same moment, Quenti's own shoulders slumped. She wasn't happy, but the relief was undeniable. Part of her feared that Runeo would go down fighting, bringing the other two with him.

Thank Sol that hadn't been the case.

The guards stepped forward, yanking Khuna and Runeo toward them and into cuffs and ropes. And all Quenti did was stand by and watch. She hated being in this position. She'd be a coward if she stood by, and an idiot like Runeo if she ran after them.

"We need to move, now," Cruz said, snapping their small group into some form of action, though Quenti didn't know what.

"What about..." Quenti started, but the words died on her lips. There was nothing to be done. She only stared out the window.

Alara was back in Ardo's arms, her face visibly pale as Khuna and Runeo were shoved beside her. The three bruyas—the three martyrs —lined up in front of Francisco. Quenti wanted to trust Ardo to keep them safe. She didn't trust him to keep the rest of them safe, but he'd do anything to keep Alara safe, right? Quenti had only known him in brief stints, but he clearly had nothing but love for Alara. She prayed that would extend to Khuna and Runeo.

"Come, now." Mena's voice was soft behind her and she felt a hand gentle on her shoulder. "We need to hide."

Mena pulled her away from the window, not by force but with the softest nudge as her arm wrapped around Quenti's shoulders.

"There is a ladder to the roof through the back hallway," Mena said, leading them out of their room. "We can go there just until the guards have gone. They might do a sweep of the inn, but I don't think they'll be looking too hard."

She led them across the balcony, overlooking the courtyard of the inn, the commotion already having subsided within its confines. It was as though nothing had ever happened. It was as though the person she loved hadn't gotten thrown into shackles to be forgotten by the whole of Sombria.

The group slipped through a shadowed hallway and up a slightly untrustworthy ladder until they came out onto the large flat roof of the inn. Even up here, red and orange sand spread across the plaster, a miniature landscape. From this height, Quenti could just see the line of black on the eastern horizon where the magia died and the Ruinedlands began. She looked away, stomach souring.

It had been all but two minutes since the events transpired, but she already missed the warmth of her partner beside her, and in its place, a near-wild panic that threatened to overtake her completely.

"You can make people forget," Quenti said to Mena, who still stood by her side, a silent companion. "You can make them feel... different, right?" She let the implication linger in the air.

"I can, but I would never use that to erase fear or grief. We have our emotions for a reason. Right now, you need to remember why you're fighting, even if it hurts."

"Why was she so desperate to sacrifice herself?" Quenti said bitterly.

"We don't get to choose whom we fall in love with, but that would be nice, wouldn't it? I'd find myself a nice wealthy merchant or maybe a pirate."

"You'd leave Sombria?"

Mena hummed lightly. "I suppose not," she finally said, "but we can always dream."

CHAPTER 35

ARDO

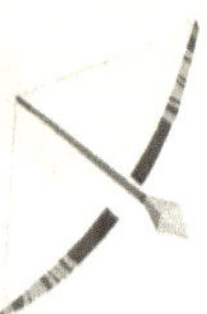

ajor Francisco threw around orders almost violently, and his men followed suit, sweeping the plaza in search of the remaining rebels—if there were any.

Ardo could only hope the others in the inn had used their chance to escape. There may not be another. He could feel the trembling in Alara's body, even as he held her in his grip. It took everything in his power to not pull her closer. To wrap her in his arms and ensure her she was safe.

It was a promise he could never keep. *No one is safe in Sombria anymore. Her least of all.*

Instead, he stood rigid, eyes following the other guards, trying his hardest to forget the prisoner he was holding on to. To do everything in his power to treat her as he would anyone else. It was difficult to ignore the curses she spat under her breath as she watched Runeo and Khuna tied.

"Who taught you those words?" he said, the words barely a whisper.

"Adelmo," she said.

The name made Ardo's chest tighten. He had never been as close to the old man as Alara had been, but he had spent countless hours with them both, sitting by the fire or training in his barn. It hadn't been until days after the battle in the Haven that he heard the news of his death. His body had been burned with the rest before Ardo could even pay his respects.

He hadn't been sure if Alara even knew of the man's death, but after hearing the pain in her voice, it was all too clear.

He squeezed her arm, hoping it might give some comfort.

"You," Major Francisco said, waving his hand at Ardo and the others holding Runeo and Khuna. "Come with me. I want to process these prisoners personally."

Ardo swallowed back the bile in the back of his throat at the words and the look Major Francisco was giving Alara. He knew the major had known Alara and Emaru back in the Haven, but if there ever had been any warm feelings between them, they'd been replaced by sour disgust.

As they moved away from the main plaza and toward the edge of the city, fewer and fewer people peeked out their windows and from behind their doors as they passed. If they were watching, they did so in secrecy, with the subtle movement of curtains in dark windows.

They moved through the southeast part of the city, which always felt lifeless. The buildings here were just as colorful as those throughout Lejon, but they were worn down and dulled with age. Walls were adorned with cracks and exposed stone, evidence of hundreds of years of history. The street turned from stone to red sand and even as they walked, the buildings suddenly gave way to scattered bushes and the sweeping landscape east of Lejon.

The wind blew hard, sending sand scattering across the roads and into their faces. Every so often, black grains cascaded past them, blown in from the Ruinedlands that sat just beyond the rainbow mountains. He wondered if Alara could feel the difference

—if any mage or bruya could feel their powers drain from them on contact.

The walk down the path to the base and the mines beyond felt natural. He'd taken this path plenty in the weeks since he'd been transferred to Lejon.

But for the first time, he felt the dread settling through him as the palisade walls came into view and the dust and smoke from the mines blocked out the southern sky, turning it a sickly yellow.

Alara stumbled in front of him, her breath suddenly coming in shallow bursts as they neared the mine.

"Keep moving," he said, the words rough. She gave an almost indiscernible nod, tilted up her chin, and fell back in step with the rest of the group.

The mine spread out before them, an ugly gash, as if El'dyo himself had come down and ripped open the earth with his spear. Ardo had only been around the mines a couple of times and never more than a single level down—the guards that kept the mines were separate from those who worked the rest of the base and Lejon. At most, standard councilguards could get permission to escort prisoners to their assigned floor. As such, information, even among councilguards, was scarce. But he had done his best to befriend those who worked the prison. He knew of some of the horrors that went on in the lower levels and could only wonder at what indescribable atrocities went on in the secret levels. His stomach turned, knowing he was leading Alara directly into it.

A narrow path switchbacked across one side of the canyon, down from the top where the base campus was spread out to the different levels of the mines. Ardo had learned on his one and only tour that the first two levels were accessible via this path. After that, a series of lifts within the mines allowed guards to move about freely, while keeping the prisoners in their respective zones.

As they came to the second level, Major Francisco led them

inside, the light of the bright sun disappearing behind them. Ardo's eyes took a second to adjust to the dark tunnels even as the smell hit him, pungent and bitter. It smelled of human waste, sweat, smoke, and something else. Perhaps the very stones they mined. He choked on his breath, even as he felt Alara tense up with her own reaction. The smell only worsened with each step.

The tunnels themselves bustled with life, hundreds of prisoners shuffling in chains, with guards standing on the edges surveying their efforts. The number of guards to prisoners surprised Ardo the most. They were easily outnumbered, even as the prisoners lugged around axes, shovels, and giant stones. With the despair that lingered heavily in the air, he could only wonder with dread as to how the guards kept order in the tunnels and stopped the prisoners from turning on them. It wasn't as though they were far from freedom, after all.

Perhaps he should have been happy. The numbers would make a prison break easier. But if it were so easy, wouldn't it have been done by now?

The lifts themselves were as Ardo imagined: small metal platforms behind locked doors, guarded by a set of soldiers at every level. The descent was jerky and made his stomach twist. These were nothing like the few lifts in the depths of the Haven which used air magia to raise and lower. There was no magia here keeping these upright and functioning, but pure human ingenuity and prayers.

Ardo stiffened as they trudged through Level Three, waiting for the inevitable moment when Major Francisco would send him up. But that moment didn't come.

By the fourth level, Alara was no longer feigning bravery and he could feel her shaking. He placed his hand on her shoulder, but it did little to help, as evidenced by the blood draining from her face with every step they took.

On these lower levels, the prisoners weren't chained or even cuffed. Was it arrogance on the part of the councilguards? Any thought of this evaporated as he felt the weight of despair within these tunnels, which had heightened significantly from the levels prior, though Ardo couldn't understand. Perhaps it was that escape was no longer within their grasp, or maybe something else.

His heart lodged in his throat. The others—Runeo and Khuna—looked just as sick, while Major Francisco's mouth only stretched in amusement. When they entered the last lift to the fifth level, Ardo pulled Alara back into the corner, his lips barely moving as he whispered into her ear.

"Breathe."

The lift jerked as it came to a stop and Major Francisco opened the doors. Ardo moved to step after Alara, but the major's hand came out to rest against his chest.

"Thank you, soldier," he said. "You don't have clearance for the fifth level. In fact, you don't have clearance for the past two. Keep this knowledge to yourself."

Ardo couldn't tell if this was genuine. Did he actually want Ardo to keep his knowledge of the floors to himself, or was this how he had been leaking rumors—rumors to instill fear.

"Meet me back in my office this afternoon. I'd love to chat with you about your current duties."

Ardo nodded, his entire body stiff as he saluted and handed Alara to another guard. Her eyes flashed back for only a second, but he saw the wild panic. Hand twitching at his side, he forced himself to swallow and turn as the doors closed behind him, and the lift jerked back into motion.

He tried to ignore the fact that he'd just left Alara all on her own, to live or die.

A L A R A

A hollowness opened up inside of Alara.

She'd felt herself growing weak when they had descended to Level Three, but assumed it was the anxiety of the mission she had thrust herself into. With each level, she was reminded of all of the obstacles she'd have to overcome to break back out. On the fourth level, her legs nearly buckled beneath her, with only Ardo to keep her upright.

He probably thought it was anxiety, but it wasn't just that.

The same queasiness was etched on Runeo and Khuna's faces, whose eyes frantically searched for some explanation for the heaviness that was suddenly pressing on them. Even they knew it was more than the fear of being trapped, buried beneath the ground.

As they stumbled down a tunnel on the fifth level, Alara tried to reach for her core of magia. It had felt sluggish since Ardo had slapped the cuffs on her wrists, but with each passing moment, it faded...

She pulled at nothing. There was nothing. No magia left in her. It was like someone had taken a part of her, like an arm or her leg, or as though someone was smothering her from the inside. For the first time since Runeo had tried to convince her that magia was truly a part of them, she realized what he had meant. Tears prickled behind her eyes, unbidden, and she tried to stifle the claustrophobia that threatened to overtake her.

To think she'd spent most of her life hoping her abilities would leave her altogether. Now, she'd never wish this on her worst enemy.

They took a series of turns into the mine, passing the dead and sullen faces as prisoners looked them over. But there was no emotion on their faces to read. No anger, no malice, no hope. Their eyes were as empty as the gaping hole where Alara's magia had been.

She tried to keep track of the bends and offshoots the group took, but the nausea from the loss of her magia kept her mind from focusing for more than a few seconds at a time. She could only hope the others were faring better than her. After countless turns, they came to a small chamber carved out from one of the tunnel walls.

They were shoved forward without instruction and Alara could only let out a short growl of protest as her arms were grabbed and the cuffs removed with unnecessary roughness. She'd expected relief, even just the slightest bit. But there was none. Even with the cuffs off, her magia was nowhere to be found and it only confirmed what she already knew.

They weren't getting out of here with their powers.

"Strip," Francisco said.

Alara twisted back to look at him, an argument already on her lips. But the whip in his hand stopped her cold.

Runeo and Khuna looked just as pale. Trying to protect her modesty, Alara turned to the back wall and carefully took off her tunic and trousers.

She felt a pair of rough hands pat along her body and she tasted copper as she bit into her lip. To her surprise, even the work the guard did felt careless and completely devoid of emotion. It was as though he was as sullen as the prisoners. The hands disappeared and a drab tunic and pants were dropped at her feet.

Khuna let out a curse beside her a moment later.

"No talking," Francisco said, voice cold.

Alara wanted to scream. She very much doubted he personally witnessed every prisoner as they were processed. The moment she was dressed, she turned around, eyes boring into the major.

There was a smugness she didn't understand. He had been faithful to Sombria in the time she had known him, yes, but why such malevolence? What did she or Emaru do to warrant the scorn, and had it always been there?

"Welcome to Level Five, Prisoners 5-9832, 5-9833, and 5-9834," another man said, from off to the side. He was wearing a red uniform and a chiseled countenance to match Francisco's, though there was a hollowness in his eyes that resembled the prisoners Alara had seen. "You've been sentenced to work until further notice as permitted by Sombria Emergency Code 92.3.6. You will be tried for your crimes at such time when the state of emergency in Sombria is withdrawn. Until then, you're mine." He punctuated the last sentence with a lopsided grin that could barely be made out in the dim torch and geode-lit cavern.

"Like hell," Runeo muttered, so low that she doubted if she had actually heard him.

Alara barely saw the guard move, but there was a crack as his club came down across Runeo's shoulder. She was sick at the cry he let out as he stumbled forward next to Khuna.

"Stand up," the Man in Red said, stern, unreasonable, but calm. Somehow, in the darkness of the mines, he was in his element.

Runeo complied, his face clenched, jaw tight, eyes piercing the Man in Red, though Francisco continued as if he hadn't been interrupted.

"There will be no talking during work hours from breakfast until night. You'll get two meals a day at six in the morning and six at night. It is your responsibility to make it to your assigned main tunnel at the proper time. If you miss it, you don't eat. No exceptions."

Alara clenched her jaw.

"Your work duties will be assigned tomorrow after morning meal. Since you didn't work today, you won't get evening meal. You may sleep anywhere within the tunnels, as long as you are back at the main tunnel for work duty in the morning."

"How do we tell what time it is?"

The question came from Khuna, and unlike anything that Alara or Runeo would have said, it didn't sound like insubordination.

All the same, the Man in Red eyed her, holding up a glowing geode to her muddied face, sizing her up. He pointed to a series of lines and pulleys along the ceiling of the chamber.

"You will find these scattered throughout the tunnels," he said. "Attached are a series of bells in every sector. Councilguards will ring bells fifteen minutes prior to each meal. From there, it's your responsibility to be where you need to be. And you should be grateful for that much." His eyes flicked over the three of them with cold indifference. Without another word, he turned on his heels and left the chamber. It took only a second to realize he expected them to follow. Khuna stepped forward first, her eyes narrowed and chin held high. Alara and Runeo trailed after.

Francisco didn't follow. Alara couldn't help but turn to watch him as they walked away. He was smiling as he disappeared from view.

The Man in Red directed them farther down the tunnel, right, left, left, before the guard waved.

"This is the main tunnel where food will be served. Again, you're expected to report to work at 6:15 tomorrow morning. Do not be late."

With that, the Man in Red left, moving back to where they had come, only this time, Alara was sure they weren't meant to follow.

They weren't alone. A few guards stood off to the side, looking bored. They didn't so much as acknowledge them. The implication was clear: that was the only instruction they would get. Going forward, they'd be expected to follow everyone else's schedule.

Ignoring the chatter of the guards, the three of them moved without needing to talk, turning down one of the thinner tunnels to the left. She half expected them to follow, yell at them, anything. But they only continued their bored conversation, leaving them to... to what? The next bell? And then labor?

Alara couldn't think about that right now. They had to learn as much as they could and then find a way out. Her eyes scanned the corners of the tunnels, where the walls met the ceiling. There was a single torch every dozen yards or so, interspersed with the occasional geode, leaving plenty of places where shadows allowed for a semblance of privacy.

"What in El'dyo's name were you two thinking?" Alara tried her best to keep her words a whisper, but her voice came out sharp. She wanted to grab them both and shake them, but she kept her fists clenched at her sides.

"I needed to make sure Runeo didn't get himself killed," Khuna admitted, looking sheepish at Alara's anger. The words weren't a surprise, and she barely registered them as she rounded on Runeo.

"And you?"

"You're welcome," he said. His voice was cold and his face was a mask of indifference, but Alara didn't miss the flinch as he massaged his shoulder where the guard had hit him.

"I'm not so incompetent that you needed to sacrifice yourself to save me." She blinked as she felt her eyes sting, her anger burning behind them.

"You know that's not it," he said, voice low.

"Do I? Because you've spent every moment since we met reminding me what a useless bruyita I am."

"I wouldn't have sent *anyone* down here alone," he said, his jaw flexing.

"I was fine. As a reminder, I've been a captive before."

Runeo's eyes narrowed at the jab, well aware of the role he played in her previous imprisonment in Arbol.

"Francisco looked like he was ready to kill you himself."

"But he didn't."

"Fighting isn't going to fix any of this," Khuna said, her voice steady in a way that Alara couldn't even fathom in that moment. "We're here now. The end goal doesn't change."

Alara went quiet, annoyed to feel chastened, but unable to garner the energy to argue. Perhaps it was a reminder of their goal or the softness of Khuna's voice that finally hit Alara, and she realized just how exhausted she was.

Giving in, she let her knees buckle and her body fall against the tunnel wall. Runeo and Khuna followed, neither any more graceful than she was.

"We should rest while we can," Khuna said, voice less steady as she leaned her head back against the tunnel wall. "I still have to face Quenti when we get out of here."

Alara's lip twitched at the soft joke, glad for the small release of tension.

That evening, when they saw the other prisoners shuffling off into their respective corners, the three of them followed a few until they found a small alcove in the tunnels that allowed them to lay down without crowding the main walkway. There were two others already there, but they laid down, nonetheless. Without pillows or blankets, the three of them pulled themselves close. Alara allowed the warmth of Khuna and Runeo's bodies to calm her rushing mind.

She closed her eyes, but sleep didn't come. Despite the exhaustion from the past few hours, the dread of what tomorrow would bring didn't release her mind. She kept remembering Francisco's smile, the touch of Ardo's hand on her shoulder, and his face as the lift doors closed. Acid twisted in her stomach, a mixture of anxiety and lack of food.

She could feel Khuna's breathing behind her, her chest just barely brushing up against her back. Runeo was on her other side, facing her. She watched him in the dark, just able to make out the rise and fall of his chest with each breath.

"Thank you for coming after me," she whispered, unsure why she knew he'd hear.

"You're welcome."

She didn't even see his lips move.

"You're still an idiot," she said.

"And you're still a bruyita."

Alara closed her eyes and prayed for sleep to come, but her lips were bent in the smallest of smiles even as the stone of the tunnel floor dug into her hips.

CHAPTER 37

ARDO

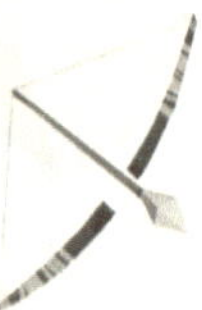

Ardo controlled his breath as they walked, timing the in and out of his lungs every few steps, letting the air expand downward within. This was the first time he had been back in the mines since he had seen Alara being pulled away, looking half sick with fear. He hadn't quite forgiven himself for allowing her to get captured and had spent most nights in the guard bunk praying to El'dyo that she was safe.

He hoped to find out for sure today.

"So there's no pathway to level three or below?" Mena asked, voice soft as they passed a set of guards walking in the other direction. They had made it onto the pathway down to the second level without incident, but they still moved carefully, Ardo almost certain they'd be caught before they took the next step.

Mena's face was carefully concealed beneath a black scarf, as if to keep out the sand and grit of the mine, even though it was purely out of disguise. Ardo was wishing for a scarf of his own as he breathed in another lungful of dust and smoke. That couldn't be good for his training.

"The pathway descends to the third level, but there was a cave-in a few years ago and they never opened the passage back up," he said, his voice as low as hers. "There's two lifts now between the remaining levels, and they're located at opposite ends of the mine from each other."

"For a functional mine," Mena said, "they spent a lot of time making sure it worked better as a prison."

Ardo couldn't argue with her. He had been in Lejon for over a month, and for all intents and purposes, the mine was a prison more than a mine. The only free people that worked here were guards and a few supervisors. The rest of the labor was involuntary, with sentences ranging from four months to life. Though he had a sneaking suspicion they found reasons to keep those with mild sentences in there longer. Of course, since the Haven Massacre (as the Council had taken to calling it), all rulings on bruya and rebel sentences had been suspended. Which meant any bruya that went into the mines didn't come out.

Like Alara.

She'd looked terrified as the doors had shut in front of him and the lift ascended into the dark tunnels above, taking him far away from her.

He refocused on his breaths and steps again. In. Out. Left. Right. He nodded to a guard they passed as they ducked into the tunnels on the second level. He needed to get them in and out today safely and then soon, Alara and Emaru would both be safe and away from the Council and Francisco. Though that was assuming Alara had been able to find Emaru and whatever else they needed. Some compass—a viajera, they called it—the importance of which he didn't fully understand.

The thought of this whole thing made him laugh. A year ago he was striving to become a general. Now he was trying his damndest to get the hell away from anything to do with the Council. At least anything to do with its current iteration.

"Do you think they've had enough time?" Mena asked, breaking him from his thoughts.

He knew what she was thinking because he was thinking it, too. If they had gathered enough information and connected with the others, could they get everyone out today?

Ardo shook his head, throat tight. "I have no idea. They've had a few days, but I don't know what the intake process for prisoners looks like. It may have been a day or two to be placed in rotation on the work shifts. But I don't know how many are down there, how big it is, or what other challenges they may be facing."

Mena met his silence with her own.

"Now stay focused," he said. "We might need you soon."

She rolled her eyes, but said nothing as she followed him through the dim tunnels. Ardo focused on counting the councilguards as they went, noticing the pattern at which they were scattered. While the tunnels felt like a maze, it seemed there was one main pathway from the outside to the lift with a few dozen offshoots along the way. Each of these had a set of guards stationed. They always stood in groups of two or three, and based on the uniforms they wore, it didn't look like there was a mage among any of them.

That would make it easier for the mind-walker, wouldn't it?

He asked as much as they stepped into the lift, alone for the first time since getting through the palisade gate.

"Maybe," she said, hesitant. "I can work easier with one or two people at a time, but with the number of groups—I don't know how far I can make it before I'm drained."

Ardo could only nod in acknowledgement. He still wasn't sure what it felt like to run out of magia, though he assumed it was like trying to use a fatigued muscle or to train after not eating for days.

Would he ever be able to truly understand these differences?

Growing up with Alara, the divide had always seemed so small, but these past several weeks had done everything to throw a wedge into that divide, making it seem greater and somehow insurmountable.

The lift shuddered to a stop and Mena stumbled sideways.

Ardo caught her in his arms and was surprised to feel how heavy she was. It was as though she had gone completely slack, not able to hold herself up. As far as he knew, she had only used her mind-walking once that morning.

"Are you okay?" he said.

"Sorry, just not used to being underground," she said as she picked herself up. "I'm not from the Haven like you. Let's go."

She walked out of the lift with confidence, though she was moving slower than before.

As they made their way through level three, Ardo's breathing was no longer regulated, his steps faltered as Mena's anxiety coursed through him.

She looked sick as she stumbled along, and as they passed torches and geodes within the walls, he could somehow make out the wan complexion around her eyes.

Finally, after passing a few unchained prisoners moving out of a dark tunnel, he pulled her toward him, tucking them into the shadows of an alcove.

"Are you okay?" he asked again.

This time, her response wasn't immediate or defensive. "Something's wrong," she said.

A set of guards passed by, one of them staring at the two of them with suspicious eyes from beneath his face wrap. Holding his breath, Ardo waited for them to walk past, but at the last moment, the woman with the uncovered face stopped short, turning toward them.

"What's the matter with her?" she asked gruffly, motioning to Mena who was leaning heavily against the wall.

Ardo straightened his shoulders, as if his stance could make up for Mena's. "New recruit's not taking well to the smell."

The man stepped forward, his dark eyes visible between the black folds of his scarf.

"New recruits aren't allowed down here. Who gave you orders?"

Ardo's heart beat fast as he felt his stomach turn. That was a stupid, stupid mistake. His eyes flickered to Mena, trying to signal her silently. They needed her powers—now. But she was sweating and breathing shallow breaths. He doubted she could have noticed her expression.

So he stepped forward, giving the woman what he hoped was a charming smile.

"My sergeant and I thought it might help the overexcited recruit to spend some time deeper in the mine. She was getting a bit cocky upstairs."

"Did the major approve this?"

He knew enough to look sheepish at the glaring guard. "Can we just keep it between us?"

"Get the hell upstairs and pray to El'dyo we don't report you *and* your sergeant. I don't care if he outranks us. No one is above the law down here."

Ardo's gut twisted, but he nodded quickly, not having to pretend to look shaken by the threat. He grabbed Mena by the arm to pull her away, but she resisted, instead stumbling directly into the two guards, eyes closed.

It was only after the guards stepped back and walked away without a word that Ardo realized what she had done.

"Why didn't you do that sooner?" he hissed under his breath, not wanting to bring the guards back.

"I promise it's not that simple," Mena said, still hunched over. "Give me a minute."

Her shallow breaths turned heavy, in through her nose and out her mouth, and each inhale felt like an eternity as Ardo continued to scan their surroundings.

"I'm not going to be able to do that again," she finally said after several deep breaths.

"Already?" Ardo tried to hide the panic in his voice, though he wasn't sure how well he succeeded.

She shook her head. "There is something wrong with these tunnels. I can feel my magia being suffocated—starved out."

Ardo looked around. "Because of all the cuffs around us?"

"No. There's something more. I'm not going to be able to mind-walk us in or out of here."

Ardo's jaw clenched. "What, then? So, we just turn around?" He almost choked on the words, knowing the answer, but not wanting to admit it to himself.

"No!" Mena insisted. "We're down here now, and nothing's going to change between today and tomorrow. We need to at least try."

Ardo couldn't tell what emotion he was feeling. Was it relief or dread? Was this a good or bad idea? The soldier in him knew the answer. This mission would kill both of them, and it would kill Alara too when they failed. Still, Ardo found himself looking into Mena's eyes—just as desperate and stubborn as his own.

"Okay. Then we keep going."

Ardo stood up straight, ready to move, but Mena didn't look any better. Her body still hunched and her breaths were still heavy.

"I can't pretend to be a guard," she said. "I think this is only going to get worse."

"Give me your scarf," he said. "And take off the vest."

She followed directions without arguing—a very distinct difference between talking to her and talking to Alara... or Emaru for that matter.

"And I'm going to apologize now for this," he said before stepping forward and ripping the sleeve of her tunic. He smeared a bit of dirt across her bare arms before wrapping the scarf around his own face.

"Did you just do this all to steal my scarf?" Mena said with a weak and humorless chuckle.

"You know, it does block out the smell a bit." He grabbed the cuffs that hung at his belt. "Last step."

Mena didn't argue. She was quick on her feet and understood exactly what Ardo had been thinking from the moment he took her scarf. She turned, letting him buckle the cuffs over her wrists.

"Is this going to be okay?" he asked, as she gave a shudder.

Mena only shrugged. "I can barely feel my magia as it is." She gave a sideways smirk. "You're pretty smart for a councilguard."

"*Ex*-councilguard," he said, returning the smirk. "Sort of. Let's go before we run into more trouble."

With that, he grabbed her arm, leading her toward the second lift. She was still looking green, but she stumbled along beside him, at least no longer needing to pretend to be okay.

They made it through the rest of the third floor easily, with Mena's patched skin almost paving the way for them now. It was as though they were scared she carried some disease with her, the guards too busy staring at her to even notice Ardo. No one questioned them as he moved her forward through the mines, even as they entered the lift to Level Four.

When the caged lift jolted to a stop, Mena let out a soft groan, but she stood up straight even as the gate opened and revealed an even more desolate level. Ardo was surprised. He had thought there would be *more* guards as they descended. He supposed he couldn't believe everything he read in the tapestries. As it turned out, the Haven was getting into the habit of hiding secrets from itself.

The two guards stationed at the entrance only looked at Mena with raised eyebrows before waving Ardo through. They barely even looked at him, too focused on examining her like she was some specimen.

So he was surprised when the shorter guard initiated conversation. "Your catch?"

"Er—yeah. Found her just outside of the city."

The guard groaned, but Ardo couldn't tell if it was in disgust or exhaustion. "So many bruyas lurking around recently. Probably a good thing, though. Our production levels have been skyrocketing." The man said it like it was a personal accomplishment. His eyes settled on Mena. "And this one looks strong, too." Then, noticing the patches on her skin for the first time, he recoiled.

Without another word, Ardo shoved Mena forward, all too happy to get away while the guard was spooked. His hand on her arm was gentle as he led her away. To his relief, the guard did not follow.

This level was quieter than the ones that came before. The tunnel they walked down was almost empty, with only a few prisoners stumbling by, backs hunched and faces smeared with dirt. After leaving the lift, he didn't see another set of guards. This deep in the mines, it was as though they trusted the walls and whatever was killing magia to keep everyone subdued. Based on the faces of the people trudging by, it was working.

Ardo stumbled into Mena as she stopped short in front of him. "What?"

She was staring at one of the walls with an intensity that startled him. As if she might see through it.

"Take off the cuffs," she said, breathily.

He didn't question her, unlocking them and freeing her hands. She ran a finger along the wall and it came back dark with powder.

He opened his mouth to ask what she was doing, but before he had the chance, Mena's head snapped up.

"I can feel him."

Chapter 38

Ardo

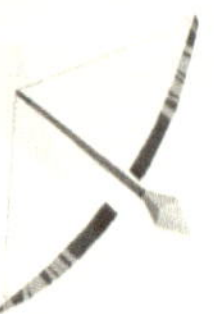

Mena leaned against the rock wall, using it for support as she trudged down the tunnel.

"Mena?" Ardo said, whispering after her, half expecting another guard to pop out of the shadows at any moment. "Who? Who can you feel?" Though the second he said it aloud, he knew. The look on her face was unmistakable. "He's supposed to be on Level Five," he said instead. "And you're not a mind-stalker, how can you feel him?"

"Twin things," she said, as if that explained it.

He didn't have time to ask further, as a moment later, they turned a corner and ran into a young-looking man with the same intense eyes and patched skin as her.

This was him. This was the elusive Benicio they had been searching for. Or Beno, as they'd called him.

Ardo didn't have time to express his surprise because the two guards who had been dragging the man along both looked up in shock at the sudden intrusion. Mena sent a punch straight into the face of the shorter guard, snapping his head back.

Not missing a beat, Ardo ran forward and grabbed the club from the other guard as he moved to swing it toward her. He used the momentum to twist it around the man and against his neck, pulling tight. It took thirty long seconds, but the guard finally slumped forward for lack of air.

Letting the man fall to the ground, he turned to see Beno and Mena standing over the other guard, face bloody and eyes closed.

Mena didn't bother with hellos or explanations. She threw herself at her brother, wrapping her arms around him and pulling him close, even as he stumbled forward.

"Mena, be careful," Ardo said, looking at Beno's leg where blood was already seeping through a new, but not quite clean, bandage. "He's hurt."

Beno's eyes widened with confusion and then fear as he took in Ardo and his attire. He rushed to push Mena behind him and stood up straighter as he met Ardo's eyes. It was all the more sad, given that the man probably weighed less than Mena, and was about five minutes from collapsing from his injury.

"Don't worry," Mena said, placing a hand on Beno's shoulder. "He's a friend."

He shook his head, still staring daggers at Ardo.

"He's a councilguard."

"*Ex*-councilguard," she said, before Ardo could correct him. "Sort of."

Beno looked over his shoulder, eyebrows furrowed. "What in the underworld are you doing down here? When did you get caught?"

"I didn't. We're here on a rescue mission. For you."

Mena was scrutinizing her brother once more, eyes pausing on every bruise, scrape, and scar. Her hand reached out and touched his left lobe with a look of sorrow Ardo couldn't quite understand. The man reached out and grabbed her hand roughly.

"Are you insane? You need to get out of here, now!" he snapped, eyes now wild as he looked around them.

"We still need to get down to Level Five for the others," Ardo said, perhaps sterner than he should have.

"And hope these two don't go talking?" Beno said, waving at the two guards on the ground.

"We can *stop* them from talking," Ardo said.

"And then we'll have two bodies to worry about," Mena said. She was still weak, but seemed to find some energy in finding her brother, her normally attentive mind returning as she scanned the tunnels. "He's right. We should leave now while we have the chance."

"I'm not leaving Alara," Ardo said, face heating up. Of course, now that she'd found who she was looking for, she was ready to head back. Only moments before, she was insisting on continuing. "If we take him out now, they'll be alerted to a breakout. It'll only be harder to get the others out later."

"The guards downstairs will assume I died," Beno said. "They were bandaging my leg after an accident. I'm supposed to be sent straight back down to continue working, but plenty of injured don't make it back. It happens every day, and with all the soot everyone is covered in, it's hard to keep track of anyone, let alone a specific prisoner. If we mind-walk out of here carefully, we can do it without alerting anyone."

"Why should I trust you?" Ardo snapped, grabbing the bruya roughly by the tunic. "And what in the underworld were you doing up on this level anyway. You're supposed to be on the fifth."

Mena set a calming hand on Ardo's shoulder, but her tone was sharp. "We need to go."

"We can't abandon the others."

"And we aren't," Mena said, voice soothing even without her abilities. "No one is going to let them stay down here, but we gain one more ally if we escape now. One more ally and more intelligence on everything happening down here."

Ardo took a deep breath, feeling the helplessness spread. It was the same feeling he'd had watching Linda Emaru tied to the pole and flogged. Swallowing back his emotions, he brought forth the soldier that he had been trained into his whole life.

Objectively, she was right.

Objectively, they were already in over their heads.

Objectively, the best course of action would be to retreat now and come back later. He'd seen what happened to soldiers who rush in without thought. He couldn't let that happen here. Not when the stakes were so high.

"Okay," he finally said. "Let's go." He pulled the cuffs back from his belt, motioning for Mena. Beno looked ready to punch Ardo, but Mena raised a hand to stop him before simply offering her wrists.

They didn't need to do anything to make Beno look like a prisoner with the stained rags hanging off his body and the dirty cuffs on his wrists.

"Don't make eye contact, keep your heads low, and pray we run into some stupid guards," he growled out the instructions, wishing to El'dyo their plans had involved more than just, "Mena will save us with her mind-walking skills."

When they arrived at the lift, Ardo tried not to even acknowledge the guards. He had almost wished there had been a shift change in the short time they had been in the tunnels, but he had never been one for luck. Every ounce of success he'd ever had had been hard-earned after too many cuts and bruises.

"What's going on?" The shorter guard was looking carefully at Ardo now, eyes flashing between him and the two bruyas. "Where are you taking these two?" Again, the guard flinched when he saw their patchy skin, taking another involuntary step back.

"Major Francisco's orders," he said without hesitation. "I'm to take them to him for interrogation."

"You just brought that one in," the taller guard said, voice thrumming with suspicion.

"How else would we have been able to find her sibling?" he said. "Down here, everyone looks the same."

The two guards looked at each other, unconvinced.

"Look, I'm just following orders," Ardo said pushing forward even as they tried to step in front of them and block the open lift gate.

"Do you have proof of these orders?" one of the men sneered.

"Of course," Ardo said, reaching for his pants pocket with a sideways smile. He slipped the club from his belt and cracked it across the face of the taller guard. The shorter guard lunged forward, grabbing him by the arm before he could do the same to him, twisting it behind him.

"Drop the club," the guard snapped.

Ardo only gripped the handle tighter, struggling to free his arm. To his surprise, the guard held his arm firmly in place.

"Drop it!" the guard repeated.

And then a loud crack rang out within the tunnels. The guard's grip on Ardo's arm went slack and he crumpled to the floor, a pool of blood expanding from his head.

Ardo's eyes met Mena's who stood over the guard, one of their clubs in her cuffed hands, and a stern expression on her face. There wasn't the look of shock he had expected. This woman was a trained soldier.

He stumbled up, avoiding a side glance at the two guards they were leaving behind as he stepped onto the lift. Beno and Mena followed, and he moved the crank up. With a jerk, the cage surrounding them creaked and ascended, leaving Level Four behind.

"This isn't going to end well," Beno said, breath heavy as he leaned against the metallic barrier that kept them in. "They're going to find those guards."

"Then we better walk fast when we get off," Ardo said, ignoring Beno. "Mena, give me your hands. I think we might need you uncuffed. Just keep your hands behind you."

The plan wasn't a good one. It wasn't even a plan. But what else could they do?

The guards at the top of the elevator didn't question them, and Ardo counted his blessings as he shoved Beno and Mena forward, cursing them under his breath, just loud enough for the guards to hear. They walked as fast as they could with Beno's injured and freely bleeding leg.

Ardo held back a growl at the sight, trying to ignore the fact that Beno was being sent to continue mining after suffering such an injury. Ardo's superior in training had always called him soft; he said he wasn't cut out for the life of a soldier. Maybe he was right. Maybe Ardo had too much of a heart to truly be a councilguard for Sombria.

"Hey!" a voice called out from behind them. Ardo did his best to ignore it as they turned the corner to enter the last lift, only to run into another pair of guards.

"Stop them!" the voice continued. "There are murdered guards on Level Four!"

Mena reacted first, sending her fist into one of the guard's sides as he moved toward her. Ardo blocked a swipe from the other guard's dagger with his club.

Beno grappled to get a hold of the guard's arms, but only succeeded in distracting him for the briefest of moments—which was all Ardo needed to land a blow to the head. He sent another messy swing to the other guard fighting Mena, hitting him in the gut and sending him sprawling, choking on air.

They didn't bother finishing the fight as a small group of soldiers came running around the corner. The three of them scrambled onto the lift and slammed the doors. As they cranked the lift upward, Beno let out an exhausted and crazed laugh.

"Shut it, Beno!" Mena said.

"If I can't laugh at all this now, what's the point?"

Beno may have been injured, but that didn't stop Mena from giving him a shove with her shoulder, which only made him laugh that much harder.

After a few seconds, Ardo found himself smiling. He was starting to like these two.

As the lift ascended to Level Two, they rode in silence, saving their energy for whatever came next.

"Can you use your abilities yet?" he said, watching Mena flex her fingers.

"Not yet. But I want to be ready."

"They're fighting us here," Beno interrupted, still leaning up against the crank that sent the lift upward.

"What?" Ardo said.

"I can feel them fighting." This time, he pointed to the switch with his free hand.

"The second I let go, we'll be heading downward."

Ardo held on to the lever and could see exactly what he meant. He had no idea how, but he could feel the resistance. "Get ready to disembark," he said, gripping the switch even harder.

Beno followed orders, hobbling toward the gate.

Ardo's shoulders tensed as the lift slowed and came to a stop. He turned and looked up to catch the eyes of another pair of guards looking over at them.

"Hey," he called over to them, praying to El'dyo they wouldn't question him. "Give us a hand, will you?"

To his relief, they both walked over, curious. "What's the problem?"

"This thing is causing us some trouble. Can you pull up the switch on your end?"

"Sure thing," one of them said. They reached over to another switch outside of the caged lift.

As the other guard opened the gates, Ardo felt the tension lift on his own switch.

"You ain't kidding," the guard at the switch said. His teeth were gritted and his breath strained. "We're going to have to report this."

Beno and Mena stepped over the threshold onto the second floor, and with an anxious breath, Ardo let go.

Nothing. No movement.

Without wasting another moment, he stepped onto Level Two, pushing his two prisoners forward with a forceful hand.

The guard removed his hand from the switch, and the lift descended downward, disappearing into the darkness.

"I'll be sure to log that when I'm done here," Ardo said. "Thanks for your help."

But the two guards were already preoccupied, testing out the switch and looking at where the lift had been only moments before.

Another push on Beno and Mena's back, and they were moving down the tunnels, Ardo doing his best not to look back.

The trio was silent for several long seconds before any of them dared to take a breath.

It was Mena who exhaled first, and Ardo quickly followed.

"How much time do you think that will buy us?" Beno said.

"I don't know, but I'll take every second I can get," Ardo replied. Every second was one less second spent fighting and one less opportunity to get their heads caved in by a councilguard.

Step, silence. Step, silence. Step, silence. The three of them moved quickly enough to cover ground but slow enough not to draw any unwanted attention. Every moment felt like an hour, and as they turned one of the corners and passed another set of guards, Ardo knew it was only a matter of time before the lift made its way back to the floor. It was only a matter of time before—

"Stop them!"

Not wasting a moment, Mena darted forward, hands landing on two confused-looking guards ahead. She didn't bother softening their falls as they crumpled to the ground.

But she didn't stop there. She moved quickly, hands fluttering as she placed her fingers along their temples, closing her eyes.

After another few seconds, she stood up, only stumbling slightly. "I cleansed their memories."

"You can't cleanse everyone's mind," Beno said, voice strained.

"We need this to be a clean escape," Ardo said, voice firm. "We have to return, so we can't have anyone set off any alarms."

"You're right, but we've already left people beaten and bloody," Beno said, turning to his sister. "Mena?"

She nodded, eyes focused. "I can do it."

"Do what?" Ardo said, his chest tightening.

"Beno's right," she said. "I can't cleanse *everyone's* mind, but I can make a convincing story and implant in the minds of those we need. Minds are malleable. So long as it's convincing enough, they'll fill in the blanks where needed." Now that they were on a floor where Mena had her abilities, her eyes looked brighter.

"But do your best not to kill any of them," Mena said with a smile. "But knock them out if you can. The ruse gets more difficult the bigger the lies I have to plant. Understood?"

Just as she finished, five guards turned the corner, only to be met by a pair of clubs from Ardo and Beno. As the guards crumpled over from the assault, Mena pressed her fingers to their temples, allowing the other two to take the battle to the remaining soldiers in the narrow tunnel.

It was slow, it was sloppy, and it was terrifying. But they somehow managed, leaving their enemies with the most minimal of blunt force trauma before having Mena finish the job. Between that and the scuffles on the lower floors, Ardo could only hope that Mena could plant a story that could justify it all.

How powerful was she, and how far could she stretch her abilities? His unasked question was answered the very next moment when the fifth guard finally fell. Almost in direct response, Mena folded onto the ground, head between her hands.

"How many can you do?" Ardo asked, a soft hand on her shoulder, hoping she couldn't feel it shaking.

"I think we're about to find out," she said between breaths.

The next wave of guards was larger, with seven having answered the frantic calls of their comrades. Like before, the trio had the element of surprise, but that didn't make the fight any less messy. When all was done, Mena bled from a gash in the side and Ardo leaned heavily against the wall, head spinning from the smack of a guard's club. But even as she bled, Mena went to work pressing fingers against temples, hands getting shakier with every guard. When there were two left, she shook her head, sweat blooming across her forehead.

"I can try," Beno said, voice quavering with uncertainty. He leaned down, careful on his leg and pressed the palm of his hand to another guard's forehead, even as the man began to stir.

"Shit," Mena said, leaning over the last guard and pressing her fingers to his forehead. Ardo watched this all, trying not to feel useless. Even after having taken most of the guards down himself, he felt so small compared to the power they wielded.

So he kept watch, waiting for another wave of guards to turn the corner or just wander by at the wrong time. What could they even do if that happened? Ardo could barely keep his balance, and the mindwalkers' abilities were all but spent after the last fight.

A minute later, Mena collapsed on the smooth ground, eyes closed.

Ardo moved to help, but Beno was there first. "Are you okay, Mena?"

Her eyes didn't open, but she fluttered her hand weakly and hummed.

"Time to leave," Ardo said, trying his best to hide the anxiety in his voice. "Now."

Beno attempted to pick his sister up, but only got his arms under her before stumbling to the side.

Ardo tried not to roll his eyes. These two were like a pair of wild dogs, pushing themselves beyond exhaustion, willing their bodies into submission until they had less than nothing left. "Just worry about yourself," he said, scooping Mena into his arms. She was heavier than she looked, and he tried not to show the strain on his face. "We need to get out of here without drawing any more attention."

"We need to find a cart," Beno said, looking around.

"We need to draw *less* attention," Ardo said.

"They carry the dead out in carts. It's the easiest way for a prisoner to get out of the mines," Beno said with a dark smile.

"Right," Ardo said, "Well let's start moving. There were some carts near the entrance."

They moved slowly, Beno peeking around every corner to make sure the way was clear. They were only a few turns from the entrance and while there were more guards, most seemed preoccupied with all of the prisoners chained and working deeper in the tunnels.

As Ardo turned the last corner and saw the carts sitting unattended, he shot a prayer to El'dyo and half ran forward. He dumped Mena into the cart a bit clumsier than he should have and waved for Beno to get in with her.

He laid down without question, face down and arms askew. It was an uncomfortable scene to see both mind-walkers slumped in a heap. He turned away from it with a small shudder and grabbed the handle of the cart, pulling it forward and out of the tunnels. The air outside was warmer than before, but the sun was blocked by the steep sides of the canyon as they moved up.

"So how am I supposed to just walk out of the gates with two dead prisoners?" Ardo said, teeth clenched and lips barely moving as he talked.

Beno's muffled voice came from the cart. "Just take us somewhere we can be alone."

Ardo followed the directions, heart racing, but hands steady. He was back to being a soldier, following orders and pushing aside his worries until after. There was something calming in letting others make the decisions, even if he'd still be the one to carry the brunt of the consequences.

He was still lost in thought as he came out of the main mine, back on the first level teeming with guards and workers. One guard dressed in dark red, stepped in front of him, a hand raised.

Ardo kept his eyes down as the guard walked around him and the cart, leaning over the two mind-walkers. He hoped the blood seeping from both of them would help sell the lie, but he saw the man lean over a finger pressing into Beno's neck. He crept his hand closer to the club at his belt, muscles tensed and ready to fight.

But the man only gave a grunt and waved him on.

He moved quickly before the man could question his decision, his cold soldier persona only barely holding him together.

"Shit, shit, shit," he whispered under his breath as he walked, moving toward the south of the campus where he knew there was a garbage dump—likely where the bodies were left until they could be burned. He only hoped that the other guards had better things to do with their lives than guard their trash and the dead.

CHAPTER 39

ALARA

Alara woke to the sound of bells ringing and the view of a small pale face only a few inches from her own. She didn't startle, having accepted the girl's wake-up call after the first morning in the mine. It turned out the other two people they shared an alcove with at night were mother and daughter.

As Alara blinked awake, the girl's face broke into a wide smile, the gaps in her teeth noticeable. "Good morning, Sol," she said, trying not to groan as she sat up slowly, every muscle in her body protesting. She could have sworn even her bones ached as she moved. It was a pain she hadn't felt even following her hardest days of training.

"Rise and shine," Runeo said from a few feet away. He was already standing, eyes shadowed and face grim. "We need to head out if we want to eat."

Alara nodded, well aware of the consequences of showing up late to morning meal. Runeo's eyes were soft, even as he watched her with hesitation. They hadn't brought up their first night in the mines since it had happened, too scared of breaking the delicate truce they had formed. It wasn't that she wasn't angry that they had willingly gotten themselves into this mess and she doubted Runeo had quite accepted he was in the wrong for it, but there was no changing the situation now.

Alara hadn't had many connections growing up outside of Emaru, but she was starting to accept that having friends meant not being able to stop them from doing stupid things for stupid reasons in the name of love.

"I'm sorry about Sol," a woman's soft voice said from a few yards away in the shadowy tunnel. "She wanted to eat with you."

Standing on creaky knees, Alara patted the child on the head. "No problem, Dez. I'm always glad for the extra wake-up." If she was honest with herself, she was surprised that she could sleep through the bells and welcomed the extra reassurance of their morning meal.

The little girl beamed up at Alara. While the child rarely spoke, it was clear she understood everyone fine. Though, part of Alara wished Sol was deaf so she could have been spared the guard's sharp words.

From what she had learned over the past few days, Sol was Dez's daughter and had been born down in the mines.

How the woman had managed such a feat, Alara had no idea, but the child herself was a ray of sunshine despite having likely never seen the sun. Her limbs were thin, but she worked as hard as her mother.

When Alara had expressed her disgust at the situation during her second day, Dez had laughed darkly, noting that the guards didn't care who was working, particularly if they had bruya blood. Alara had found that particularly hateful considering the girl had never left the lower two levels of the mines, and therefore there was no way of knowing if she had been born with magia or not.

Could a little girl's core even develop down here in the dark if it was always suppressed? Even Alara, who spent the majority of her life wearing magia-suppressing cuffs, was given the freedom to exercise her abilities on a near daily basis.

On their third night in the mines, Sol whispered into Alara's ear that she was named after the sun god, and although her mother had always promised someday they'd be free and she'd see it, she thought it was a myth her mother had made up.

"But sometimes, I hear the sun whispering to me," she said, conspiratorially, "so maybe it isn't a lie."

Sol was both a light in the darkness of the tunnels and Alara's reason for being sick to her stomach most days. The little girl spoke of gods like they were walking the earth and visiting her in her sleep to tell her of far-off lands where the sun never set. She almost wanted to believe the girl.

To tell her the truth about the world above almost seemed cruel.

Before Runeo could usher them out for morning meal, Khuna rounded the corner carrying a stack of clay bowls.

"I brought food." She passed out the bowls, making sure Sol got a proper helping. She, like Alara, had noticed Dez would give the little girl extra of her own food if she was worried there wasn't enough, which usually left the mother weak and almost dead on her feet by the end of the day.

Alara only had time to stuff down a few mouthfuls of slimy gruel before the bells echoed through the tunnels in violent harmony with the screams of the councilguards.

Their workday had begun.

No one spoke as they left their alcove, heading toward the central tunnel. If they didn't make it there before the bells stopped ringing, there was a lashing waiting for them.

In the main tunnel, Alara traded her bowl for a pickaxe, not for the first time debating the worth of sending it directly into the man's neck. She'd be killed by the other six guards before she could even dislodge the weapon from his bleeding throat, but at least it would wipe the smirk off his face.

Sol took a pickaxe as well, the handle nearly the size of her torso. But she dragged it across the ground without complaint, following the line of prisoners as they moved into their respective tunnels. Khuna and Runeo split away from her, both assigned to different areas.

It turned out there were more people down on this level than they initially realized. After they had all adjusted to the weight of whatever was suppressing their magia, they spent the next few days trying to gather as much information as possible without drawing suspicion. Not that it mattered much. The prisoners down here seemed to know only as much as they had gathered themselves, despite being held prisoner for weeks, months, or years. Information wasn't a commodity that was handed out, not even by the guards who were stationed here.

Dez, one of the oldest residents by sentence, had been a good source of information. There were several more bruyas that had been down here longer, but their minds were half-addled, and conversations with them quickly spiraled into silence. Alara had to wonder how long it might take someone to go crazy trapped in the dark without a piece of their soul.

Ironically, the only good thing about the mines was its sheer scope. Sure, the tunnels looked the same, but there was always something new, with the main tunnels leading to dozens of offshoots, each of those offshoots leading to dozens more.

As they discovered, the tunnels were laid out like a tree more than a maze. As the years progressed, its branches multiplied, reaching farther and farther out to an unknown end.

Every morning, tools were delivered in groups along the tunnel, with a specific set of prisoners assigned to a specific station for pickup. They were allowed to move around freely, unchained, but there weren't many places to run and there was always a guard nearby to notice if you tried anything. If you showed up late to somewhere you were supposed to be, you were whipped. If you didn't show up at all, you were likely dead. She had already seen two carts pulled by with bodies in the back during her time here. The bodies had been thin and sinewy, dirty and worn down from the hard labor.

After pickup, they were sent into their respective tunnels to dig or haul depending on the day. It didn't take a genius to realize they were mining for receptives. But then again, some of the pieces the guards had her hauling simply looked like black stone.

In the darkness, it was hard to tell.

They were given another bowl of gruel for evening meal, but they weren't allowed to stop work until deep into the evening. The guards themselves took shifts, but the prisoners were expected to work nonstop.

The tunnel Alara and Sol had been assigned was to the left of their main one, two turns and a small decline down to a dead end to chip away at. Another branch to add to the ever-growing tree. Sol was the first to swing her pick at the wall, not even making a dent in the stone. But she kept at it, all the same, knowing well she'd be yelled at or beaten for stopping. Alara stood beside her, arms shaky from exhaustion, but moving in a rhythm that was becoming familiar.

Today there was a new prisoner in their group, someone Alara didn't recognize as they spread out across the tunnel and took their positions. At least, he was new to them, but not new to this life of mining. His torn clothes and strong arms spoke of years of hard labor.

This was another thing she had learned while down here. They moved prisoners around occasionally, likely to stop any one group from working a bond or getting any ideas. Dez had told them when Sol turned seven, she'd be separated from her mother and moved around just like the others. The idea turned Alara's stomach. She didn't even know why Dez had been sent down here and she hadn't gotten up the nerve to ask. She, Runeo, and Khuna had been lucky and persistent in making sure they found each other at the end of the day, even if it meant an hour less of sleep each night.

But how long would that last?

The first few nights they had spent bone-tired, but exchanging information about what they had seen or heard. The last few days, there had been nothing new to say. It was as though they'd hit a wall of information that was impossible to penetrate. Though, still, they were relieved. Relieved everyone was present and safe.

"You have to work harder," Sol said.

Alara jumped, for a second wondering if, lost in her thoughts, she had paused her labor. But Sol wasn't looking at her. She was looking at the new guy standing on her other side.

He was halfheartedly smacking his pickaxe against the wall, not even scratching it—hardly even going through the motions of faking it. Alara looked behind them to see if there was a guard present, but the small party had been left alone.

"What are you trying to pull?" Alara said.

She expected a snarl of defense or a dead stare of exhaustion from the man. What she didn't expect was the smirk.

"They send the weaker ones up a level or two, give them easier work," he said. "I've seen it happen. You just have to make them think you can't do the work. There are other tasks like cooking and healing that some prisoners do."

Alara looked at him with a raised eyebrow. The muscles on his arms didn't speak of someone who needed to be assigned easy work, but she didn't say as much, only shaking her head. Whatever he needed to do to get by down here, so long as it didn't affect her or Sol.

She turned back to her wall, tossing the pieces of stone behind her as they chipped away. If the piece was small enough, Sol would pause from her own attempts and carry it to the cart behind them, helping her mother who hauled and piled the stones as they went.

Several minutes later, as the cart filled out, the guard returned, barking orders for a few of the prisoners to get ready to roll it to the main tunnel. It was a pattern that had played itself out a hundred times over the past week.

It was almost a welcome respite from the mundane swing of a pickaxe.

But then the guard's voice turned cold and came up close behind Alara's group, a curse on his lips.

"What're you trying to pull, bruya pig? Work harder!"

Alara turned to see the guard spit on the back of the man's neck, even as the prisoner continued to feign a struggle.

"I can't," he said. Alara wasn't sure the quiver in his voice was an act, but it sure sounded convincing.

"Try," the guard said, crossing his arms and leaning back as he watched the man, making no move to leave him alone. The prisoner gave another few swings of his pickaxe, each one connecting but somehow making less of a dent than Sol managed just beside him.

The guard moved with surprising speed, snatching the pickaxe from the man's hands and throwing it behind him.

The others in the tunnel jumped away as the tool clattered to the dirt floor, the sound covering up the scream as the guard yanked the man by his shirt and threw him down alongside the pickaxe.

Alara expected him to pull out a whip, but he reached for his club instead, and in an instant she knew what was about to happen.

She instinctively dropped her own tool and grabbed Sol around the waist, pulling her into her body and tucking her face into her chest. She pressed her hand over her ears, even as the crunching of bone breaking under wood echoed throughout the tunnel.

If anyone screamed, it was muffled by countless successive blows.

Long after the prisoner's body stopped moving, the guard gave the body a few more hits, as if caving in the man's skull hadn't finished the job immediately. Blood coated his club and pooled at his feet as he stood straight up, taking steady breaths as he scraped bits of flesh onto the ground.

"Get back to work," he said before walking away, leaving the still body of the man behind.

<h1 style="text-align:center">CHAPTER 40</h1>

<h2 style="text-align:center">QUENTI</h2>

Quenti spent the first few days after Khuna's capture jumping at every sound from within their new accommodations: basically a closet in the back of an old bar's dirty kitchen. It was windowless, loud, and smelled of ferment, but it was hidden, and most importantly, Mena trusted the owner.

Still, she couldn't stop waiting for Khuna to come bursting through the door having escaped the mines in some brilliant plan she just hadn't had time to explain to Quenti. After day three, she started to accept that Khuna wouldn't be escaping without help.

To add to her frustration, no one would listen to anything she had to say. She had been all but cast to the side and forgotten as Mena, Cruz, and Dante sat around, making escape plans. Even Ardo—the *councilguard*—was given more room to add his thoughts than her. She was left sitting by, listening as the blameless went about their lives, completely undisturbed by the prison camp of bruyas only a mile south of town.

On the fourth day, Ardo burst into the room, Mena unconscious in his arms and another strange-looking man limping in behind him. It wasn't difficult to recognize the new bruya as Mena's twin, his patched skin matching his sister's down to the pale around his lips.

Quenti's heart leaped into her stomach and she ran to the door, opening it wide, waiting as the other three prisoners passed by. And waiting...

But no one followed in behind them. The crushing weight of disappointment made Quenti's knees weak. She shut the door and turned back to the room. Dante had gone out earlier that morning to keep an ear out for gossip, so it was only Cruz and Quenti here as the three others collapsed in the center of the room.

Cruz didn't ask questions, but went to work immediately, taking stock of the injuries between the three. She checked Mena's pulse, seemed content and went over to look at Beno's leg which was wrapped in a stained cloth, which had all but failed to stop the trickle of blood.

Quenti grimaced as Cruz unwrapped the bandage, revealing the ragged slice beneath. The smell of iron in the air brought her back to the wound she had acquired in the Haven and she fingered the knotted scar below her tunic.

"Get me a clean sheet," Cruz said.

Quenti jumped to attention, assuming the order was for her alone. She moved, grabbing a sheet from one of the beds and ripping it into thick strips, handing them to Cruz—or Lena, as the ex-councilwoman had constantly been reminding Quenti to call her.

Once Beno's leg was wrapped and he was looking only slightly worse for wear, Cruz focused back on Mena and the councilguard still holding her.

"What happened?" Cruz said, attention focused on the passed out Mena.

"We can talk about that later," Ardo said. "But for now, you need to focus on the wound in her side."

Cruz nodded, lifting the woman's shirt to see the clean gash below. It leaked blood and Quenti turned away as she suppressed a gag.

"Any earth mages in here that I don't know about?" Cruz said.

"I am," Beno said with a heaving chest, "but it's going to take some time before I can do much of anything."

Cruz nodded, wrapping Mena's waist in a perfunctory manner, not bothering with the woman's modesty.

"It looks like our fight in and out of the mines is going to be harder than we thought," Ardo said, turning away, even as he continued to talk.

Quenti scoffed at his chivalry.

"There was something down there," Ardo said. "It suppressed their magia, even without cuffs."

Quenti's heart sank into her stomach. No magia? Khuna never had to suppress her abilities. How would she survive?

"How?" Cruz said, her face stiff and stern. She finished with wrapping the wound and sat back against one of the small beds.

"It's the Alkay stone," Beno said, voice low.

Cruz shook her head, dismissing the bruya immediately. "There isn't enough Alkay in the entire realm to do that."

"Yes, there is," Beno said, sharper this time. "There is more than enough in one tunnel of that mine alone."

"It's a by-product," Cruz said. "Barely useable."

"You're wrong."

Quenti almost jumped at the sound of Mena's voice.

"He's right," she said. Her eyes were open and she carefully pulled herself up to a seat, noting the bandage around her middle with a grateful smile. "The feeling was the same I get with the Council's cuffs. Well, the same, but different. It was... more. Like being suffocated instead of just being pinned down."

"Either way," Beno said, "it's Alkay stone. I promise you."

"I'm sorry to interrupt," Quenti said, "but what in Sol's name is Alkay?"

"It's the material that makes the cuffs work," Ardo answered. "It blocks magia. It's created in the process of making receptives, but as Senye Cruz said, there shouldn't be enough to suppress magia at that level. And it shouldn't occur naturally."

"It wasn't until we got down to the lower levels that the effects took hold," Mena said slowly. "So the Alkay stone is down there. Natural or not. I spent enough time there to know."

"Down in the restricted and secret level of the mine," Cruz said. "Fancy that."

Beno stood, helping himself to a large cup of water from the basin in the room. "I think that Alkay stone is more than a by-product of the receptives. It's a stone unto itself. And they've found a whole vein of the stuff. When you're down there—your core is just gone. Like the tunnels itself have sucked it dry. It feels like a plunge in the River Muerte but worse, so much worse." He shuddered even as he spoke.

Quenti remembered the strange and sickly feeling of crossing the river weeks back. She could only imagine living with the feeling for weeks or even months.

Khuna.

"So our magia will be useless in getting the others out," Quenti said, the others answering her uncertain question with nods. "How did *you* get out? Where are the others?" She looked at Beno accusingly. She knew it wasn't his fault that Khuna had walked in after them, but this wasn't making sense.

"They're on Level Five," Ardo said. "We never made it down that far. Once we were on the third, Mena was too sick to even pretend to be a councilguard."

"So you turned around there?" Cruz asked.

Ardo paused, hesitant with his answer. "No. We pretended Mena was another prisoner and made it to Level Four, which is where we ran into him." He nodded at Beno.

"They got lucky," Beno said. "I was only there because of the injury. There's a torture chamber they pass off as an infirmary on Level Four."

"So, the others are still down there," Quenti said. "On Level Five." She was just stating a fact, but her words were like an accusation.

"Right," Ardo said. If he detected the accusation, he didn't show it. "Beno didn't see them while he was down there, but the prisoners on each level are kept separated into small groups and shuffled around every so often."

"So we don't even know what they've learned," Cruz said, her voice suddenly sounding tired. "And you've now staged a breakout that will probably garner more attention and more eyes on the mines."

"No," Mena said, her voice tired, but firm. "It wasn't a breakout. Beno tried to stage a revolt. He managed to attack several guards, but was taken down and killed."

"What?" Cruz said, eyebrows furrowed as she turned to the very alive Beno.

Mena wiggled her fingers. "That's all the guards will know. It'll remain an incident isolated to a select few, all too embarrassed and scared to report it to the major."

"You can instill seeds of emotions as well?" Cruz said.

"If you managed to do it perfectly," Beno added, his tone admonishing.

Mena closed her eyes, lips pulled into a soft smile. "And I usually do."

"Even if our breakout went unnoticed, we still don't know anything about the others," Ardo said.

"Except that the mines are magia-proof and even more difficult to navigate than we thought. And, of course, we still have three—four," Quenti corrected at Ardo's sharp look, "of our own down there."

"Yes," Mena said, her voice pained. She took in a slow breath because she spoke, turning to Beno. "I'm afraid to ask, but do you have the viajera?"

In the chaos of the last few minutes, Quenti had completely forgotten about the little trinket that had brought them all here in the first place. The reason Khuna was gone—again.

Beno shook his head. "It was taken from me when I was captured. They search all the prisoners." He shuddered at the memory. "I don't know what happened to it, but I doubt it left the mines."

"Why is that?" Cruz asked.

"I don't think they understood what it was, but they could tell it was powered by magia when they took it. My clothes and a few of my other personal effects were kept separate."

"So?" Cruz said, not amused by his logic. "They could have been taken out separately, then."

Beno spared her an annoyed glance. "So, if you had spent any time down there, as I have, you'd know there was something else happening in those mines. It's almost as if normal rules don't apply. Blameless and magia wielders don't coexist. Blameless rule over magia wielders. It's as if the world has gone back hundreds of years, where magia is treated like a novelty or an unknown. As if hundreds of years of exposure meant nothing to them. Everything is being re-examined."

"I still don't understand," Cruz said, her tone growing sharp and her patience thin.

"I'm saying there are experiments going on down there. They try to distract you, but I noticed certain people—not guards or prisoners—moving in and out at odd hours. Sometimes, they carried with them strange objects. Sometimes receptives or other magia-enabled trinkets. It's like they're bending backwards to experiment and test the most basic of things, as though any explanation given up here is a lie. If they so much as suspected the viajera had magia, I think they would have kept it for testing."

"But we don't know for sure," Cruz said. She looked at the others, as if for reassurance. "That's a lot of assumptions and speculation."

"And even if we knew for sure, we're still going in without our magia," Mena said.

"You have any better ideas?"

The room descended into silence, and in it, Quenti's mind started to race. First in panic, and then in what she could only call enthusiasm. It was like her mind was latching on to an idea, but without knowing what that idea was yet.

"What's the reason for the mines?" Quenti asked.

She was met by a few puzzled stares.

"What is the *official* reason?" she clarified.

"Mining receptives," Cruz said. "This is the only known place in all of Sombria where receptives exist. It's why it's been so valuable to us."

Quenti blinked. She could still feel it in the back of her mind. Some idea forming.

"So there is a cache of magia-holding stones just... waiting for us down in those mines?"

"I see where this is going." Cruz spoke up this time. "But no. There is a refining process for the receptives to be useable to store magia. That's where the Alkay stone comes from. They're as useless as ordinary stone before that."

Quenti thought back to her times listening to her father complain over his dinner—a cup of ferment—about the traders that sold receptives and the constant struggle with the supply chain because of how regulated they were by the Council.

"Where are they refined?" she said, ignoring the lack of enthusiasm from anyone else. "It would probably be close by, right?"

"Are you suggesting we smuggle receptives into the mines?" Cruz said.

Quenti's heart sank. "Is it that stupid of an idea? If we can somehow bring our abilities down with us, we can increase our chances of escape once down there."

"It's not as though it's simple to steal receptives," Cruz said.

"I know," Quenti said. "They're highly regulated. I get that. But I know for a fact that even some receptives fall through the cracks. And we're at the best possible place for that to happen, right? Just after they're refined, before they're put into circulation."

Cruz looked back and forth between the others, unconvinced, but thinking.

"You asked where they are refined," Cruz said, crossing her arms, her back to the bed. "I truly don't know. The specifics weren't exactly handled at my level." With this, she turned to Ardo with a raised eyebrow, but he only shrugged.

"I don't know either. Maybe mage councilguards would, but..." he let the sentence hang.

"Even if we got a hold of a bunch of receptives, we don't even know if they'll work down there," Mena noted.

"But you," Quenti said, pointing to Beno. "You mentioned they have receptives down there. Why would they bother with receptives if they were useless?"

"Another thing we don't know for sure," Cruz said. "But it is a thought worth considering. Thinking back to the logic of the cuffs we use, the Alkay stone there never interfered with our receptives at the Haven, no matter how close, but we don't know the effects on a grander scale," Cruz said. "We'd have to test it out. But none of that will matter if we can't find a way to get our hands on some receptives without getting caught."

Quenti was standing now, heart pounding with something other than dread for the first time in weeks. "So, where do we start?"

"I think we start at the source," Ardo said. "We need to ask for more information from the guards in the mines."

"*You* ask," Mena said. "Beno and I are both injured and technically dead. And Cruz will be well known to anyone who's visited the capital."

She didn't mention Dante and no one seemed ready to correct her, particularly Ardo.

"And that's assuming your memory erasing trick worked," Ardo said. "I guess I'll have to find out the hard way."

"I can help," Quenti said, regretting the words the moment they left her lips. All eyes turned to her in puzzlement and surprise. She stood up straighter. "My father was a trader and a merchant. Well, a fisher. And then a trader and merchant when times got hard. Either way, I grew up in the world of receptive sales and the market. I might... I *will* be able to help. And no one would recognize me."

"Well then, we start at the source," Ardo said again, smiling warmly at Quenti. She only frowned back at him, not wanting to give him the satisfaction. But she'd do anything for Khuna and Alara, even if it meant spending time with some bull-headed blameless councilguard.

Chapter 41

Quenti

The under-sized mat in the corner of the room felt empty without Khuna. Despite her exhaustion, Quenti couldn't close her eyes—couldn't silence her mind and let herself drift off to sleep. Unwelcome thoughts still raced through the events of the day and the idiotic idea she had had about helping Ardo.

What was she doing?

She had barely been outside of her hometown growing up and now she thought she was some kind of bruya spy, ready to take on the Council?

It was stupid. *She* was stupid. Even more stupid than Alara and Runeo had been when they got themselves captured by the council-guards. Even more stupid than Khuna, who threw herself in front of them, knowing full well what the outcome would be.

Maybe all of this was Khuna's influence. Or maybe this was just a desperate move from an idiotic kid.

Quenti couldn't see anyone in the darkness of the room, but she heard the steady breathing of the others in their respective corners. After resting for a while, Beno was able to heal himself and Mena from their more critical injuries. It would still take a week or two for the internal damage to repair itself and for their magia to recover to full strength, but at least now their bodies weren't barely clinging to survival. Quenti remembered how exhausted she had felt after the amount of magia she had used in the Haven, and she had only used a fraction of what Mena had been forced to. And none of them even knew the long term impact of the mines on their magia.

Compared to those two, Quenti was nothing. What could she expect to do with the help of an overzealous councilguard? And after what happened in Arbol, how could she learn to trust someone like him, who slipped away after their conversation to run off to the barracks like the good little councilguard he was. He'd already gone above and beyond what she had expected of him, but that oddly made her trust him less. And tomorrow she'd be right there with him —an idiot girl and some stupid councilguard. How could the two of them hope to make a difference?

How could the two of them hope to rescue their friends? Perhaps more importantly, how could the two of them play such a vital role in the future of this godsforsaken realm?

It would be much easier to run. Sprint to the Ruinedlands and not look back. That would be simple. That would be peaceful. That would be... perfect.

Quenti wasn't sure she dozed off, but one moment she blinked, and the next, the room was awash in the light of two torches.

Over a breakfast of sliced fruit that tasted a few days past its prime, she grilled Cruz about anything the councilwoman could tell her. Which was close to nothing. As it turned out, in the name of checks and balances, there were pieces of information that were split among different members of the Council.

"The receptive regulation was headed by the blameless councilmembers," Cruz said. "To them, it helped ensure safety if mages were to declare war on the blameless one day."

"You mean a way for the blameless to control the flow of magia and those who wield it." Quenti's tone was acerbic.

"I didn't make the rules, child," Cruz said, her own tone biting back. "This is a partnership that's existed for hundreds of years."

"Sombria was built on balance and trust between blameless and mages," Dante cut in, not trying to hide his own annoyance at the "child" who had "butted into adult business" by volunteering for this mission.

"It seems more like it was built on a bitter distrust of magia and mages," Quenti said.

"We can have no idea what the world was like after the Bruya Wars," Cruz said, as if quoting a textbook. "Millions died and the country was nearly destroyed, as the black dunes east of here can attest to. There was a rightful amount of distrust, and we, as mages, did our best to gain it back."

"And how is that working out for us so far?"

Quenti met Ardo in one of the smaller plazas. A plain-looking tiered fountain splashed in the center of the square, the water tinged pink from the red sand that had blown in over time. He was already there when Quenti arrived, looking strange without his uniform. Almost like a normal person.

"Good morning," he said as she walked up.

She responded with the slightest of nods before sitting down on the edge of the fountain a few feet away.

"Unless you want me to yell," Ardo said, "you're probably going to want to sit closer."

She reluctantly followed his advice. They had to choose between meeting in an extremely public place where there was enough noise to allow them to speak privately or in a deserted one in hopes of being alone. Quenti chose the meeting spot, still not sure how far to trust the man next to her. While the location gave her security in numbers (though how secure would she really have been if he'd called in his councilguard brethren?), she regretted the feeling of exposure the plaza gave them.

"Any chance you had any magiaful revelations of our next steps while you were sleeping?" Ardo asked, with an annoying smirk.

Quenti returned his look with a saccharine smile. "You need to go ask someone where the receptives are refined."

"I thought you'd say that. Listen, I don't have the rank to go around asking questions about things I have no business knowing."

"Then take me in there with you and I'll ask the questions."

"And the moment someone suspects something and looks into who you are, we're both arrested and all that information we wanted becomes double locked-down."

"And if we don't ask the questions, then we never get the information anyway," she said. "I am not leaving Khuna and Alara down there while we hide in the shadows and twiddle our thumbs."

"I'm not saying that. I'm saying we need to be smart. We screw up once, or someone suspects us, and it's over. I'm lucky as it is that your friend's lies seemed to take."

"Who, Mena?"

Ardo nodded. "I spent most of the night tossing and turning. Waiting for someone to march in from the mines after our escape. Waiting for some evidence that the dead bodies down there led back to us. But everything's been... silent. So forgive me if I don't want to go pushing my luck, asking stupid questions that'll get us all killed."

"Fine," Quenti said. "Then maybe we don't ask. I don't care how secretive all this is, there still has to be some way they keep track of receptive refining. Somewhere in that base of yours, there has to be a record of where they're sending the receptives. A weave trail of some sort. They're too valuable for the Council to throw around."

"You said you knew the trading community, right? The merchants in town will know just as well as the guards."

"And this is exactly why you need me, blameless." She said the last word almost as a curse. "Merchants don't go around telling friends, let alone strangers, where they get their wares from. They're tightlipped and paranoid bastards who are always looking to get the advantage over a competitor."

"So the merchants won't tell us where their receptives come from?"

"Exactly. And they'll send their muscle after us if they think we're trying to get in on their supply or regions."

"Then we steal the receptives from them," Ardo said plainly.

"When was the last time you bought a receptive?" she asked.

Ardo only narrowed his eyes at her.

"Outside of the Haven, supply isn't so plentiful," she said. "And even if it was, the market isn't exactly thriving. They go for a high price, and with them being so regulated, there's a limit to how many any individual merchant can sell in any given month."

Ardo shook his head in disbelief. "I've seen merchants sell them by the handful—"

"—in the Haven," Quenti said.

That shut him up.

Quenti tried not to let her pleasure show. "All of Sombria is not the Haven. In Hurazon, a merchant would be lucky to sell one a month. And, if what you're saying is true, we're going to need more than one if we're going to use them in the mines, right?"

Ardo bit his lip and looked over at the water spouting from the fountain.

"Besides," Quenti continued, "with the tensions the way they are, I doubt any blameless are willingly running around selling them, as is. I wouldn't put it past the blameless to dry up the supply voluntarily."

"Merchants wouldn't do that."

"Do what? Control the flow of magia to their enemies during a war? I always told Alara you were stupid."

"Not all blameless view those with magia as the enemy, you know. I'd like to think you know that by now."

Quenti might have felt guilty, but as she did, her mind returned to the stupid little girl who turned Alara in. The girl who was the sole reason Khuna was down in the mines to begin with.

"I barely know you," Quenti said, pointing an accusatory finger toward his chest. "And just because Alara's gone all doe-eyed for you doesn't mean I trust you."

Ardo raised in hands in surrender, but she couldn't help but catch the blush on his cheeks at her words.

She rolled her eyes.

"Look, what's the point of having a councilguard around if we can't even use you to dig around for more information?" Quenti said. "Admit it, the best plan is to use you to find out everything we can from our enemies themselves. We ask some merchant, and even in the best case, we'd only get hearsay information."

Ardo's jaw was clenched and he remained silent for a long time. Finally, he spoke. "Fine. But this isn't just a one man job. Believe it or not, I do have responsibilities."

"So, what are you suggesting?"

"Senye Emaru would kill me, but I think I have the perfect idea for you."

"What does that mean?"

"If we're going to turn the base upside down, I'll need some help. With the twins out and Senye Cruz as one of the most recognizable figures, that leaves you."

"Why are you looking at me like that?"

Ardo smirked. "How would like to play the part of a councilguard?"

CHAPTER 42

QUENTI

Quenti yanked at the crotch of the black councilguard trousers, trying to stop them from riding up too high again. Ardo had dug the outfit out from one of his old trunks. He said he had planned to dress Emaru in the garb after her escape from the mines, but who knew when or if that plan would ever come to fruition.

Instead, Quenti now wore the awkwardly cut outfit, wondering how she hadn't noticed that the councilwoman had stood multiple inches shorter than her despite her threatening presence back in the Haven.

"Name?" Ardo asked, not bothering with pleasantries as he and Quenti walked down the empty desert trail.

"Lucía Canchaya."

"Rank?"

"Blameless sergeant."

"Sergeant will do," Ardo corrected.

"Sergeant who just happens to be blameless, then," Quenti said, unable to bite back her sarcasm. "I've been with the councilguards since I was five and am apparently a crazy amazing prodigy. Either that, or I look damn good for my age"

Ardo only threw her an annoyed look.

"Where is the real Lucía anyway? Does she even look anything like me?"

"Lucía doesn't exist," Ardo said. "If she did, you *definitely* wouldn't be able to pull this off."

"And a made-up name works better how?" Quenti said.

"Not made up—at least not completely. She has a tapestry trail going back at least seven years before she was even recruited for the councilguards."

"But she doesn't *exist*." Quenti said again, slowly.

"Not technically, no."

"Is it that hard to say no?"

"You'd be surprised what a series of tapestries can do. As far as Sombria is concerned, she's more real than most bruyas."

"That's stupid."

"And the realm's stupidity gives us an advantage," Ardo said. "Senye Emaru created Lucía nearly a decade ago, when she started to suspect distrust among the other councilmembers."

"So even she admits the Council is a crap pile."

Ardo ignored the jab and continued. "She wanted an identity she could use if she ever needed information that wouldn't be allowed of a mage councilwoman. Like, for example, anything to do with receptives. Even you have to appreciate the genius in that."

"I really don't," Quenti said, inspecting her nail beds as they walked, making a show of how bored she was. "You're telling me she created a fake person and couldn't even get them promoted to something higher than a sergeant?"

"She needed to be high enough to have some sway and access to information, but not so high in the ranks that she could be missed."

He eyed Quenti. "Just *don't* throw your weight around with the wrong people."

"And who in the underworld are the wrong people?"

"Anyone above you: sergeant majors, lieutenants, captains, majors like Francisco, colonels, and the apukispay general."

"In what world would I be crossing paths with the apukispay general?"

Ardo groaned. His frustration was oddly satisfying. "Just promise me."

"And pass up the opportunity to command Francisco to tell me everything I need?"

"You remind me of Alara, you know?" Ardo said, voice suddenly softer. The words made Quenti's stomach lurch. "Only infinitely more annoying."

"I'd like to think I taught her how to remove that staff stuck up her rear end."

"That and stage an uprising against the most peaceful ruling body in our country's history."

"Oh, you can thank your lady Emaru for that," Quenti said.

The two fell silent again, and for several long moments, only the sound of boots on dirt echoed between them.

Quenti was thinking of Alara, but every thought of her brought with it thoughts of Khuna, remembering the way her she'd looked at her right before she had gone bursting out the inn doors. Like she loved her, but had no choice but to throw her life at the councilguards.

The idea was absolute l'lama dung to Quenti. It was Alara who had made the first move and Runeo who had followed in his pure, hotheaded stupidity. Khuna had always shadowed Runeo around like a little sister, eager to take drastic measures to ensure his safety.

When she and Khuna were reunited again, she was going to have a serious discussion with her about her friendship with Runeo and her need to constantly follow him off cliffs.

"Isn't anyone going to notice how young I am?" Quenti asked, breaking the silence between her and Ardo.

"All we can do is hope everyone thinks you look good for your age," Ardo said. "Which is why the less attention you draw to yourself, the better. But if anyone asks, you're twenty-seven."

Quenti looked down at herself with a small snort. For once, she was glad not to be smaller. Maybe she could pull this off.

"Just don't talk too much."

"Is that the best spy craft advice you've got?"

"For you?" he said. "Yes."

As they trudged toward the base, Quenti took in the stark surrounding landscape. This close to the Ruinedlands, the ground and limited flora looked drained of color. Even the sky didn't look blue, but a pale gray. Smoke and sand blew up in clouds from the mine just east of the base, making the air feel heavy and dirty. She could only imagine what it was like closer to the mines. Or *inside* the mines. Did the sand and dust choke Khuna's lungs even as she slept?

"Look alive," Ardo said, and Quenti realized how close the walls had come. The trail they had been following had turned into a road when she wasn't looking, and men and women were lined up, waiting to enter the gate that led into the surprisingly large walled mini-civilization that made up the base.

The wait took forever, with Quenti constantly feeling the need to fidget with her pants and Ardo jabbing her in the side to stop. By the time they made it to the front of the line, she was close to jabbing him back with the dagger on her belt.

"Name and rank," the guard at the gate said, barely glancing her way. He was wearing the uniform that denoted him as a footsoldier, the lowest rank in Sombria. An ugly scar cut across his face and she wondered if he got that during his service for the Council or before he enlisted.

His scowl in her direction made her realize she hadn't yet answered, and Ardo stood tense beside her.

"Right," she said. "Lucía Canchaya, Sergeant."

The man looked up at her name, eyes suddenly focused and sharp on her face.

Quenti bit her tongue, keeping her face neutral even as her heart jumped erratically in her chest. She wasn't sure what he was looking for, but after a long pause, he turned to Ardo.

He answered without hesitation. "Everardo Gomes, Runner."

"Purpose?"

"I'm escorting Sergeant Canchaya for an overview of the mines. She has orders straight from the Council."

The guard nodded, writing the information on his parchment. He handed a red ribbon to Quenti to tie on her sleeve before stepping aside for them to enter. Even after they were inside and the guard had turned to speak to the next person in line, she walked carefully, waiting for him to call back and tell them to stop. It never happened.

"Step one down," she said, letting out a shaky breath.

"Now for the hard part: finding the information we need," Ardo said.

They headed toward the main building at the base's center first. If they were right, there would be weaves or tapestries somewhere indicating the amount of receptives coming out of the mine, along with where they were being sent. Quenti had to admit when she thought about helping with the mission and becoming a bruya spy, she didn't expect reading weaves would be her first mission.

The building itself was multiple levels tall, built of stone, with no eye for design or beauty. It was gray and square, stretching across the heart of the campus. The whole base was an egregious eyesore, with slate and brown buildings connected by sand walkways. There wasn't a single tree or bit of plant life to be seen. Though perhaps this could be attributed to how close the Ruinedlands were, rather than an active decision by the councilguards.

Inside was somehow even more lifeless, with narrow halls stretching inhumane distances without windows or color in either direction. Maybe coming from the Haven, they didn't miss the natural light, but the darkness made her lip curl. Every door looked the same, with only small signs indicating what was inside.

There was just enough room for two people to move abreast through the halls and Ardo fell behind her every time a guard or group had to pass. In the dim light it was difficult to see the different uniforms apart, the dark reds and greens and blacks blending into dark blurs of fabric.

Maybe this would do her ruse a favor.

After the fourth group passed them, whispers coming in the wake, Quenti stepped back beside Ardo.

"Why is everyone staring? Am I doing something wrong?"

"Gossip moves fast here. There probably aren't many visitors coming out here."

Quenti shook her head. There had to be something more. They were stepping aside for her like she mattered. She was just a sergeant. From what she understood, that rank was pretty low.

"Who exactly is this Lucía I'm supposed to be playing?"

Ardo didn't answer immediately, eyes not quite catching hers. Wait, was he actively *avoiding* eye contact? "She's technically a bit of a war hero."

"What...?" Quenti said, stopping in the under-sized and over-long hallway. "How can she be a war hero? She doesn't even exist! And since when has there been an actual war?"

Ardo took a right at the next turn, all but forcing her to catch up as he spoke. "It was Senye Emaru's idea. She's been planting seeds and stories for Lucía a little each year. There are tapestries back in the Haven recounting her deeds."

"What happened to lying low?"

"It's all we have to work with," Ardo said. "And with Lucía's history, it's all the more reason for you to *not draw attention* to yourself."

"Don't say it like that."

"Trust me, I already had this discussion with her years ago. She wanted to have some clout and power to make the character more real."

"Because nothing says real like a seventeen-year-old war hero."

"You're twenty-seven."

"How can—" Quenti stopped talking as another woman in councilguard garb passed them, eyeing her curiously as she did. Quenti lowered her voice to a whisper. "How can you expect me to go unnoticed?"

"It's easy," Ardo said. "Just don't talk to anyone. 'Yes, sir.' 'Yes, ma'am.' 'I'm under strict, confidential orders.' Keep your head down."

"I'm afraid to ask, but what ridiculous story did she come up with for Lucía? What am I meant to have done?"

"Two years ago, you were a part of a platoon of soldiers that went into the forests east of Attalea after you heard about a planned invasion by a sect of bruyas. Your entire group fell in battle, but you killed seventy bruya rebels in the process and stopped the uprising. You also found plans on the dead indicating they planned to march to Cielo."

"That's the biggest load of—" Quenti cut herself off as another group passed them, eyes following her as she gave an awkward nod and kept walking.

"For what it's worth, the conflict was real. Lucía is the only fictitious part of it."

"And why I haven't heard of it?"

"It was kept secret for fear of inciting fear and unrest amongst Sombrians."

"That's the stupidest thing I have ever heard. Why that of all things? Couldn't she have just picked a normal councilguard who rose through the ranks like a normal person?"

"Senye Emaru came up with it. I think she enjoyed the drama of it. But I don't think even she realized how well the story would spread."

"That explains how I'm a sergeant so young, I guess.

"Have you forgotten that you're supposed to be twenty-seven again?"

"Right," Quenti said. It was surprisingly difficult to remember she was supposed to be ten years older.

"And if anyone asks, you turned down the promotion, refusing to take credit for a mission that ended the lives of so many."

"How honorable of me."

They took a set of stairs down at the next dead end. The torch-lit dimness didn't change, but the air did, feeling heavier as they descended. In their silence, her thoughts once again returned to Khuna and her chest tightened.

Ardo stopped abruptly, raising a hand across her chest, as they came to a double set of doors. The sign above the door read "Weave and Tapestry Library."

"Here goes nothing," Ardo said as he opened the door, a smile stretching across his face. "And here we have our archives. All our weaves and tapestries are up-to-date and checked regularly for accuracy."

Quenti realized he was making a show of talking to her and nodded along as she followed him into the small room beyond. Looking around the cramped space, she assumed they had to be in the wrong place. There was only a small desk with a short, pale man sitting behind it, looking at them with a mixture of surprise and happiness. She couldn't blame him. If the hallways felt miserable, this room felt like a prison cell.

"Sirs!" he said, standing up to greet them. Quenti could have sworn she heard his knees creak with disuse as he stood. "How can I help you?"

"Runner Gomes, here. I'm giving Sergeant Canchaya a tour of our operations here and she wants to check with the recent archives."

"Sergeant Canchaya?" the man said, face turning slightly pink, though he made no show of it in his voice. "Sergeant Lucía Canchaya? Of course."

The familiar tone made Quenti tense, but he didn't press the matter, and he didn't even question her age.

"This way," he said, coming from behind the desk to open a door in the corner that Quenti hadn't even noticed. As she followed, she felt a slight twinge of panic. The room beyond the door stretched dozens of meters in either direction, with shelves a couple of feet taller than her filled with boxes, and hanging weaves and tapestries as far as the eye could see in the shadowy room.

"Give me a minute," the man said, moving forward in the darkness. "We need to use receptive torches down here because of the risk to the l'lama wool. I just need to..."

A moment later, torches flickered to life along the walls. The room wasn't as endless as it had appeared at first, but it was large, and Quenti was starting to dread their next steps. Part of her wondered if anyone would notice the receptives in the archive going missing.

"Anything specific you're looking for?"

Quenti glanced at Ardo briefly. They had known it was too

suspicious to ask for exactly what they were looking for. "Sorry, but that's classified," she said.

"Right," he said. "Of course."

"How are the files organized?"

"Anything from the past year to six months will be hanging among the weaves. Anything older has been converted into the tapestries and bound. They are then organized by topic—prison records, work histories for guards, finances, shipments, so on. *Those* shelves are labeled. I hate to admit our weaves are a bit haphazardly arranged at present. We're understaffed and over-whelmed with the increased activity over the past month. Our weavers can hardly keep up with the transition from one format to the next."

The term haphazard was an understatement, Quenti realized an hour later when she was still sorting through hanger after hanger of weaves, half of them fraying at the edges and hard to decipher.

"I found something!" Ardo practically shouted a few rows away. While Quenti had been wading through the weaves—the only recording language she was completely fluent in—he had been looking among the more historical tapestry records for the receptives. He came around the corner, holding a giant bound book with a set of codes written on the cover and "Receptive Relay" beneath. Inside, were dozens of pages of tapestries. From what Ardo told her, they were mostly rows and rows of numbers and codes, and after a few minutes of analysis, Quenti was able to—she hoped—understand what the numbers meant.

There were dates, the name of the guard in charge of shipments, the inventory at start, and the inventory at the end of the journey, which was almost always a little less—though she couldn't tell if that was normal. She could also barely decipher the differences in the numbers. Finally, their payments were tracked in a separate column.

"No location of delivery? What kind of records are these?"

"The information is likely kept separate so it's harder to track." Ardo shook his head.

"Suspicious."

"Or smart," Ardo said. "Remember how deep the distrust goes with the blameless councilmembers." He let out an exhausted sigh. "I'll keep looking. I haven't seen anything yet, but it has to be nearby."

"But you just said they were paranoid," Quenti said. "Wouldn't they keep them separate?"

"El'dyo, I hope not."

Quenti looked back at the book cradled in her arms, focusing on the neat columns laid out in front of her in all their woolen glory. They looked... familiar, even to her untrained eye. And not just because they looked like every other piece of tapestry she'd laid her eyes on in over the past hour.

"Wait," she walked over to one of the earlier weave columns she'd sorted through. "I think I saw..."

She rummaged through hangers and hangers of weaves, ignoring the dryness and chafing that came with rubbing your hands on wool for extended periods. Finally, she found what she was looking for.

"Ah!" she said, not bothering to soften her excitement. "I wondered why these were kept separate from the rest of the weaves."

"What am I looking at?" Ardo said, unfamiliar with the language of the weaves. Although most people had a basic understanding of the tapestries, only merchants and translators knew how to read the weaves, the patterns of colors and knots, a completely different language.

"I think," she said, "this whole row of weaves is a cipher to certain tapestries."

"Huh?"

Quenti tightened her lips, annoyed that Ardo couldn't read her mind. "The librarian said the weaves were over there, yes?" She motioned to the other location in the room where the most recent weaves were stored. "So why are these kept within the tapestries?"

Ardo crossed his arms, but after several long seconds, the logic seemed to click, and he started to chuckle. "This country really was founded on paranoia, wasn't it?"

Quenti wanted to disagree, but with every passing moment, it grew harder and harder to argue with his logic. Why else set up a library like this other than to hide information? As Ardo had said, you'd be hard-pressed to find a councilguard who could read the weaves, and Quenti knew that most merchants thought tapestries were a luxurious waste of time.

It took at least another hour for her and Ardo to put together the rest of the pieces.

It was clear the weaves they read held identifying information for the numbers in the bound book, columns registering the different shipments. And then, with a flip of the weave was another layer, this one a payment chart to the guards, along with information on the cart and merchants making the shipments. At the very top of the weave, in script were the words: Rimpia.

"It's tracking shipments to and from Rimpia."

"That's north of here," Ardo said, frowning. "It's on the way to Uodora, at least a three-day journey without l'lamagas."

"And where do they go after?" Quenti asked, flipping through the pages of the tapestries.

"I doubt these records would say. That information would be kept up in the factory or in Sombria after they were shipped there."

"Why?"

"Need I remind you that the Council was founded on paranoia?"

"So, we've got nothing."

"We know Rimpia is where the majority of receptives are being treated and processed. That's a start."

"And we know it'll be another week at least just to get there and back, not taking into account finding a way to steal the receptives we need."

Quenti's shoulders slumped. She locked her fingers beneath the giant tome she held in front of her, letting its lower half rest below her belly button. She could feel what little optimism she had had drain away, her body becoming heavier with every breath.

What had she been thinking? Learning where the receptives were stored hadn't helped them. It wasn't as though they could steal from what was probably one of the best guarded factories in the country. She'd done nothing but waste all their time.

"We should leave," she said, hauling the book back over to Ardo. "At the very least, we can tell Cruz what we found out. Maybe she'll have an idea."

Ardo pursed his lips and nodded, looking equally as disheartened.

Somehow, that made it worse, knowing that someone, even Ardo, was as lost as she was.

As the councilguard rounded the corner to return the enormous book to its resting place, Quenti turned to clean up the rest of the weaves she had waded through.

She almost didn't hear the soft clearing of the throat from the entrance.

Standing in the doorway of the library, a looming shadow among shadows, was the imposing figure of Major Francisco.

Chapter 43

Quenti

"Sir!" Ardo said, saluting without hesitation as he caught sight of Major Francisco.

Quenti mimicked his motions, trying to keep her face neutral—never mind how much she was screaming inside. Thank Sol the man was just a blameless with no ability to read what she was thinking in that moment. It was stuck somewhere between "Get out now" and "Kill him immediately."

"Runner Ardo," Major Franciso said. "What are you doing here?" The words sent a knife through Quenti's chest, even though he couldn't more clearly be speaking to Ardo.

Ardo met the Major's gaze, not flinching under his curious stare. "Sir, when you're given the opportunity to escort Sergeant Canchaya around the base, you take it." He was giving the man the same boyish smile and charm he used with Alara. It almost annoyed Quenti to see it work again, despite it being in her best interest.

The corner of Major Francisco's lips turned upward and he slapped a hand on Ardo's shoulder before turning to Quenti with a small bow of his head.

"I heard the rumor you were here, but I had to see it myself," he said, holding out his hand. Quenti took it with a smile she hoped would pass for comfortable. His handshake was stiff, oppressive, and she fought the urge to squeeze his hand back or jump forward and rake her nails down his face. Someone like Lucía would never puff up to meet the approval of a common major like Francisco. She hoped her repressed rage and anxiety could pass for confidence.

"After all these years of hearing about you and never getting to meet you in person, I was beginning to think you were a ghost," he said, finally letting Quenti's hand go.

Quenti laughed, the sound brittle to her own ears. "I was real and alive last time I checked."

Major Francisco's face remained unreadable. "Your story is truly incredible. Unbelievable, really, what happened. My old colleague explained it to me a while back and I never forgot it."

"And I'm sure it's a story that gets bigger with every retelling," she said with a swallow, tasting bile in the back of her throat. "It's been twisted so much, I hardly even recognize it myself. You of all people should know how that works."

After a few more seconds of his bland stare, he smiled and nodded, and Quenti felt the tightness in her chest unfurl.

"So, why are we being blessed with your presence on our base, Sergeant? Not many in Sombria care to make it out this far, what with the superstitions around the Ruinedlands."

"Superstitions that only impact those who wield magia," Quenti said. "Besides, I'm not what most would call superstitious."

"And what would they call you?"

Quenti blinked. She hadn't the slightest idea what she was saying. Where was this conversation even going? "Lucky to be alive," she finally said.

Major Francisco stared back at her, his square jaw set and stiff, eyes piercing. If that response had worked, she had no way of knowing.

"So, why are you here?" he said, almost as though the interaction prior hadn't happened.

Quenti hummed noncommittally at this. "I'm not at liberty to discuss it," she said, mimicking something she had heard a council-guard say to the head of their village when she had been younger. Major Francisco narrowed his eyes.

"As Major of this base, everything happening here goes through me, including whatever mission you've been sent on." The cold threat was clear in his tone and she saw Ardo going stiff behind him, looking at her with wide eyes.

Run. The urge moved through her like a bolt of magia before she pulled it back and gave the man a placid smile.

"*Everything* happening here goes through you?" she asked. "So, you must know that for every shipment of receptives that gets sent to Rimpia for refining, a small percentage mysteriously vanishes in transit."

He looked back at her, jaw slackening, but the suspicion not quite gone from his face.

"I've been sent to lead the next shipment to Rimpia."

"Oh?"

"To ensure no bruyas are involved in these small discrepancies."

Quenti kept her face still, even as her mind raced and her heart threatened to beat through her chest. She had never spewed so much l'lama dung in her life, and she had no idea if anything she was saying made sense. Was her story with Lucía threatening his whole opera-tion or aiding it? She couldn't tell.

And then the major's face morphed from suspicion to annoyance.

"So they've sent you to babysit me."

"Of course not," she said, shocked by the outright admission, but still unsure what he'd admitted. "But the Haven recognizes that Lejon has been historically underfunded. Given its importance, they want to improve conditions, particularly as the threat of the bruyas continues to escalate."

Quenti held herself up against the urge to collapse or sprint out of the room and not look back.

No. She could do this.

She *would* do this. For Khuna.

And for herself.

"We keep perfectly good watch over the receptives, and the Haven has always understood that a certain percentage get damaged during shipment. But we've always kept this number at an acceptable percentage."

There was something in the way that Francisco was talking, a defensiveness that made Quenti wonder if she had stumbled onto something. Something he was sensitive about.

She doubted it was actually bruyas causing the problems. Someone like Major Francisco would have taken the opportunity to complain about them and defend his strict policing.

"Yes, the shrinkage figures are low," Quenti said, "but they are present. And in these uncertain times, the Council wants to make sure their investment in the mines is secure."

Major Francisco didn't bother hiding his sneer. Lucía may have been a war hero, but he still outranked her. The idea of sending a lowly sergeant to oversee this likely bothered him to no end.

"Then again," she said, "I'm sure they'll also be happy to learn how much worse things would be were it not for your hard work."

It was the right thing to say.

He nodded, looking mollified. "I would never do anything against the Council's wishes." Though he looked appeased, his voice was still tinged with ice.

"So I've heard," she said. Her eyes lingered on every part of this

Major Francisco. This man who had caused them so much trouble—not to mention the countless deaths he was no doubt responsible for. They traced every hardened wrinkle on his face. The stubble on his chin. The way his pressed uniform conformed to his chiseled frame.

He reminded her of men she had met when living with her father. Men who made themselves feel big by squashing those around them, holding their heads high in triumph when someone else failed. Men who stroked their egos with their own self-righteousness.

"In fact, I've heard lots of good things about you," she said. "I know you play things by the book and always consider what's in the best interest of the Haven. I came here to make sure our guards weren't in danger and you're telling me they aren't. I won't take that lightly."

"Is that so?" he said, eyes still narrowed, jaw set, untrusting.

Quenti didn't know what came over her, but she felt the sudden urge to gain his approval. This was a man who could and would move mountains to get what he wanted. Perhaps taking just a little extra risk...

"By the way," Quenti glanced around the library, as though checking to make sure no one but them three were present. "Know I am appreciative of the work you've done for the mines," she said in a conspiratorial whisper. "As well as all of Sombria. Without you, we'd be overrun with bruyas and magia."

Major Francisco's expression remained chiseled and impassive, though Quenti thought she could see his eyes widen ever so slightly. As if taking in *Lucía* for the first time.

Or perhaps she had imagined it.

"In addition to the receptive shipments," she continued, "I also want to make sure we're taking into account the rise in bruya activity. My hope is that I can return to the Council with news of your success in spite of your limited resources. They may see cause to fix that issue."

His eyes went even wider. This time, she knew she wasn't imagining it. She had caught his attention. It was as though it took mountains of gold and copper to bury people alive in the mines against their will.

"You're a smart soldier, Sergeant Canchaya," he said, smile thin on his lips. "You know, many fools think the only way to rise in the ranks is to be imposing and merciless. To cut an imposing figure and throw your weight around. But you..." He squinted at Quenti, taking in her face, her figure.

It took all of Quenti's willpower not to flinch at his gaze. She'd always felt too big growing up. Other girls had mocked her for her size, telling her no man would fall for a woman the size of a l'lama. But under this man's eyes, she felt physically small for the first time.

"...your youthful appearance," he continued. "You truly understand its usefulness."

Quenti smiled, caught between the thrill of lying and the fear instilled by the man's piercing stare.

"Where are you staying during your time here?" His tone was suddenly light, and free of judgment. She would have thought this would put her at ease, but she didn't trust the shift. "I didn't see any record of guests in the barracks."

"I'm staying in town," she said quickly. From the look the major gave her, this wasn't the normal protocol. "I didn't intend for my time here to be made public knowledge. You say appearing unimposing is an asset. I prefer not being seen at all."

"Ah," he said, "well, you've failed your mission, Sergeant. There's a reason the Council entrusted me with the security of the mines."

"You truly live up to your reputation, Major."

"You as well." He stepped forward, placing a hand on her shoulder. Being caught in the man's gaze was bad enough, but having his hand on her shoulder froze the blood within her veins. "I'd like to invite you to dine with me before you leave again."

"I don't know… I have a lot to tend to." Quenti spared a glance at Ardo, who looked as uncomfortable as she felt.

"Nonsense. You'll have time for a single dinner. I have an estate just off base, so you don't need to worry about *drawing more attention*. At least not from the wrong kind of people. In a few days' time, I'm having a party to celebrate the opening of a new series of tunnels in Level Three. Come. I insist. In fact, it's an order."

Quenti felt a hand twist around her chest and heart, cutting off the blood supply to her brain as she nodded, smile bright. "Of course, Sir. It would be my pleasure."

"Perfect! Where might I direct your formal invitation?"

"You can relay the information to Runner Gomes," she said, careful to keep her face neutral. "My accommodations don't know of my status with the councilguards. I don't want to draw any more attention than I already have."

"Understood," he said, placing an elbow onto a crossed arm and a hand to his chin as he gave her another once-over. "Better not to be seen, as you said. Hm." Another long bout of silence passed. "As you were, then." Without another word, Major Francisco retreated from the over-sized chamber.

Quenti made it a full two minutes before she flew to the small copper trash bin in the corner and vomited. Her breakfast emptied into it with a sour smell and she half sat, half fell onto the ground. Ardo stood behind her, laying a comforting hand on her back that she didn't want to admit appreciating in the moment.

"You did good," he said softly. "Really good. You're a regular spy."

"My mouth tastes like vomit."

"It smells like vomit too."

"What in the underworld just happened?"

Ardo gave a small huff of a laugh. "I think you just got invited to the major's house for dinner."

"How did any of that work?"

"I think he follows the book so strictly that it takes extra energy to think others might not."

Quenti nodded, though her head still lay low in the metallic bin. "But the receptives *are* going missing. You saw that, too, in the weaves and tapestries."

"Yeah, I saw that. That was quick thinking. Dangerous, but quick. You practically accused him of negligence. Or outright stealing."

Quenti shook her head, annoyed. "You said he's too by the book. He wouldn't steal—"

"Against the Council's wishes."

"You think the Council is behind the missing receptives?"

"I think *part* of the Council is, yes," he said. "After that interaction with the major, I'd bet my spear on it. In case you didn't realize, there's a lot the Council is hiding from its own people."

"You don't think I know that?" Quenti said. Of course she knew that. She'd known her entire life. What irked her beyond this world was that Ardo was the one telling her. "But let's say you're right. The Council. Sorry, *half* the Council—the blameless half—smuggles receptives. Why? It's not like they can use them."

"Who says they can't use them?"

Quenti could have thrown herself off a cliff for how stupid she was being. Of *course* they can use them. All they need are willing or subservient magia users to fill the ore... but where did that leave them?

Tired, for one thing. Quenti was strung out and exhausted. She could feel the very weight of her body as she wiped her mouth with her sleeve.

"Any chance the major won't notice if I just disappear without taking him up on his dinner?"

"I doubt it."

"Maybe I can get sick. When's the last time there was a plague around here?"

"You need to go," Ardo said, his tone serious. "He doesn't take no for an answer. And trust me, you *will* be missed if you don't show. Besides, you might learn something that can help us. Maybe you'll learn about their plans with the receptives."

"Or maybe I'll vomit all over his dinner table."

Ardo helped her to her feet, pushing the trash bin behind a shelf with his toe. "If you're going to vomit, at least make sure to hit him."

Quenti laughed, the queasiness in her stomach not quite gone, but lessened to the point where she could smile without fear of throwing up again.

She hated how much better his jokes made her feel. She hated that, despite everything, he was the one person in the world she not only had to trust, but she found herself *wanting* to trust.

Chapter 44

Alara

Alara's eyes adjusted to the dimness of the tunnels almost too well. Even at night, when she and the others tucked themselves away in the alcove to sleep, it didn't feel quite dark—as though they were living in the space between pitch black and shadow. Difficult to differentiate.

The only thing that truly signified the night, was the soft and steady breathing of the others around her as they drifted off to sleep, hopefully far away from the tunnels in their dreams. Most nights, her own dreams were filled with the screams of prisoners and the snapping of whips. Every morning she woke from her nightmares, unsure if she was truly awake. She wished she could dream about other things—the trees and bridges of Arbol, or the colors of the market in the Haven. Instead, she saw Adelmo's hollow eyes and relived the sensation of Lili's core disappearing into nothingness.

Heat traced across Alara's cheeks and she realized she was crying, silent and alone in the dark. She bit the inside of her cheek hard and blinked rapidly, trying to push the tears away before they could drown her. If she started crying now, if she let the small lock box in the corner of her mind open, she wasn't sure she'd survive the tidal wave. She wanted to scream until she couldn't feel the pain anymore. Instead, she focused on the dull pain in her cheek where her teeth gnashed, and she held her breath until she was forced to let it go.

She jumped at the feel of a warm, rough hand on her shoulder and turned to see Runeo's black eyes blinking at her in the dark. She resisted wiping at her face, the tears invisible in the semi-darkness. But there was a knowing in his look that told her it didn't matter. It only made her stomach twist and her eyes burn hotter. She moved to turn away from him, embarrassed at the show of emotion, but even as she did, he moved closer and pulled her into his body.

He was warm, a sharp contrast to the cave air, and she could just make out the steady beat of his heart and the cadence of his breathing against her back. She told herself she should move away, but she only settled in closer, letting his hand wrap around her own. His fingers traced along the veins in her hands, and she focused on the feel of his calluses against her own. She closed her eyes and let her breaths fall into pace with his own. With her eyes closed and the heat of Runeo's body wrapped around her, she could almost pretend they were in the cloud forest, beneath the dark night sky.

She tucked the grief, rage, and hopelessness back into the small box in the back of her mind where it couldn't hurt her.

Not yet. Not right now.

As Alara slowly came to the next morning, she noticed a warm arm beneath her head. She turned as Runeo blinked awake, pulling his arm from under her head. They sat up and pulled apart without comment, too exhausted to feel shame or embarrassment.

She'd been in the mines while she dreamed, but at least no one had died.

She hadn't seen anyone die since the man whose head had been smashed in, but it featured in her dreams plenty. And there was a plethora of whippings and beatings throughout the day. Some were a result of a worker falling behind an unspoken and arbitrary schedule. Some were for looking at a guard the wrong way. They didn't take kindly to being looked at, as the yellowing bruise on Alara's face reminded her daily.

But the fading ache in her cheek barely cut through the other pains and aches that had settled over her body. She had forgotten what fullness felt like, the sharp hunger of her stomach now a constant companion, along with the inherent weakness that came with it.

It was only her anger, simmering low and hot in her stomach, that kept her moving. And the small bitter knowledge that Runeo had chosen this for himself, too. But even that was getting more difficult to hold on to as she saw his face grow sallow and pale alongside Khuna's. There were no mirrors down here, so she was protected from having to see her own slow transformation into the shambling corpse.

Khuna came through the tunnels, bowls balanced in her thinning arms, the routine of their mornings an uneasy comfort. Alara had even managed to get used to shoveling the cold and slimy grit down her throat every morning out of pure desperate hunger.

They didn't speak as they ate. They never spoke while they ate. They rarely spoke at night either. In fact, Alara was almost sure they didn't speak at all the night before. They had only given the perfunctory greetings when they came back to their small alcove before laying down to fall asleep. There was no discussion of plans for escape. No new revelations. No hope. Just. Exhaustion.

She wanted to say something, anything to reaffirm their plans, but she couldn't hold her thoughts long enough to form the question, every ounce of energy needed to be saved for the day ahead.

Instead she gave a cracked smile to the others as they lumbered to the main tunnel, cradling their empty bowls.

Alara stumbled as she rounded the corner, the main tunnel brighter than normal, with an extra couple of torches held by red-robed guards standing along the wall. The others behind her slowed as well, turning the corner with careful steps.

"5-2425, Tunnel 7-B2," one of the guards said. "Prisoner 5-1345, Tunnel 7-C4."

Alara felt numb at the realization that they were shuffling the groups. Sol's small hand landed in hers and she gave it a small squeeze of reassurance, though she had little to offer. The guards moved down the line of prisoners, calling out the assignments in some system Alara couldn't find the energy to understand. She noted that the tunnels were labeled based on where they split off and that their main tunnel was apparently Tunnel Seven. Not that this helped her in any tangible way, but she stored the information nonetheless.

As the assignments went on, she noticed the scowling Francisco standing behind the other guards, watching over the progress with sharp eyes.

It wasn't the first time she had seen him down here. She was actually surprised with how often she had caught glimpses of him marching through the main tunnel on random mornings and evenings, sometimes watching prisoners, but more often eyes cast down and feet moving fast, as though he had places to be.

She could always pick him out down here. While the rest of the guards wore red uniforms and scarves masking their faces, he wore his normal councilguard major attire, with its shining gold embellishments.

Alara only realized she was glaring at him when their eyes met, and she saw the recognition in his gaze as he sneered.

His eyes shifted quickly between her and where Sol stood beside her, hand still warm in her own.

Alara let the girl's hand go, heart pounding as Francisco stepped forward, snatching the board the guard was reading from.

The guard only gave a small start and stepped back, eyes lowered as the major came to stand a little too close to where Alara stood, head down.

"Prisoner 5-6252, Tunnel 7-B4," he said, eyes focused on Sol.

Dez gave a small bow of her head, holding her hand out for Sol to follow. Before the girl could take a step, Francisco stood between them. "Prisoner 5-7942 is assigned to Tunnel 7-B3. *Only* Prisoner 5-7942."

The blood drained from Dez's face.

Alara had heard the woman speak of this day with dread: the day Sol would be ripped from her grasp and forced to work separately.

"No—"

The word had barely escaped Dez's lips when Francisco's meaty hand cracked against her cheek. The metal knuckles of his gloves cut across her skin and blood bloomed instantly.

Sol let out a silent gasp and lurched forward, but Alara grabbed her quickly, wrapping her arms around her.

"Did you just say no to me?"

"I'm s-sorry," Dez stuttered out, blood dripping across her lips. She stumbled up, eyes still focused on the ground. "She's only five."

"And we're short one hand in that tunnel." His voice was cold, almost bored.

Alara gave the girl a squeeze and whispered in her ear. "You'll see your mom and me both tonight. Don't worry." She pushed her forward, wondering how empty the promise she had made was.

She knew one day they'd be gone. One day, she wouldn't meet Sol or Dez in their alcove.

The little girl's shoulders were straight and stiff as she moved forward, following a guard with dark eyes. It pained Alara to see her not look back, not even look at where her mother stumbled away in a different direction.

"Prisoner 5-9832, tunnel 7-F5," Francisco said.

Alara could almost smell the sourness of his breath as he sneered down at her. She knew he couldn't miss the twitch of her jaw as she fought every muscle in her body to stop herself from lashing out at him. He seemed to pause, as though daring for her to do it. Tempting her to lash out so he could retaliate.

But when she only nodded and turned away, he passed the board back to the other guard.

"The rest may continue as previously assigned."

Alara's nails bit into her palms as she looked for her new *group* outside of tunnel F, marked only by a guard with a carved board. As assignments were completed, the groups for tunnel F followed, eyes down as a number of guards led the way, each group breaking off at their respective turns. Her group—five—was the last, and she realized, looking around at the men standing at least a foot taller than her, with muscles sinewy and well-honed, that she looked decidedly different from everyone else in her work group.

"Rojo, your new assignments," the guard that had led them there greeted the man already standing in the narrow alcove.

"What in El'dyo's name am I supposed to do with that scrawny rabbit?" He waved a hand at Alara, his voice rough and low beneath his scarf.

The guard shrugged. "She'll be good for the tight spaces. Major's orders."

Any questions Rojo had were clearly swallowed back up with this declaration. He only mumbled something under his breath before waving to the others.

"You five, pickaxes. You four hauling. And you," he looked at Alara. "Haul until we need you. And I expect you to work just as hard and fast as the others, little rabbit."

Time passed in a blur. Without any meals or passing of the sun to break up the monotony and exhaustion of the day, it seemed to go on forever, all while passing by in the blink of an eye.

As Alara's muscles started to grow numb, the guard, Rojo, grabbed her by the arm.

"Rabbit," he said, dragging her with him as if she were a l'lama to be led. "Your turn to be useful."

She bit back the bitter remark that she had already been ten times more useful today than him. Instead, she let him guide her, knowing nothing would be gained by fighting back.

He pulled her to a far corner where some of the diggers had made progress in breaking apart a small crack in the stone—a crack that went deeper inward. They stopped in front of it without comment and Alara looked back at the guard, wondering what he expected from her.

"Go," he said, shoving her forward. "Crawl in there and see if you can see any crystals."

"What?" The word left from Alara's lips with a gasp. He could have only been pointing her to the narrow crack that led into the stone. The space was barely wider than her head and grew pitch black just a foot or so in.

"Get in," he said, losing patience quickly. "Now." This time, the shove came from the tip of his club, and she winced at the implication. She stepped forward, hesitant, but also understanding she had no choice. Prisoners had been beaten for less.

"If that bruya lover causes you any trouble, don't hold your punches."

Francisco's voice echoed behind her and she found herself throwing a glare over her shoulder before she could think better of it.

Rojo caught the look and she felt his club sharp and fast across her shoulder.

Pain shot down her arm and back, draining what little energy she had left in her. Embarrassingly, her knees hit the floor before she could catch herself, and even after, she could do nothing as her face smacked onto the cold, dirt ground. Where there would have once been defiance, there was a stark coldness throughout her body. A paralysis.

"Get up," Rojo said.

Alara tried to move her arms. Nothing. She tried to move her legs, but was met with the very same resistance. It was as though her body was no longer hers to control.

"Get *up*," Rojo repeated, this time yanking Alara up by her arm.

She settled back onto her feet, taking shallow, yet steady, breaths letting her mind take back control. A spare glance toward where Francisco stood saw a smug look painted over his face. She would have been mad if she had room to feel that way. Instead, she turned back around, clenching and unclenching her fists, confirming control over her faculties once again.

Then, without another word, she slid in through the crack. It was okay. She could do this. She could ignore the scratch of stone across her stomach and back as she moved. She grew up in the Haven. She'd crawled through tighter areas when she was younger.

Much younger.

As she took a deep breath, the walls pressed in around, gripping her chest like a vise.

"Take the torch, you idiot." Rojo's voice was closer than she expected and she carefully turned her head to see she was only about a foot from the opening. He held a small torch out for her, something to light her way. Instinctually, she felt herself pulling for the threads of her magia, wanting to reach out to the small flame. But there was nothing there except a hollow ache in her chest.

Biting her cheek until she tasted blood, she took the torch, maneuvering it painfully to her other hand. She continued the slow process of moving deeper into the earth. Every time her mind threatened to run off into the darkness, she remembered her time as a child, squeezing through the crevices in a fit of exploration. She'd done this before, and she could do it again.

It worked, keeping her breathing calm and steady until she came to a dead end in the crack, the wall coming together too closely for even her to pass.

"What do you see?"

"Rock," she said, biting out the words. She was too far for them to reach and she let the venom seep into her tone.

"Are there crystals or veins of anything in there?"

Alara was tempted to simply ignore the question, but she took a steadying breath and maneuvered her eyes around the opening as best she could. All she saw in the dim, dancing light of the flame was black stone.

"Nothing," she said.

Rojo cursed as Alara once again switched the torch to the other arm, shimmying out of the crack the way she had come.

Somehow the journey back felt longer, but finally, the torch was pulled from her hand and she came stumbling out of the crevice, knees shaking, drops of sweat darkening the dirt below her.

Before she could even catch her breath something else was placed in her hand.

"Be quick about it," Rojo said. "You don't want to be in there still when that wick runs out."

Alara's eyes focused on the object in her hands. It looked like a tall thin candle, but the wick burned fast. Too fast.

"What?"

"Take the damn thing and stick it back there as far as you can. All the way."

She looked back at the crevice she had just freed herself from and let out a groan of frustration. But she moved before Rojo or Francisco could react to the small bit of defiance.

It was almost easier slipping through the crevice this time, which she was all too happy about, as the wick on the small candle continued to burn down in the darkness. When she could no longer push forward, she wedged the candle between the rocks and pushed her way back. Somehow, she got faster each time.

As she exited the crevice, she noticed that the rest of the crew and guards had retreated. Understanding the urgency, she didn't question this, but joined them, feet moving quick now that she was out of the narrow space.

Just as she made it to where Rojo was standing, deep into the tunnel and around the corner, a roll of thunder coursed through the cave behind her, and the ground shook violently beneath her feet. She cursed as a stone fell from the ceiling, slamming into the ground just behind her. And then, as quickly as it came, it ended.

The rest of the group, guards and prisoners alike, were completely unfazed as they moved back toward the work area, picking up their pickaxes and shovels from the ground. The guards led the way with torches, shining a light on where there had once been a wall.

The crevice was gone along with the wall. Instead, it was replaced with a concave opening, large chunks of stone littering the area. The haulers moved without instruction, picking up the boulders and passing them over to the half-full carts further down the tunnel. She stood for several seconds, trying to understand what had just happened.

The candle had destroyed the tunnel wall, like a receptive bomb of air and fire, but without any magia. There was no magia, right? There couldn't be any magia down there.

And yet...

She knew the councilguard had been developing tools for blameless use beyond the spear and bow, but controlled explosions?

A sharp crack of pain coursed through her back and Alara felt herself collapsing to her knees again with a strangled gasp. The whip cracked a second time. She bit back the cry that sprang from her throat, ignoring the sharp cut of stones on her knees as she moved forward, away from the whip and Francisco behind her.

"Stop standing around gaping and get to work," he said, voice hot with anger.

Alara moved robotically as she clambered onto shaky legs. She grabbed the nearest stone, too heavy for her, but she struggled to wrap her arms around it nonetheless, dragging it along the ground and down the tunnel, toward a cart. She refused to look up to see where Francisco still stood, whip still in hand behind her.

She had met the man less than a handful of times in her life, yet he seemed to hate her so bitterly. Was it simply what she stood for that made him angry, or did he truly associate her with Emaru?

After what felt like an eternity, one of the male prisoners scooped up the boulder that Alara dragged along and dumped it into the cart without a word.

"Thank you," she said, under her breath, but he turned away without acknowledging her.

She continued her work, trying not to think of Emaru or the Haven or the Sunday dinners with her guardian. She was the reason she was down here—in more ways than one—and the thought left a sour taste in her mouth.

Instead, she focused on the pain in her back as she bent over another stone, on the blisters that ripped and bled on her hands, and on her simmering rage for the major and what his face might look like smashed in with a club.

If—when—she made it out of here, she was going to personally see that Francisco died, painfully and slowly.

Chapter 45

ARDO

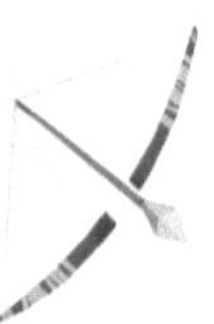

The day after their run-in with Major Francisco, Ardo and Quenti met in the plaza again. They didn't bother with secrecy now that Major Francisco knew *Lucía* and he were working together. And Ardo couldn't deny he appreciated sitting by the fountain and letting the wind blow a cool mist across his face. After years working in Cielo and the mountains of Sombria, Lejon's heat was killing him slowly. And after weeks of working in solitude and in secrecy, there was a relief to not being confined to dark alleys.

"What do we have to do today?" Quenti asked, not bothering with hi or hello as she practically threw herself onto the fountain ledge next to him.

"Good morning to you too, Lucía," he said, drawing out the name a little too long. The deadpan stare he got in return was worth the jab, though it didn't quite have the twinkle of humor he was looking for. "We need to discuss your dinner with the major."

"So the plan is still for me to walk straight into the pumisi's den. Should I show him my throat or play dead?"

It was Ardo's turn to give her a blank look, holding back the snide remarks he would have made had their relationship... well, existed at all.

"You're going to do neither. You're going to show him your teeth."

"So I get to stab him?"

"*Show* him your teeth," he emphasized. "Don't use them. You're going to pretend to be pumisi too, only a different kind."

"A different kind?"

"He already has a picture in his mind of how you work—of how you actively work to let other people underestimate you. So you're going to show your teeth, but you're still going to play nice. I'll do what I can to protect you."

"And I'm supposed to trust you?" she said, turning to face him. "Trust you to protect me from your boss."

"Ex-boss," he said.

"You still collect payments from him, don't you?"

Ardo couldn't argue with that. Sure, he may claim to be an ex-councilguard, but he was still fully employed and owned by the Council. But still...

"I'm undercover just as much as you are, war hero," he said.

"Except no one has ever questioned where my loyalties lie."

"Oh?" he said, eyebrows arching. "Did Alara know exactly where you stood with Sombria from day one?"

"I didn't hide it," she said. "It's not my fault she's a blind idiot. Which is exactly why I'm struggling to understand why I should trust you just because she does."

Ardo stood up with an exhausted exhale. This conversation was getting them nowhere. "Come with me."

He didn't wait for her to argue, and walked away immediately. He knew her curiosity wouldn't let her stay behind. Sure enough, when he was halfway across the plaza, he heard the pitter-patter of her footsteps fast behind him, catching up.

"Don't do that," she said.

"Do what?"

"Command me like I'm your soldier."

He turned down an alley, not looking at her. "It wasn't a command. It was a request. Besides, I think you'll like this one."

"Where are we going?"

"We're going to go somewhere you can hit me," he said. "Repeatedly."

The copse of half-dead trees was just as empty as it had been when he had sparred with Alara what had felt like months ago. Months ago in a different world, where she was free. The thought of her being stuck down in the mines was almost as oppressive as the heat, even under the shade of the trees.

He stopped when they came to the small clearing, tossing a small club at Quenti. She fumbled, trying to catch it.

"What in the underworld?"

"Fight me."

She looked at him like he had grown a second head. "I'm not Alara. I don't fight." She waved the club through the air with such an exasperated sigh he couldn't stop the laugh that bubbled up.

"Don't laugh at me," she snapped.

"Sorry, I'm just used to Alara getting excited every time she has a weapon in her hand."

"Alara has a problem," Quenti said. "She has *many* problems."

"You have a point," Ardo said, smirking. "But you're telling me you haven't fought *anyone*?"

"I don't fight as much as I just hit something when I have to."

"Well, there's a start. For now, don't worry about knowing how to fight. Just hit something."

He didn't need to explain further, Quenti lunged forward, swinging the club clumsily. He blocked it easily with his own, not bothering to parry the blow, but rather just let her readjust and hit again.

Her hits were all over the place, but easy to predict. She threw her entire body into each move, telegraphing what she'd do before she swung. But he had to give her credit for the strength behind each swing. She was only a couple inches shorter than him and she used her weight to her advantage. With some training, she'd probably be a formidable soldier.

"I don't trust you, you know," she said, after a particularly hard swing.

"I know I haven't earned your trust yet, but I am trying. You're Alara's friend and I wouldn't do anything to hurt her," he said. "I think that's one thing you can trust."

"You did." She swung her club to the left. He blocked it without trying.

"I did what?"

"You hurt her. Back in the Haven when you fought against us. I know how much that hurt her."

"And you don't think it hurt me?"

"I don't care what it did to you," Quenti said with another hard swing.

This time, Ardo did parry, throwing her off balance and to the side. Despite the anger in her face, Ardo couldn't help but smile.

He'd spent countless nights wondering about Alara. Wondering if their friendship had truly meant nothing to her, and that it was worth nothing more than a romp through the woods with the bruyas. To hear Quenti say that filled a part of him that he hadn't realized was empty.

"What's so funny?" Quenti said, breath heavy.

"Nothing," he said. "Keep it coming. You still have a long way to go."

He lost track of time as Quenti continued her barrage, but his arms were aching by the time she finally dropped her club, knees collapsing under her.

He let his own arms relax and sat down across from her, silent and waiting.

"I hate not knowing what's going on down in the mines," she said after a while. "I hate that we don't even know if they're okay or what they're doing."

He could only nod his head, his thoughts straying too close to Alara and sending a sharp stab through his chest.

"And you know what pisses me off more?" she asked, looking at Ardo as if expecting an answer. He only gave a small shrug and waited. "Khuna chose this. She decided to step out into that square and get herself captured because Runeo was being an idiot. And once again I was left behind. I should have gone after her. I could have. Instead I just stood there and watched her get arrested. And now I can't do anything."

"You are doing things," he said softly. "You're playing the role as spy. Do you realize how brave that is?"

Ardo wondered if Quenti was even aware of the tears flooding down her face. She didn't bother to wipe them away, instead letting them run across her lips and drip onto the ground.

Finally, she met his eyes, her lips pressed together tightly.

"It doesn't feel brave being ordered around by that man. Sitting around, 'Yes sir'ing him, and attending his stupid dinner is enough to make me sick. If it were up to blameless like him, we'd be wiped from the face of this country."

"Not everyone—" Ardo started, feeling a shame eating away at his chest.

"You don't need to defend yourself to me," Quenti said. "I know you wouldn't, if only because you're madly in love with Alara."

Ardo opened his mouth to argue, but she quickly continued. "But you can't deny that there are enough of them out there set on taking away our power. This whole thing started because I wanted to run off to the forest and live in peace. And they just couldn't let me. They dragged me back to the Haven. They burned down Arbol. Yet, they say we're the threat."

Her voice cracked, the tenseness suddenly draining from her as her shoulders slumped.

Ardo watched the shift, feeling a fraction of the helplessness she felt. He'd spent his entire life adamant that the blameless and magia users were the same. That it took both to make up a complete Sombria. It was what he'd been taught all his life and was a law he'd hoped to one day enforce. But what experience did the bruyas and mages face? Bruyas are told from day one that their existence is a mistake—that there was only one path, and that was the path to El'dyo. And Alara? Alara spent all of her life wallowing in self-hatred.

He had no words for Quenti. No way to express how he felt. Instead, he pulled Quenti to him, wrapping her in a hug. She allowed it, muscles tensing and then softening.

"I know that none of this is really your fault, you know," Quenti said.

"Maybe part of it is though," Ardo said. "As a councilguard, I've fed into this system for most of my life. Maybe had I seen things in a different way, I would have been able to help Alara before. Maybe I could have been someone she could have told these secrets to. I could have been more than an obstacle to her the last time we met."

"I don't know," Quenti said, laughter in her voice. "She's pretty stubborn."

Ardo smiled. "Point being, I'm on your side now."

Quenti's own smile slackened, as though reminded of a cold truth. "You're on Emaru's side."

"Senye Emaru is on your side too. She wants peace between the mages and the blameless. Things are changing in Sombria. And when the dust settles, she wants to make sure there is balance again."

Quenti was silent for several long seconds, her gaze intense as if studying him. "And when the wind blows the wrong direction? When it comes down to blameless versus magia, whose side will you be on?"

"It won't," Ardo said. "I wouldn't be here, helping you all and putting myself at serious risk of being caught for treason if I didn't think peace was possible."

She shook her head. He could see the stubbornness in her face, the same cold, hard determination that Alara had when she wasn't going to back down.

"You're not answering the question," she said. "I'm saying *if* you had to choose? If you have to go against your self-interests, what's to stop you from giving up and betraying us?"

"Alara." The truth slipped from his lips before he could question it.

Quenti didn't look surprised, only validated.

"I won't betray you—any of you," Ardo said, "because I won't betray Alara, no matter what that means for me. I have to believe there is a world where we can be together, in peace." The words were earnest—almost embarrassingly so.

Quenti didn't respond one way or another, letting the hot breeze fill the empty air.

"We should go meet with the others," he said. "We need to make sure you get out of the major's home alive. And then, I want a drink."

Quenti nodded, standing from the ground and dusting herself

off. She shone with sweat from their fight, but already seemed calmer and more assured. She didn't wait for Ardo to collect the clubs before she was marching out of the clearing and back toward town.

"Come on, then," she said. "If you want to create this little world of yours, we don't have time to stand around and talk."

CHAPTER 46

QUENTI

Quenti wasn't sure she felt any better about the plan or her situation after meeting with the others.

She would still be alone in Major Francisco's home, hoping to Sol the pumisi wouldn't scratch out her throat.

But it did bring with it the potential to simplify their mission. With Major Francisco being a high-ranking military officer from a rich family, there was a chance that they may find receptives within his estate, and with it an opportunity to forgo their long-term, overly-elaborate scheme to snag receptives in transit.

All of that amounted to more pressure on Quenti to perform. Quenti, who wanted nothing more than to run into the mountains and never deal with another blameless again.

So when Ardo declared he needed a drink, Quenti followed him without so much as a question. Between Cruz's silent contemplation and Dante's brusque negativity, there wasn't much in the way of pleasant company. While the twins weren't so bad, they were still recovering from their injuries in the mines, and didn't have much to contribute.

Somehow, the sole blameless became the one Quenti became the most interested in speaking with—if nothing else, simply being around.

The two didn't even bother leaving the bar they resided in, simply slipping through the kitchen and into the main dining area. The smell of ferment and oily food was even thicker out here, but Quenti tried not to focus on it. The lighting was dim and the press of bodies allowed her to feel invisible as she and Ardo slid into a pair of chairs at a long table.

He wore his councilguard uniform, but Quenti settled for a scarf wrapped tightly around her hair and face, hoping to not draw attention as Lucía tonight. Part of her wondered if it would be wiser to hide in plain sight as the war hero, as it would at least save her from the anxiety of being discovered as another bruya, but she was glad for the disguise when she counted at least a dozen other off-duty councilguards drinking and talking around the room.

"Wine or ferment?" Ardo asked, waving down a server.

"Wine," Quenti said quickly. He nodded, ordering them a small bottle before turning back to her.

"You're going to be okay," he said.

"I know."

"Are you sure? Because you look almost green."

"I just don't like the smell of bars much," she said, shrugging and hoping he'd drop the subject.

"How long have you and Khuna been together?" he asked, after a few beats of awkward silence.

Quenti couldn't help but roll her eyes. "Can we stop with the small talk now?"

"You didn't step out of that closet to talk?"

"No, my honorable councilguard. I came here to drink."

She smiled as the bartender flew in with a bottle of honey wine and she reached for it before Ardo had a chance, pouring them both two large glasses.

It was sweeter than she preferred, almost sickly so, but she took two deep gulps of the stuff before setting her glass down.

"Now that was better than any conversation we could have," she said, giving him a bright smile.

"Just don't make yourself sick," Ardo said. "I don't know how I'd explain Lucía getting drunk at a bar in Lejon and tossing her dinner up on the server."

"I'm sure Lucía can hold her liquor."

"Yes," he said. "I'm sure *she* can. But how well can *you*?"

Quenti made sure to exaggerate her eye roll, but took a smaller sip all the same.

They fell into a not quite companionable silence after that, both nursing their drinks and letting their eyes wander over the crowd as it shifted and moved, Quenti's ears wandering in and out of the various uninteresting conversations around them. More often than not, variations of complaints of a hard day's work or the blistering dryness that came with Lejon.

Before long, the couple who had been sitting next to them at the table was replaced by another pair of off-duty councilguards that made Quenti shift uneasily. She pulled her scarf down lower across her forehead as if she might be able to disappear behind it.

As her ears again wandered in and out of conversations, the sound of Major Francisco's name tugged at them, making her heart jump. She couldn't stop herself from casting a glance to the side. They were both men, their uniforms indicating lower ranks, though she didn't remember which ones. And they were engaged in what seemed to be a heated argument, heads bent together conspiratorially.

"I swear I'll kill the pig myself one day," one of them whispered.

"Don't joke about that, Nico. You're going to get yourself arrested and locked in the mines with the bruyas."

"I'll be taken in one day on false charges either way. Did you hear they arrested Trinidad's family under suspicion of aiding his escape from the Haven? No proof needed."

"They're coming after blameless now?"

"If they're associated with mages or bruyas," Nico said. "I got word that my cousin's on the run now after they tried to arrest him."

"The wind mage? Shit. For what?"

"Are you not listening? For nothing."

Quenti sipped at her drink. Across the table, Ardo raised an eyebrow at her. She caught his gaze before slowly moving her eyes to her left side where the two guards spoke.

"...where he is?"

"No," one of the guards responded, "but I don't blame him for running. The Council's started to lose its mind, Sol, curse them."

Quenti recognized the venom in his tone and she saw the woman standing just a foot behind him turn with a look of open disgust.

"What did you just say?" she asked, lip curled up. Quenti's back went rigid along with the two guards'.

"None of your business, *civilian*," Nico said, loudly. "This is military talk."

"You curse the Council and speak Sol's name and you call me civilian? You're a shame to that uniform."

"Mind your own business," Nico's companion said, trying to turn back to their drinks and their table. But the woman yanked the guard's shoulder back.

"Anyone who curses the Council is my business."

More faces turned their way, curious at the rising commotion, and three others stood behind the woman, their faces twisted with aggression.

"What in El'dyo's name is going on over here?" a councilguard said, walking between the two groups.

"This bruya lover is speaking treason," the woman said.

Quenti's hand clenched her glass and her eyes were wide as she looked at Ardo, trying to communicate—anything that might get them away from this situation. But she couldn't read the look he was giving her or understand the wave of his hand.

"What?" she said, the word hissing out from behind clenched teeth.

His lips moved in something akin to words, but she could only guess at what he was saying. Her blank stare must have conveyed as much because a second later, he shook his head.

"Sergeant Canchaya and I," he said, standing up, voice raised, "have been sitting here the entire time and we didn't hear anything but a few drunken ramblings."

Quenti's entire body tensed as all eyes turned on them. She wanted to send a dagger straight into his neck, but instead she unwrapped the scarf from her head and turned, letting Lucía take control of her face.

"Sergeant Canchaya?" the councilguard said, coming to attention immediately.

No one likely recognized her face—and why would they?—but with the onslaught of hushed whispers, it was clear they recognized the name. Quenti tensed her jaw, but stood. There was no point in staying hidden now.

"They made some comment about bruyas forcing the Council's hands and cursed them for it," she said. "But I heard no talks of treason."

"I know what I heard," the woman said, voice low.

"Perhaps," Quenti said, eyes narrowed on the woman, "some of us have had a little too much to drink."

The councilguard hesitated for only a moment, looking between Quenti and the woman whose face grew redder by the second.

"I—" she sputtered out, but before she could finish the councilguard had grabbed her elbow and led her out of the bar, her companions trailing behind her, looking pale and confused.

Quenti turned to the two loose-tongued councilguards who sat beside them, both faces a shocking white as her eyes focused on each of them in turn.

"Both of you," she said, "out back, now."

To their credit, they listened, jumping to attention. Quenti could get used to the obedience.

Ardo raised an eyebrow as she passed him, following behind the two other guards without question. They walked through the bar, the others stepping out of their way as they passed. She led them through the kitchen and out to the back alley beyond. The sound dropped away immediately as the door closed behind them.

"Nico, was it?" she said, turning on the taller of the two. His eyes were wide, but after a few seconds he finally nodded. "And your name?"

"Manny," he said, voice choked.

"Stop looking at me like I'm going to murder you," she said, annoyed at the wide-eyed stares they were giving.

"Perhaps you should stop looking at them like you're *planning* on murdering them, Sergeant," Ardo said from behind her.

"What in S—El'dyo's name were you two thinking in there?" she said, finger wagging in a way her mother's used to when she was *disappointed*. But she couldn't help it. These two blameless guards were going to get themselves killed, and all because they couldn't hold their tongues in public. "How stupid do you have to be to talk about the Council like that, in public? Now, of all times?"

Nico and Manny looked no less confused at her reprimand. They looked to Ardo, as if he might explain.

"She has a point," he said simply.

"Go home," she said finally. "And don't do that shit in public again, or it may be your last drink."

"Yes, Sergeant," Nico said, voice hesitant. But he followed her directions quickly, grabbing Manny by the shoulder and half-walking, half-running down the alley. She watched them until they disappeared.

"How many stupid councilguards are there?" she said, rounding on Ardo.

"More than we'd ever guess," he admitted. "Well, that ruined my buzz. I'm going to bed."

"Same." Quenti turned back to the door to return to the small closet she now called home, but before she could reach the handle, she threw a small smile over her shoulder. "Quick thinking back there, by the way. It was stupid. Kinda like them."

The right side of Ardo's mouth raised into a lopsided grin. "There's a lot of us out there. I promise." With that, he followed the other two into the dark.

CHAPTER 47

QUENTI

Quenti's stomach churned as the l'lamaga-drawn carriage pulled up in front of the large, stucco hacienda, its verdant garden and sprawling orchard laid out like a painting. It was the most green she had seen since entering Lejon, and she wondered where they got the water to feed the land to such perfection. Major Francisco may have come from a long line of war heroes, but as Ardo told her, he was still an army man, raised and bred. Shouldn't he eschew such extravagances for a bedroll and tent?

She was learning a lot about the councilguards and the system during her time here, though she still hadn't quite gotten over the two idiots from the bar the other night. Where were they now and how long would it take before they got themselves killed? The major would have gladly done the honors, she was sure.

As the carriage came to a halt, Ardo gave her a smile that she thought might be meant to be reassuring, but it only came across as grim. He was slumped in the shadowy corner of the carriage, Mena across from him, looking tired but determined.

Quenti gave them both a nod. She was about to open the door when it swung forward, Dante giving a small bow on the other side.

"Sergeant," he said, with a lopsided smile.

"This is ridiculous," she said under her breath as she stepped down, begrudgingly allowing him to help her.

"Why feed your people when you can water your garden?" Dante said. "It's the Council's new way."

"You're a fool if you think this is *new*," Quenti said. "What rock have you been sleeping under?

Ardo only gave a small chuckle from his seat in the carriage behind her. He was tucked into the shadows, hidden from prying eyes.

"He brings with him a new low," Dante said in a rare show of aggression toward someone Quenti hated. "Little Francisco may be a prized soldier, but that doesn't change the fact that he's nothing more than an opportunist. He operates while safely ensconced in his pretty painted walls, all the while sleeping on his wool bed at night."

The bitterness in his voice was raw. It was as though he held a personal grudge against the major. For once, it was an anger she was happy to have on her side.

"I know you want to prove yourself to Senye Cruz and the rest," Quenti said. Even she couldn't help but notice his constant need for approval from the former councilwoman. "But don't do anything stupid."

"Do I look like those idiots in the mines to you?" he said, staring straight into Quenti's eyes, as if she were responsible for what had happened.

She glared daggers back at him, but almost out of pure stubbornness, he refused to look away.

"Don't worry about me," he said. "I know how to follow through with a mission when someone else is on the line. Besides, it doesn't end here. We need *everyone* for what lies ahead. For now, just worry about yourself."

"I've got that covered."

"Good. Then don't get caught." Dante said those last words with a slamming of the door. As he climbed back into the front of the carriage, Ardo's head poked out.

"I'll echo his sentiments," Ardo said. "But in a nicer way. Stay safe. Stay alive."

"That goes for you too."

"Hey, I'm not *really* an ex-councilguard, remember?" he said with a smirk as he handed her a handbag that housed her forged documents. And then the carriage pulled away, into the darkness and toward where the stables resided. From there, they'd carry out their part of the already dangerous mission.

At the very least, the carriage seemed to start them off on the right foot.

They had acquired it from a particularly friendly merchant with the help of Ardo's uniform and wallet. Ardo thought it would be more legitimate to show up at Francisco's house with an actual carriage rather than by foot. Now looking up at the opulent hacienda with its sprawling garden and intricately carved balconies, she was glad for the advice. No one had been out there to greet her, but her arrival had been visible to the doorman dozens of feet away. If she had simply sauntered up to the estate after hiking through the desert landscape, she was sure Major Francisco would hear about it later. But that didn't make the sight of the elaborate estate any easier to approach.

She tugged at the tunic of her uniform, feeling out of place.

She almost wished Ardo had stayed with her—to have the comfort of having someone nearby who knew her. But the emotion was fleeting, as the desire was quickly replaced by anger. She didn't need a blameless guard to protect her.

I am a bruya.

She didn't dare say the words out loud, but she repeated the sentence in her mind, a mantra with every beat of her heart. She could do this.

The sand and gravel crunched beneath her feet as she walked, the boots making it difficult to feel the ground—a sensation she wasn't accustomed to. She missed her sandals and her skirts, but she let the uniform of the soldier remind her of who she was. She was Lucía: sergeant and war hero for the Council. When Lucía walked, she *needn't* feel the pebbles beneath her feet, just as Major Francisco didn't notice the lives he clambered over to remain perched at the top of his little mountain. That was who she needed to be.

She tucked Quenti—the bruya and rebel—neatly away, letting her anger and hate for the Council stay there, unacknowledged, with no way to endanger the mission at hand. She focused instead on being Lucía. A warm smile came to her face just as the neatly dressed man opened the door with a small bow.

"Lucía Canchaya," she said, her voice firmer than she expected.

"Of course," he said with a nod. "The major is eagerly expecting your arrival."

She didn't know whether she should be happy or terrified. Either way, she smiled back as he waved her through the small atrium and back out into the courtyard beyond.

A large, carved staircase twisted up and around to the second floor. Trees and flowers blossomed just as verdant and bright here within the confines of the house. They turned left, following a staircase, and Quenti noticed the tiles beneath her feet were covered in elaborate, hand-painted plants.

She also noticed, with a satisfied smile, the number of receptives glowing in various parts of the house. She noted the few tucked into planters and vases, realizing the lush green of the estate might not be attained through hard work alone. The lights also were set with receptives, flickering on with colorful glows as the sun dipped low enough to leave shadows stretching along the walls.

They passed through a wide arch behind the stairs and into a large dining hall, where music filled the air. Even in the enclosed space, a steady and soft breeze blew through the room, and Quenti couldn't help but roll her eyes at the receptives hanging in the open windows executing the work.

"Lucía," Major Francisco said, standing from the carved chair at the head of the table. His was larger and more complex in its design, but even the other chairs set around the table were carefully carved to look like birds and palms rising up from the ground. It was an extravagant and ridiculous detail. "So nice of you to join us."

He motioned to the others as he spoke, and Quenti let her eyes drift across the other guests. This so-called party he had described was thus far only five others. All men, all as tall as her or taller, all dressed in formal wear, well beyond anything she had ever seen in her village growing up or even in the Haven during her short stint. Perhaps her uniform hadn't been the best choice for outfits, though she decided Lucía didn't care for formality.

The men sat with a mixture of gold-colored wines and pipes, emitting swirling smoke into the air, only for it to be softly blown away by the receptive-created breeze.

Major Francisco looked just as ridiculous as the others, draped in a cape that covered a heavily embroidered tunic that hung to his knees.

"Everyone, welcome Sergeant Lucía Canchaya," he said. "She's in Lejon for a short time and was kind enough to honor us with her presence this evening."

In turn, he motioned to each man as he introduced them. There was a head Council judge, an investigator for internal corruption, two colonels, and a man from Rimpia with a position that Quenti hadn't even heard of, but she could only assume was associated with the receptives. She also knew there was no way she'd be able to remember any of their names, and hoped she wouldn't be put in a position to call on them. Regardless, there was no denying the influence that practically oozed from within the walls of this estate.

The major had put together a dinner for some of the most important people in Lejon, if not Sombria, and it was enough to make Quenti vomit. Right after she passed out.

The youngest of the men, the man from Rimpia, looked around the age of her father, his hair only just graying at the temples. But he held himself with the importance of someone who knew his place. Even pretending to be in her twenties, she was young enough to be every one of these men's daughters. What must they think of her?

I am a bruya.

No.

I am Lucía Canchaya. I am a war hero. I am a sergeant. I am blameless.

She straightened her shoulders as she moved forward, taking the proffered seat between one of the colonels and the judge, and she just hoped her smile didn't look as wobbly as it felt.

She passed on the offered wine and tobak, stating she preferred to keep a clean mind while on the job. The sweet and smoky smell of the hall was still enough to make her lightheaded. She had heard of the imported leaves before, but her father had preferred to spend his money on ferment, and she had never been so close to the pungent smelling mixture, even in spite of the receptive's breeze.

"The great Sergeant Canchaya!"

"I never expected to meet the famed war hero."

"She's so young. I have daughters older than her."

"What's a war hero doing in Lejon?"

They spoke of her as though she wasn't there, and it was only the Judge, Reymundo, who directed a question at her.

"Still only a sergeant after all this time," he said. "Are you not ambitious enough to petition for a promotion?"

"I am happy with where I'm at," she said. "And as your friend pointed out," she said, trying not to show her annoyance, "I am still young. There is plenty of time for bigger and better opportunities."

"And how old are you?" one of the men said.

The colonel, Quenti thought, though his name escaped her.

His pipe hung loosely from his lips as he spoke. "I may have an unmarried son around your age."

Quenti couldn't stop her eyebrows from arching up and the flush of her cheeks. "Oh—I'm... not interested in relationships."

Khuna's face flashed in her mind and she felt her gut clench. But the answer felt right and true. How could someone like Lucía ever focus on relationships?

The colonel—Colonel Opiz, Quenti remembered—only shrugged, unaffected by the rebuke.

"I, for one," Major Francisco said, cutting into the conversation for the first time, "would love to hear the story of how the great Lucía saved Sombria from the bruya threat. From what you've said, the rumors we've heard aren't the most accurate portrayal of what happened, no?"

A murmur of agreement echoed through the room and Quenti felt herself lose all the color in her face. She had expected this. Ardo had coached her to expect this. But her stomach twisted inside all the same as she sipped from a glass of water in front of her to bide her time.

"As you said, the rumors have made me out to be a hero," she said. "And I wouldn't want to break the illusion."

"Nonsense! Hearing it from your own lips will only make the story more legendary, I'm sure," Reymundo said.

She gave them a wan smile and took another sip of water.

"It's not a very inspiring one," she started, trying not to sound too rehearsed in her telling.

"I was only a corporal at the time, helping lead a small group under my sergeant. We were down patrolling the southern border after a number of bruya sightings from the locals. It was more of a training exercise than anything. The Council was sending down another larger platoon in a few days, but we were to gather information on the bruya movements and plans east of Attalea."

She paused, taking another drink of water and allowing the men to wait for her. She felt a small thrill of power as they watched.

"Things didn't go to plan. We ran into a bruya rebel group just east of where the rivers Sur and Arrib merge." Quenti was all too glad of being able to picture the spot, just north of where Arbol used to lie, a thought that sent a twinge of pain through her heart that must have shown on her face.

"Bruya rebel," Reymundo said with a scoff. "A bit redundant, don't you think?"

Quenti blinked, fighting irritation, but also trying to remember her place in the lie. She managed to find a smile in the confusion. "Yes, that's true, I suppose. Anyhow... where was I?"

"It must be difficult to recall," Major Francisco said, face showing none of the empathy he was expressing.

"Yes. And as you've all heard by now, the bruyas attacked, unprovoked. We were forced to respond. My platoon was only lucky that we had the higher ground. There were twice as many bruyas to our mages, and my archers were able to take out a good number before they crested the hill. As you know, bruyas are poorly trained." Quenti had to stifle a swallow as her mind escaped to the destruction of Arbol, and the bruyas pathetically fighting the councilguards amid the flames. "Our mages still had the advantage and our blameless with their weapon skills were unmatched."

She bit her tongue as she paused again, emotion choking her

throat. She had feared not expressing enough emotion in this story's retelling, but now she was in danger of breaking down in a manner unbefitting a decorated soldier.

"We thought victory would come easy. But we were unprepared for another wave of bruyas that showed up. I never even saw the sergeant fall. I was focused on my own fight. It came down to me and two bruyas. I took a nasty wound to my side."

She lifted her tunic to show the jagged scar left behind from her fight in the Haven and wondered if Ardo would be annoyed or proud of the ad lib.

"I killed the last bruya and passed out. When I came to, I was in the forest surrounded by a mountain of dead bruyas and my own soldiers. I was lucky a hunter from Attalea ran into me as I was trying to make it back to the town."

She stopped there, giving a tight smile. "As I said, not a hero, only a survivor."

"Huh," the judge said. "You were right. That wasn't much of a story."

"Now, now," Major Francisco said, a glass balanced lightly in his hand. "You seem to forget that Lucía isn't a trained storyteller like some of those war-cry profiteers who spread the tales. Besides, every soldier knows how hard it is to share one's exploits."

The colonels in the room grunted in agreement.

"Too true," Colonel Opiz said. "You can always tell a liar from the glee with which they speak."

"And, at the end of the day," Quenti said, finding her voice, "all I did was survive. Nothing more."

"So humble," Major Francisco said, wearing a smile Quenti didn't trust. "You should enjoy the acknowledgement of your gifts. A toast, to our Lucía, here."

He raised his glass, and the others followed his lead. Quenti raised her own glass of water with a queasy smile.

"Now," he said, as though bored with the conversation already. "I did want to sort something out before evening meal, and I wondered if you could help me."

"Help you?"

"Yes, I sent a runner to Cielo to ensure we were allowing you everything you needed for success in your mission—you know, for the receptive escort? Yet, when they returned today, there was no record of such orders anywhere to be found in the weaves." His eyes flickered over to Quenti, piercing her. "Strange, isn't it?"

CHAPTER 48

QUENTI

"Major," Quenti said, slow as to keep her voice steady. "Are you implying something?"

"Of course not, *Lucía—*" he said, voice just as careful and controlled, pausing on her name in a way that made her stomach twist. "I just want to clear up any confusion."

"I have my documents with me, if you would like to check again," she said, lips pursed. She didn't think she needed to pretend to be unbothered by this interruption to the evening. "Perhaps your runner was mistaken or spoke to the wrong people. You know as well as I do how messy the Haven gets with its weavework."

Francisco gave a noncommittal hum. "Of course, but I'd prefer that we clear this all up once and for all—since we're all here."

Quenti eyed the group of men around her. The rankings of those around her, as well as the investigator had seemed odd. They weren't just guests. They were witnesses.

She grabbed the bag at her feet, happy to have the table in front of her to hide her shaking hands. The small page of forged woven tapestry was there for just the occasion. She hoped the fact that there were absolutely no matches within the Haven wouldn't ruin the evening.

As talented as Senye Cruz and Ardo had been at forging everything, there was no way for them to plant them within the records system kept within the Haven. All the same, Quenti set the page on the table, pushing it toward Francisco, forcing him to lean over to snatch it up like a hungry monkey.

"Rogelio," he said, motioning to the man who had answered the door earlier. "Take this to Leon and have him check them with our records in house."

The man gave a small bow and took the tapestry without question. All Quenti could do was watch them disappear around the doorframe.

"You keep a library in house?" Quenti couldn't help but say.

"What better place to ensure their safety?"

It had answered one question: what had happened to the weaves of all the orders of the soldiers on base? They had spent hours, but were unable to find them in the Weave and Tapestry Library. It was why they couldn't plant her own.

The hall was silent, everyone having watched the exchange with only muted curiosity.

Two other men, larger than necessary for house servants, had taken Rogelio's place at the door back into the courtyard.

"Let us drink while we wait," Reymundo said, the first to finally break the uneasy silence. He poured himself another generous helping from the decanter at the center of the table, motioning for Quenti. "Come, Lucía, you must try a taste of this, at least. It's honeyed wine imported from the Xacanillo region of eastern Berde, just beyond the Ruinedlands. I insist."

She forced a smile as the man tipped some of the wine into a glass, pushing it toward her even as she shook her head. Major Francisco's sharp eyes never left her, as if waiting for her to break into a run. As tempting as it was, another, more bitter, part of her wanted to sit here and watch the man squirm. Watch him question his decision to confront her, even if it was the correct one.

"If you insist, Judge." She grabbed the glass delicately and made a show of smelling the aromatic drink. It smelled sweet, and she was happy the honey-scent blocked out any scent of alcohol that usually made her stomach churn at the memory of her father. She took a sip and surprised even herself with the exhale that escaped her lips. "This is quite delicious. I don't often take time to indulge in drink. My travels don't give me the chance to learn of these fancy imported goods I'm sure you're all used to. My work has me relegated to no further than the outskirts of Sombria."

"Well," Major Francisco said. "You're clearly speaking with the wrong people. Pull on the right levers, like the indelible Judge Reymundo here, and even you can find gems like this in the darkest of *mines*." He smiled and pointed to one of the colonels, who chuckled at the play on words, though even Quenti could tell it was one of an anxious underling.

The judge also followed up with a good-humored laugh of his own, but Major Francisco's eyes narrowed on her as he took another sip from his glass.

The minutes ticked by with growing unease and forced small talk among the group. As each second passed, an anxiety spread among them, that their little party would be ruined by something much more serious. And yet, everyone remained civil—by blameless standards, at least. It seemed as though the major had crafted this little scenario all on his own.

He remained silent, his gaze still fixed and untrusting on her, every moment his men were away with her forged orders. But she continued to smile and engage in conversation with the other men at the table, not wanting to sit in silence and count the seconds by her heartbeats.

As she was reassessing her plan of not sprinting for the door and praying for the best, Rogelio returned, floppy tapestry in hand. His face was blank and gave nothing away as he leaned down and whispered into Major Francisco's ear. Her breath stuttered in her chest and she found herself holding it as she waited. But, waiting for what?

Rogelio stopped speaking for a moment, and in it, Quenti thought she was finished. But the old man simply turned his head to the side, let out two stifled coughs, and continued.

Quenti took a deep breath. If she was going to make any difference in this final moment before she was inevitably found out, this would be it. But what was she going to do, jump on him? She didn't have so much as a ceremonial staff to threaten him with.

At last, Major Francisco nodded, sending Rogelio away. He looked at Quenti, the tips of his ear turning a dark shade of pink.

"It appears," he said, "that I was mistaken." He looked up, eyes meeting Lucía. "Or, at the very least, the sloth-like nature of our records-keeping system was mistaken."

She tried not to show her relief as she nodded. "Well, of course they were." She sank deeper into her seat, taking the first enjoyable swig of her honey wine that evening.

"I apologize, of course, for the disruption of our evening," he said, the tinge in his cheeks showing a genuineness to his apology that she didn't expect. His gaze then turned to his guests and then back to her. "But I am sure you understand. We can never be too careful in these times. After what happened in the Haven, there's no more denying the prevalence of bruyas with cursed magia within the realm."

Quenti tasted blood on her tongue as she bit down hard. "I'm all too glad to see your caution at work. Men like you are the reason Sombria remains safe."

Major Francisco didn't smile, but there was a smallest shift in his expression that Quenti couldn't mistake for anything other than pride. "Then you, of all people will appreciate this," he said. "Just yesterday, I received news of a large civilization of bruyas wiped out south of Attalea. What are the chances they were the same savages who attacked your platoon?"

She felt the blood drain from her face. "The Council was able to eradicate an entire civilization of bruyas? No easy task."

"I only wish the Council could take credit," he said, sighing heavily as if the words truly pained him. "It was a *wildfire*, of all things, that destroyed them."

"A wildfire?" she asked, keeping her breath level. "I thought the Council had made moves against the group of bruyas who caused all that trouble in the Haven."

Major Francisco shrugged, looking at the other men for any confirmation or argument, but both colonels shook their heads.

"If the Council or councilguards were behind it, I didn't hear anything about it," Colonel Opiz said. "And I'd like to think I would have. I'm usually stationed in Cielo with Apukispay General Juanez."

"Strange," Quenti said, chest tight, "so the rumors I heard must have been mistaken. So, how did the Council find out about this?"

"The fire was seen all the way in Attalea and Hurazon. It was reported to the Council and they sent a platoon down to ensure it didn't spread to the villages. They found an entire city built into the trees, burnt to a crisp."

Colonel Opiz gave a laugh. "They were living in the trees? El'dyo, bruyas really are nothing but brutish monkeys."

Quenti flinched as her hand clenched sharply into her leg under the table.

"Were there any survivors?" she asked, barely able to bite the words out.

"Not from what I heard," Major Francisco said, leaning back in his seat, "but they found graves housing charred remains. I'd bet coin that this was some sort of in-fighting between bruya tribes. You don't live in the trees without some sort of measures against this sort of thing."

"Oh, my dear Francisco," Judge Reymundo said. "I think you give the bruyas too much credit."

"How else can we stay one step ahead?" he said. "The day we underestimate them is the day we lose."

"Then," Quenti said, suppressing a scream in the back of her throat, "we are blessed by El'dyo to have a man of your intelligence among our ranks." It was all she could do not to leap at him and claw his eyes out like a wild animal, but even she knew that would solve nothing.

Before anyone else could speak, a red-faced Rogelio pattered into the room. He ignored the others, going straight to Major Francisco and whispering something into his ear.

Quenti's fear was bitter on her tongue as she waited, expecting the men to look at her, accusations ready. But the major only shook his head, whispered a few sharp words in response, and sent Rogelio back on his way. Even as the man raised his glass, ignoring the interruption to their conversation, Quenti took a deep breath and tried to swallow back the bile in her throat.

"Salud!" he said. "To the eradication of the vermin that haunt our realm."

"And may the blameless return to their former glory," Colonel Opiz added, raising his own glass.

The others followed suit, Quenti feeling stiff as she repeated the words. She realized for the first time that she was surrounded, not just by some of the most powerful men in Sombria, but blameless men who didn't just hate bruyas, but all magia users. The irony of them sitting in a house full of receptives was not lost on her, and she had to bite back the sneer from her face.

I am Lucía Canchaya. I am blameless.

"May Sombria rise to greatness once more," she said, sipping from her own glass.

CHAPTER 49

ARDO

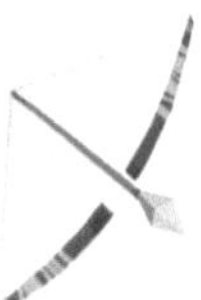

Ardo was happy to see that, despite the opulence of the estate, there wasn't a legion of staff wandering the grounds. Once Dante had dropped the carriage off at the stables, leaving it in the hands of a half-attentive l'lamaga handler, Ardo had joined him in the back gardens. The estate stretched out behind the house in a maze of paths and a personal training field larger than some of those he had seen on bases around Sombria.

"Get over here," Dante said, half hiss, half whisper. There was a wide trellis along the wall of the house, which stretched to the second floor, only a few feet from a balcony.

Ardo watched as the man started to climb, the rustle of leaves and wood creaking beneath his feet. He waited until Dante had both feet on the balcony before he followed, trying to ignore the shaking of the trellis with every move. When he finally made it over the railing, he couldn't help the release of breath that escaped him. He grimaced, trying not to think about the fact that they'd have to climb back down.

Dante peeked through the door before waving him over.

"It's empty, but the door's locked."

Ardo nodded, pulling his picks from his pocket. "If only I could tell my old sergeant I was using the skills he taught me to break into a major's house."

"You and me both," Dante said with a shifty smile. "Only I would revel in shoving it in his face. Just focus on getting us in there."

Ardo rolled his eyes, hidden from view as he crouched at the door, but he followed the instructions, focusing on the ticking of the tumblers in the lock. With a final *cah-chick*, the door swung open and he gave a small bow.

"As you wish," he said, happy to see the other man scoff at his tone.

Dante pushed past him without comment and into the room beyond. Ardo followed, jaw clenched. What in Sombria had made this man so dead serious?

The room beyond was a guest bedroom. There was a bed and vanity, but the closet was empty of clothes and the shelves devoid of any personal effects. Yet, the room was bigger than any Ardo had ever owned or lived in.

"This is ridiculous," he said, the words slipping from his lips like a sigh.

"Not the sort of accommodations you're used to?" Dante said, running his hands along the wall where a receptive was set in to light the torches.

"I was happy enough not to have to share a bunk," Ardo said. "And you?" Dante was one to happily condescend to any one of the group's opinion, but never seemed to share much about himself.

"When I was younger, I would have coveted a place like this," Dante said. "But now, I can only see the waste. Think of the families that could be fed with the metal and receptives in this one room. Even in the Haven, the receptives used were for public places, enriching the lives of those for the greater good. But this? This is pure opulence."

For once, Ardo agreed. "Well, in this case it's lucky for us. Otherwise missing receptives might be noticed right away."

"You read my mind. And from the look of it, this room isn't exactly used regularly," Dante said with a flourish as he used his knife to wedge the first receptive out of the wall. "Now take this and get moving."

Ardo snatched the gem out of the air, slipping it into the small pouch on his belt.

As much as it annoyed him, he followed the man's directions again moving toward the bathing room, where he knew a number of the receptives would be in use. Sure enough, just beyond the small door, an adjourning room held three receptives just for moving water and another two for heating.

"How many do you have?" Dante asked as he placed an imitation gem in the original's slot.

"Two fire, three water, but they're all small."

"There have to be some larger receptives somewhere in this house."

"The farther we wander, the more likely we are to get caught. And as you said, this room doesn't look like it's used for much."

"Hm," Dante said shaking his head. "Disappointing. Especially for a councilguard."

"I'm trying to be reasonable," Ardo said, the frustration clear in his voice. "I thought it was something you of all people would understand."

"What does that mean?"

"It means that up until now, you've been the rational voice in the group and now you're ready to jump in front of an arrow."

"We need larger receptives if they're going to do us any good," Dante said matter-of-factly. "According to Beno, they'll drain a bit every minute we're down in those mines thanks to the Alkay stones."

Ardo stepped toward the other mage, his patience wearing thin. "I know what Beno said. And like you, I want to get what we need. We just need to be careful."

A shadow passed over the man's face as Ardo leaned closer, nose tipped down to stare at him. He held Ardo's gaze for a moment before looking away with a sigh.

"Sorry," he said, surprising Ardo. "I haven't slept well the last few nights and I don't want to let Lena down."

"Cruz respects you."

Dante scoffed. "That woman only respects those who can get her what she wants."

"What does that mean?"

"It means we've already had three of our people caught and taken down the mines, the viajera is still missing, and we're no closer to getting it than we were weeks ago. No matter how you try and twist it, we've failed more than we've succeeded." Dante took another breath before nodding. "But you're right. It'll do us no good to get caught now. Only further continue the string of failures."

Ardo felt a pang of respect for the man for the first time since he had met him. He hadn't liked the way he sneered at the others in their group, but perhaps he had judged the man a little too quickly.

"You're right, too," Ardo said. "In order to succeed, we need more receptives, and we need to look around some more. But let me go first—" he raised a finger as Dante began to argue, "I have experience with stealth as a trained councilguard." He waited for a reaction from Dante, but received none. The line had been something of a test, in which he half expected Dante to claim the very same. In all their discussions, Dante had remained something of an enigma. There were occasions where he spoke and acted like a councilguard, and others where his actions skewed closer to that of a bruya. But now wasn't the time. "I'm going to check the hall and surrounding rooms first."

Dante nodded his head in acknowledgement, teeth clenched behind lips, and he stepped out of the way.

Ardo opened the door with a soft click, swinging it open just far enough to hear beyond into the hallway. Then he waited.

Other than the soft rhythmic breathing of Dante behind him, there wasn't another sound in the hall outside. He slid through the door, still open only just wide enough for him to fit and padded down the hall, landing gently on the balls of his feet.

There was no sound of footsteps, and as he passed each room, there were no receptive lights illuminating the gaps under the door jambs. With a light touch, he opened another door, seeing much of the same setup as the room he had come from.

Another guest room. Good news was that it didn't seem the major entertained very often. But with that was the inevitable fact that they'd likely get more small, poorly maintained receptives.

He slinked farther down the hall to the door at the end. This one did have light leaking into the hall from under the door jamb, but seemed as silent as the others. He pressed his ear against the door before opening it, making sure there were no footsteps or shuffling on the other side. As he cracked the door, light filled the hall and he saw that it opened up onto the second floor balcony overlooking the inner courtyard.

The balcony itself was empty, but he saw the occasional staff member crossing the courtyard below. It would be more difficult to move around beyond the hallways, but he could already see the door of a library opened up across the way, where he imagined more receptives were sure to be.

"Follow me," Ardo said quietly as he found Dante back in the guest room. "And keep your steps light."

The mage's eyebrow rose at Ardo's words.

"Sorry," he said. "I probably didn't need to point that out."

"Let's just go," Dante said, pushing them both out the door.

Ardo went straight to the balcony door, peeking an eye through the crack he had left before pushing it back open.

The courtyard below was empty, but who knew how long it would stay that way. He moved quickly, not bothering to give Dante instructions. The man was hotheaded, but seemed reliable. He would follow.

He stopped at the first door, pressing his ear against it before cracking it open, still in a crouched position. He peered into the shadowed space from a low level, and it took a second to realize it was the back staircase down onto the main floor. Not much use to them. He shut the door and moved on to the next one. And the next. And the next, until a door opened into a large office space.

Without a word, he slipped in, Dante following behind and closing the door with a whispered click.

Standing tall, Ardo took in the surrounding space. The moonlight pouring in through the large window lit it without the need for torches and Ardo smiled when he saw some large receptives along the window for wind and moisture control.

"*Buenísimo*," he said with a grin. Dante saw the same receptives and they both moved as one, using their blades to carefully shimmy the receptives out of the crevices they were set into.

"Still no earth receptives." Dante glanced around the room, eyes narrowed.

"There weren't any in the gardens, but maybe the courtyard below."

"Now who's being careless?"

"We need to go down there either wray and check in on Quenti."

Dante pursed his lips, but nodded. "The main stairway is too exposed though; we should take that back staircase."

"Which we have no idea where it opens back out to," Ardo

noted, but shrugged and headed that way regardless. Either way, Dante was right. They couldn't go down the large sweeping staircase that circled down into the courtyard without being seen by at least one staff member.

The back staircase was still dark and quiet as they descended, careful to feel for each step in the dark. As they came to the end, he pressed his ear against the door and heard the muffled sound of voices. He had assumed the stairs opened up somewhere near the kitchens, but the question was how they could sneak out without being seen.

He sent a quick prayer to El'dyo as he turned the knob and gently opened the door. Light shined in, but not from the room they were entering. He waited, but the quiet hum of conversation didn't change or stop as he pushed the door open farther. He could see the wall opposite the door, only a few feet away. They were entering into a narrow hallway, probably between the kitchen and another room, though the kitchen itself was only separated by a curtain, with shouts and clattering extending just beyond.

He motioned for Dante to wait while he moved forward again, expecting to be heard with every movement. Finally, the hallway opened to a darker and quieter room.

It was a quaint morning room with its small table and sitting nook.

Ardo turned back to Dante, mouthing the words more than speaking them. "Look for more receptives; I'm going to check on Quenti."

They both padded to the large arch that opened into the inner courtyard, each tucked in the shadows on either side. Ardo didn't wait for Dante. The moment there was no one there, he ducked out of the doorway and sidled along the edge of the courtyard toward where he could hear the sounds of panpipes and men talking. Before he made it two steps, there was the clipped sound of a man trudging toward the courtyard with purpose.

Ardo ducked behind the staircase and into the shadows of some large ferns there.

"Leon," a man's voice said. "The major would like you to check this document against the weaves he pulled today."

"Where are they?"

"In the downstairs office."

There was the sound of shuffling and then two sets of footsteps hurrying away. Ardo cursed silently in his mind, looking back toward the morning room where he hoped Dante still was.

He waited a beat to make sure the silence had truly fallen in the courtyard and then dashed back to Dante as quietly as he could.

CHAPTER 50

ARDO

"They're checking her orders," Ardo said

"You said they were good forgeries," Dante said.

"They are. Any trained eye would be fooled, but once they cross-check her orders with what they have on file, they're going to find discrepancies."

"And what do you want from me?"

Ardo couldn't tell if it was a challenge or a genuine request, but he had not time to guess. "I know this was a last resort," he said, "but we need Mena. They're going to check them against documents they have in a downstairs office on the east side."

"You're sure?"

"I... think," Ardo said. The truth was, he never saw them enter, but it was as good a guess as any. "There are three rooms. One of them must be it. Retrieve Mena. Once I'm in, I'll open the shutters and signal for you both for the correct room."

Dante didn't bother with stealth, going straight to the large window at the back of the room, unlocking it and slipping out. Ardo closed the window behind him, but didn't lock it. He made his way back into the courtyard, descended a set of stairs and tried to focus on the direction he had heard the footsteps walking. There were three closed doors along the east side of the courtyard.

As he got closer, though, he could hear the distinct sound of two men talking behind one of the doors.

Taking one more deep breath, he ducked into the room, closing and locking the door behind him with an almost silent click.

The office beyond was twice the size of the one upstairs, with bookshelves that reached the ceiling on either side of the room and a large desk in the center. The floor was stone and there was no rug to dampen the echoes of his harsh breaths as he stood there. The two men leaned over the desk looking at the forged tapestry, next to a hanger of weaves and a box of more tapestries.

One was young, probably only a few years older than Ardo, but the other man's hair was graying at his temples.

"What in El'dyo's name?" The older man said. "Who are you?"

The younger man's hand rested on the small club hanging from his belt.

Fighting the urge to pull out his own weapon, Ardo raised his hand in salute. "I'm glad I caught you both. The major had a question about the assignment status on her orders."

Both men looked more confused than before, but the younger's shoulders relaxed and his hand dropped from where his club hung.

"What?" the older man asked, voice more impatient than confused.

Ardo stepped forward, his mind racing, yet unable to settle on anything to say.

"Sorry," he said instead, lunging gracelessly at the younger man, locking him in a chokehold and snatching the club from his belt. Before the older man could yell, he whipped the club in his direction, driving it into his diaphragm and sending him sprawling and coughing onto the ground.

He twisted the younger man in his grip, dropping the club and grabbing the dagger at this own belt.

"Don't make a sound," he whispered, digging the tip of the dagger into the man's throat. The soldier in him didn't care about the small whimper from the man's lips, but another voice inside told him he didn't deserve this. It wasn't too long ago that Ardo himself was in this very same position: confused, unaware, and a victim of circumstance.

"What do you want?" The old man said, breath heavy.

"That goes for you too," Ardo said. Ignoring that guilty voice inside, he dragged the captive to the window and unlatched the shutters. They swung open easily, letting in the dust air and sun from beyond.

It took only a minute for Dante's face to pop up in the window, Mena standing beside him, face wan but smiling.

He passed the trembling guard to Dante and grabbed the older man off the floor where he was still coughing harshly. Ignoring the man's breathy curses, he pushed him against the window and let Mena lay a hand on his. She closed her eyes, the lines etched deep in her forehead, and the man fell silent.

Dante and Ardo watched, not wanting to disturb the woman as she worked. She hadn't quite recovered from their time in the mines, and Ardo could tell this little bit of magia use was already exhausting her. There was a reason they had left her behind in the carriage, hoping they wouldn't have to further impede her recovery. Dark circles were as prominent as ever beneath her eyes, smeared like warpaint.

The minutes ticked by slowly as she modified both men's memories. When all this was done, they would forget all about this assault and only remember finding the matching weaves on file. The only remnant of this moment would be a nick on the neck and an unexplained cough.

Finally, Mena let go of the younger man's hand and waved to Ardo and Dante.

"That's it. Are you ready to go?"

Dante led the two men out, their minds in a slight haze still as he handed Lucía's forged tapestry back to them. Once they were gone, he shut the door behind them and turned back to Ardo and Mena.

"We still need earth receptives," he said. "I'll grab them and we can leave out this window."

Before Ardo could argue, Dante ducked from the room, leaving the door cracked. Ardo moved forward, carefully watching as Dante grabbed a handful of receptives from the planters along the edge of the courtyard. Apparently, the mage had noticed that a few larger receptives were responsible for the branches winding up and growing into the columns that held up the balcony above.

Ardo almost hoped their loss would lead to this place crumbling around Major Francisco.

Dante kept his head low as he moved back toward the office, receptives balanced in his palms.

"You! Stop right there." A voice rang out across the courtyard.

Dante was only a few yards from the office door, his eyes swinging up to meet Ardo's through the crack. He could see the thoughts flitting across his face as they looked at each other. Ardo could almost see the moment of decision in Dante's eyes as he turned away, dropping the receptives into the planter nearest him and raising his hands in the air as he faced the men.

"What are you doing in here?" An older man, dressed in the uniform of a councilguard asked as he strode across the courtyard. Dante took two large steps forward, away from where he had dropped the receptives, his hands still craised.

"Calm yourself," he said in a very un-Dante-like demeanor. "I was just looking around. This is a lovely home, truly"

"How did you get in here?"

"The door?" Dante said, taking another step toward him.

"Stop there," the man said, closing the distance between them in a quick stride and grabbing Dante's arm. He twisted him to the ground in one move. His knees hit the stones with a crack.

"Rogelio," the man called. "Get in here now. We have an intruder!"

Ardo watched from his place behind the door as the man tied Dante's hands behind his back and Rogelio rushed in, looking just as confused to see a stranger there.

He should have moved forward. He should have fought the two men. He could probably have taken them. But they were in the middle of the courtyard and barely a cry away from others. There was no way they wouldn't draw attention.

He looked again at the planter where Dante had dropped the receptives. The last of those they needed.

"Shit," he cursed, nails biting into his palms as he watched Dante get dragged away. He knew it was what the mage had wanted. He left the receptives for Ardo, knowing he was already caught. But it felt as though he had lost another soldier in battle.

The moment Dante and the others disappeared around the corner, he darted out, grabbing the loose gems and running back into the office on soft footfalls.

Mena took the bag of receptives from him as he climbed out of the window, pushing the shutters closed behind him.

"Where's Dante?" Mena asked, voice low and urgent as Ardo started moving away from the office.

"We need to get back to the stable, now," he said, not bothering with answers. He was doing the math in his head and knew the guards would figure things out too quickly if Quenti's driver was suddenly missing after finding a strange man wandering the estate.

Mena read his unspoken mood and followed behind him without another question. He expected to need her abilities when they returned to the stables, but the hand, half asleep along the wall didn't even recognize that Ardo wasn't the man who had originally dropped the carriage off.

"Hullo," he said, giving Ardo a small nod.

Ardo gave a tight smile as Mena crept in through the back door and tucked herself and the receptives into the back of the carriage where she had come from.

"Interested in a card game?" Ardo said, moving to sit next to the man. "I could use the extra coin. My mistress doesn't pay nearly enough."

This perked the man's attention and he sat up, smirking.

"I'd be glad to take some of that coin away from you."

Ardo smiled, sitting on the bucket across from him and placed the small pouch of coins from his belt onto the board balanced between them.

"You pick the first game," Ardo said.

Chapter 51

Quenti

The night dragged by slowly, the voices of the other guests growing louder with every pour of wine. Quenti had to admit it was sweet on the tongue, but she kept her sips small and infrequent, too tempted to allow the alcohol to soothe her nerves.

The conversation twisted and turned from one story to the next, never wandering far from the superiority of the blameless and the Council. They spoke of other countries where magia didn't exist, where only the blameless lived. It sounded like a soulless place to Quenti, but she kept the smile plastered on her face.

"It's getting late and I fear my wife will wonder where I've gone off to," Reymundo said, pushing his chair back from the table.

The others took this as their cue, the group moving as one to finish their glasses and stand up. Quenti followed their movements, only half-conscious of her body. She could feel the blood beating through her heart and through her head, and she wondered if the others could hear it too.

She was the last to leave, trailing behind the others. She hoped to disappear into the background, forgotten, but feared Major Francisco would pull her aside any moment, calling her out as the liar she was.

Her heartbeat quickened as he followed her outside, standing directly beside her as the carriages lined up in front of the estate.

"I must ask, Lucía," he said, voice too close to her ear.

She had to hide her flinch as she turned to look at him, "Your orders only show you escorting the receptives in a few weeks' time. What else are you doing here?"

"I'm sorry, Major," she said, trying to clear the catch in her throat. "There are some things I've been asked to not share with anyone."

"Anyone?" he asked with a tilt of his head.

"Anyone beyond the Council, that is," she corrected. "And part of it was my own curiosity. I wanted to understand the atmosphere here and see how things are being handled. Needless to say, I have plenty of wonderful things to report back."

Major Francisco smiled. He wanted to say more. The look of curiosity was all too apparent in his face, but being the good soldier he was, he wouldn't push her to defy the Council. That much had been made clear. At least not the blameless of the Council. Quenti noted for the first time that with Senye Cruz and Senye Emaru gone, there was only one mage left in their ranks. She'd heard nothing of new appointments being made. Had things really gotten so bad? Would they simply leave those two seats unfilled?

She couldn't ask, having supposedly been in Sombria more recently than Major Francisco, but she made a mental note to try and figure that out later.

"I am sorry again, Sergeant," he said, "for the circus earlier. I needed to be sure. As you can understand, I'm quite careful about our security here. You wouldn't believe the issues we've had over the past several weeks. That mess in the Haven has brought out the worst in everyone. Do you know how many attempts I've had on my life since then?"

"No need to explain, Major," she said. "And I wouldn't expect anything less. I might have questioned you had you not been so thorough."

"After tonight," he said, turning to face her with a look in his eyes that she couldn't quite read. "I'd like to be able to trust that you'll be on the right side of the coming war."

Quenti tilted her head. "Which side would that be? The Council's or the blameless's?"

The question made him smile. "Aren't they the same?"

"They are now."

"El'dyo bless the blameless of Sombria, then," Major Francisco said, his smile a twist that made her stomach lurch.

The first three carriages picked up the two colonels and the judge. The fourth in line was Quenti's, and she stepped forward, ready to greet Dante.

She barely faltered when she saw Ardo sitting lazily on the driver's seat.

"Runner Ardo," Major Francisco greeted him with a smile. "I didn't realize you were here."

"I should apologize," he said, smiling warmly. "I just stole a couple handfuls of coins from your stablehand as we waited. He should practice his card skills."

Major Francisco laughed at this, helping Quenti into the dark carriage before stepping away.

"Have a wonderful night."

She waved, shutting the carriage door and holding her breath as they moved away. The moment they were out of the gates, she squinted into the dark.

"Mena? Dante?"

"It's just me," Mena said, voice soft. "We lost Dante."

Quenti remembered Major Francisco's expression when Rogelio had whispered in his ear. She thought of the sharp eye the he had kept on their carriages as they rolled up. His eyes were always piercing. Searching for deceit. Now, Dante had been caught. Quenti could only pray he wouldn't give their game away before they finished.

She took a deep breath and did what she had been wanting to for most of the night. She bent out of the carriage window and vomited.

CHAPTER 52

ALARA

"I don't like the look you have in your eyes," Khuna said, staring at Alara from across the darkened alcove. They should have been asleep. The others were, but Alara hadn't managed to calm herself down enough for that. Francisco had spent another few hours in her alcove barking unnecessary orders, cracking his whip if they weren't followed immediately. She had a few scabs across her back where the blood had dried, her tunic ripped, and the skin left unattended.

"I'm just thinking about the best way to kill him." Her voice was low and unfamiliar to her own ears. She realized she hadn't spoken to anyone in the last two days, save for a few grunts to her fellow prisoners during the working hours. That realization, more than anything, sent a shard of ice through her chest.

"That's not the plan," Khuna said, inching closer to Alara in the dark. "But I promise, he'll get his."

"It's not enough," Alara said. "I want to see his eyes when death comes for him."

Khuna only placed a hand on Alara's. "Get some sleep. You'll do none of us good if you're a walking corpse tomorrow."

"As if any of us are doing any good down here." But she turned over and closed her eyes nonetheless. Khuna was right. She needed to sleep if she was going to fight Francisco. If she stood a chance at winning a war against all this.

"We'll get out of here," Khuna said, her voice a whisper in the dark. "We need to be patient. And to trust the others to get us out."

"Maybe," Alara said, unable to stop the words from escaping her lips.

She didn't know if she actually fell asleep. Before she knew it, others around her started the familiar movement that came with early morning. The stretching, groaning, and yawning. Had it really been five hours?

Runeo groaned from nearby and she saw him struggling to stand up, his hand clutched to his side. He had narrowly dodged a boulder a few days ago when it had broken loose from the ceiling above him. He'd continued to claim he was fine, but Alara had seen the way his movements had slowed and the sharp intakes of breath when he twisted the wrong way.

She resisted the urge to reach out to him or give him a word of comfort. He'd only get angry. It was his go-to emotion recently, except for the moments in the middle of the night when he reached out to her, silent but soft. As angry as she'd been for Runeo throwing himself down here with her without discussing it with anyone, she wasn't sure what she would have done had she been trapped down here without Khuna and Runeo.

The next few days, Alara tried to follow Khuna's advice as best she could. She still fantasized about cracking a club over Francisco's head or thrusting a spear into his gut every time she saw him, but she didn't act on her thoughts or even so much as glare in his direction.

Instead, she did what everyone else did and sat by as he continued to abuse any prisoner who so much as walked too closely to him.

All the while, she tried not to forget that this wasn't permanent. No matter how she felt, Khuna was right.

As she, Khuna, and Runeo toiled away, Ardo and Quenti and others were above ground working to get them out of here. At least she could only hope. Every time the guards walked a new prisoner in, her stomach tightened, afraid of seeing Ardo or Quenti or any other person that would highlight their failure. All these weeks later, they were still on their own. To make matters worse, they had so far failed to find Beno or Emaru, and hadn't so much as glimpsed any sign of the viajera. What had been the point of all of this if they couldn't even find those things? If the others did manage to break them out, what would they have to show for it?

"Morning meal!" the call of the guard echoed down the tunnels. Alara was already awake. Even if it weren't for the constant barrage of thoughts bouncing around her brain, the aches of the day's work before would have made it plenty difficult to get comfortable on the hard ground. She had caught a rock to the shoulder during one of her crevice crawls, as she had taken to calling them. It wasn't serious, but prevalent enough to make her wince if she moved the wrong way, though that wouldn't stop them from forcing more of these crawls onto her. With them constantly expanding the branches of the tunnels, someone of her small stature was always in demand.

Better her than Sol.

Khuna was the first of them up and moving, and Runeo and Alara followed behind her. Dez and Sol trailed close, Sol wrapped in her mother's arms as she sniffled into her shoulder. Francisco still hadn't let the two work together again, and Sol spent each morning crying in her mom's arms before pulling herself together to work. It made Alara sick to see how easy it was for the small child to push down her emotions when the situation called for it.

The bowls were set out by the time they got to the main tunnel, a few guards sitting off to the side chatting merrily and ignoring the prisoners elbowing each other for the cold gruel.

Dez picked up two bowls, struggling with the little girl clinging to her pants. She passed Sol one of them before moving her along the line with a gentle nudge of her shoulders. Alara watched, even as she grabbed her own bowl and started to eat. So she saw the moment the little girl, so focused on holding her food in one hand and her mother's pant leg in her other, tripped over the uneven floor.

The bowl clattered along the floor as she fell with a soft thud, clumpy gruel spilling across the stone.

"Sol!" Dez whispered, picking the girl up as she let out a soft cry, the sniffles she had been holding back earlier turning to true sobs.

"Shut her up," one of the guards said, not moving from where he was leaning against the wall.

Dez pulled Sol away and toward a corner, shushing her along the way. Alara hated the way the guard's eyes followed them, looking put out by the child's muffled cries.

"I said shut her up," the guard snapped again, pushing off the wall, hand following to his club in threat.

Alara bit her tongue, stopping herself from yelling back.

"What's going on here?" The voice rang out, cold and echoing down the tunnel. It made her stomach churn as she recognized it.

Francisco rounded the corner, hand already fisted around the whip on his belt.

"Just an accident with the kid, Major," the guard said, giving a small salute to his superior officer. "She's done crying now."

The second statement was directed at Dez and the threat was clear. She pressed Sol's face deeper into her chest, whispering in her ear. The girl's cries softened into nothing after a couple of seconds.

Even still, Francisco took measured steps toward them, eyes sharp and scowl set firmly on his face.

Dez pushed her bowl into Sol's hands, encouraging the girl to take a bite. Alara watched uneasily from her place along the wall as the major sneered, looking between the dropped bowl and the mother and daughter pair.

"Eat your own food," he said, staring down at them.

"It's okay. We can share," Dez said, not meeting his eye.

"She dropped her bowl. She can go hungry. Eat your own food."

The command was cold and Alara's teeth ground together.

Dez didn't move right away, confused by his words, even as Sol took another bite of the gruel in her lap.

Without warning, he slammed his hand across her face, sending her and Sol sprawling across the ground. The little girl let out another cry.

"Shut her up," he said, kicking the fallen bowl away from them, upending the rest of the food. "Fine. They both can go without today." He spoke to the guards, who were watching the exchange in half boredom.

Alara realized she was tasting blood, her tongue still held sharp between her teeth. Yet, she held herself back, Khuna's words chanting through her mind.

But as Francisco raised his hand to strike Dez a second time, Alara couldn't stop herself.

She moved forward, not even knowing if the plan was to throw herself between Dez and Francisco or to attack him here and now.

Either way, Khuna moved faster, her hand shooting out, gripping Alara's arm like an iron vise. She pulled her back, shoving herself in front of Alara as she stumbled back into the wall.

"Stay down," Khuna said between her teeth, a hand pressed to Alara's chest.

A small voice in her mind told her she should listen to Khuna, but the louder part of her was screaming for revenge. Before she could make a conscious decision, a pair of guards pulled her and Khuna apart.

They wrenched Alara's arms behind her and pressed her face against the cold stone floor, dirt coating her exposed tongue. She turned her head to see Khuna held in the same manner, the other prisoners backed away against the walls. No one was going to intervene on their behalves.

Francisco moved toward them, his steps careful and un-rushed. He stopped in front of Khuna, though his eyes were focused coldly on Alara.

"It seems Linda's rebel instinct was passed on to you."

"Emaru doesn't get any claim on my rebel instinct," Alara said, unable to stop the words. The idea that her old mentor could take any credit for where she'd ended up made her chest burn.

"And what were you doing?" he said, turning to Khuna and ignoring Alara's comment. "Trying to protect your friend?"

With a signal from Francisco, Khuna was pulled up by her arms and set kneeling in front of the major. Her face was neutral as he looked down at her, lips curled in disgust.

Without warning, his fist cracked into Khuna's face, sending her falling backwards. The guards holding her arms picked her up immediately as Francisco sent a booted kick into her side.

"This," Francisco said, emphasizing his word with another kick, "is what happens when we get rebels." Another kick and this time Khuna wasn't pulled back up, blood mixing with dirt as she tried to push herself up with shaking arms.

"If you rebel, it isn't just you who gets hurt. Anyone standing next to you, anyone behind you, anyone who so much has passed by you in the tunnels, will be punished."

Alara tasted acid on her tongue as Francisco pulled the whip from his belt. She could have closed her eyes and turned away, even with the arms holding her down. But she refused to as the whip came down again and again, splitting the shirt and skin across Khuna's back until all Alara could see was red.

Francisco didn't stop until Khuna stopped moving, the only sign of life the shallow movement of her shoulders as she breathed. It was only then that Alara realized her throat was burning, and she found herself spitting up the acid that had curled up from her stomach.

Francisco didn't let Alara help Khuna until after she finished her work shift that day. She found Khuna still slumped in the main hall, taking shallow breaths with closed eyes. She could only tell she was awake from the strangled sounds she made with every small movement.

"Rojo," Francisco said, voice calm, "take the prisoners up to the medical room to get that one looked at. Make sure she can work tomorrow."

By the time Alara and Khuna were escorted back down to their level, the tunnels were dark and silent. The medics had fixed Khuna up just enough to allow her to move, but they had done nothing for her pain. The bruya limped, leaning heavily against Alara.

They left the guard behind, slowly making their way to the tunnel they normally slept in. But the moment they turned the corner and left the torches of the main tunnel behind, Alara stopped and gently set Khuna against the ground.

"We should sleep here," she said, voice strained with the guilt and anger sitting heavy on her chest.

Khuna didn't argue. She laid against the ground on her stomach, using her arm as a pillow.

Alara stretched out beside her, their sides brushing—enough to give each other warmth, but not enough to aggravate the bruya's wounds.

"I'm sorry," she whispered into the darkness.

She wasn't expecting an answer; didn't think she deserved one. But after a few minutes she heard Khuna's words like a sigh.

"I know."

"We're going to get out of here," Alara said. "I'm going to get us all out of here."

Even as she said the words out loud, they didn't feel like truth, but a raw and ragged hope. She repeated them again in her mind, over and over. If she said them enough, she might believe them.

CHAPTER 53

ARDO

The room was overly warm with the door closed and their entire group huddled together. Even with Dante gone and their numbers dwindling by the day, it felt too crowded. It had been two days since the dinner, and Ardo still hadn't seen the mage's name come through the weaves for prisoners in the mine, which didn't make any sense since they were sending everyone there. Either he was dead, or Francisco was keeping him somewhere else for reasons unknown.

None of them wanted to dwell on either scenario for long.

The news seemed to disturb Senye Cruz the most, and while she had never been the most verbose among the group, the silence following her protégé's capture didn't go unnoticed.

Beno still looked pale and weak from his time in the mines, but he was sitting up and moving around more over the past day. Mena had almost fully healed from the wound in her side, although her magia was still weak and difficult to grasp, particularly after pushing it again at Major Francisco's hacienda.

Ardo could only imagine the feeling as a sore or weak muscle, and he still had the sense of not belonging to the rest of the group. Being surrounded by magia wasn't anything new to him—he'd been in the Haven since he was a young teen, and entered the School of Protectors to train—but in all his years, he had never been the only blameless in the room. He would never say it aloud, but the feeling seemed a bit unnatural to him.

The receptives they had gotten away with were spread and sorted between them in the middle of the room as they argued through potential plans. Ardo had chipped in occasionally, when his knowledge of the guards was needed, but for the most part he had sat silent as they argued over the use of the receptives and their ability to retain magia underground. Back at the Haven, magia theory had only made his head spin.

"Even with the receptives," Quenti said, "we're walking straight into the lion's den. The mines themselves are full of guards and the only exit is straight onto the councilguard campus."

She ended her piece with a deep breath, eyes slightly wild as everyone turned to look at her. Ardo winced as she went back to biting at her nail beds and staring down at the ground. Her anxiety had only gotten worse since her confrontation with Major Francisco, along with the growing fear they'd never form a plan crazy enough to work.

"She has a point," he said, drawing the attention to himself. "We need to have another plan, other than 'don't get noticed.'"

"So, us fighting our way out probably isn't an option?" Beno said, waving at their small, tired group.

"We need a distraction," Ardo said, thinking back to his days in the School of Protectors and the endless strategy classes. "We need to pull some of the guards away, preferably on a wild guan chase."

"I can just run through the streets shouting about bruyas coming," Quenti said. "That might get some attention."

From the smirk on her face, Ardo knew she meant the suggestion as a joke, but his mind began to whirl as he looked across the group.

"Hang on a second. What if it wasn't just you reporting bruyas?" he said, lips pulling into a smirk. "If you had a few people with you claiming a bruya attack, we may be able to get a few dozen guards off the main campus and across town, where they can't cause trouble."

"Aren't they going to notice pretty quickly that there are no bruyas?"

Beno leaned forward now, seeming to read Ardo's plan in his face. "We can use some of the receptives to cause a fuss. We make a show of magia. No one will care if they actually see anyone wielding it."

"You think a lone soldier will be enough to grab anyone's attention?" Quenti said.

"I think we might be able to find help closer than we think," Ardo said, giving Quenti a weighted look. The bruya clearly didn't have a clue as to what he was referring and simply returned it with a blank stare. "Your councilguard friends from the bar."

"Those blameless idiots?"

"Those blameless idiots who owe you a favor and already hold a grudge against the Council and the major. Those blameless idiots who have friends and family already being affected by everything that's been going on."

Senye Cruz's face was flushed and taut as she looked between the two of them. "What is this and why did we not hear about it sooner?"

"Because it was nothing," Quenti said.

"A small bar fight that Quenti got a couple of councilguards out of after they were overheard criticizing the current Council."

"So you're suggesting we just tell these random strangers that we're rebels looking for a distraction to get our treasonous friends out of prison?"

"I was thinking something a little less straightforward than that," he said. "Quenti still is Lucía, the great war hero, after all."

Quenti opened her mouth to argue, but it was Senye Cruz who cut her off with a sharp wave of her hand. The woman might have been an ex-councilwoman on the run, but she still knew how to command a room.

"So we get these soldiers to cause a distraction to draw focus and resources away from the base. That's one part of the plan, but it still leaves us trying to get out of the mines without being seen with a group of escaped prisoners in tow."

"Once we're down there," Beno said, "we can hopefully get a few of them, at least, into guard uniforms."

"I should be down there with you," Mena said.

"You need to be at the top of the mine to send the receptives down through the ventilation shaft. It would be too dangerous for you to go in after that and try to find us."

"Then I want to help find Dante," she said, voice firm. "If the distraction works, I want to use it to see if there's even just a weave trail at Major Francisco's estate. As you said, there's a lot more that man is hiding there than we originally thought."

Ardo wanted to argue, but couldn't. He and Quenti had spent time in the library looking for some sort of hint of where Dante was being kept, but found none. If there truly was a weave trail, Major Francisco's estate was the next best option to look.

"You can't do that alone," Senye Cruz said.

"And you can't go into the mines, either," Mena said, chin raised in defiance. "You can't be seen by anyone. So come to the major's estate with me."

"Walk into the house of the one man who is sure to recognize me?"

Ardo shrugged. "If it gets to the point where he's there to recognize you, then we're already caught and doomed to fail."

The entire group fell silent at the thought.

"All of this," Quenti noted, "is again assuming we have a distraction."

The group looked around, as if one of them might hold a secret answer to fixing all of this. It was Ardo who finally broke the silence, the soldier in him telling him it was his duty.

"It looks like we have some blameless guards to talk to, Lucía."

Ardo left the meeting a few minutes later. He'd do no good with their continued debate on how to best use the receptives, but he could look through the weaves and tapestries and find out where Manny and Nico were stationed. At the very least, Quenti taught him how to recognize their names within the weaves, and him paying them a visit would do the rest of them good and give their plan much-needed momentum.

He might have felt guilty about dragging the two young men into the war, but with the way they spoke at the bar that one evening, they'd be a part of it soon no matter what. At least this way, they'd be involved by choice.

At night when he laid in the barracks and tried his damndest to fall asleep despite his anxiety, he wondered how many of the boys and men surrounding him he'd see in battle in the future. What side would they be on? He wasn't the only disaffected councilguard out there, but then again, most complaints would go no further than chatters and whispers in loud bars.

To actively speak out and work against the Council, in the open, was a death sentence for a councilguard.

Finding the two councilguards was easier than Ardo expected. He had known their ranks and their names from their interaction, and he expected to find plenty of Mannys—or some variation—in the weaves. And he was right. But there was only *one* Nico at the rank of stationeer currently working in Lejon.

And it was clear he'd found the right dorm when he walked in to see Nico and Manny sitting on a bunk, playing a game of golpeado. They didn't look up until he cleared his throat, but the moment their eyes met his, the blood drained from both of their faces and their smiles fell. Ardo's eyebrow hitched up as they stared, before jumping to attention and saluting with shaky hands.

"We need to talk," he said.

Neither spoke and Ardo had to bite back the laugh that bubbled up. He shouldn't have felt so much joy at watching the two men shaking in their boots, but it would also be a lesson in discretion to have them question the consequences of being overheard talking the way they had.

"Is this a good place to chat or should we go somewhere more private?" he asked.

They exchanged a glance before Manny waved to one of the bunks across from them without a word. He had taken on an air of indifference as he watched Ardo sit, but the shake in his hand was still evident. They waited for him to speak first.

"The way I see it," he said, looking between them, "you both owe Sergeant Lucía and me a favor. And I might have an idea on what you can do."

"You're blackmailing us?" Nico asked, voice indignant, even at a whisper.

"If you want to see it that way. Or, you can see I'm offering you an opportunity to piss off some of the people you're not happy with."

Manny's eyes narrowed. "Meaning?"

"You're going to meet Lucía, me, and some friends," Ardo said. "We'll chat about how we might help each other. Are you both off tonight?"

"Tomorrow," Manny said, face still twisted with suspicion.

"Meet me at the southern plaza fountain tomorrow at sunset. I'd tell you not to tell anyone about this conversation, but I know you both understand the importance of keeping it quiet. At least I hope you've learned that by now."

He didn't wait for them to agree and slammed the door behind him.

CHAPTER 54

QUENTI

Quenti and Ardo waited along the edge of the plaza, hidden in the shadows as the sun began its final descent. Beno sat near its center, scarf loosely wrapped around his neck as he pretended to play a game of solitaire.

Ardo had described the two men to him, and it was his job to make sure, with a brush of his hand, that they didn't have intentions to betray them. It wasn't a guarantee. Beno noted that even Mena's ability to suss out intentions wasn't perfectly accurate. But Quenti refused to trust them without some evidence, as fleeting as it may have been.

So when Beno gave the signal, she found herself more confident walking out with Ardo to meet the two men.

Nico gave a violent twitch and elbowed Manny as she and Ardo approached.

They took a seat on the bench across from the fountain, a few feet from the two guards, who startled when Beno sat himself beside them.

"This is our friend," Ardo said, giving a nod to the bruya. The guards eyed him with suspicion, but didn't argue.

"We're going to do this here?" Nico said, eyes darting around the half empty plaza.

"Do what?" Beno said. "Meet some friends and talk?"

"It's less suspicious to meet in public than be seen sneaking around," Ardo said, leaning forward to speak low. "So long as we're careful about what we say and how loudly we say it." He eyed them, and to their credit, the two men had the self-awareness to look embarrassed.

"So?" Quenti said, blinking at Beno, needing the confirmation. Beno nodded.

"So, what?" Nico said.

"I'm going to be blunt," Quenti said, trying to muster her courage. "We need help distracting the major and as many guards as possible somewhere away from the mines and base."

Nico's look was blank, but Manny seemed to put the pieces together quickly, and his face quickly turned into one of horror. "Why? And what would we be distracting from?"

"You don't need to know that," Ardo said before Quenti could open her mouth.

"So you want us to risk our positions and lives distracting a superior officer and our own men so you can do something that you won't explain to us."

"Yes," Quenti said, smiling widely. "And keep your voice down."

"No," Manny said, eyes sharp, but voice now in a whisper. "Not going to happen."

"Afraid to act against Major Francisco?" she said, raising an eyebrow.

"Yes," Nico admitted, even as Manny scoffed.

"And you know who I am?" Quenti said, relishing the way they both flinched back from her gaze.

"Yes, Sergeant," Manny said.

"Then you should know, I have a good reason for wanting to act against the major." She let a bit of her contempt for the man leak into her words. The guards stiffened, but she could see Manny's mind turning over the admission.

"Perhaps we can tell them a little?" Ardo said.

Quenti opened her mouth to say no. The denial was automatic and her gut told her it was the best way, but she was seeing the same hesitation Ardo was. They weren't just afraid to act against Major Francisco, they were worried about what they'd be acting on behalf of.

She bit her lip, focusing a second on the pain as she thought. Alara would have told them immediately. She'd trust them to do *good*. But Quenti wasn't Alara. Quenti didn't trust blameless blindly, particularly ones dressed in councilguard black. And, if they were being honest, not everything Alara did turned out well. Still...

"Fine," she said finally. "But Beno's keeping an eye on them."

"I'll do what I can," Beno said. "But based on what I've felt in them, I believe their hate for Francisco will outweigh any fear."

Nico blinked at this statement, sliding away from where Beno sat beside him. "How did you—"

"Our friend here is a mind-walker," Quenti said, relishing in the new fear blooming in their eyes. "We don't appreciate the way the Council has been leaning recently, either. We have friends—family members who've been impacted."

"We have people in the mines," Ardo said when Quenti's voice faltered. "And we're going to get them out."

"And you think we'll just say yes?" Manny stood up. "We may have made a mistake, but we still have things to live for. With all due respect, Sergeant, you're sounding like you've been shadow cursed."

"I assure you we aren't," Quenti said. "And I don't believe in El'dyo's shadow."

"You're a war hero," Manny said, not sitting back down. "You've killed bruyas on the Council's orders."

"I've done my job to protect Sombria and I plan to continue that. There are bigger threats to our country now than simple bruyas."

"You're suggesting treason," Nico said, slowly. Quenti was beginning to notice he was usually about two steps behind his friend.

"I'm doing more than suggesting. And besides, you act like you've never suggested treason yourselves. We're just calling on you to act on your words."

"You're asking us to go on a suicide mission."

"I don't plan on dying," Quenti said. "I don't expect you to do so either. And if that isn't enough, I'll be there with you."

Ardo and Beno both snapped to attention at this. This hadn't been a part of the plan—at least not that she had told them. But she knew that the soldiers would want support—proof of their commitment to not just sending them off to die. And she wanted to keep an eye on them anyway.

"A sergeant is going to be a part of the distraction?" Manny asked. He still hadn't sat down, but he hadn't moved to leave, either.

"And a war hero, as you said."

"What kind of distraction are you thinking?" Manny said after a beat, sitting back beside Nico.

Quenti smiled.

CHAPTER 55

ARDO

"There are a million ways this plan can go wrong," Senye Cruz said. This wasn't an argument. She was simply stating facts.

"There are," Ardo agreed. "And I don't know how I feel about Quenti going off alone as a distraction, but it's what we have."

"I won't be alone," Quenti said. "Lucía will have her lovely blameless friends."

"And we trust them?" Mena asked, nervously glancing between their groups. Beno and Ardo were dressed in the red uniforms of the guards in the mines. It had been easy to get access to fresh ones through Manny. Quenti was dressed as Lucía, ready to meet her "new friends" on the edge of town for their distraction. Mena wore the black uniform of a standard councilguard. She'd be entering the base before anyone else, using her magia to send as many receptives as she could through a ventilation shaft that led down into the mines. After that, it was up to Beno and Ardo to retrieve them on Level Three through the narrow openings from within on their way down.

Mena would then meet Senye Cruz outside of Francisco's property in search of Dante. This plan, more than any of the others, was based on chance. There was no way to confirm where he was and no way to confirm that Francisco would stay on base, especially when alarm bells started ringing. But Senye Cruz was firm in the fact that they wouldn't leave the mage behind without even trying.

For his part, Ardo hadn't wanted to argue; his own guilt at leaving Dante behind in the hacienda had not been quelled by his hours of searching for any sign of his arrest or imprisonment.

"No matter what happens, anyone who can, meets back here by midnight tonight," Senye Cruz said, jaw tight. "If someone is compromised, we'll leave a red scarf in our room. In that case, we are then to meet in the secondary location outside of Lejon."

Ardo knew the place—it was the same copse of trees he had taken Alara and Quenti to. But if all went well, they wouldn't need that second location, so long as none of them were captured.

"And don't forget, the priorities are obtaining the viajera, Alara, and ensuring the dagger is safe," Senye Cruz said. "Everything and everyone else is secondary," she said with a tinge of regret in her voice. Ardo had never heard the woman sound so uncertain, and he was ashamed to admit to himself that it unsettled him.

The dagger in question had been buried outside of town under a marked tree to protect it from falling into Major Francisco's hands. Ardo hadn't questioned why a dull dagger was so important to everyone, and he wasn't going to argue about getting Alara out of the mines first, but it still made him sick to think all the others weren't a priority. There was no guarantee that all of them would make it out of this town safely.

As if Senye Cruz's words were a reminder of the stakes, Beno and Mena clasped hands and pressed their foreheads together. There were no words exchanged, although with two mind-walkers, perhaps he just couldn't hear them. It was strange seeing the two dressed in uniforms, standing together. Except for a few small differences in their bone structures and the unique splotchy patterns of light skin, they looked like mirror images of each other. He turned away, not wanting to interrupt their parting.

In doing so, he made eye contact with Quenti, who was avoiding looking at the twins just as actively. He was surprised by the small smile she gave him as she took two steps toward him.

"Don't get yourself killed, soldier," she said. "I don't want to listen to Alara whine about it later."

"Same to you," he said, hesitantly placing a hand on her shoulder. "You've been good for her, I think. Even if you've turned her into a treasonous rebel."

"Treasonous rebels are the only good Sombrians left, I think."

He laughed at this. "Maybe Manny and Nico can convince you otherwise."

"Sol, they are just as treasonous as the rest of us! They just don't know it yet."

"I'm sure you'll teach them."

"That's the plan," she said with a smile.

"Be safe," Ardo said. "Don't use your powers unless you have to. It's safest to keep Lucía's cover for as long as possible."

"I know, *Dad*" she said, giving him a wry smile. "You don't have to remind me how dangerous being a bruya is."

Ardo could have laughed at his own ignorance. All of this was new to him, but everyone here, in some manner or another, had been hiding their true selves from the Council their entire lives. The thought left a pit in his stomach.

"Are we ready?" Beno said, pulling Ardo's attention away. He and his sister were separated again, though their hands were still clasped tightly together. "It should be sunrise soon."

Stiff nods circled the group, no one looking thrilled at the day to come—no one relishing the uncertainty in their plan. Ardo and Beno moved first toward the door, but before Beno could grasp the handle,

Mena grabbed him once more and pulled him into a tight hug, tears choking her voice.

"Be safe and don't do anything stupid."

Ardo watched the exchange with a strange ache in his chest. He thought of Senye Emaru and Alara stuck below in the mines, waiting on them. He just hoped they hadn't lost hope in the weeks it had taken them to form the plan. More importantly, he hoped they had found each other amid the darkness.

Beno said something muffled into Mena's shoulder before letting go and motioning for Ardo to leave with him. His throat was tight, but he didn't look back as the door closed behind them and they shuffled to the back alley. The others would leave soon enough, but at spaced intervals. From here forward, their small groups were on their own. All they could hope is they saw each other again at midnight.

Ardo sent a prayer to El'dyo as they walked, moving through shadowy streets, purple with dawn light. And then he sent one to Sol and another to the old god of wealth and good fortune.

Just in case.

CHAPTER 56

ALARA

It had been a few days since Khuna's beating and she had healed just enough to move without her face twisting in pain. But it did nothing to soothe the growing anger and hopelessness in Alara's chest. Khuna still couldn't sleep on her back and by the end of each day her steps were uneven and dragging. There was no reprieve from the mines and the work, but Alara didn't complain or raise her gaze too high in defiance, even when Francisco walked by, smug and satisfied at his handiwork.

Khuna wasn't the only one looking worse for wear. Runeo only grew grayer and more ill from the suppression of his magia as the days wore on. His eyes were hollow and his lips pale as he moved through his work routine with little notice of the others around him.

Still, at night, in the anonymity of the dark tunnels, Alara would whisper to them about everything they would do once they were out again. She no longer pointed out that Khuna and Runeo had jumped into this danger willingly. None of that mattered. They just needed to make it back out alive.

"Thank you for defending Mama," Sol said one morning, voice raspy with sleepiness. The others still hadn't woken, savoring the last few minutes of rest before work.

"It didn't help," Alara said. In fact, it had only made things worse. She hated to admit it, but throwing herself at Francisco had only gotten more people hurt. Her heroism hadn't saved anyone.

"It didn't stop him," the girl said, voice thin, "but it helped to know that... someone cares." Alara was reminded again just how young the child was, despite the depth of grief in her eyes and weariness of her words. "I hope you get out safely."

Alara startled at the words. "Get out? I'm not—"

"I know I'm not supposed to listen, but at night I can hear you talk. You're not supposed to be here."

"No one is," Alara said.

"I was born here," Sol said. "Where else would I belong?"

"Sol... don't—"

"You're looking for something." The words were so matter-of-fact that Alara found herself looking back at every conversation they whispered into the dark, assuming they were the only ones left awake and alert.

"Something and someone," Alara said in a hushed whisper, knowing it was pointless to lie to the girl. She clearly had been listening from the beginning. If she had wanted to get them into trouble, she would have done so already.

Alara described Emaru to the girl. "Have you ever seen someone that looks like that? She'd have come in the day or so before us."

Sol shook her head, the movement just visible in the dim torch light from down the tunnel. Alara's heart sank. She had no idea why she had put so much stock in their conversation. The weeks in the mine had truly gotten to her.

"But," Sol said. "I might know where *things* are kept."

Alara chuckled. "Things, huh?"

Sol frowned. "You said you were looking for some*thing*, right? I've seen a room that the guards sometimes go into when no one is looking. And they take these things with them."

"Then how come you've seen it?" She was half teasing the girl, and she knew part of it was out of self-preservation. As much as she adored Sol, she was prone to letting her imagination get carried away.

"Grown-ups don't notice me," she said.

Alara looked back at the girl, and she could tell even in the darkness that Sol's eyes were focused back on hers. "Do you think you could show me? Maybe tonight after evening meal?"

The smallest of smiles revealed itself across Sol's tiny face, present even in the murky darkness.

That night, as Alara explained the plan, Khuna and Runeo only frowned in response. They didn't take kindly to being left behind, but eventually she convinced them it would be too difficult to sneak around with either of them in tow. They agreed with reluctance.

It wasn't that they weren't allowed to wander the mines after hours—there were no rules as long as they didn't go near the lifts or bother the guards—but if there really was an important room where Sol thought there was, it wouldn't be a good idea to get caught sneaking around it.

So after Alara had choked down the cold gruel and they had turned back into their normal tunnel, she and Sol waited for twenty minutes, silent and patient. Eventually, the sounds of pickaxes on rock and depressed chatter went quiet as the night guards settled into their respective positions.

Sol slipped into the tunnel first, her tiny feet not making so much as a whisper against the stony ground as she creeped. Alara followed with as much grace as she could muster despite the exhaustion and twitching of her muscles that hadn't stopped for days.

The main tunnel was better lit than the side tunnels, with small torches set up high against the ceiling. A determined prisoner could probably grab the torch and use the fire to attack the guards, but then what? They'd still be stuck with four levels of prison between them and freedom.

Alara's thoughts strayed from the pointless escape tangents and back onto the object at hand. It wasn't difficult to follow Sol's small silhouette through the darkness, her eyes having adjusted to the constant dim lighting over the weeks within the mines. Or was it months? Surely, it couldn't have been longer than months, right? Time had grown meaningless without the passing of the sun overhead, and Alara was beginning to forget what that ball in the sky even looked like.

Alara was so lost in her own self-pitying thoughts, it took a second to realize that Sol had turned down a tunnel and was inching along the left wall, her steps more careful, somehow quieter than before, as silent as a field mouse.

After a few more feet, she stopped, her hand pulling at Alara's tunic, yanking her forward to where the shadows darkened like an illusion. In fact, Alara wasn't even sure if there was an opening at all, the crevice was so slight. It was a tight squeeze, but after a hefty exhale, Alara was able to pull herself through.

It was black as pitch inside, and she felt around with her hands, noting the small cave that they had ventured into, large enough to fit three people standing.

Large enough for a small child to curl in a ball and hide when she could escape.

"How did you find this?"

"When I was little," she said. The words sitting uneasy with Alara —the girl was still little. Too young for the life she'd lived. "Before I could work, they let me wander during the day. But if they saw me sitting too long, they would yell at me. So I found somewhere to hide."

"And the door you found?" Alara looked around, as if her eyes might pick up something important in the dark. But she could only feel the air around her and the movement of Sol next to her.

"If you look out the crack," her small hands moved Alara six inches to the side, "from right here, the wall isn't a wall."

She squinted into the outer tunnel, the darkness lightening to a simple black, but she saw nothing amiss with the shadowy stones.

"I don't see anything?" she couldn't hide the questioning tone.

"It's hidden with magia!" Sol said, voice strained. This clearly wasn't the first time she'd defended herself over this mysterious doorway.

Instinctively, Alara reached deep within herself, hopeful to find something. But any hope the girl had given her disappeared into the darkness the very moment she tried. Why had she thought...

"There's no—"

"—I know there isn't magia down here," Sol said. "But I've seen it! They press a rock into the wall and the stone disappears."

"They press a rock? What kind of rock?"

The girl might have shrugged, based on the pause. "I dunno. It's just a gross rock."

"Gross?"

"It's green like the moss that grows in the dark corners here."

The hope that had escaped her grasp just a moment before rose again, though just ever so slightly. If what Sol said was true, perhaps they had been more right than they'd thought.

A "rock" being activated by touch was fairly common in the Haven. It was so simple, it was almost foolish in its simplicity. They were using receptives to hide the door and receptives to open it. She had assumed every guard in the mines was blameless, but her mind-stalking ability had been suppressed before she could confirm that. Maybe some of them were, in fact, mages, though the thought made her stomach churn. Both at the thought of a magia user having a hand in this, and in the blameless continually using magia users to do their bidding.

She might have been more horrified by the hypocrisy of it, had she not grown up in the Haven surrounded by hypocrites.

El'dyo, she had been one of those very hypocrites.

"And you said you've seen people go in and out?"

"Uh-huh."

"When?"

This time Alara could feel the shrug as the girl's shoulders brushed against her side.

Alara couldn't blame her. Time down here was measured in meals, sleep, and the workday. There was little to distinguish nine in the morning from four in the afternoon.

It had almost felt like a lifetime, and yet no time had passed since they'd made it down into the mines.

"Thank you, Sol," Alara said, swallowing back the emotions threatening to flood her eyes. "This was very helpful."

The following night, Alara had to explain to the girl that she needed to return to the secret spot alone. This way, Alara would have room to lie down in the cave and wait.

That last part was an inadvertent lie, as Alara found out. She squeezed herself back into the alcove and tried to adjust herself into a comfortable position before realizing with a groan that there would be no lying down. The best she could do is sit with her legs bent and head resting in a rocky nook in the wall. Then again, maybe the discomfort would keep her awake long enough to see someone go in or out of the door.

However, the long day of carrying rocks had drained her more than she realized. When she opened her eyes, woken by the distant sound of bells, she realized morning meal was being called. She had to wait until the tunnel was empty before wedging herself out. She missed the meal and was quickly shoved into her duty group with a self-satisfied smirk from one of the guards.

The next night was more of the same, with Alara going in and out of consciousness, struggling to notice when her eyes were closed or just coated by the inky darkness.

By the third night, Alara regretted not allowing Khuna to take her place. Runeo would have never fit comfortably through the crevice even with the weight he had lost from too little food and too much work, but Khuna would have. All the same, Alara was too scared of what a night of sitting twisted in the small space would do to Khuna's healing back.

So instead, Alara found herself crouching in the alcove again, trying to find a different position than the one she had fallen asleep in the night before. But every way she twisted, her hips throbbed and her back ached.

So involved in her positioning was she that she almost missed it when a shadow shifted on the other side. Another shift, twist, and turn of light on darkness, and before she knew it, the flicker of a flame in someone's palm was too blinding to deny.

She stopped moving, holding her breath as she watched the man. He was dressed as a councilguard, his face covered in a red scarf, but there was something about him that made Alara doubt he was one of the guards she normally saw making rounds. Unlike the others, he was short and squat, not widened by muscle, but with fat.

She was also able to see that while the fire sat in his palm, clearly controlled by magia, it hovered directly over a small green stone—a receptive. He raised his other hand and pressed it into the wall, just as Sol had described, and a moment later, the image of the stones that stood there flickered, and the man disappeared behind a thin door.

Though he was gone in what felt like an instant, he hadn't left before Alara had stolen a glance into the room beyond. She could only see a sliver, but it was brightly lit with torches. A scattering of objects rested on a low bench along the wall. She had only just been able to make out the vaguest of shapes before her view flickered, turning back into stone before her very eyes.

It was probably stupid of her, but Alara couldn't stop her curiosity. A minute later, she slunk out from the pitch black alcove and ran a hand along the wall where the man had disappeared.

Though she had just seen the image flicker and the door clearly behind it, her hands could only register the cold, rough stone of the wall.

Why were the guards hiding a room behind a hidden door on a hidden level of the mines? What could they possibly be hiding behind that door that was so important to keep secret?

Alara had a few guesses.

It was tempting to wait until the man came out. Her hand itched to feel the weight of the fire receptive in her palm. To wield her magia for even a moment. But she knew it would be a stupid move. There was no guarantee the man would come out alone and, as always, it came down to being stuck five levels underground with little to defend herself.

So, instead of giving herself up to certain death, she focused on the bite of nails in her palms before slipping back into the crevice that had become her watchtower, and she waited with growing impatience.

He did leave eventually. And he was alone, too. It was hard to see in the dark, but as he exited, Alara noticed with a small lurch the splatter of something dark and wet across his chest.

Oil? Water? Alara couldn't tell.

She counted to five hundred after his footsteps disappeared before she moved once more, giving the hidden doorway a look once before shambling back toward where the others would be waking soon. For the first time in weeks, she allowed that small core of hope in her chest to bloom ever so slightly.

There had been no rhyme or reason to the objects in there, but that had only been to her mine-addled brain. Maybe—just maybe—that room housed the belongings of hers and countless other captured mages. Maybe it held the ever-elusive viajera.

And Emaru and Beno… well, they had done their best to find them over the past weeks. From what Alara could tell, they weren't down on this level. They'd have to deal with that problem when it came. She allowed herself the smallest celebration at this minute discovery. In her time in the mines, they had been hard to come by.

Khuna, Sol, and Dez were still asleep when she returned to their small alcove, but Runeo sat up against the wall, face twisted in the shadows.

"Are you okay?" she asked, voice soft as she sat next to him.

He didn't answer right away. His eyes remained focused on a point in the distance that didn't exist.

"I keep dreaming about Micos." His voice was a rasp and Alara felt his words in her chest.

"I dream about Lili sometimes," Alara said. "I have nightmares about watching her die. About being the one who…" She couldn't finish the sentence. The nightmares had been plaguing her since their first night in the tunnels, but she had refused to admit it to the others. She could deal with the dreams where she watched the woman die. But she couldn't admit to how many she had where her own fire burst from her, engulfing the tierren.

"Do you think he's still in the Haven?" Runeo asked.

Alara bit her lip. "Maybe. But no matter where he is, we'll get him back."

"Why do you do that?" Runeo said. "Give me hope when there is none?"

"Because there is hope," she said. "If my memories could come back, so can his."

"Maybe I don't want him to remember everything. I failed him. He should have never been captured. I should have protected him." His words cracked and Alara felt her own chest aching. "He'll wake up knowing it was my fault."

"Don't put all the blame on yourself and take away Micos's agency. He made his own decisions. He wouldn't want you to take those on yourself."

Runeo's hand found hers in the dark, and she squeezed back as their fingers intertwined.

"I'm sorry for all the times I've underestimated you." His words were so quiet, Alara thought she might have misheard.

"Say that again when we're out of here and I don't think you're just lying to make me feel better."

"What are you two whispering about this early?" Khuna said from a few feet away.

Alara didn't answer immediately, letting Runeo decide on what to share. But he didn't speak, so she cut in. "I found a room."

"Oh, a room?"

"There are... things in it."

"Things... love it," Khuna said, her sarcasm clear. "What things?"

"I don't know," Alara said. "But I'd like to think it's where they keep top secret things. A magiaful compass, for example."

"You're sure?" Runeo's voice had changed. Gone was the earnest pain of the past several weeks.

"No," she admitted. "But it's the first lead we've had."

It was with this small bubble of hope that they stepped into the main hall for morning meal. Alara was almost excited for the lukewarm and sticky gruel, happy for the energy boost. Eager for the opportunity to return to that dark alcove. So, when a hard voice called her prisoner number, she wasn't prepared. She wasn't ready for the spike of fear. Had she been seen sneaking around the hidden room? But the guard continued, calling Runeo and Khuna's numbers, as well.

"Prisoner 5-9832, Prisoner 5-9833, and Prisoner 5-9834, come with me."

The guard stood a ways down the tunnel, away from prying eyes. Away from the only other witnesses—not that it mattered down here. He only waited long enough to see them step forward before turning and marching away. Not knowing what else to do, they followed. Alara only gave a quick glance behind her to where Dez and Sol stood in the food line, Sol's eyes wide as she watched them leave.

Their breath and light footfalls reverberated around the tunnel walls, heightened by the sound of her heart beating. Alara couldn't tell if it was just exhaustion or plain terror that made every step sound louder than the last.

The distant guard turned down one of the tunnels, and the three of them followed, too timid and obedient at this point to resist, but still wary. Alara's eyes grazed the corners of the hallways, and she wondered if she could dislodge a loose rock to, what, hit him on the head?

Then what?

Alara did her best not to shrink at the question, but he was smiling widely.

"But I have to ask," Beno said, looking each way down the tunnels, if making sure no one would mysteriously appear, "what's the status of your mission?"

Alara nodded. "I think I may have a lead on the viajera—assuming, of course they kept it down here. Were you able to find anything on your end?"

"We've pored over the weaves and tapestries in the base," Beno said. "There are no records of it. But then again, there were no records of my time in the mines, either. A lot of what happens down here is kept off the weaves and tapestries."

"So, it could be anywhere," Alara said.

"Or it could be down here," Beno said. "It sounds like if we want to find it, this is still the best lead we have, and one we should act on immediately. After all, we don't want to keep everyone waiting."

"Everyone?" Khuna said, hopeful.

Beno turned and smirked at her. "Yes, Quenti too. You'd be surprised, but she's turned into quite the councilguard."

"What?" Khuna and Alara said in unison.

"See? I knew you'd be surprised."

Alara's mind boiled with dozens of questions. Questions about Quenti and Ardo. About how they planned to escape the confines of the mines. But with this resurgence of hope, the soldier inside her returned, along with her motivation to complete the mission.

"Well," Alara said. "If we're going to head back up, we have to make sure we're not empty-handed."

"So where are we going first?" Beno asked, everyone's eyes turning to Alara.

"Back the way we just came and down a few tunnels. Without being caught or questioned by every other guard in here." Alara's words were sharp with exhaustion and anxiety.

"Luckily, you have me," Beno said. "I'm more than familiar with the routines and protocols. Anything else?"

Alara took a deep breath. She was almost too scared to ask what followed. "Is there any chance you have a set of receptives with you?"

Beno smiled wide, his face lighting up in the same familiar way Mena's did. He tugged at a small purse that hung from his belt, letting the sound of stone on stone inside speak for itself.

"I could kiss you," Runeo said, eyes bright.

"I'd settle for a shrine in my honor," he said. "But I'll hold onto these until we get past the guards. Can't have the prisoners playing around with magia. So, where do we go again?"

Getting back to the tunnel with the hidden entrance was easier than it should have been, but with a guard beside them, no one much questioned them. The other prisoners had already gone off on their daily assignments and only a few other guards were left in the main hall, eyes questioning as they settled on their approaching group. Beno passed them with a few words about a special assignment before moving on.

That seemed to satisfy the guards, who moved on to their own daily task of keeping the rest of the manual labor in check.

While Beno kept the lead for appearances' sake, Alara followed close behind him, hissing the directions through the tunnels.

She watched the left wall carefully, waiting until she saw the small shadow of the crevice.

"Here!"

They stopped as a group, Alara running her hand along the wall, trying to estimate where she had seen the man enter the prior night.

"It's somewhere around here," she said.

Beno followed her hands with his own, eyebrows furrowed. "They used a receptive, you said?"

"He was holding a green stone—an earth receptive—and he

pressed his hand against..." she paused, scowling at the wall, "...well, the door."

"The door. Right," Beno said, his skepticism undisguised.

"I think there's some kind of magia making an illusion of the wall. Or I was that tired last night and hallucinated the whole thing." She hated that a part of her thought the second might be true.

"An illusion?" Beno asked, wrinkling his eyebrows. "A mind-walking stone could do that, theoretically." He fell silent, digging through the pouch at his side until he pulled out a moss green stone with a smile. He glanced around at the others and took a deep breath before pressing the stone to the wall, his own palm almost shining with the magia as he did so. Alara's own chest twisted with envy at the sight of it. An almost animalistic hunger awoke inside her.

Soon.

She wondered for a brief second what past Alara would have thought of this ache at missing her magia. She let out a small snort and only realized how strange that might have seemed to the others as they turned to look at her.

"Sorry," she said, face heating. "I'm... tired."

"Are you all planning on coming or waiting around until you get caught?" Beno's voice came from a few feet away, but Alara could no longer see him. He read the confusion in all their faces and Alara had to stop herself from yelling out before Beno's hand suddenly appeared, stretching out from the wall like a disembodied demon.

Runeo was the first to step forward, carefully stretching out his hand. The tips of his fingers met the wall, but rather than stopping, they slipped through and disappeared into the stone, the image flickering on and off as he did.

"That is disturbing," he said before shrugging and slipping through the stone. Khuna and Alara followed behind, only flinching a little as they passed through the barrier.

Alara's eyes widened as the scene became visible before her. She stood in the doorway she had only briefly glimpsed the night before, and beyond was a long hallway, not a room. A bench stretched along the wall, cubbies holding a random arrangement of items, including ponchos, sets of keys, boots and sandals. Jackets and sweaters hung from hooks on the wall above the cubbies.

It definitely wasn't the storage room she had been hoping for. Based on the inconsequential items strewn about she assumed this was simply storage for guards or whoever used this hall. Before she could so much as sigh in disappointment, she noticed the others walking ahead, already eyeing the pair of doors at the end of the hallway.

"Which way?"

They all had frozen, as if realizing how vulnerable they were, wandering around without weapons or disguises in a place they clearly weren't meant to be. Someone could walk in at any point, and it would all be over.

"I'd wanted to save this for the escape," Beno said, pulling open the pouch and lifting the stones from inside. "But you should all take a receptive. You're a fuegen, right?" He handed a few red and black stones to Alara. They felt almost hot under her hands and she could almost hear the magia inside singing as her core stirred at the presence. It felt stilted in her chest, much like it had for the years she'd worn her magia-blocking cuffs, but it still sent a thrill through her.

She looked at Khuna and Runeo and saw the same light of hope and warmth return to their eyes. It had been too long since she'd seen that look from them.

"All receptives are full—or at least they were before coming down here—but we don't have much beyond what you're holding to get us the viajera, find Emaru, and get out alive. So just... be prudent with your powers."

"So we're doing it, then?" Alara said. "We're finding Emaru?"

Beno gave her a sidelong glance. "Unless you truly want her to spend the rest of her life—or what remains of it—underground like the rest of you."

"But don't you realize what she's done?" Alara said, still unsure about how she was feeling about this whole thing.

"I know it's hard," Beno said. "I understand your concern, trust me. I share it. But Senye Cruz believes Emaru could still do some good. She wields enough power on the surface to make a difference. That much is irrefutable."

"And you think it'll be for the right side?" Alara said.

"We won't find out if we keep waiting around," Runeo said.

"That's right," Khuna said, moving toward the door closest to her. "So, let's go. I have a girlfriend to grovel at the feet of after all of this."

They followed, a new lightness to their steps in spite of the questions still plaguing Alara. But they would cross that bridge when they got to it.

One thing at a time.

The door Khuna opened was to a washroom, which they might have been disappointed by, had it not been weeks since the three of them had had such a luxury.

Through the second door, they found another hallway lined on either side with even more doors.

"Great," Alara said, though they didn't slow down.

They moved forward, opening each door carefully, ready to defend themselves at the first sign of trouble. One after the other, the rooms revealed themselves as empty and dark. Some had barren tables and chairs, others were stocked with weaves and tapestries that they didn't have time to peruse. One near the end of the second hall appeared to be a workshop, with a few receptives scattered across the table's surface and schematics laid out etched in l'lamaga skin.

Alara stopped, unable to ignore her curiosity as her eyes grazed the contents.

"Are they experimenting on receptives?" she asked, trying to understand the drawings she was looking at—colored stones surrounded on all sides by a series of darker ones.

Beno looked over her shoulder, running a finger along the picture. "They aren't studying the receptives, they're studying the Alkay stone within the receptives."

"The what?" Alara asked, brows furrowed.

"That line, along the stone here," he said, picking up a golden-hued receptive. "It's the same stone that's stopping us from using our magia down here. The same stuff in those beloved cuffs of your Council."

"But the Alkay stone was lost shortly after the first bruya war," Alara said. "They used all the rest up making those cuffs. There's only so much left."

"A finite amount, I'm sure," Beno said. "But much more than they've let on. And maybe, just maybe, what they've found here is an entire vein of the stuff. How else do you explain what happens when you get below the second floor of this place?"

"It would explain why they've continued to have such interest here, even beyond simple receptives," Khuna said.

"Shit," Runeo said, his voice loud behind them.

Alara turned to see him looking over her shoulder at the table.

"I don't want to think about what the Council could do with an endless supply of this stone."

"And they're extending the mine," Alara said, looking up at the wall above them. A vertical map of the mines hung on the wall above them, fresh cochineal ink laying out a sixth level below where they were now.

"We should keep going." Everyone turned to where Khuna stood. "The viajera isn't in here." It was clear she was the only one who had bothered to look around the rest of the room.

Beno nodded. "But let it not be said this was a waste of our time." With that, he swept the few scattered receptives from around the room and threw them to their respective wielders. Alara smiled, catching three new fire receptives that all felt at least partially full. Maybe this wouldn't be impossible, after all.

"What in El'dyo's shadow?" a stranger's voice called from the doorway.

CHAPTER 58

ALARA

The man in the doorway wasn't a guard. Nor was he the man Alara had seen the night before. He wore a cream tunic that felt completely out of place in the dirtiness of the mines. To make matters worse for him, he had no weapons on his belt.

Beno moved first, the only one among them who'd had proper nutrition and rest over the past few weeks. Though, instead of an actual attack, he threw the fist-sized earth receptive he was still holding in his hand.

"Catch!" he said as the man fumbled to do just that, utter confusion painted across his face.

Beno crossed the room in a few wide strides and wrapped his large hand over the man's mouth as he pulled him into his chest, his other hand pressed to his temple. Alara could just make out the small stone between his fingers—a mind-walking receptive. The poor man couldn't so much as think about calling out until Beno had him pinned, and after only a bewildered grunt beneath the bruya's hand, he went still.

A few seconds later, Beno let him go, dragging the man to sit in a chair along the wall. His eyes were unfocused and he remained silent.

"I know where we're going," Beno said with a self-satisfied smile. "Follow me."

He didn't wait for their response, moving forward and turning out of the doorway with bold decisiveness. The others followed at his heels. There were no more hesitations and explorations as he strode past two doors without so much as a glance before turning through the third into another hallway. This hidden area felt nearly as expansive as the main mine, though that might have simply been Alara's anxiety.

Beno stopped them in front of a door, a small panel on the wall marked with a carved flame.

"You're up, little fuegen," Beno said, waving Alara forward.

She took out one of the smaller receptives in her pocket and pressed it against the wall. She didn't even need to call to her own core. The panel heated and the door swung open.

"Do they have mages working down here?" she said, tucking the receptive back in her pocket.

"Who knows?" Runeo said. "Either way, I hate them all."

"No arguments here," Alara said as they continued through the door and saw where Beno was now standing.

In front of him stood a large cabinet, its doors open. A mass of items littered the shelves inside: daggers, cuffs, stones, and carvings. Each carefully placed in its own section of the shelf in some apparent organization, though Alara couldn't place it, and she didn't have time to ask.

Among the trinkets, Beno picked up a small gem, carved into the crescent of a moon. It was the same bright blue of the gem Mena wore in her right ear. With a soft smile, he ran it along his fingers and put it in his left ear where a small empty hole had been. Any semblance of sentimentality was quickly pushed out when he took a sharp intake of breath, grabbing another small bronze object on the lowest shelf. It was smaller than his palm and intricately carved along the face, though a uniform dirt color that would threaten to blend in with the blandest of landscapes. As he ran his thumb along the edge, it popped open and she saw the movement of a needle inside, spinning wildly.

"Got it," he said, smiling.

"That's the viajera? That's the whole reason we're here?" Alara didn't know what she had expected, but part of her thought it would be bigger or... more important looking.

"Is it supposed to be doing that?" Runeo said, eyes focused on the spinning needle.

"Probably the Alkay is messing with its powers down here. We'll have to wait until we're above ground and hope to Sol it still works. But it would take a lot to separate it from its twin, and I doubt they'd know how."

"Let's not doubt anything the councilguards are willing and able to do with a little persistence," Alara said, moving forward and happily plucking the two daggers off the shelf. She couldn't tell if they held magia, but the blades were sharp, which would do well down in the rest of the mine.

"Be careful with those," Beno said, eyeing the blades. "We don't know what they're testing or working on down here, but what I did see in that man's mind—I didn't like."

"A pointy blade is a pointy blade," she said as she slipped them into the band of her trousers. The metal was cold against her skin, but she'd have to find a belt or sheaths later.

Alara jumped as a clatter echoed from across the room and she turned to see Khuna stumbling after a few receptives she had dropped.

"Sorry," she said, sheepishly. Alara might have snapped at the girl, but she saw the difficulty in which she still moved and the stiffness in her shoulders as she collected the stones. She was still clearly in pain, even if she wasn't saying anything.

Alara opened her mouth to say something, but stopped when she heard a muffled yell from... somewhere.

Her eyes flickered across the room and she saw Beno standing at attention, his own gaze landing on a closed door along the wall nearest them.

Another muffled yell.

Alara and Beno moved as one, though with his longer stride, he easily made it to the door before her, swinging it open and letting the light from this chamber bleed into the next.

With only a little bit of concern for using too much of their receptives, Alara produced a flame in her palm to light the room and entered, steps soft and silent.

It was empty except for a single long table at its center and a small cabinet with tools she didn't examine too closely, because on the table, a figure lay strapped down with their face hidden by a sack. She could tell by the cuff on their wrist that they were a bruya—although why they needed a magia-suppressing cuff in an entire mine system surrounded by Alkay stone, she couldn't fathom.

"What is it?" Khuna asked, moving through the doorway, followed by Runeo. Alara could tell the moment they had noticed what was in the room by their sharp intake of breath.

It was Runeo who stepped forward first, hand reaching out to pull off the sack from the prisoner's head. "Sol help me," he said, voice caught between anger and disgust.

Finally summoning the courage, Alara peeked over his shoulder, and her mouth hung open, wide in recognition.

"Emaru."

Chapter 59

Alara

Emaru's head snapped to the side at Alara's voice, eyes finding hers in an instant.

"Alara," she said, voice cracking with disuse, and Alara felt her chest ache with a twisted sort of empathy.

It was only then that she noticed the cuts all around the woman's body, and the blood stains on the table.

Runeo looked down at the former councilwoman like... well, like she had killed his brother, but Alara couldn't help but look back at her in pity. It was as though she were looking at a shriveled old woman wearing her old mentor's face. Emaru's hair had gone completely gray and stuck to her face with sweat and oil. The skin along her eyes and forehead held wrinkles that Alara didn't remember and her eyes' cold attentiveness had gone dull.

Alara and the others here may have felt broken from their times in the mine, but Emaru *was* broken.

Yet, isn't this exactly what Emaru had been working toward—treating bruyas as less than human? She had simply landed on the wrong side of the table somewhere along the line.

But Alara couldn't quite muster the hate and anger she had been holding on to since their escape from the Haven. The stuttered rhythm of her heart reminded her that this woman had raised her— had been the closest thing to a mother she knew.

Because she killed your parents.

Runeo and Khuna, on the other hand, didn't have any problems summoning their disgust, their glares burning hot even as Beno pulled Runeo away and started unbuckling the woman from her restraints.

"Why did we agree to break her out, again?" Runeo said, face red with withheld rage. "I prefer her like this."

"We've already been through this," Beno said, undoing another strap and allowing Emaru to sit up. "Besides, we made a deal with Ardo. And in spite of what the Council thinks, bruyas keep their deals."

"Ardo?" Emaru said sharply, looking between them, eyes settling on Alara. "Where is he?"

No one bothered answering her question, Beno instead focusing on undoing the last strap to free her completely.

She almost fell from the table as she moved to push her legs over the edge, shoulders shaking with the effort. Alara stepped forward, as if to catch her, but Beno was there first, supporting her as she stood.

"Are you going to be able to walk or do you need some healing?" he asked, looking her up and down.

"I'm fine," she said, managing to look just as cocky and self-assured as ever, even as she leaned against the taller man beside her, dressed only in rags.

"What did they do to you?" Alara asked, the words slipping from her lips even as her mind screamed that she didn't care.

"You mean after the whipping?" she said, voice cold and sardonic. She hadn't changed one bit beyond her physical looks. Even as she stood there, Alara could see the woman's old bite returning. "As it turns out, a blameless faction within the councilguards have been experimenting on ways to temporarily and permanently suppress magia. Something I perhaps could have done something about had I stayed in power and not been arrested under the false pretense of helping *you*."

"Oh, I'd be glad to tell them how little you helped me," Alara said.

"Can we get back to the experiments aimed at ridding us of magia?" Beno said. His hands had tensed around Emaru's arms and Alara could see her flinch, even as she tried to hide it.

"I've already told you all I know," Emaru said. "It was all I could garner from their conversations."

"Blameless pigs," Alara said. The words that spewed out shocked even her. In her entire existence, she couldn't recall ever saying anything so... hateful. But she didn't feel sorry.

Emaru met Alara's comment with a smirk. "I'm glad to see you finally see magia in a new light, though I hate it took a band of bruyas to teach you. You never wanted to listen to me."

"They're better teachers," she said. "And a better family than you ever were."

If Alara had seen a pained expression in Emaru's eyes for the briefest of moments, it was gone before she could believe it.

"We should get moving," Runeo said, eyes bouncing around the room as he refused to look at the mage before them.

Beno agreed, letting go of Emaru as she moved to stand on her own. Alara watched with a pinched expression. She moved the same way Khuna had been after her beating.

"It's not easy being on the wrong side of the law, is it?" she said, finally feeling the anger and betrayal she knew was inside her after everything. "Especially when you know you're right."

Emaru's eyebrow raised, face holding that imperious air she always projected so well. "So you think I deserve this for trying to protect the peace of Sombria? For, what was it again... selfishly claiming power with lies and fear. This is exactly what I've warned Sombria against—one side claiming control over another without checks and balances."

"Lies and fear could never lead to balance and peace," Alara said.

"I've failed as a parent if that's still what you think I was doing. You think you've conquered your fear? You now fear and hate the blameless and the Council just as you once did your magia. You haven't changed at all."

"I was just thinking the same of you," Alara said, waving her hands at her bedraggled appearance. "After what they did to you, you'll still defend the Council and Sombria."

"I defend what Sombria and the Council stand for."

"Are we sure we can't leave her?" Runeo said, voice tight. "I'll happily tell Ardo we couldn't find her."

"We made a promise," Beno said. "*I* made a promise. Ardo's waiting for us on the third level, and we would never have made it this far without him."

Alara felt a flare of warmth in her chest, knowing that Ardo was nearby—or at least nearer than he'd been in weeks. He'd kept his promise and come back for them.

Emaru seemed to read something in Alara's expression because her smile turned almost feral. "Perhaps I was wrong," she said. "Maybe you're seeing less black-and-white than you used to."

She threw a glare at the woman before marching forward, leaving her to stumble behind them. Runeo was already ahead, Khuna following close. Beno took up the rear of their small parade, making sure to grab a few more of the receptives sitting along the edge of the room where they had found Emaru.

"May I have those?" she asked, though her tone didn't hold much question.

Runeo turned to argue, but Beno tossed her the receptives before he could even open his mouth. As they moved through the empty halls back toward the mysterious tunnel entrance, Beno explained the plan, which boiled down to using the receptives to get out fast and secretively.

"We just need to take down any guards we can't mind-walk as quietly as possible," Beno finished.

A pang of guilt bloomed inside Alara's stomach with each step. Sol's large, sad, and somehow resilient eyes stared back at her in her mind. She halted, stopping Khuna in her tracks.

"What's wrong?" Beno asked, voice impatient.

"We can't just sneak out of here and leave everyone behind."

"That's exactly what we're going to do," Beno said, voice brooking no argument. Not that Alara cared. She was already riding high on rage from Emaru's attitude after they'd agreed to save her. Even now, the woman looked at Alara like she was stupid. It made her want to scream.

"We have receptives and a chance to get others out. If we leave them behind, Francisco will only punish them for our escape. We need to do something."

"We have a handful of receptives, two potentially cursed blades, a club, and one half-empty mind-walking receptive. What do you think we can do against a mine full of guards and a military compound?" Beno's tone was curt, but the pale patches of skin were turning pink, likely to match her own heated face. The others watched the exchange silently.

Alara looked between Khuna and Runeo. "We can't leave Sol here. She's just a kid. And you know they'll be the first ones to suffer once we're gone."

Khuna bit her lip as she looked away, unable to meet Alara's pleading eyes.

"Maybe... maybe we can grab Sol and Dez, too," she said.

"We are not *grabbing* a child on our way out," Beno practically growled. "We've already spent too much time talking as it is."

"I don't want to help a single child escape," Alara interrupted, surprised at her own stubbornness. "I want to shut this entire cursed mine down."

"Alara," Runeo said, his voice gentle in a way that made her uncomfortable. He was never gentle. If anything, he was the one normally saying these things long before she'd even thought of them herself. "Beno has a point."

"So, what? We ditch everyone and give our prayers to Sol and El'dyo that they all stay alive? I thought you were better than this, Runeo."

She expected an argument, but as she looked at him, he could only match Khuna's downcast glare. The mines had taken a toll on him as well.

"You're just like the rest of the Arborelis," Alara said. "Ready to run and hide to save your own skin rather than stand and fight."

"Or perhaps," Emaru said, voice cold. "Your friends are finally seeing the bigger picture. This isn't about saving a few people down here. It's about saving all of Sombria."

"You," Alara snapped, "don't get a vote."

"And you," Emaru said, "are the only one advocating for insanity. What good do any of us do if we die in here trying to destroy one prison—one *mine*—that they will rebuild the moment we're gone? This isn't about a single mission or a single person. Sombria is crumbling and we need to stop it before we lose our country."

"Our country?" Alara said, turning to face Emaru directly. It felt good to release some of the anger building up in her now that her guardian looked less pathetic and weak. "Why should we listen to someone who's spent years pitting bruya against mage, brainwashing anyone in her way?"

"I wasn't the one who saw the world in black-and-white. That has always been your flaw, my child."

"Don't call me that! This *is* black and white. What's happening down here is wrong, and we can stop it."

"We're wasting time," Beno said, voice raising above their argument. "Unless you have some extra mind-walking receptives in those pockets of yours, then we have no hope of leading a prison break. So let's get ourselves out alive and we'll worry about next steps when we know we're free."

Alara clenched her teeth, looking at the others around her. No one was making eye contact besides Emaru with her told-you-so smirk. They were all siding with *her*. With the woman who had tormented their people for decades.

"I can't believe you're all going along with this," she said, unable to hold back the words. She felt her voice crack and she swallowed back the burning behind her eyes, refusing to show weakness.

"We came here for the viajera," Khuna said, voice soft. "We need to get back to the mission. *You* need to get back to the mission. It's the bigger picture."

Alara was sick of hearing about the bigger picture and greater missions. She hadn't signed up for a war. She only wanted to save lives and stop getting stuck on the wrong side of battles. But it seemed she was here, once again, caught up in a greater mission that meant leaving others to die.

"Fine," she said, finally. "I can't stop you all from running."

She wasn't giving in. She couldn't wrap her mind around walking out of these mines without doing something.

"Are we done waiting to be caught?" Beno asked.

Runeo gave a grunt in affirmation for everyone, continuing forward down the stretch of hall.

"Subtlety is key," Beno said to Alara. "We need to be careful and not draw any attention."

There was a click and swish as the door at the end of the hallway opened, three guards stopping at the sight of them marching down the hall in a line, very much not belonging here.

"What were you saying, Beno?" Alara asked as the three men reached for their weapons.

Chapter 60

Quenti

Quenti had planned to meet Nico and Manny just outside of town on the east side facing the Ruinedlands. She had tucked herself in the shadows of the last street out of town and waited until she saw them. The moment she did, she also noticed the three others walking behind the two council-guards and cursed herself for her lack of care. She should have waited until they were closer—she shouldn't have trusted them to begin with.

Without even thinking, she pulled back her hands, calling her magia to the surface and feeling for the water in the fountain down the street.

Manny read her shift in mood quickly from a distance, his own hands raising in apology.

"Don't panic," he said, eyes narrowed as he saw her empty hands twitching by her sides. "They're friends."

"*You're* not even friends," Quenti said, not dropping the connection with her powers, but not using them yet either. She'd lose their trust the moment she used her magia. "You have thirty seconds to explain."

"Good. I only need five. You needed a distraction and we've obliged. We brought backup to help with your mission." Manny still hadn't lowered his hands, as if he planned on slapping away an attack from Quenti. "You can trust them."

"I barely trust you," she said, eyes still narrow.

It was Nico who stepped forward this time, eyes dark and angry. For a moment, she was tempted to step back, but she held her ground.

"We all have loved ones we're fighting for."

"What, like your missing cousin?" Quenti said, admonishing him for thinking one missing relative constituted trust.

"Who, as it turns out, is dead," Nico said, his voice still and stoic.

Quenti bit her lip, swallowing a click in her throat, but she didn't back down, challenging Nico with her glare.

"I received an encrypted message from my tía yesterday," he said. "And it was all because of Francisco and his brand of justice. And I'm not the only one." His voice grew more intense by the moment. "Vi's mother is in hiding. Raf's brother was arrested for hiding his child's magia. So, whatever it is you have in mind, you can trust us, *Sergeant*."

She didn't move immediately, her eyes taking in the three behind Nico. There were two women—girls who couldn't be much older than her and Alara—and another young male guard that vaguely reminded her of a shorter Ardo with his curls and boyish face. The thought made her roll her eyes.

"Fine," she said. How much of a choice did she have at this point —other than to call off the plan altogether? "But you're all following my orders."

"Yes, sergeant," they said, not quite in unison.

Quenti doubted these were the best and brightest Sombria had to offer, but even she had to admit that the extra numbers gave them more of an edge. Every person counted.

"You two," she said, pointing to two of the newcomers, "Names?"

"Raf and Pedra," the man—Raf—answered.

"Are you good runners?"

"Yes," Pedra said, chin tilting up.

"Perfect. Do you know how to use receptives?"

This question had them both looking at each other without answering.

Great. This would all turn out great.

Quenti gave an exhausted sigh before passing them the bag of receptives. "When you get to the ravine on the northwest of town, you're going to set off one of these. You can throw it against another rock or use a club to break them, but don't stand too close to any of them when they break. They are mostly fire and air—ones that will make the biggest visual impact. After you set off the first one, wait until we come back with guards and then throw a few others. We just need to convince them that there are bruyas around."

Raf rummaged through the bag curiously as Pedra listened, eyes focused dead on Quenti's.

Quenti appreciated the attentiveness of her stare as she explained.

"And if we're seen?"

"Don't be," she said. "I'll do my best to lead people away once we're there. You can come around the back and join us when the receptives are gone."

"What about us?" Nico asked.

"You and…"

"Vi," the second woman said.

"Vi will be on the edge of town," she said. "Hopefully, some villagers will see the commotion in the ravine, but you're there for extra insurance. The moment you spot the receptive firing off, you run to base and explain we're under attack. Manny and I will take things from there."

Quenti allowed them five more minutes of questions before her anxiety got the best of her and she chased the four off to head north. She and Manny turned south toward the base. She wanted to get there with enough time so that it wouldn't look suspicious when they had to run off again.

"So, how long have you been a councilguard?" Manny seemed uncomfortable with silence and hadn't stopped small-talking since they had left the others.

"None of your business," Quenti said, not bothering to hide her annoyance.

"You look quite young."

"You're one to talk. I'm still not sure you're old enough to have been initiated."

Manny gave a small huff, but dropped the subject.

They didn't move far onto the base, as they wanted to make sure they were some of the first to hear about the "attack." So they found a small set of logs a few yards from the fence and set up a game of dice.

Despite the cool façade, Manny appeared just as nervous as Quenti, with both of them simply going through the motions of the game. She had planned to playact more—something she'd grown used to as Lucía—but she couldn't get up the energy. She couldn't take her mind off of what was at stake and what might be happening underneath them, even now.

If everything went well, she'd see Khuna tonight.

If everything went perfectly and the god of fortune was on their side.

"One of your friends—" Manny said, voice soft, "they're important to you."

She didn't need to ask who he meant. "They're all important to me."

"You know what I mean."

She looked at him, surprised to see the empathy in his eyes. "Yes," she said, not thinking the admission would matter. Lucía had no known family.

He nodded. "I've lost a few friends recently, too. We all have."

She only nodded in acknowledgment, not knowing what he expected. Maybe this was exactly the type of reaction someone like Lucía would give anyway.

"Thank you," he said.

She hadn't expected that.

"For what?"

"Doing something," he said as he took his roll. "I'm sure you get it. The frustration of working in a system that is happy to sit by as innocent people are slaughtered and enslaved. I never thought things would get this way, you know? I joined the guards because I believed in balance... not this."

Before she could respond, she heard the sound of pounding feet and a shout from just beyond the gate.

"Bruyas! Bruyas attacking."

Quenti recognized Nico's voice as it joined Vi's yells, calling for backup due north.

Manny and Quenti exchanged glances before jumping up, their nonsense game left behind. She didn't even have to help rally the troops. Within two minutes, all of the guards nearby had grabbed weapons and were forming up.

She was the highest ranking officer in the immediate vicinity though, so no one questioned her when she asked Vi to stay behind and gather more reinforcements, just in case.

The girl let a small smirk slip before saluting and sprinting to the main building.

"Here goes nothing," Quenti said.

They raced forward, the guards forming automatically into a makeshift unit as they moved through town.

She couldn't stop the smile as she saw the chaos their abrupt journey was causing within the large town. People stood in open windows, gawking at the display and whispering among themselves. Based on the small snippets she heard as they marched along, news of the "bruya attack" had already spread.

By the time they made it to the edge of town and could see the trees of the ravine ahead, there was a burst of fire somewhere along the south border. She didn't bother hiding her smile as the guards came to attention.

"You," she said, pointing to the back half of their group with an authority that still didn't feel natural. "Run along the left side of the ravine. The rest, follow me."

She moved forward, keeping toward the opposite side of the ravine where the last explosion had come from. She sent another prayer to every god she could think of that Raf and Pedra were being smart with their hiding spot.

They moved through the woods quickly, but by no means quietly. If there had been bruyas in the ravine, Quenti knew they would easily have run away by now, adept at avoiding the sound of stomping councilguard boots.

"At our ten o'clock!" Manny said, waving at nothing in particular, "I saw movement."

Quenti gave a sharp wave of her hand, sending the others in that direction, just as she caught movement out of the corner of her own eye. To the right, she saw Pedra ducking behind a tree. A moment later a flare of fire went up and immediately disappeared just north of them. The guards paused in confusion for a moment, torn between following orders and moving toward where the receptive had flared.

"Keep moving," she snapped. "It's a distraction."

She smiled as the guards turned and moved away from Pedra. She could get used to the simple power of being listened to.

CHAPTER 61

ALARA

Runeo, at the lead, acted first, throwing his arm out and sending a gust of wind and dirt up from the ground and into the guards' faces. Alara could see the bright smile of satisfaction at being able to use his powers for the first time in an eternity.

She felt her own magia pulling at the torches lined along the hall, eager to be used, but she hesitated, the narrow hall wouldn't allow for any error in aim. She was out of practice and too exhausted to trust herself. Instead, she grabbed the daggers from her belt and moved forward, pushing Khuna back behind them. There wasn't nearly enough water in the room for the water bruya to be useful.

"Save your receptives, as much as possible," Beno said, pushing forward with Alara, a club raised in his hands.

They struck together, Alara's blade swiping at the lead guard's side at the same moment Beno cracked him in the head with the club. The councilguard dropped before he could yell out.

"Alara!" Runeo said, just behind her. She instinctively tossed him her second dagger before whirling around to fight the next guard. He was a large man, at least a foot taller than her and had his own dagger drawn and ready. She grimaced at the almost maniacal smile twisting his face as he sneered down on her.

Oh, she had missed this.

Lunging forward, she twisted at the last moment, ducking under his arm and kicking him at the back of his knee. The guard stumbled forward. She swung her dagger, attempting to slash his side, but she just missed the break in his armor, the blade uselessly bouncing against the thick leather of his vest.

He growled as he turned on her, eyes flashing with satisfaction as she attempted to feint to the left, only for him to call her bluff. His dagger sliced into her forearm, drawing a line of blood that she could barely feel. For the past several weeks, she'd lived in pain, and so fueled was she by adrenaline and anger that the cut barely made her flinch. Instead, she used the momentary distraction his own satisfaction caused to drive her knee into his crotch. Her dagger sank into the space between his neck and shoulder as his knees buckled.

With a flick of her blade that saw blood splattering onto the dirt floor, she turned to see Runeo and Beno finishing off the third guard. Runeo's ear was bleeding from a blunt hit, but the guard was clearly worse for wear, with her leg bleeding freely. Beno knocked her down with a final blow to the head, sending her sprawling to the ground, unmoving.

"So, subtly?" Alara asked, unable to hide her grin. She had been itching for a fight for weeks and it was wonderful to get it out of her system. Based on the sparkle in Runeo's eyes, she wasn't the only one. It was almost enough to make her forget that they had just ended three lives.

After everything she'd been through in the mines, though, she was having a hard time finding sympathy.

"Not bad for a little thing," Beno said, giving Alara a nod of approval. She looked over at the guard that Runeo and Beno had taken down and realized how short the woman had been. Muscular and strong, yes, but much closer to Alara's size than the guard she had fought.

"How did you two end up with the short one?"

"As if you've ever been one to judge by size," Runeo said.

"Stop talking and get these uniforms off. We can put them on," Beno said, looking over the three guards and noticing the blood and tears in the uniform of the guard Alara had taken down. "Well, two of them, at least."

It took a few minutes of shifting around clothing to discover the uniforms fit Alara and Emaru best and they were able to salvage two scarves to wrap their faces, though Alara had to ignore the tang of blood that soaked into the scarf wrapped around her own face.

"We can't risk cuffing you two if we end up needing to fight," Beno said, looking Runeo and Khuna over, the pair still dressed in their prisoner rags.

"They won't expect cuffs down here, anyway," Khuna said. "It'll be more of a problem when we get to the upper levels."

"Then we'll address it when we get there," Alara said, anxious to get moving. The adrenaline of the fight was coursing, restless beneath her skin, and with the receptives nearby, she could feel her own core of magia chafing to answer the call.

As they moved forward, toward the door that led back to the main mines, Beno turned.

"Remember, keep your heads down and don't draw attention. The goal is to slip out of here without being seen."

Leaving behind hundreds to suffer and die, Alara thought, remembering their argument—one that had never come to a satisfying conclusion. But she bit back the words, understanding that pushing the issue further would only delay them.

With a silent affirmation across their group, Beno nodded, pushing open the door and stepping back into the mines, his own scarf pulled over his face. Before they left the narrow tunnel, Beno, with a careful look around, borrowed Alara's dagger to wedge the mind-walking receptive from its place above the door. Instantly, the ghost of an opening came into view, no longer hidden. He motioned for them to continue.

Alara held her breath as they walked, as if not taking in air might prevent them from being seen. They passed two guards who only gave them a cursory glance, eyes barely skimming over Khuna and Runeo in their prison garb and downcast eyes. It was easier to become invisible in the mines than Alara thought. She thanked both Sol and El'dyo that Francisco wasn't down there. If he was, there would be no slipping by undetected.

Beno marched ahead, playing the role of guard and leader. Alara realized as they moved down the main tunnel that she had no idea where the lift was. The main tunnel, as they had come to know it, wasn't even the longest one on Level Five. It was simply the widest area near their work zone where the guards had always gathered for food. Past the main area were another dozen tunnels stretching out in every direction. And one of them led to the lift. It had seemed so long since they first came down that it was almost a distant memory.

Beno moved with confidence, but every turn and tunnel looked the same to Alara's exhausted eyes, despite having spent the past several weeks living within them. A part of her was overwhelmed by the idea of seeing the sky again and escaping. Another part of her was nauseous at leaving the others behind. She would shut down these mines eventually, she told herself. Even if it was the first thing she did after they crossed back over the Ruinedlands.

All of Sombria had already forgotten everyone here. She wouldn't forget them too.

"Runeo! Khuna!"

Their entire group startled at the small voice, Alara going stiff as she recognized it. She almost opened her mouth in an automatic response, but she bit her tongue at the last moment, instead tightening the scarf around her face.

She watched as Sol padded up to Khuna and Runeo, eyes furrowed.

"Where's Alara?" she asked. "Is everything okay? She's supposed to be working with me today again."

The group was silent, Khuna's eyes meeting Alara's over the small girl's head, wide with regret.

Good, Alara thought. She wanted them to look at the girl and realize what their decision to escape meant.

"Get back to work," Beno said, voice raspy beneath his scarf.

Alara could do nothing but watch as he pushed the girl away, scolding and muttering mild threats. But Sol was persistent, eyes bright as she looked up at him.

"Where did you take Alara? She's supposed to be working."

"Sol," Khuna said, voice tight. "She'll be there soon, I'm sure. Just go back to work before you get in trouble."

"If she's not going to get back to work," Alara said, trying to drop her voice, "then she should come with us."

Beno's eyes flashed in her direction and Emaru grasped her arm, tightening her fingers into flesh.

"Let the child get back to her duties," she said, practically hissing the words in Alara's ear.

Sol watched the exchange, pale face growing anxious, as if she just realized she was surrounded by a group of suspicious councilguards.

"Never mind," she said, taking an uneasy step away from them. "I'll... I'll go back."

"Wait," Alara grabbed the little girl by the shoulder.

"Leave her alone!" a woman's voice called from down the tunnel.

It wasn't Dez, but another of the female prisoners Alara had grown familiar with over the weeks, even if they'd never spoken. Instinctively, Alara's grip loosened, and Sol slipped free, scrambling behind the woman.

"Get back to work," Emaru said, her voice harsh. She was losing patience, yes, but Alara was also reminded of how weak she was.

"Where'd that little brat run off to?" Another voice emanated from the tunnel as a guard appeared, a torch raised above his head and a scowl on his face. "What's going on out here?"

"Nothing. Everyone get back to work," Beno snapped. "Except you two!" he added, as the guard with a torch stepped toward Khuna and Runeo, who stood still against the wall.

A crowd was now gathered, with a handful of prisoners watching from the sidelines and the woman standing between Beno and Sol.

Three more guards joined the first, trying to wrangle back the prisoners to their respective jobs, but no matter how much they yelled, no one was listening.

The first guard was all too happy to take advantage of the situation. With a grunt, he shoved the woman out of the way and grabbed Sol by the arm, throwing her down onto the ground. Alara couldn't hide her horror as the guard's whip came down with a crack against Sol's back.

"Get. Back. To. Work." Each word was another hit, the sound of it cracking something else in Alara's chest.

"Stop," she said, her voice cracking. Emaru only tightened her hold.

"The bigger picture, child. We need to get out of here." The words were warm against her ear, but they sent a chill down her spine.

Sol's back was bleeding freely, and she lay unmoving on the dirt floor. The other prisoners had gone silent, watching the display in disbelief.

Then there was a scream, and Dez emerged from the crowd. Two guards grabbed her before she could make it to them, pushing her against the stone wall even as she thrashed and screamed.

"Get back to work, you useless rats!" the guard with the whip screamed, his face spattered with flecks of Sol's blood.

Alara tasted bile on her tongue. She couldn't watch this. She couldn't bear it any longer. But even as she tugged against Emaru's hold, retrieving a receptive from her pocket and pulling at the threads of her magia, a flash of red and black blocked her vision.

The guard flew across the tunnel, a root wrapping tightly around his throat, choking off his scream before it even began. Beno, his face scarf fallen and forgotten, stood over Sol, his hand outstretched and face twisted.

"Sol help us," Khuna said as Alara met her eyes. Runeo didn't need to think. A second later, a blast of wind was propelled down the tunnel, knocking the other guards aside.

It was like a fire receptive had been set off. The tunnel exploded in cries as prisoners jumped guards, taking pickaxes to necks and skulls without hesitation.

Emaru let out a muffled cry and her hold on Alara loosened as she was tackled.

Alara snatched the scarf from her face, throwing her hands up as prisoners rushed them like ants.

"We're not guards!" she said loudly, throwing her hands up. "We three are not guards," she said, motioning to Beno and Emaru. There was a moment of hesitation before the faces of the prisoners twisted from confusion to recognition, and then back to confusion. They had spent weeks with Alara, but clearly couldn't piece together what in the underworld she was doing in a guard's uniform. Still, they released Emaru, backing away with their weapons lowered.

"What in El'dyo's name were you thinking?" Emaru turned on

Beno, her fury palpable. "What happened to the bigger picture? You could have *mind-walked* him into stopping."

"I couldn't help it," he snapped back. "I saw what he did to the child and didn't think."

The child.

Alara threw her body onto the ground next to where Sol lay. Dez's arms were wrapped around the girl and, Alara saw with a huff of relief that the child's chest was rising and falling. Dez's face was still pale and drawn, and she brushed Sol's hair from her face.

"We need to get moving, more guards are coming," Emaru said. Alara had heard this tone plenty of times in the past. It implied she was no longer content with Beno's leadership and was more than happy to take charge.

"We can't just leave now," Alara said.

"You can't be serious," Emaru said.

"Once the other guards see this, they won't hold back." Alara met Emaru's gaze with an equal intensity. She'd spent her entire life being pushed around by this woman. She wouldn't let her do it again. "They'll kill or punish everyone."

"Don't be a fool."

Alara pulled out the half dozen receptives tucked into her pocket and looked out to the confused crowd that had gathered, doing her best to ignore the dark pools of blood forming all around them. "Who here is a fuegen?"

There was a shuffling of confusion before a few of the prisoners raised their hands, though hesitantly. Runeo and Khuna caught on quickly to what she was doing and pulled out their own receptives.

"Don't give them all away," Beno said before tossing a few of his earth receptives to a nearby man. The others followed suit, passing out the stones to any prisoner willing to take them.

"Find others able to use them," Alara said, passing all but her last two receptives off. "Dez." She turned to the woman still holding Sol.

"Once the level is taken, there is a secret room Sol knows about. There are probably more weapons and receptives inside, but be careful. There may be more councilguards there, too."

Alara was happy to have judged the mother correctly. She looked up from her position on the ground with a face of pure resolve. "We have it. Go."

Alara nodded before lurching forward to hug the woman. She looked down at Sol's face. In spite of the pain she was likely in, she somehow looked peaceful with her eyes closed. With a squeeze, Alara made an internal promise that this whole mess would not be in vain. "There should be healing supplies in the lab halls, too."

"Thank you," Dez whispered.

With one last look at Sol, Alara and the others ran, Beno at the lead, each of them many receptives lighter. But Alara didn't care. She was feeling better than she had in weeks. For the first time since the Haven, she felt like they were doing the right thing.

CHAPTER 62

ALARA

The commotion from the small revolt hadn't yet spread to the lift hallway yet, which Alara was grateful for. Living day in and day out in near darkness, she often forgot how big the underground ecosystem was. Explosions could go off at one end of the same level without anyone at the other end noticing.

Alara prayed their luck would hold out.

As they turned the corner toward the lift, the guards stood at attention, though no more alert than Alara remembered.

"Is something wrong?" one of them asked.

Beno grabbed the nearest guard by the back of his neck and whispered something into his ear before turning to the others.

"Sorry," Beno said, "but you three are needed down in the main tunnels, immediately."

The shorter man closest to the lift took a step backward. "I'll sound the alarm."

"No!" the guard directly next to Beno said. "You heard him! We're needed now. He'll sound the alarm."

With that, the man next to Beno ran off, leaving the other two to look between each other before following his lead. Alara hoped they'd be sending those guards to their certain death once they ran into the spreading revolt.

Without another word, the group filed into the lift. Beno switched the lever outside of the lift upward, tying it in place before following the group.

Alara hadn't noticed this initially, but it looked like the lift had a fail-safe system in place, requiring both the switch outside of the lift and inside of it to be pulled upward before it rose.

With a breath of exertion, Beno pulled the lever, and their journey upward began.

Alara didn't release her breath until they made it to the next level and the gate swung open. The guards here stood straight, bored, but still attentive. She didn't know how long they would have before the chaos below spread.

"Get on with it," she said, voice dropping low as she pushed Khuna forward and off the lift. The guards barely spared them a glance as they walked past them, allowing Beno to take the lead once more.

Alara tamped down the hope that blossomed in her chest as they made their way through the tunnels, one turn after another. Each time a guard's gaze landed on their group a little too long, Beno stepped over to them, sliding a hand onto their temple or neck, and a second later they were wandering off in a different direction. Still, she could see by the press of his lips each time he put his mind-walking receptive back in his pocket, that he was worried. It didn't take long before the first stone emptied, and he started working from one he stole from downstairs.

"You there," a guard's voice called out as they rounded a corner. Ahead, Alara could see the lift for Level Three sitting behind three guards, one with sharp black eyes hovering above his red scarf. He stared at them, focused and sure. "Where are you taking these prisoners? Do you have documentation?"

Beno didn't bother with answers, walking up to the man and placing a hand on his shoulder. Alara could see the brush of his bare fingers across the man's neck. "We're under the major's direct orders," he said, putting on a show for the other two guards.

Their group didn't slow down, pushing forward with the comfort of knowing they'd be let through anyway. But the guard's face only hardened at Beno's comment, his shoulder jerking out of the mind-walker's reach.

"I don't care whose orders you're under," he said. "Prisoner exit above Level Four requires special documentation."

While Beno's face remained impassive, his shoulders stiffened at the man's words. Something had gone wrong. He stepped forward again, reaching out to brush his hand against the guard's bare skin, but the man lurched back, a snarl on his face.

"Hands up," he snapped. "Up against the wall."

The other two guards by the lift stepped forward, drawn by the change in tone. Alara's muscles tensed, heart beating a deep rhythm in her chest. She wasn't ready to go back down. She wasn't ready to be caught. Trapped again.

The guard's face only grew harder when Beno didn't move, his eyes blackening in rage as he pulled out his club. "I said, against the wall. Now. All of you."

Emaru moved first, throwing the man against the wall with a sharp wave of her hand.

"Very sneaky," Khuna said, running forward and pulling the dagger from Runeo's belt before lunging at one of the other guards. Alara didn't bother with her own dagger, pulling the fire from the nearby torch and launching it at the face of the guard who'd first spoken.

The battle took little time. Even in their bedraggled state, they outnumbered the men, and their powers granted them a surprise the guards weren't expecting. It served as a reminder to Alara of just how powerful Emaru was with her airen abilities. They rushed forward, leaving the three men alive, but unconscious behind them, much to Emaru's annoyance.

They used the scarf from one of the guards to switch the lift controls upward on the outside and began their ascent.

Two levels down, three to go.

Though that didn't even take into account the base they'd have to wade through on their way out, all in hopes of not being questioned.

That thought didn't last long.

The silence as the lift ascended was cut off by the sounds of screams filling the shaft. If they were coming from above or below, Alara couldn't tell, but the increasing tenseness of the rest of the group made it all the more clear.

"This isn't going to be easy anymore, is it?" Khuna said.

"I tied that pretty damn well," Beno said. "Assuming they aren't able to cut it immediately, we should be good to reach the third level." He pulled the club from his belt. "But something tells me word has spread."

No one argued. Khuna readied her dagger and the others prepped their receptives.

The outer gates were already open to Level Three as the lift fell in place, the feet of a dozen guards coming into view first.

There went their easy escape.

CHAPTER 63

QUENTI

The distraction was going as well as they could have expected. Despite not having seen a single bruya in person, the guards she had led into the ravine were still sweeping through the trees. Another group showed up after they had, Nico tipping his chin as he passed Quenti and Manny.

Major Francisco wasn't among the group, and Quenti couldn't tell if she was happy or disappointed. She had no desire to see that man ever again, but she also didn't want him to muddy up the work in the mines. If the gods were on their side, he would be none the wiser in his over-sized estate.

Then again, this would cause extra problems with Mena and Cruz, who had still insisted on searching for Dante. Quenti wondered if they had been successful. For a plan that hinged on luck, it still shocked her that they'd be willing to take such a risk just to save the stupid man who had been little else than a thorn in Quenti's side from the beginning.

As they continued to fruitlessly sweep the trees for the elusive bruyas, her mind swung from one concern to the next. She wouldn't know if Khuna and the others had made it until hours from now, making every second feel like a lifetime.

"Sergeant," Manny said from beside her, his voice low so as to not be overhead.

"Yes, Stationeer."

"I have been informed by a few men who just arrived that there is an alarm sounding on the base. There's a potential escape attempt at the mines."

A terror passed over her face as she looked back toward the town. She could just barely hear the bells ringing in the distance. She had assumed they had all been in pursuit of the bruyas, but this proved otherwise.

Her mind cycled through the possibilities. Were they out? Were they caught? Was it a good sign or a bad sign that the alarm had been raised?

"What are your orders, Sergeant?" Manny asked, eyes seeking out hers, even as her mind spun. "We could continue our search, but you should return to see if you're needed by the major."

Her thoughts were moving slow, heart a stuttering beat in her chest. But she nodded.

"Yes."

She turned, her body catching up to her plan before her brain had. Manny's hand on her shoulder stopped her.

"And Sergeant," he said, softly. Kindly. "Good luck."

After sounding off a quick series of orders to the next in command to continue the search until the culprits were found, she was moving. She didn't bother with stealth. The townspeople didn't even notice as she passed by, too busy moving among themselves, confused as to what they should be trying to do, if anything. After all, this wasn't an alarm that sounded every day. Or ever.

A few tried to wave her down to get her attention, but she ignored them. No one here would know what in the underworld was going on. She needed to get to the base. Only there would she find answers. Only there could she actively help Khuna.

Before Quenti knew it, she was through the gates, only slowing when she ran the risk of running into the councilguards scrambling within the compound.

Her blood ran cold when she saw Major Francisco barking orders from outside the main building. She didn't want to speak with him or approach him, but she knew he was her best bet at getting information. No one bothered her as she marched forward, waiting until the group he was speaking to raced off with their orders.

"Major," she said, giving him a small salute as his eyes found hers. "I heard the alarms from north of town. Is this related to the bruya attack?"

"The bruya attack?"

"There was a bruya sighting, north of town." She stopped herself from saying how many guards were currently up in the ravine searching for these mysterious bruyas. She didn't want him deciding to call off their search for reinforcements here.

"Probably friends of the traitors," he said under his breath. "But no. There's been an attack from within the mines. An attempted escape."

"By who?"

"That we don't know yet."

"And has anyone escaped?" Quenti prayed her tone was one of contrition and not hope.

"No," Major Francisco said, easily. "And they won't. I've already sent the Receptive Unit down. No one is getting out as long as I'm here."

She wanted to ask more. She wanted to know anything and everything he could tell her. Where were the prisoners? How did they know of the attempted escape? What had gone wrong in their plan?

"Orders, sir?" she said.

Major Francisco eyed her before shaking his head. "Not yet, Sergeant. But stand by." He walked away, leaving her anxious and unsatisfied.

She barely made it to an alley between two buildings before she was collapsing on the ground, hot tears running down her face.

The others weren't out yet. The major seemed sure they wouldn't make it. And what was a Receptive Unit?

She dug her fingers into the sand beneath her until she felt the coolness below, focusing on the sensation of the two temperatures against her skin. A deep breath in and a deep breath out. She scrubbed the back of her hands across her face, trying to wipe any trace of her tears away.

After a minute, she was able to pull herself up, straightening her uniform and venturing back out into the sunlight. It didn't take long to find a stationeer dressed in the red uniform of the mine guards. She stepped in front of him before he could pass, giving him a sharp nod.

"Stationeer, where is the Receptive Unit?"

The boy blinked, confused and startled as he took in the insignia on her vest indicating her rank.

"I... the Receptive Unit is already in the mines. I—I think," he stuttered, "Sergeant," he added.

"Absolute negligence," she said, letting her annoyance show even as the poor guard vibrated with nerves. "They forgot to sign out their supplies. Where are they in the mines?"

"I—I think the Level Two lift, but we've been told to evacuate."

Quenti waved her hand in dismissal, raising an eyebrow when the guard only looked back with wide eyes.

"They don't want anyone else on Level Two during the explosion."

The explosion. "They're going to destroy the lift?"

The guard's eyes gave a questioning look—as if this was information she should have known. "Protocol E."

"Of course," she said. Her voice might have wavered. She didn't even know, as she walked away, feeling dazed as the information processed slowly through her mind.

Of course they wouldn't escape. Major Francisco was planning on blocking off the bottom levels of the mine where Khuna and the others were still trapped below.

And what was his plan after that? Would he leave the prisoners and guards to die, or was there another secret exit? Even if there was, how would she get the others there and out without being seen?

Quenti questioned if she should bolt to the major's estate to ask Mena and Cruz what to do, but there wasn't time. She'd need to make these decisions on her own.

Rope.

She needed a rope. It's what Mena had used to drop the receptives through the ventilation shaft. She knew from the diagrams Ardo had stolen for them that the shaft was plenty wide for a human, but the openings to each level were barely wide enough for a small animal to fit through. But if they realized the lifts were caved in, the shaft would be the next place to go.

That would be their only plan.

With a new sense of resolve and purpose, Quenti turned on her heels and headed back to the main building.

CHAPTER 64

ARDO

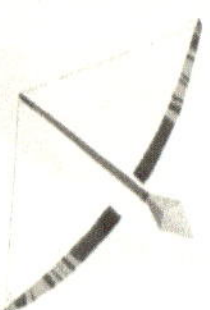

Ardo thought he knew anxiety.

He remembered waking up after his run-in with Alara and the other bruyas when they had broken into the Haven. The sick twist of his gut when he realized what had happened and who was responsible. Nothing should have been able to top that sense of horror and fear.

He had himself half-convinced that a mind-walker had manipulated her actions. But then he saw the passion in her eyes in the worship hall, and in that instant, he had known. All of it had been her.

And then she was gone. His best friend. The girl he had spent too many years thinking about, even when she wasn't around, was a traitor to the realm and a fugitive.

The next day, he watched as Senye Emaru was cuffed, tied, and led away, face wan and body barely healed from her injuries in the escape. He knew the only reason he wasn't being dragged away with her was because of his previous demotion. Apparently, his inaction when Quenti had grabbed Alara on the cliff so many weeks before had been a blessing in disguise.

Who would assume the man she had unceremoniously fired from his position would still hold any allegiance to her? It had been a lucky turn of events that spared him from any suspicion, despite his loyalty to her. But it all led to his being alone in the Haven, without a single friend. Even Adelmo was gone—a loss he hadn't expected to sting as sharp as it did until he found himself wandering through Cielo after the battle in the Haven, trying to understand what he wanted to do and where he could go.

He had a small handful of friends outside of the councilguards, but after Senye Emaru's arrest, none of them wanted to be seen with him. They knew better than to assume where his loyalties lay. So he'd ended up in Adelmo's abandoned house, staring at the fighting dummies and the dirty clothes left strewn about the small home, recognizing the tunic Alara had been wearing.

He had spent the next two weeks in pure fear. Fear for himself, fear for Senye Emaru, and a twisted fear for where Alara was and if she was okay. He couldn't quite convince himself to hate her for what she had done. He only knew the fear of not knowing if she was safe.

He thought that would be the peak. That there was no way he could ever be more scared or feel more helpless.

When he'd made the decision to chase after Senye Emaru and find a way to free her, he had taken control. He requested a transfer and his new life began. He'd never feel helpless again.

Yet, here he was, pacing in front of the lift gate, trying not to bleed anxiety as the guards stood next to him, near dead with boredom. He couldn't even differentiate which anxiety was worse—them getting caught, killed, his cover being blown, or the old gods awakening and coming down to claim Sombria as their own.

"El'dyo, I can't wait to get a mug of ferment in town tonight," one guard said, eyes half lidded as she leaned her head against the wall. "I haven't had a real break in three weeks. I'm over this whole influx of prisoners. You think Major Shithead wants to create a whole civilization down here?"

"Don't be disrespectful, Nina," the male guard snapped. His eyes threw a glare at her and Ardo, as well, as if he had encouraged her disrespect with his blank face. "That influx is our insurance that the Council is finally ridding Sombria of these traitorous rats."

"Were they not trying before?" she said, voice somewhere between bored and annoyed. "What were they spending all their money and time on before?"

"Probably trying to keep useless guards like you in line."

Ardo watched the exchange with tight lips. But he tried to keep his eyes blank, expression only showing the barest hint of annoyance at the conversation.

"Code Black!"

The yell came from down the hall, a frazzled looking guard turning the corner as he continued to yell.

"Escaped prisoners with magia!"

The male guard moved quicker than expected, grabbing a tube in the wall along the lift. "Code Black," he repeated. "Escaped prisoners wielding magia."

It took only thirty-five seconds. He counted them out in his mind, as he tried to think of a way to trick them into leaving their posts at the lift.

And then bells started to ring, the ground vibrating with their call.

"Damn," Nina said, rolling her eyes. "So much for my night off."

"This won't last long. These attempts never do," the other guard said.

"There'll still be hours of weavework and debrief after all of this though, even if we never even see the escapees."

"We should go down to help the others," Ardo said.

"Command is to stay at our post, new kid," the male guard, Lazlo, snapped, impatient in his apparent babysitting of his two fellow guards.

Ardo bit his tongue and tried to distract himself from the impatience growing inside him. The tunnels had become unusually quiet, and he realized why when he saw a set of guards march by down the hall, a line of prisoners following, subdued.

A sharp pain shot through his temples and Ardo doubled over, a hand against the wall to hold himself up.

"All guards, remain at your posts until given further orders." The voice was harsh and half-garbled in his head, nothing like the mind-talking he had been subjected to in the Haven. "The receptive unit will be working on Level Two." It went on to describe the escaping prisoners, and Ardo felt any small bit of hope drain from him as he recognized the descriptions all too well. At the same time, he noted with a flicker of relief that it seemed Senye Emaru was among the escapees, though she wasn't named. None of them were.

"El'dyo I hate when they use the mind-talking receptives," Nina said, looking green as the message came to an end.

"What in the underworld is the Receptive Unit?" Ardo asked, not caring if the question might give away his ignorance of the base. But the two guards only shrugged, just as much in the dark as him.

"They don't pay me to care," Lazlo said, looking a bit more anxious than he previously was. "They've never needed to go farther than temporary lockdown to stop an escape before. Makes me wonder what those bruya traitors got into."

Ardo had to assume it had to do with the receptives they had smuggled into the mines or the escaping ex-councilwoman they had in tow. No longer able to tamp down on his anxiety, he paced, assuming the others would see it as a reaction to the escape attempt. The guard that had come running with the alert seemed to imply the group had made it to this level. So where were they? The lift to Level Four wasn't so far from the lift to Level Two.

They would have easily been able to get to Ardo by now. At the very least, he thought he would have heard some hint of a struggle within the tunnels immediately surrounding them. But apart from the frantic guard and envia communication, there was nothing.

He jumped at the scraping of metal on metal behind him and turned toward where the gate to Level Two lift vibrated.

Not good.

He clenched his jaw and wrapped a hand around the club at his waist. Lazlo and Nina looked completely unaffected by the arriving lift, but Ardo could only assume it was backup coming to catch Alara and the others before they even made it out.

They already had enough to fight against as it was without this new group.

But then the vibrations stopped and the gate didn't open. Even Lazlo looked unnerved as he walked over, sliding it open carefully. The lift wasn't there. Had it stopped somewhere between the levels?

"Is everything all right up there?" Lazlo called up into the shaft.

The distant voice that answered was sharp and impatient. "Stay at your post and shut up, soldier."

Lazlo rolled his eyes—the first indication of any annoyance—before turning back and giving the other two a shrug.

"You heard him," he said, leaning back against the doors.

"I don't like this," Ardo said.

Nina looked just as uncomfortable as they heard the rattle of the lift above them and the heavy bang of stone on metal.

Lazlo refused to make eye contact with either of them, his position held against the gate.

Nina and Ardo looked at each other as another bang rattled through the shaft.

"Maybe we should check on the others on this level," Nina said. "We haven't seen anyone since the first alert."

"Hold your position and follow orders, Specialist."

Ardo shook his head. He was over playing along with this ridiculous game.

"I'm going to see what's going on."

"I'm coming too," Nina said, a couple steps behind him.

Lazlo gave a grunt under his breath, but he didn't follow or try to stop them. Ardo had no doubt he was already planning how he'd write them up later for insubordination.

They were only a few yards from the lift when the ground shook with a force beyond a simple rumble. Nina fell to her knees with a crack and a second later, Ardo was thrown against the ground as a wave of dirt and air exploded down the hall from where they'd just come. His ears popped with the sound of the earth splitting and he heard Nina give a muffled scream beside him.

As soon as the first rumble stopped, there was another softer crack and he looked up to see a large stone dropping from the ceiling a few feet from them.

"Shit," he said, stumbling to his feet, "Run!"

He could barely hear his own voice. He wasn't sure if he had even shouted or if there was anyone to hear him, but Nina's body came into view through the clouds of dust, and he saw she was bleeding freely from her shoulder, but standing. Her eyes met his and she nodded before following the orders and disappearing into the tunnel ahead.

Ardo looked back at the lift for a second, questioning if he should check on Lazlo. They might be on different sides of this battle, but the councilguards were still his brothers-in-arms. But as another large stone fell from the ceiling, the dust parted to give a brief glimpse of where the lift had once been. There was only a pile of stones there now, no sight of the guard beneath the rubble.

So he ran, trying to remember the way to the next lift amid the ringing in his ears. Ardo tried to hold back the bile on his tongue.

The lift to the second level was gone. The shaft was gone. They were stuck down here until the soldiers decided to dig them out. Their only means of escape had been blown up.

Chapter 65

Alara

Alara was regretting her years of refusing to train her magia. The tunnels were winding and thin, so even with plenty of torches to feed on, she was too afraid to let go of her powers fully. She'd be just as likely to burn them alive as save them from a guard's attack. It was something she'd been working on prior to their capture, but the weeks of suppressed magia had left her as uncoordinated as before.

Instead, she was relying more on the dagger she'd found than her receptive, only using small bursts of fire to distract the guards she was fighting.

They were outnumbered three to one, and most of them were either exhausted, injured, or running low on magia. Alara had seen Beno throw down his last mind-walking stone as the man he tried to manipulate into dropping his weapon fought him off with ease.

Alara ducked and a club soared overhead as she jammed her blade into the guard's ankle below the leathers protecting their legs. Her dagger bit through the tendon and they cried out as they crumpled.

She plucked the club from their loosened grip and knocked them across the temple.

She was about to turn and swing at the guard attacking Khuna when the earth shifted beneath them and nearly all of them went sprawling to the ground. The rumble that followed sounded like the world around them was crumbling and Alara instinctively covered her head, as if she might catch the earth as it consumed her. But other than a few loose stones, the walls and ceiling didn't fall.

The guards they were fighting didn't look any less confused or disturbed by the sound, and they took advantage of the distraction to run down the hall and toward wherever the explosion had come from. Somehow, the escaped prisoners were no longer the most pressing matter to attend to down in the mines, and before long, their group was left with a few spare moments to breathe as Runeo knocked the last remaining guard out with a stolen club.

"What in Sol's name was that?" he asked, turning to look at the rest of their pale faces.

"Nothing good," Beno said. "We should move."

The others didn't need to verbalize their acknowledgement before they were running, following him toward what Alara could only assume was the next lift.

Every other turn, they ran into another set of guards, their receptives and energy slowly draining with each encounter. Maybe it was a good thing she limited her magia use.

The guards didn't look much better, though. One female guard who came running around the corner was already bleeding and covered in dirt by the time they'd engaged her. It seemed their small battle wasn't the only one being waged and she remembered again that Ardo was supposed to be on this level. Had he been responsible for this?

The thought had barely slipped through her mind when she saw the tanned skin and messy mop of hair she knew all too well turn the corner.

Alara hesitated in her lunge toward the woman, suddenly unable to look away from Ardo. His eyes were wild and his hair was covered in dirt. The guard took her moment of distraction to swing at her with her own blade. It was Runeo's body that pushed her out of the way of the dagger's arc. He jammed his stolen club into the guard's injured shoulder, throwing her back and onto the ground.

"Nina," Ardo said, "stand down."

The guard let out a groan of pain, eyes swiveling to him in confusion.

Ardo barely looked at her, his eyes focused on Alara, gaze heavy. "Go check on the others and see if anyone has gotten follow up orders on what we're supposed to be doing now."

"Are you blind?" she shouted. "These are the escaped prisoners!"

"Do as I say if you have any hopes of a night off after all of this," he said, voice icy in a way that Alara had never heard before, even when she had betrayed him in Cielo.

The guard seemed to understand the threat and looked between their group before stumbling away down a side tunnel, shoulder cradled in her hand.

"She'll get more guards," Runeo growled, pointing his club threateningly at Ardo. "Are you stupid or trying to get us killed?"

"The guards have bigger problems," he said, not quite looking at Runeo. "We all have bigger problems."

"Bigger than the prison guards ordered to kill us?"

"They blew up the lift to Level Two," he said through clenched teeth. The words had Runeo snapping his jaw shut.

"What?" Beno asked, his words echoing everyone's thoughts. "What does that mean?"

"What do you think it means?" Ardo said, voice annoyed in a way Alara rarely saw. "I mean, the lift is gone. The shaft is gone.

Some Receptive Unit, as they called it, ripped a damned hole in the mine and collapsed the tunnel."

"So where do we go, now?" Khuna asked, voice tight.

"There has to be another way out," Runeo said. "Otherwise, they've buried the guards down here with us."

"I think that's exactly what they did," Ardo said, face showing what he thought of their strategy. "They even buried one of us... one of their own with it."

"So we're trapped down here?" Alara said, her voice an airy squeak. The adrenaline that had been keeping her moving until that moment was beginning to drain away, a wave of hopeless dread crashing down to replace it.

"What about the vent?" Ardo asked, turning to Beno. "The one we smuggled the receptives through?"

Beno shook his head. "The shaft may be big enough to fit a human, but that's only if we can get into it. The opening was barely big enough to fit my arm."

"At this point, we have nothing to lose, so blowing it open is an option."

"I don't think we have much of a choice," Emaru said, speaking up for the first time since running into Ardo.

Alara felt her heart skip at the sound of his voice, so familiar and yet so foreign. Ardo's eyes fell on her, his lips pulling up into a small smile.

"Alara," he said.

She couldn't tell if it was from infatuation or weakness, but all she could do was let out an exhausted breath before Ardo's eyes settled on Emaru.

"It's good to see you, Senye," he said.

"It's good to see you too, even after that whole mess at the Haven." Emaru gave a smile that Alara had only been on the receiving end of a handful of times in her life. "I'd apologize for demoting you, but then where would we even be if I hadn't?"

"Let's go," Ardo said, moving forward to place a hand on Emaru's shoulder. The gesture made Alara's lip curl and she turned away so as not to be seen. Hot acid burned up her throat.

Their group moved, following behind Beno as he traced his path back to the ventilation shaft. Eventually, he came to stop in front of a dead end, and he waved at a small crevice carved into the wall. After taking a moment to look it over, it was clear the opening wasn't natural. It's edges were too straight, too clean.

"Oh, why didn't I think of this?" Runeo's words were biting as he stepped forward measuring the small crevice with his hand. It was a single palm's width wide.

"Not helpful," Khuna said, her voice short.

"Could you use your dagger?" Beno said.

Alara didn't wait for Runeo to respond, shoving him out of the way, and picking away at the wall with the short blade. A high pitched scratch of metal on stone echoed in the tunnel, but the wall didn't even seem to notice the edge in the slightest.

"Move aside," Khuna said, shuffling forward with more timidity than Alara. She pressed a hand against the stone, her receptive clutched tightly in her other.

For a minute, they stood watching in anxious silence, Emaru and Ardo continually looking down the tunnel, expecting an ambush any moment. But for now, all seemed quiet, the councilguards likely figuring out what to do with themselves now that they were trapped. Alara had to wonder how long it would be until a guard remembered the vent shafts could reach the surface. Or was that even common knowledge among them? She could have counted the number of things most councilguards didn't know about the Haven, despite being stationed there.

And even if they did... they likely didn't have receptives to exploit the opening.

"You're a genius." Beno's words pulled Alara from her own thoughts, and she noticed the stone around the ventilation hole was darker than before.

Then she realized what was happening. Khuna was pulling water to the surface. Beno reached out with his own receptive and Alara saw the tension on his face as he pulled at the earth and whatever roots he might find nearby. She wasn't surprised when his complexion turned a pale green, even as the earth around the opening barely shifted. She doubted there was much life to be found in the stone this deep and so close to the Ruinedlands.

"Runeo, do you have any receptives left?" he said, letting go of his magia with a small gasp.

"A bit," he said.

"I could only form a few cracks, but if you can push the air through them, with the water Khuna surfaced, it may be enough to crumble the stone."

"Here," Emaru threw the receptive before Runeo had even turned, but he snatched it out of the air without looking.

"Thanks," he said, though his tone didn't speak of gratitude. A second later, the tunnel was buzzing with a new air current that shivered along Alara's skin and moved the tangled hair across her face. It was going to take days to brush out the tangles from her curls when this was all done. An almost manic laugh bubbled up from her throat at the out of place thought.

"We're about to have company," Ardo said, voice soft, yet stern.

She was so focused on her own thoughts she hadn't noticed Ardo's change of posture as he peered down the tunnel.

Alara could just make out the shuffling of footsteps getting gradually closer to their tunnel. They were too loud to not be the booted feet of guards.

"Don't they have anything better to do?" Khuna said.

"I almost have it," Runeo said, not letting go of his powers even as the others shifted into fighting stances.

"Even if we get the opening widened before they get here," Beno said, "we don't have time for all of us to get climbing."

"Then we fight," Ardo said, face set in a determination that sent an ache through Alara's chest. The last time she had seen that look had been in the Haven when they had been fighting on opposite sides. The realization didn't warm her feelings for the ex-councilwoman standing next to him.

"Give me your club and dagger," Beno said, moving to stand beside Ardo.

"What?"

"We don't have enough energy or time to fight and we don't know how many guards are headed our way. Someone needs to distract them."

"Then we can both do it," Ardo said, still gripping his weapons.

"*You* need to help lead them off the base. You have the best chance of getting them out of here without being seen."

"And you're going to get yourself killed by running off alone."

"This whole thing is my fault anyway," Beno said. "Besides, if I can get back to the lab, there are more receptives inside. I'll have a fighting chance." That escape plan was even more foolish than the one they were actively pursuing.

Descend back two floors and then climb back up amid this chaos?

It was clear what his plans truly were.

Beno looked back at the vent which was slowly cracking. "Well, climb!"

"You'll have a better chance of walking out of here if one of us goes with you," Khuna said, lips pinched in the type of disapproval normally left to parents.

"No offense to any of you," Beno said, raising his eyebrow. "But I doubt that."

He turned back to Ardo and put his hand out. "Now give me your weapons. We don't have time for argument."

Alara knew he was right. The footsteps were growing louder, and it was impossible to tell when the guards would turn the corner.

Ardo shoved more than handed the weapons over, but not before he grabbed the bruya by his tunic. "I better see you at the end of this. I am not answering to your sister."

Beno only gave a cocky smile. It was an act, Alara knew, but she couldn't help but be comforted by the small bit of optimism. With only time for a tilt of his chin in goodbye, Beno ran and disappeared around the corner, his dagger scraping loudly across the stone as he did.

CHAPTER 66

ALARA

They decided Khuna and Emaru would go first into the shaft, with the rest of them worried their injuries would prevent them from being able to move easily and quickly in the space. Having them in the lead allowed the others to keep an eye on them and make sure the escape plan was feasible.

It was clear even crawling through the newly opened hole was difficult for Khuna, her movements stiff and jerky. But when Runeo tried to point this out, she quickly told him off, stating that she had spent two months of her childhood climbing trees with a broken arm and this couldn't be much worse. Alara wasn't so sure as she carefully wedged herself in the vertical portion of the shaft, which likely dropped at least two levels deeper.

"How do you feel?" Runeo asked, his tone quavering with a nervousness Alara wasn't accustomed to.

"I'm okay," Khuna said, voice echoing. "It's a tight fit though. We'll see how the taller of you fit."

"Senye Emaru, you're next," Ardo said, motioning for her.

The others didn't argue, but stepped aside to let the taller woman through. Not for the first time since finding her, Alara recognized how fragile the woman looked. She averted her eyes, not wanting to see her struggle through the opening.

"Make sure your feet are flat against the wall and use your upper back on the other end so—"

"—I know what I'm doing," Emaru said.

"Right," Khuna said. "What was I thinking?"

"Who's next?" Runeo asked.

"You go," Alara said, waving him on.

"No." He stepped back away from the opening. "I should go last. I have a bit of receptive left and we may need my powers to help in the climb."

"Alara, go," Ardo said, a hand on the small of her back, pushing her forward.

Alara tried not to linger on the feeling too much, especially as she caught Runeo's glare toward Ardo.

With only a small moment of anxiety, she ducked down and pulled herself through the opening, shuffling along on her hands and knees. It was easier going for her than it had been for Emaru or Khuna. Even still, when she made it to the end of the tiny tunnel, her heart gave a swoop as she caught a glimpse of the shadowy darkness stretching out before her. She had made it into the shaft and had come face to face with the drop down into near blackness, somehow even darker than she was used to in the mines. The light from above, blocked now by Emaru and Khuna barely illuminated the walls of the tunnel. She couldn't decide if the darkness helped ease the anxiety or made the unknown drop worse.

"How did you..." she spoke softly, not wanting her voice to echo through the vent. She knew the other two would easily hear her whisper.

"Shuffle out carefully and use your hands to brace against the far wall as you turn." Khuna spoke just as softly as Alara, and it somehow sounded as though she was whispering directly into her ear.

For all her years running around in the tunnels of the Haven, this was a new experience for Alara, and she held her breath as she followed Khuna's orders. Inch by inch, she moved her body forward, catching herself on the opposite wall and crawling her hands up until she was positioned diagonally in the shaft, Emaru's trousers just above her, brushing her hair.

"Just like climbing trees?" she asked, as she turned herself to press her shoulders against the wall and bring her feet into the shaft.

"Not in the least," Khuna admitted.

Alara chuckled, happy for the distraction.

"Lili would have volunteered to stay behind with Beno," she said, voice soft. She didn't know where the thought had come from, but she couldn't help but express it in the moment as they shimmied upward.

"Yes, she would have." Alara could almost hear the crack in Khuna's voice.

"Ready for me?" Ardo's voice echoed eerily from beyond, but muffled and yet louder than even their whispers.

"One minute," she called back, experimentally twisting her shoulders as she stepped *up* the wall. She felt sturdy in her movements, but with all the awareness of the death fall that waited below her at a single slip.

It was difficult to measure distance in the shadowy darkness, but after a handful of steps, she let Ardo know he could follow. She paused long enough to hear him squeeze through the tunnel, tiny pebbles freeing themselves from the wall and descending into the shaft below. The moment she could tell he made it in, she started her slow ascent once again.

Her heart never quite settled into a normal rhythm as they

continued to climb. She could hear the others, Khuna and Emaru above, Ardo and Runeo below, but it was difficult to make anyone out clearly in the constantly shifting light. The only moment of affirmation that their steps were getting them anywhere was when Alara's toe caught on a small square hole in the wall. She squeaked at the sudden change and heard Ardo's sharp intake below her.

"Are you okay?" he said.

She shushed him before tilting her head down to look at her feet. They had made it to the next level's vent. She could see light on the other side, but no indication of movement.

"I think we're at the second level," she finally hissed when she was sure there was no one directly outside the vent. "Should we slip out here?"

"No," Ardo said, voice rough with exertion. "I don't want to run into the Receptive Unit and find out any other tricks they have up their sleeves. The vent goes all the way to the surface. We can slip out from there."

Alara hated the idea of climbing two more levels, but she couldn't argue his point. She didn't want to run into anyone holding the same explosives she had seen used in the expanding mine shafts. She had felt the reverberation from those explosions one too many times. So she shut her mouth and kept moving, one shuffling step at a time. This was their chance to make it out without being noticed.

They had been climbing for countless minutes, when a sharp yell sounded and then cut off somewhere below her. She strained her neck, trying to see around where Ardo was braced and heard the soft sound of pebbles tumbling down the shaft.

"Runeo!" she whispered, trying hard to balance staying quiet with her anxiety.

There was a groan below and she saw Ardo shifting carefully, trying to look below himself.

"Do you need help?" he asked.

"I'm fine," Runeo bit out, the tension clear in his voice. "Just slipped."

"Should we pause?" Alara said.

"No, we need to keep going. I'm not dying down here. Especially with Micos out *there*."

They fell into silence at the words, no one willing to argue with the declaration. So they continued.

"Are the walls getting smoother or is that just me?" Ardo asked after a few more minutes of tension. The comment made Alara's lips twitch with amusement. He'd always had the ability to make her laugh no matter how stressful things were. She'd missed that.

"That might be the least of our problems," Khuna's voice came from above, a strange echo in the vent.

"What does that mean?" Ardo and Alara asked at the same moment.

"I think the vent is getting wider too. And we still have a bit to climb," she said, voice slow. Alara could hear the careful control she was keeping over her fear. "I don't know if I'll be able to make it to the top."

"What about the Level One vent?" Alara said. "Can we slip out there?"

"I didn't see a vent for Level One," Khuna said.

"There might not be a vent since the first level already has multiple openings," Ardo said, answering the unasked question.

"So we either climb up and pray to the gods we can make it or we climb down and... pray to the gods," Alara said.

"We pray to whatever god we believe in," Ardo answered. "Any and all of them."

"I'm going to keep going," Khuna said, already moving based on the sound of her voice. "I might be fine."

"Might be fine," Alara said. "Love those chances."

But she kept moving too. She couldn't see Khuna with Emaru in the way, but she quickly understood what the bruya was talking about. After a few more feet, Alara noticed she was starting to stretch out across the shaft, no longer cramped. If she wasn't terrified she might have been relieved by the extra space.

She stopped for a second, twisting to see if she might be able to turn in the shaft. If she could use her hands to crawl instead of her shoulders, she'd have another foot or so of height. But she wasn't sure how she'd twist around or how long her arms would hold her.

"Um," Khuna said and Alara could hear the slight waver she was concealing, "I think I've reached my limit. What are the thoughts on crawling back down?"

"Shit," Runeo said from below. "We passed the second level a bit back, but we still need to find a way to crack open the vent. I don't have much magia left."

"Then we're stuck," Alara said, voice strained. She hated how defeated she felt, and even more that it came across in her voice.

"Give me a second to think," Ardo said.

Khuna's laugh was thready from above. "Now I'm really glad Lili isn't here. She'd have died about now."

"She could have just grown some roots to pull us out," Alara said, biting back the sadness even as she felt the fond smile on her lips.

"We're not giving up yet," Ardo said. "Just give me a minute." But Alara knew he was speaking out of more desperation than confidence.

They stayed like that, in silence, bracing against the walls and knowing for every second that ticked by, their strength waned and the chance of falling increased.

Alara wondered where the shaft ended. Did it end at Level Five or did it go lower than that? Not that it really mattered.

Khuna's voice broke through her dark thoughts. She was only too glad for the interruption.

"Uh..." she said. "So, should I trust the rope that suddenly appeared from above us?"

"What?" All four of them spoke in unison, even Emaru's voice tight with incredulity.

CHAPTER 67

QUENTI

Quenti could feel her heart in her chest as she leaned over the wooden slats that separated the shaft below from the air above. She had already pried two of the planks away, throwing them to the side so she could look down into the depths below. She thought she could hear the faint sound of talking, and she knew it was them. It had to be. Her heart couldn't take another option.

The rope was curled beside her. She needed to tie it to something. It wouldn't reach the bottom of the shaft by a long shot, but if she could get it partway down...

Her mind whirling with all the potential hiccups, she looked around, desperate for somewhere sturdy she could trust to hold her weight with the rope.

Perhaps it was because of her focus, so sharply pinned on helping Khuna escape, that she didn't notice the other councilguards until they were practically on top of her.

Major Francisco stood only thirty yards away, dressed in his black uniform, pristine despite the sand. Even the unit of guards at his back looked grubby and bedraggled in comparison, as if his ego wouldn't even allow the filth of Lejon to touch him.

"Lucía," he said, a smile that Quenti could only describe as serpentine stretching across his face. He said her name slowly, with such disgust and bite that she didn't bother to put on her Lucía face and pretend. She stood, shoulders back, sneer evident.

"Emiliano," Quenti said, verbalizing his first name—one she hadn't even heard spoken aloud before. Only in the weaves that she and Ardo pored over had she seen it written. She hated the way it sounded almost as much as she hated his expression.

"I believe I have some friends of yours," he said, flicking a bored hand at the line of guards behind him.

Two grim-faced women stepped aside, allowing a perfect view of the three prisoners on their knees just beyond.

Mena, Cruz, and Dante all looked worse for wear, but Dante looked particularly haggard, his eyes black and a line of dried blood caked along his chin from a split lip already beginning to heal. Mena and Cruz were pale, but Mena's face was screwed up in determination and Cruz's eyes burned with fire. They hadn't yet had the hope beaten from them like Dante.

"When I was informed of the break-in at my estate, I realized that none of this could be a coincidence," he said. "Between your appearance, the bruya sightings, and an escape attempt, one obvious factor to look closer at was you. I'd be lying if I didn't say I was the slightest bit disappointed."

For a moment, she wondered if she should lie and slip back into Lucía's persona. But she knew it was useless. Instead she reflected Francisco's hungry smile, eyes sparkling as she saw his anger shift.

"Upset that we interfered with your murder spree?" she said.

"I knew something was off with you," he said, voice infuriatingly cold and unfeeling. "I suppose I should have known better. I should have pushed further, even after the evening at my estate."

Quenti was choking on fear, but she refused to let the man see that. "But I had you. Makes you wonder, doesn't it?"

"Wonder what?"

"How many others you've missed," Quenti said. "I know you don't like to believe it, but even within your tight-knit blameless club, there will always be bruyas like me."

"Perhaps," he said. "But at least, after today, there will be fewer of you to worry about. In fact, I should thank you all for giving me an excuse to get rid of so many at once."

"You'll destroy your own mines just to kill some bruyas?"

"We'll give them a few weeks, and when we know everyone's starved to death, we can dig out the mine and restart."

"And your own guards?"

"They know the risks of working in the mines, and their families will be well compensated."

Quenti bit her lip, infuriated by his casual tone.

An echo of words behind her drew her attention, and she turned without thinking, eyes finding the open shaft at her feet. The voices she had thought she had heard were clearer now. They weren't just in the shaft, they were climbing upward.

"Miguel, Josye," Francisco said, "grab the rope."

Two men larger than Quenti thought possible, stepped forward from the group, ignoring her even as they passed her.

"Go ahead, Lucía," Francisco said. "Drop it down for our friends."

Feeling sick, she did just that, letting the end of the rope snake down into the dark shaft below her. The two towers Francisco had called Miguel and Josye braced themselves as something—someone—tugged on the rope.

"Hello?" Khuna's voice called from below, and she couldn't stop the leap of happiness from sending her stumbling forward.

"Yes!" she said, voice shaking even as she caught a glimpse of her partner below. "Sol, you're alive."

She didn't even realize she was crying until her vision of Khuna below her blurred. She needed to say something—to warn them. Perhaps they could go back down and find another way out. But before she could even think the words, a cold bite of steel crossed her neck.

"Step back, Lucía," Francisco hissed. "If you so much as make a peep, I'll have my guards here drop your friends down the shaft before you have a chance to reunite."

Quenti bit her tongue, letting the sharp pain of it focus her thoughts. She was lightheaded, unsure if the oxygen from her lungs was even making it to her brain. Once the others were out, they'd stand a chance at fighting. But there was nothing they could do now as they hung below.

Khuna emerged first, her eyes not so much as glancing at the others, but finding Quenti immediately. And then they settled on Francisco, her eyes flashing with a mix of anxiety and anger, though the blade on Quenti's throat kept her from calling out to the others.

She surrendered as another set of councilguards threw her onto her knees, pulling her hands tightly behind her back.

Quenti twitched at the brutal treatment, but Francisco still held her tight. She was helpless as Emaru climbed up out of the shaft next, looking even worse than Dante. She didn't even put up a fight as she was cuffed and half dragged to where the others kneeled. One by one the others materialized: first Alara, face twisting in hate at the sight of the guards, and then Ardo and Runeo. There was an unending stretch of tension, of waiting. But then Miguel pulled the rope up and out of the shaft, backing away.

Quenti's eyes searched out Mena behind her, looking sickly now. Any hope or determination seemed to have drained from her.

"Cave the shaft in," Francisco said. "This'll end all of this faster for us, anyway." He didn't even wait for his orders to be followed, waving to the guards holding their group to start walking away without a second glance, leaving the hundreds of bruyas and blameless to die. He dragged Quenti along by the collar of her uniform, not bothering with the blade at her throat. The safety of everyone else was enough to keep her in check, and she wished she were heartless enough for that not to be the case. There was nothing she could do except let herself be dragged along.

As they passed by Dante, Francisco's hand brushed back the man's hair, who flinched with a pained grunt. "Thank you again for all the information, young man," he said. "Too bad our prison is out of order or else I would have let you live. I do want to thank all of you for allowing me to know the weaknesses of our mines. We'll have to do better when we rebuild and restart."

Quenti's jaw tightened. After all of that talk, it was Dante, of all people, who squealed on them. She would have been mad had it not been for the already-dead expression on his face. "So, that's it," Quenti said to Francisco. "You kill everyone down there and you kill us. And you think this all goes away?"

"Don't worry, bruya," he said, hand tightening along her arm. "We'll be ready when more of you come, skittering to the surface like rats in a flood. And we'll squash each and every one of you until there is nothing left of your people. This land hasn't belonged to your magia for centuries. It's time you realize that."

An explosion rocked the ground from behind them and Quenti felt herself fall forward, caught only by the vise grip of Francisco.

"The citizens of Lejon and my soldiers have been getting restless. A nice public execution will be just what they need to remember everything the Council does for them, even out here."

"This won't end with us."

"I don't imagine it will," Francisco said. "But it will end someday.

And when it does, the blameless will be the ones left standing. Your magia and superstitions will be nothing more than relics of the past."

CHAPTER 68

QUENTI

As they marched through the base, the chaos of before was gone. Guards were grouped together by unit, some silent and standing at attention, others chatting as if thousands hadn't just been murdered in cold blood. Beyond the main base, toward where the mines were—had once been—a funnel of smoke and dust snaked into the air. Other than that, there was just silence.

Francisco sent a small group of runners ahead of their miserable parade, drawing the attention of each unit as they passed. And just as they were moving into the open land that sat between Lejon and the base, the bells of the city rang once more, calling out a mandatory gathering.

The walk across the sands and into town felt both endless and immediate. And through it all, the grip on her arm never faltered, a constant thrum of pain in the back of her mind.

The same makeshift, wooden platform that Emaru had been whipped on was already standing in the center of the green. The crowds were still gathering in the square and along the patios of the buildings overlooking the plaza, but they moved with a silence that spoke of an unsettling knowledge of what was coming. The air didn't quite hold the excitement it had during Emaru's initial punishment. Perhaps it was news of what had happened in the mines spreading already or the fear from the supposed bruya attack still dampening the town's spirit. She doubted they were mourning for the bruyas lost, but some of the guards left down in the mines had to have family and friends.

The councilguards spread out as they came through the square, clearing a path and pushing the crowds back to encircle the stage. And that's what it was: a stage for Francisco to perform his little act of supporting peace in Sombria as he tore it down from its very foundations. They were lined up in front of the platform, facing out toward the crowd of blameless. Bile rose in Quenti's throat as she took in the dark stains along the wooden planks beneath her. Old blood—and not just Emaru's from her whipping.

Francisco finally released his grip on her and she stumbled forward, even as another grabbed her arms and tied them behind her back with unnecessary force. She hissed out a curse as her shoulder twisted. Her head turned even as her knees ached trying to keep her balance.

Cruz was kneeling beside her, face blank, now as distant as Dante's had been. For once, no longer calculating. Khuna was three down, her own eyes focused on Quenti's. They were filled with a pain that shot through her own chest and made her hands shake.

There were a hundred words she wanted to tell Khuna, but instead she just kept her eyes focused on her, refusing to look away even as she felt Francisco pacing behind her. He was giving a speech again, calling out the crowds below. He was speaking of treason, of balance and peace, and a need to shed blood to keep the country safe. Quenti let the words wash over her, feeling nothing even as he called for blameless to forsake magia and those with it who act against Sombria.

She only had eyes for Khuna, with her wide, almond eyes and pink lips that looked pale in the sunlight. She could see the dark circles beneath her eyes and the fading bruises along her skin from her time in the mines. She was thinner than she'd been, her collarbones sharp underneath her skin. But she could also just make out the pale freckles along her brow and the small curl of her hair along her forehead from the humidity of the day.

She barely even registered when Francisco called out Senye Cruz's name, and the woman beside her was dragged up and away, somewhere behind her.

Even still, she kept her eyes focused on the only thing that mattered. She kept them focused on Khuna.

CHAPTER 69

ALARA

Alara flinched as a set of thick fingers pulled at her hair and forced her to face where Senye Cruz was now kneeling in front of Major Francisco. A weight dropped in her stomach, and she felt she might be sick. For the second time in a month, a councilwoman kneeled on this platform as the major leered over her. Senye Cruz's face was drained of blood. She looked exhausted, the fine lines somehow overpowering her other features, but her chin was still set in determination, eyes roaming the crowd in defiance. It was like a challenge to them all to rise up.

"Are you okay, Senye?" Alara said. It was a stupid question, she knew, but one she couldn't help but ask.

Senye Cruz's gaze remained focused forward. "My son," she said. "I die knowing he is a traitor."

"What?" Alara said, eyes blinking, her confusion somehow overwhelming her fear and anxiety, but she was kept from pursuing the subject further by a smack to the back of her head.

"I stand here today," Major Francisco's voice rang out across the plaza, "to remind everyone in Lejon and beyond what becomes of traitors who work against the people of Sombria—against the Council that has kept our lands peaceful for hundreds of years. And to remind everyone that there is no exception to our justice. All traitors, whether councilwoman, guard, magite, or *bruya*—" he said that last world with thinly veiled disgust "—will be punished."

The crowd erupted into unsettling chatter, but fell silent as the councilguards surrounding them shifted. Alara imagined Francisco was getting exactly what he wanted. The people of Lejon were scared for their lives.

"Lena Cruz, leader of the rebels, ran from the Haven as a coward and a traitor. Today she faces the punishment for her crimes in aiding and abetting bruyas in the kidnapping and murder of Sombrian civilians. She also led an assassination attempt on me this very afternoon, and it is only through the bravery of our councilguards that I still stand before you today. She is responsible for hundreds of deaths and has shown no remorse in her actions."

Alara hated the turn of Major Francisco's lips as he spoke. She was so focused on his sneer, she didn't notice Senye Cruz had opened her mouth to speak over him. It took a second for her to realize, that even cuffed, the ex-councilwoman was projecting a vague impression of her words into everyone's minds, amplifying her voice just enough to block out their captors.

The Council no longer stands for what it was created for, she said, the cold distance replaced with a determined expression. *The man speaking before you rules with fear and he'd have you convinced that the threat to Sombria is from the outside, from the bruyas. But the true threat to what Sombria is and has been is from the inside. The Council is turning our people against each other, bruya against Sombrian, blameless against mage. But this country was built on unity and a belief in everyone's humanity.*

Her eyes flashed bright as she swept her gaze over the plaza before her. *Do not forget our true enemy: division and fear.*

Cruz went silent, and Alara saw the twist of the major's fist in her hair, pulling her neck taut. She could just make out the words he hissed into her ear a few feet away.

"Such a beautiful speech. Too bad your words mean nothing. They will fear you and the threat of magia because that is the nature of the world. Because they have every right to fear all of you and what you represent."

He pulled something out from his belt, shining bronze in the waning sunlight. It was a thin cylinder, much like a dart launcher she had seen from foreigners across the sea north of Sombria. A receptive was set into the carved handle, just below Major Francisco's thumb.

"But I bring with me some semblance of hope," he said, holding the device over his head. "Something to be salvaged from this era of mages we live in. A weapon to defeat them once and for all!"

The plaza maintained its confused silence, though it didn't seem to bother the major.

"I want you to look out at the crowd and see them all standing there," he whispered so only those kneeling could hear him. "No one is running to help you. Today is the beginning of your rebellion's death, and it starts with you."

Alara didn't even see him move. With no more than the twitch of his finger, there was a sudden explosion from the small cylinder.

Blood splattered across the platform. A drop fell against Alara's lip and she tasted copper. Cruz's body slumped to the side and splayed across the ground. She glanced over for the briefest moment, just enough to see the missing piece of Cruz's forehead. It was as though a small explosion had gone off inside it. Alara averted her eyes quickly, instead focusing her gaze on the woman's chest, waiting for it to rise and fall as it had done countless times before. She had to breathe. She had to be alive. Alara couldn't handle what it meant to have seen Senye Cruz lying so still.

"No!" Dante was the sole voice ringing out in a sea of silence.

Face red and wet, chest heaving in a panic. He was expressing what they were all feeling in that moment and it made her stomach twist tighter. She'd barely even seen the man shaken and here he was curled over himself looking broken, face a mask of despair and rage.

And all the while, blood spread slow and dark from where Cruz lay, unmoving, pooling around Francisco's feet and staining his boots.

Alara couldn't stop the bile that rose up in her, and she choked, shook violently, and the only thing keeping her upright was the guard's hand.

And then the crowd was no longer silent. A few shouted out in fear at the explosion and even more were whispering and muttering, trying to understand what had just happened.

The small bronze device was still clutched in Francisco's hand, a small trail of smoke trailing from the tip. He was proud as he held it above his head, circling to let his gaze fall across the entire plaza.

"Behold, the future," he said, raising the weapon over his head once again. "This is how the blameless will regain our power over Sombria. We will no longer cower in fear of magia, but we will wield it and control it just as mages have always done. They've kept their powers from us for generations, but it is our intelligence and ingenuity that will keep our realm rising. Receptive technology is the future!"

CHAPTER 70

QUENTI

Quenti couldn't take her eyes away from the dead councilwoman who had twice over saved her from the Haven. Blood spread like a shadow from her head, the scarf she had been wearing splayed out beside her in a matching red slash.

She could hear Francisco talking, or at least she was aware of the faint buzz of his voice in the back of her mind. She could see him placing a small, delicate metal ball into his weapon out of the corner of her eye, but she didn't tear her eyes away from Cruz, even as a councilguard kicked her body to the side, a nuisance to be dealt with rather than a human. Then Quenti was being pulled up, feet scrabbling for purchase as she was dragged toward Francisco. Her knees hit the wooden platform where Cruz's body had just been, her hot blood seeping into the knees of her pants. She almost laughed at the realization that she would be executed in the uniform of a councilguard sergeant.

A strangled cry pulled her out of her daze and she saw Khuna being pulled back to a kneeling position by a broad guard. Her face twisted in agony as she made eye contact with Quenti.

Quenti would have given anything to reach out and touch her in that moment.

It was a stupid and hopeless move, but she didn't have the self-control or energy to think it through, letting out a cry and slamming her elbow back into Francisco's shin she propelled her body forward across the platform. Her hands were tied and she lost her balance before she could move more than a few feet, but Khuna had answered her sudden movement with her own cry, twisting out of the guard's grip and scrambling against the wood planks to push herself forward.

They almost touched, foreheads only a few inches away when someone—probably Francisco—pulled Quenti back by her arms, wrenching them in their sockets. She didn't bother to hold back the scream that tore through her throat as she watched Khuna get pulled away. She barely registered the warm tip of the receptive weapon placed against her temple.

"Meet your war hero, Sergeant Lucía Canchaya," Francisco said, voice a crackle in the back of her mind. "A liar. A traitor. A bruya. And accomplice to the rebel Alara Ayar."

Quenti bit her lip as the metal pressed harder into her skull.

"Even our blameless aren't safe from the corruption of magia and these rebels. They'd have you convinced they fight for both sides, but behold their lies. Their talk of balance and peace is a charade just as this child's game of playing ally. For her crimes of treason, espionage, falsifying Council documents, attempted infiltration of the council-guard ranks, this nameless and treasonous bruya is hereby sentenced to death."

That last word drained every last drop of fight out of Quenti, and her shoulders slumped under the weight of her own shame. A voice in her mind told her to fight and scream, but she couldn't get her mouth to move. Her muscles froze, no longer under her own command.

A click echoed from beside her ear and she closed her eyes, no longer able to watch Khuna's face as it contorted from anger to terror to despair. Beyond her, she could only see a sea of faces, utterly unaffected by the lies and death being spewed before them. No one came for Cruz. No one would come for her.

There was a beat.

And then another.

Francisco jerked beside her and she let out an involuntary whimper, waiting for the pain of the explosion. It was the kind of sound the likes of which Lucía Canchaya would never make. But it didn't matter. In that moment, Quenti was herself, and she would die as herself.

Another second passed, and the release of death never came. Only the hard thud next to her followed by the sound of a small rock on wood.

"Who threw that?" Francisco asked, voice burning with barely controlled rage.

Quenti looked up, blinking against the bright sky and saw a trickle of blood falling from Francisco's hairline. The crowd was murmuring and undulating with unease. And then a small stone flew from somewhere to their left, this time skimming across Francisco's cheek.

He let out a call, pointing to somewhere in the crowd. Councilguards tried to push their way through, but the crowd wasn't moving without a struggle.

Just as the guards made it to where Francisco had pointed, another stone flew from the opposite side of the plaza.

"And when will you answer for your crimes?" a voice Quenti recognized yelled out from the crowd. She couldn't see where Manny stood, but his voice was clear and firm.

"You don't speak for all blameless!" A woman's voice this time. Though she didn't recognize it, she thought it might have been Vi.

The hum of the crowd was rising, turning into something more akin to a rumbling. More rocks flew, and Francisco's face turned the shade of his own blood, eyes wide as he swung his weapon through the air, searching out a target. But the voices were faceless, the crowd working together to hide each call and throw.

With a twitch of Francisco's finger and an explosion, more screams filled the air. The crowd scattered from where a woman's body crumpled to the ground, blood seeping from her shoulder. But in the same moment that some ran away, others moved forward, breaking through the councilguard line and storming the stage as a wave.

Quenti watched, eyes wide and chest aching. The blameless of Lejon were revolting on their behalf. The blameless were revolting for their fellow mages.

Chapter 71

Quenti

Quenti only realized that Francisco had disappeared into the crowd when a new set of hands grabbed her from behind, tugging at her arms. She screamed, thrashing forward only to hear Nico giving a sharp cry behind her.

"Stop or I'm going to end up slicing you instead of the rope!"

"Nico!"

"Hi, not-Lucía," he said, cheerful somehow in the chaos of the moment.

"What in Sol's name are you doing?"

"Helping," he said. "You're really stupid. How did you ever become a spy?"

Quenti let out a half-laugh, half-sob as her hands came free and she turned, throwing her arms around his neck and pressing a kiss against his cheek. His skin was rough and hot and she saw the blush creep up his neck.

"Why does he get the first kiss?" Khuna said behind her.

Quenti felt something in her chest release as she turned to see Khuna standing behind her, her own arms unbound. Vi and Pedra were still untying the others across the platform as Manny and Raf fought off guards.

The moment Mena was free, she jumped off the platform, ignoring the fighting around her and running straight through the crowd—toward the base. She was going after Beno and the others left in the mines that Francisco had left for dead.

Quenti turned back, not caring about the screams or blood around her. At least for the moment.

She flung herself into Khuna's open arms, pressing her tight against her chest. She might have been squeezing too tight, but Khuna's own hands clenched into her back, making their embrace all the tighter.

Quenti kissed Khuna's cheeks. Her forehead. Her nose. Her lips. She tasted of blood and dust and it was all Quenti could do to keep from simply falling to the ground right then and there, still wrapped in her arms.

"I'm so sorry," she choked out.

"What in Sol's name are you talking about?"

"I didn't save you. I left you to get captured. I should have—"

Khuna cut her off with a sharp kiss to the lips. "You're an idiot."

"Told you," Nico said from behind them.

"I'm the one who ran off to be a hero, again," Khuna said. "I'm so sorry I left you."

"Can you stop that please?" Vi stood behind them, dagger hanging loose in her hands. "We can go through all the apologies later. I'm sure you owe all of us some too."

"Right," Quenti said, scrubbing a hand across her face to wipe away the remnants of her tears. "You're all helping? I lied to you—we lied."

"I mean, yes," Vi said, giving a half-hearted shrug.

"I'm not blameless. I'm not Lucía."

Manny turned from where he was standing, having just sent a

guard flying with a hit with his club. "Just because you lied doesn't mean you were wrong."

"You're putting yourselves in danger..."

"As you pointed out before, we already were. This way, at least our anger is going to something good. We're done with whispering in crowded bars."

Vi gave a nod of assent. "When we realized what was happening —when the explosion went off and they said Francisco had ordered the mines caved in—we weren't the only ones upset. Look around, half the town brought their rawk'anas and staffs to this meeting. Lejon is done with being under Major Francisco's thumb."

Quenti couldn't speak, her words choking on her emotions as she took in the scene around her. Hundreds of civilians fighting the guards using whatever tools they had. Outnumbering them three to one—they were winning. Before she could swallow back the tears threatening to spill, Vi pulled her into a hug.

"Sorry," she said, "but now isn't the time."

"I don't know how to get the cuffs off," Nico said, motioning to their wrists, which bore the magia-suppressing bands.

"Don't worry," Quenti said. "I've been practicing my blameless fighting skills."

She ignored the small eyebrow raise from Khuna, grabbing a spear from the hands of the fallen guard nearby. There was blood on the shaft, a mixture of Francisco's and Cruz's. Quenti bit her tongue and turned her eyes away from the body of the woman before she thought too hard about her death.

Khuna grabbed a club and jumped off the stage and into the melee. Quenti followed close behind, alongside Nico and Vi. Vi wielded her dagger, taking swipes at any guard that got too close to her. Quenti was baffled at how they were about to differentiate the guards on their side versus those fighting for Francisco, but then she saw that at least a dozen nearby guards had torn the Council symbol from their uniforms, leaving behind a small, but gaping hole on their shoulders.

Confident of who she was attacking, Quenti lunged toward one of the guards with her spear, point first. The guard dodged to his left, hitting her spear with his club and sending her stumbling forward. A sharp pain shot upward as his dagger made contact with her hip.

She cursed, reaching for her magia out of habit only to fumble over a barely there thread. Her teeth clenched in frustration as she gave up, bringing the spear back around and hitting the guard's leg. It was barely enough force to send him back a step.

Quenti had raised her spear, ready to strike again, when she saw Vi running behind the guard. She sent her dagger deep into the guard's side, twisting as she pulled it out. He fell with a scream and she kicked him away, readjusting the grip on her blade.

"Okay, I was wrong," she said, looking Quenti over. "Don't take this the wrong way, but we really need to get these cuffs off."

She grimaced. "One of the guards might have a key."

Her eyes gazed over the chaos around her, trying to see if any of the councilguards had the key to the cuffs hanging from their belt. But it was too difficult to see anything, let alone a specific guard. She jumped up onto the platform, looking out across the plaza. If Francisco was still—

Just as she thought the words, a flutter of black caught her eye. At the far end of the plaza, where the square met the narrow streets of Lejon, she saw Alara in her councilguard uniform running after a larger figure dressed in black.

She was chasing after Francisco. And she was alone.

Chapter 72

Ardo

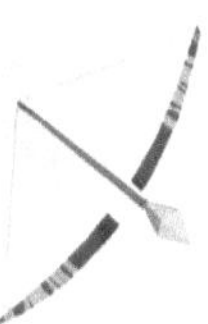

The first thing that Ardo did once he was untied was borrow the female guard's dagger to rip off the Council emblem from the shoulder of his uniform. It felt good to throw it to the ground, letting the small scrap of fabric fall through the slats of the platform and disappear. He went straight to Senye Emaru after that, helping her as she pushed herself up from the ground, arms weak and vibrating under her body with the effort.

"Lena..." she said, voice rough and raspy.

Ardo tightened his lips, not quite looking her in the eye as he led her to where Senye Cruz's body had been left.

"I'm so sorry," he said. "This wasn't part of the plan."

"It's war, my boy. None of it ever goes according to plan." Her cold hand cupped his cheek. "You've done more than you ever needed to. You came for me even after I demoted you and blamed you for Alara's own foolishness. I'd ask you how, but I'm sure it's a long story. Did I hear correctly that someone was using Lucía's name? *My* Lucía?"

He smiled. "You're right. It is a long story. But one for after this is all sorted. I should go help the others."

"I don't think I can fight," she said, face pinched, as if admitting as much had cost her dearly.

He didn't respond. There was nothing he could say. She didn't need platitudes or lies. Instead, he turned and left her sitting next to the dead body of her once friend and enemy, letting her mourn without judgment.

The others had been untied and had dispersed into the crowd, all except Dante, who was still hunched down at the corner of the platform, as though wishing for someone else to end it all for him. Ardo was almost happy to oblige. It was because of him that Senye Cruz was gone. It was because of him that everyone had been captured in the first place. He fought the urge to act rashly, and instead yanked his gaze away from the pathetic fallen rebel mage.

Ardo felt helpless looking out over the roiling crowd without a single weapon in his hand. The dead guards on the platform seemed to have already been stripped of weapons and most civilians were fighting with makeshift staffs and shovels.

He tried to locate Alara in the crowd, but it was impossible to differentiate her among the hundreds of black and red uniforms. Major Francisco and his personal guards also appeared to have disappeared from the central plaza, and he hoped, albeit dimly, that Alara wasn't chasing after the major herself.

A strangled cry drew his attention, and he saw one of the black-clad guards grabbing Dante by his collar and dragging him forward, off the platform. There was a glint of metal, and he didn't have to wonder what the guard's next move would be. Dante barely had the mental fortitude to hold himself up.

Against his instinct to let it happen, Ardo lunged forward, jumping off the platform and landing on the stones just a foot from the guard. He gave a small prayer to El'dyo that it wasn't someone he knew or recognized as he threw his punch, aiming for the woman's face. She reacted almost instantly, bringing her dagger up and catching Ardo's arm as she dodged. Dante hit the ground with a smack.

Ardo hissed at the pain in his wrist as blood welled from the cut, but he dodged her next slash, bringing his body to stand between her and Dante. The next time she lunged, he ducked, sending a kick into her shin, trying to throw her off balance. Based on how quickly she responded, the move did him no good, and he found himself dodging another series of blows, teeth clenched against each point of contact she managed with her blade.

After the fourth cut, he knew he was going to have to figure out a new strategy. Eventually she'd get in a good enough shot that would end the fight altogether, and he didn't plan on bleeding out after all the work he'd put into surviving these last few months. But the guard was relentless with the blade, giving him little time to think. She seemed determined to kill him one cut at a time.

Even after he realized what he needed to do, he hesitated for a too-long moment, dodging and almost stumbling over Dante's form behind him. The man hadn't yet managed to pull himself up and away, even with Ardo's distraction.

Shit, he thought as he clenched his teeth. The next second, the guard jabbed the dagger to the left, aiming for Ardo's shoulder. She was caught off guard when Dante's form collided into her, sending the two of them scrambling across the dirt, twisting and writhing. Ardo may not have ever seen Dante fight before, but even he could tell the attack was fully fueled by adrenaline, his form sloppy, messy, and dangerous.

Dante's knife clattered to the ground, useless to the both of them as the councilguard started to gain the upper hand in the scuffle. As she mounted him, Ardo picked up the fallen weapon and lodged it in the open spot between her clavicle and neck, hammering it deeper with his fist as blood erupted from her mouth. A few short seconds later, she fell to the ground, limp. The life drained from her eyes, yet somehow Dante's complexion was a shade paler than hers in death.

Any anger that Ardo had been grasping onto toward Dante drained from his body at the look in the man's eyes.

Ardo wordlessly draped the other man's arm over his shoulder, blood smearing across his uniform and skin. They managed to limp back onto the platform and he set Dante down next to Senye Emaru, staring out over the plaza as the fighting died down.

"This isn't what Sombria stands for," she said, voice hoarse.

"Is it not?" Dante said, his own voice barely above a whisper. "This country was built by war. Sometimes balance can only be achieved after chaos."

"So many are going to die," she said.

"So many already have." Dante's eyes rested on the still form of Senye Cruz, though they remained distant.

Ardo didn't speak through the exchange, his own eyes scanning over the crowd. The blameless villagers and few rebel guards were slowly gaining ground as the last few guards huddled into small groups, each attempting to flee the plaza. Alara was still missing, along with Francisco. And where was Quenti? Their group had all but dispersed, and he was left sitting with the injured, praying the others were still alive.

Chapter 73

Alara

Alara didn't move immediately after the rogue guard cut her binds. She stared out over the plaza, watching the people of Lejon revolting with their shovels, waqtanas, and walking sticks. These were the people she had spent her life wanting to serve and protect, but from the looks of it, they didn't need her protection. Not really.

She would never be enough to save everyone, but if she inspired others—if they spread their message and emboldened the people through their actions—they wouldn't need to fight for everyone. They could be the spark that started the fire.

And after everything she had been through, she was ready to burn all of Sombria to the ground in the process.

She stumbled to her feet, feeling lightheaded. The smell of blood was sharp in the air, and she noticed the puddle of dark red pooling out from the corner of her eye. If she turned just a few inches to the left, she'd see *her* body. Her eyes remained focused ahead, instead.

Senye Cruz had been right all along. It wasn't about being the sole person to bring down Sombria and the Council. Even someone as important as her was disposable. It was about the people as a whole.

She gazed over the chaos, her eyes drawn to the blur of black and gold from across the plaza. She sneered, seeing Major Francisco pushing through the crowd, parrying blows in order to move forward. He was running.

She could have let him go. She had promised Khuna this wouldn't come down to her killing him out of spite. But that had been before he had killed Senye Cruz in cold blood. And if he escaped Lejon today, he wouldn't give up. He wasn't just fleeing to save his skin. He was running to the remaining members of the Council to tell them what happened here. And he would come back with more guards, more receptive weaponry, and a renewed sense of purpose to rebuild the mines.

So perhaps she couldn't save everyone, but she could at least help by killing one man.

She jumped from the platform before she even thought through her plan. Her wrists were cuffed, but she could still feel the core of her magia, soft and warm in her gut. This was little different from the world she lived in not too long ago. She just needed a weapon.

Most of the townspeople around her didn't even have true weapons, fighting the guards off with whatever had been easy to grab from their homes. She saw a few coming out of the inn and the neighboring cantina wielding cooking knives and butcher blocks. But after weeks in the mine, feeling powerless and alone, all she wanted was a spear in her hands to feel whole. So she went directly toward one of the guards she saw, fighting off a half dozen towns-people with his spear. He was outnumbered but well-trained in his actions. A small part of Alara could appreciate the delicateness of his movements, the dance of the spear.

Only a small part of her though.

"Can I borrow this?" she asked, gently stopping a man from

swinging his shovel forward. His eyes widened, taking in who she was and immediately dropping the weapon, stepping back from her with a small bow.

"Yeah—yes, of course."

"Thank you," she said as she slammed the shovel into the ground and stepped hard along the neck. The wood splintered, leaving the metal behind. She was left with a terribly balanced and short staff. *Perfect.*

She didn't need to say anything. As she stepped up to the guard, the others fell back, leaving her space. The older man in the black uniform snarled as he threw himself toward her.

Alara felt alive for the first time since Lili's death—since Adelmo's death. Since this entire mess started. Their fight was more dance than scuffle, and her blood sang with every step and swing of her makeshift staff. The guard's sneer dropped from his face after only a few parries, as it became clear Alara was a true threat to him.

Her smile got wider and more gleeful with every move, as she saw the man's feet losing their balance. All she needed was a single mistake. A single swing too soon or too late. There would come a time—in only a few moves—when he'd miss his cue, and then...

Her staff caught him just under his ribs, pushing with all her strength to choke the air from his lungs. He stumbled back, but before he could even take two steps, Alara dropped her staff and used both her hands to twist his spear from his grip. She turned away without a second look.

"You can finish him," she said, throwing back the mutilated shovel to the man she'd borrowed it from.

She ran from the group without hesitation.

Major Francisco was impossible to see in the crowd. He was likely already on the edge, if not out of the plaza, but Alara had her not-so-secret skill of being small. She slipped easily through the mob, unnoticed in the wave of fighting. She was running on the adrenaline that only comes after witnessing someone close to you murdered in cold blood.

By the time she made it to the edge of the plaza, she could just make out Major Francisco turning a corner a few blocks from where she was. She let her magia flow from her, her sense of the cores around her flowing through the streets until it caught on the vague sense of someone running. The only one running in that direction.

She moved forward, pausing only to snatch a torch that was burning along the arch of the cantina door. The exhaustion and pain from the last few weeks was still there as she ran, tight and heavy in her muscles, but she pushed through. Her mind was only focused on one thing. Major Francisco.

Major Francisco who had ordered countless innocents whipped.

Major Francisco who had beaten Khuna for simply existing next to Alara.

Major Francisco who had retaliated against Sol for nothing more than being born to a bruya.

Major Francisco who had doomed hundreds to death with barely a second thought or regret.

He had a head start, but it was clear after a few blocks, he didn't think he was being followed. He slowed to a jog as Alara only pushed herself harder, twisting through the streets and alleys, following her sense of him, even as her powers strained against the cuffs.

Her footsteps must have been loud because only a few steps before she swung around the corner to meet him, she felt him pulling away faster once again.

But it was too late. She turned the corner and saw him running only a few yards away. They were on a long, narrow street, no alleys or doors for him to duck into. No where to hide, not that he could. She saw his eyes dart to the side as he slowed to a stop and knew what he was hoping for.

"Major," she said, taking two steps toward him. The trained

councilguard in him turned fully to meet her, refusing to back down from a fight.

"Traitorous pig," he said. He raised his arm, the strange exploding weapon tightly aimed on her.

She dropped the torch she had been carrying to the ground, the flame having gone out blocks before. But she didn't need an active flame. With a simple flick of her fingers, she pulled the embers from the torch at her feet, bringing them back to life and sending the ball of fire directly at his face.

He hissed as the flame hit him, the arm holding the weapon shooting up to block his face.

He screamed a curse, but she didn't stop, pulling another ball of flame and throwing it at him without pause.

He dodged, firing off his weapon at her even as he fell to the side. She flinched, instinctively, waiting for the pain. But nothing happened. He had missed.

"You'd have been better off with an arrow."

She ran forward, spear still in her hand as she moved to impale him, all her rage and desperation driving her forward. But he rolled before she reached him, throwing his useless weapon to the side and grabbing for something on his belt.

"You're wearing cuffs," he snarled. "How are you still using your magia?"

She ignored his question, jumping over him as he moved forward, trying to trip her. He grabbed at her arm and she twisted around, easily dislodging his grip.

But she had underestimated him.

With a cold snap, she felt another cuff fit over her forearm, just above the one on her left wrist. Her sense of her core spluttered out almost immediately. It was nothing like being in the mines, but she still couldn't catch the threads there long enough to use them.

She only stumbled for a beat, cold at the loss of her fire. But she still had a spear. And she still had her training.

She whirled around, bringing her spear down to meet his club even as he lunged for her. It was a good move. A perfect deflection.

But the spear had already been through countless fights and Francisco's arms were the size of Alara's legs. Only a moment after the initial block, he swung again. Not for her, but for her spear, and with an echoing crack, it snapped in her hands. She fell back, fumbling for a large piece of the end. It was just enough to raise up above her head and block the next swing, but her arms were shaking and his lips were curled.

She was losing the fight. Not because of lack of skill or passion, but because he was simply bigger and stronger.

A blow to the head turned everything black for the briefest of seconds, and Alara found herself holding up her arms to block him, only for his fist to break through and land another sharp hit to her cheek.

"You want to try to kill me?" he yelled out. "Fine! This is what happens when you try to incite a rebellion."

It was only then that Alara noticed Major Francisco had tossed his club to the side in favor of bare fists.

Bare fists, and yet he was still beating her.

"I don't care how many of you there are," he continued. "We blameless will rise up, and we will *stop* you. Every time, every bruya, every rebel. Every. Mage."

Another blow to her face, and she tried to pull at the threads of magia again to no avail.

No.

This couldn't be it. This couldn't be how it ended.

Her guard dropped, weakness overtaking her and opening her face up for another assault, the taste of copper thick in her swelling mouth.

She could feel her consciousness retreating, each blow numbing her senses and making it more difficult to breathe, let alone concentrate on… what was it?

Another hit.

It was somehow becoming harder and harder to even realize she was in a fight for her life. That each swing from the man on top of her brought her closer to eternal unconsciousness.

Only seconds earlier, she had found the thought of death repulsive and terrifying. Now, the prospect was a release. Her arms dropped at her sides and she felt herself smiling, waiting for the next hit.

As darkness took over the corners of her vision, it started to feel as though he had stopped altogether, as though the punches no longer held any power over her.

And then she slipped away, desperately clinging to the afterlife that awaited her.

CHAPTER 74

QUENTI

It took Quenti too long to make her way through the mob and onto the nearly empty street beyond. She stared down the wide sandy road, eyes tracing over each and every offshoot and turn.

"You did it again," she said aloud.

You ran off alone. Alone to die. But she wasn't alone. Alara didn't have to fight this battle alone. When would she learn?

The sandy streets were a confusing mess of footsteps, but one pair stood around among the others, small and precise and fresh. She kept her eyes on Alara's prints, ignoring all else. The fuegen was so far ahead, but Quenti was taller and faster.

Quenti turned the last corner to see Francisco on the ground, legs straddling a slight, sprawled figure. She couldn't even see the figure's face, only dark red splattered across the sand around her like spilled ink. She looked... dead.

Alara looked dead.

Quenti moved forward, acting on pure instinct as she brought the spear down, the tip aimed at Francisco. She'd expected for the spear to cut through his neck, already relishing the feeling. But with the speed of someone half his size, he twisted, forearm knocking away the spear in the same moment he sent his shoulder into her side, throwing her over him and into the sand.

She was quick to her feet, her body remembering Khuna's and Ardo's training on instinct.

Never turn your back to the enemy.

Francisco still straddled Alara on his knees, fists smeared in red, the dark spatters a map across his face. Quenti kept her eyes raised to his, refusing to look down at the lifeless form beneath him.

Get up, you idiot. You are not dying like this.

"Lucía Canchaya," Francisco said, voice breathy, somehow more gravelly than usual. He climbed to his feet, stepping over Alara, ignoring her like a husk doll on the side of a dirt road. His face twisted into a tight sneer. "You were a pathetic excuse for a sergeant. I should have never fallen for your ruse."

He was angry at himself. She could see it in the set of his shoulders and the deep lines along his face. Pride swelled in her chest and she smiled.

"Too bad you're not as smart as you think."

She lunged forward, shifting her balance and gripping her spear just like she was taught. She hoped to use the moment of surprise, but before her spear made contact, he'd sidestepped it, sending a punch into her side and throwing her off balance.

Pain radiated through her ribs, but Quenti didn't stop to catch her breath. She only turned again, bringing the spear down against his shoulder. The tip only bounced off his armor as he lunged forward. This time his fist made contact with the space just beneath her ribs, ripping the air from her lungs.

She fell back, barely keeping her feet under her. Francisco stood a few feet away, lips twisted into a sneer.

"Who would have guessed that Lucía the war hero would end up a traitor. A traitor to her own people. You don't deserve the title of hero, and you don't deserve the title of blameless."

Quenti's hand tightened along the staff of her spear, and she smiled. Dante may have betrayed their escape attempt and goals, but Francisco still had no idea who she really was.

"You're right," she said.

This time she didn't bother with her spear, dropping it as she brought her hands up.

"My name is Quenti Mandu." She called on the cool magia within her chest. "And I am an aguen and a bruya."

She took the briefest moment to savor the look of surprise and realization in his face as water coalesced from the air and houses around them, forming to wrap around his head.

She thought she might have even seen fear glinting in his eyes as the water cut off his air supply. There was no time to interpret his expression as he ran forward, heedless of his lack of air, and slammed his entire weight into her body.

Her vision went black for a single moment as her head made contact with the hardened sandy road, the impact shuddering through her bones and muscles a second later.

Again, she remembered her training, scrambling to her feet and turning to face Francisco before he could make a follow-up attack. Her body ached and shallow breaths burned her chest.

Francisco stared back at her, uniform soaked, and eyes narrowed. "Very clever," he said. "It never dawned on me that you'd be a filthy bruya. You and Ayar have a lot more in common than I thought."

Quenti refused to take the comment as an insult, instead trying to figure out something—anything—she could do to win. That sneak attack had been her only chance, and now the element of surprise was all but gone.

"You're both little girls who have bitten off way more than they can chew," he continued. He planted his feet on the ground, raising his fists in the air. "And I'm through playing war with two —ugh!"

An arrow sprouted from Francisco's left shoulder, sending him jerking forward, though he caught himself from falling, feet planting harder into the ground. He spun around, eyes wild and desperate to see who had dared attack him.

Nico's stoic face looked back at the major, eyes boring into him. "That's for my cousin."

"Who?" Francisco growled.

"Someone who you had arrested and killed. Another in a long list of forgotten."

Quenti didn't waste any time. She closed the gap between her and Francisco in a second, bringing a punch down to the back of his head. Pain sprouted in her fist, and she felt a shock run up her arm. The attack had connected, but it didn't have nearly the impact on him as it did on her.

Instead, it only seemed to further anger him. He spun around, yelling as he took an angry swing at her, only just missing as she tumbled to the sand. With the arrow sticking out of his shoulder, he looked more like an angry monkey than a person. But desperate and angry animals always proved to be the most dangerous.

A loud *thunk* rang out and Francisco's head jerked to the left as a club connected with it. Manny looked at Quenti with a smirk before swinging the club upward, trying to catch Francisco's face on the upswing.

The original blow had nearly sent Francisco to the ground, but he somehow planted his feet even harder, holding his body up as they sank deeper into the sand. Still, he managed to dodge the second swing from Manny, grabbing the councilguard in the neck with a clenched hand.

"You... traitors." The veins on Francisco's hands grew more prominent as he squeezed harder, turning Manny's face a sickening blue. Yet another arrow sprouted from Francisco, this one from his right shoulder, and Manny fell to the ground. Francisco let out a feral growl, falling to his knees.

"You traitors," he said, his whisper intense and accusing. "You sick, twisted bruya lovers. This isn't the end. You will all face the wrath of the Council. You and your families will fa—"

A final arrow through his throat choked off his words, and he fell to the ground, blood pooling and soaking into the sand beneath his body. Silent at last.

Quenti took several deep breaths, almost not believing the man in front of her was gone. Manny's eyes caught her gaze and they shared a brief smile.

"Sorry, Sergeant," Nico said as he approached cautiously, bow still in hand, an arrow nocked, just in case. "I said I may kill the pig myself one day."

"It's Quenti," she said softly. "Quenti Mandu. And I am not a sergeant or blameless, and I'm definitely not a war hero."

Nico looked down at the prone body of Fransisco, eyes darkening. "I wouldn't be so sure about that."

A weight lifted off her chest as she shared a smile with him. No longer hiding. No longer afraid.

She didn't have long to celebrate. It took no longer than a second before a fresh panic rose within her and she scrambled to the small lifeless body twenty feet away. The stupid girl who could never help but run off into danger by herself.

She looked... but she couldn't be...

"Alara," she said, her gaze settling on the girl's swollen, bloody face.

Alara's eyes were glazed over, distant. Quenti had seen that look before. The look of the dead.

No, no, no, no.

"Alara, wake up! Please, wake up." She smacked at her face, ignoring the globs of blood leaking out, slaps growing harsher and more panicked by the second. She was *not* being left behind. Not like this.

And then the girl blinked, the glaze subsiding.

Alara's chest rose and she coughed, sending a pool of blood from her mouth.

Oh, thank Sol!

Quenti set to work sitting Alara up, allowing her to spit out even more blood.

"You idiot!" Quenti said, unable to stop the tears from pooling in her eyes. "When are you going to learn not to go running off on your own?"

"Sorry," Alara said, voice uncharacteristically weak and submissive. "I promise I won't do it again."

Quenti pulled the other girl into a soft embrace, tight enough to be felt, but soft enough so as not to overwhelm.

"I really don't believe you," Quenti said, words choked with tears.

"Did we get him?" Alara said. Her voice was still distant, but firm and cognizant.

Quenti turned to look at Major Francisco next to them. Blood leaked from his wounds, sluggish but steady, his mouth opening and closing for another second before stilling altogether.

"We got him," Quenti said.

"Good."

Quenti felt a warm hand on her shoulder and she turned, surprised to see Khuna standing above her, taking in the bloody tableau in front of them, eyes a little too wide. Behind her, Nico and Manny stepped away, giving the three of them space.

"Are you two okay?" she asked, voice soft.

Quenti only nodded, not quite trusting her voice.

"Alara," Khuna said as she took in the image of the girl's face. "What in th—?"

"—she's okay," Quenti said, giving Khuna a reassuring gaze. Alara had already been through a lot. She didn't need to be scolded again. That would come later. She imagined the others would have plenty to say, too.

Khuna nodded, lips tight, understanding. "Fine. We should get back to the plaza," Khuna said, leaning forward to help Alara from the ground.

Alara was pale and shaking, but her eyes were still focused on Francisco's body.

"I'm..." Alara said, voice distant. "I'm a little jealous you all killed him."

"Is that your way of thanking me for saving your life?"

"We helped, thank you very much," Manny said behind them.

Alara gave a weak wave and slurred, "Nice to meet you," before leaning back into Quenti's side.

With that, the five of them turned, ready to return to the plaza.

Before they could take three steps, a mob materialized a few blocks ahead of them. They were dressed in black, their uniforms dusty and dirty, but in one piece, their Council emblems shining bright in the late evening sun.

As they made eye contact, the guards looked just as surprised to see them as they were. They hadn't been chasing after them, meaning they'd either been retreating or looking for Major Francisco. Either way, it didn't take them long to notice the major's prostrate form and the bloody bruyas and rebel councilguards standing next to it.

With a shout, the guards ran forward, weapons raised.

Their small group didn't need to communicate. Quenti took a couple steps back, Alara still half hanging off her. They were both a liability at this point.

The others would have to fight without them.

Khuna, Manny, and Nico raised their weapons, confident in their stances even outnumbered five to one. Alara grasped her hand tightly, as if even she was wondering where this fight would end.

But even as Quenti braced herself, yet another sound drew her attention.

Behind them, from the other side of the street, yet another mob appeared, this one wearing a rainbow of colors and their assortment of makeshift weapons raised high as they ran. This group vastly outnumbered the guards in their black uniforms, funneling onto the street like a crashing wave. The mob of black turned and ran, no longer focused on the five of them. The mob passed them by, not so much as slowing down as they rushed after the councilguards—citizens warding off the very people who claimed to protect them.

Manny and Nico exchanged a look as they watched the wave of civilians pass them.

"I don't know if they'll need saving, but you can always offer," Quenti said, smiling. Their faces showed the same light Alara's did when faced with a fight. Manny and Nico gave a brief salute before they both turned and followed after the mob.

Quenti wanted to hope they would catch the councilguards, but she didn't have the energy to do more than watch them disappear.

"It can't be that easy," Khuna said.

"Won't be," Alara said through swollen lips. "Not over yet."

Though she may have sounded funny saying it, Alara was right. Any councilguards they didn't catch would likely find their way back to Cielo and the Council. This wouldn't be the last Lejon would see of them. They'd take time to regroup and make a plan, especially with Francisco gone and the chaos that was the rest of Sombria.

But with the value those mines still brought with receptives and Alkay stone, it would only be a matter of time before they came back.

That would be a problem for another day.

"We should find the others," Quenti said with a heavy breath, hopeful everyone else was still safe.

CHAPTER 75

ALARA

They walked back to the plaza in silence.

Halfway there, Alara found herself able to walk again without relying on Quenti, albeit much slower than normal.

Her body had stopped shaking, but she still felt like death, which made sense given how close she was to dying. And all because she had yet again put herself into another stupid situation with Francisco.

She would have to work on that... but not now. Right now, all she wanted to do was curl up on a soft bed and sleep for the next month. She chose to ignore the fact that she'd be leaving to go over the Ruinedlands as soon as everyone recovered. She'd worry about that after she rested.

People were scattered across the plaza when they finally returned —the injured, the dead, and those left caring for the former. Whatever guards were left had their emblem torn from their uniforms and were helping gather weapons and bodies. Alara caught sight of Runeo helping tie two guards together, even as one continued to struggle.

She headed straight for the center of the plaza and the platform that rested there. Ardo was standing over Emaru and Dante, looking the part of mother hen as he bound their wounds and fussed over them.

Before she could decide where to go or what to do next, Ardo was looking up from his task, bright eyes meeting hers from across the space. He jumped from the platform, long strides bringing him to her in an instant. She flinched, not knowing what to expect as he looked down at her, eyes burning with a mess of emotions she couldn't untangle.

He didn't hit her. Or kiss her. He grabbed her shoulders, giving her the slightest of shakes. He opened his mouth, as if to speak, but nothing came out.

"Francisco," she said, answering the unasked question. Her tongue darted out to taste the iron and salt of her blood still trickling down her lips, and she could feel a tightness along the left side of her face, where it was swollen. Ardo snarled, looking over Alara's shoulder. It was like he expected the major to materialize from within the crowd.

"He's dead."

He looked back down at her, "Did you...?"

"No," she gave a half smile. "Quenti and her councilguard friends." It was an odd thing to say. Quenti was the last person in the world she'd expected to make friends with councilguards.

Ardo's body was tense and unmoving, looking down at her and letting the silence linger as his eyes swept across every detail of her beaten face. And then he pulled her close, cradling her face into his chest, though with a tenderness she hadn't expected.

"If you ever do something like that again. I will kill you myself."

"You can try." She smiled and then winced as it cracked one of the cuts on her lips open.

After a few short seconds—not long enough—he held her by the shoulders in front of him, eyes raking over the damage on her face. "You need to find a healer."

She nodded, looking at the people around them, beaten and bloody the same as her. "I'm not the only one."

Her breath caught as her eyes found Runeo in the crowd, glaring at them from where he stood. He glanced away the moment they made eye contact, but he made no attempt to hide his scowl. She turned back to Ardo before her mind could wonder what his look had meant.

"How are they?" she asked, motioning at Dante and Emaru. She moved toward them, letting Ardo follow.

"Fine—they'll live," he said, voice strained.

"Is that your professional opinion?" Dante said, groaning as he attempted to stand. Even to Alara, his jibe felt forced, and she did her best to ignore the errant glances he made over to Senye Cruz's body.

"Yes," he said, pushing him back down with a gentle hand as he stepped back onto the platform. "As are my orders for you two to not move until we get a real healer here. And that," he said, turning to Alara and pushing her gently to sit beside them, "goes double for you."

The next few days went by in a blur. Quenti helped the blameless set up a triage center at the inn in the plaza, treating the number of wounded, townspeople and guards alike—including Alara. Quenti didn't have any particular skills in healing, but she joked she was better at it than she was at fighting, so it was where she wanted to spend her energy.

Any guards willing to denounce the Council were given free leave, while those loyal few who had survived the battle were kept in the town's original jail. The small building hadn't been used in years, not since Francisco had taken over the punishment in Lejon, using the mine for every infraction, bruya, mage, or blameless.

Alara and the others had spent that time, as ironic as it felt, back in the mines, digging and moving stones. After the dust of the battle had settled, Quenti had told them she'd seen Mena running off toward the mines right after everything had started. They found her there, fingers bloody, face pale, as she shoveled away the rocks and dirt, digging at the collapsed hall that had once been a shaft and lift. She wasn't the only one, either. A handful of other townspeople and guards had chosen to start the rescue instead of taking part in the battle in town.

By the third day of digging, the vast majority of folks able to stand and lift had taken to helping with the rescue, moving rocks in a slow progression, chipping away at the mess Francisco had left behind. They did it all manually, any tierren well enough to use their magia assigned to the medical tents.

Ardo worked beside Alara. Everyone had been eating and sleeping in shifts, and they hadn't had more than a few seconds to themselves. More surprisingly, Runeo and Ardo had spent hours working next to each other, any disputes either forgotten or left unmentioned. Even Runeo's sharp looks of disdain had softened.

"I hear something!" A shout went down the line and suddenly everyone within the caves was running toward the heart of the cave-in. Mena was at the forefront, shakily lifting away another boulder. Alara wondered, not for the first time, if the woman had slept since the battle. If she had, Alara suspected it was inside the mine and standing up, just in case she was needed.

Ardo, Runeo, and another man pushed forward to help Mena move a rather large boulder. And with that, a pale hand shot up from between the stones, sending a ripple of gasps through the crowd.

They moved quickly after that, the last few stones pulled aside and the opening stabilized. After the first man emerged from the rubble, he was followed by a never-ending line of survivors.

Those who could walk were pointed toward the town, where the healers waited. Others were worse for wear, barely able to pull themselves out.

Khuna ran into town and grabbed Quenti and a handful of healers willing to set up a second triage center on the base. There was a healing ward already set up in a secondary building, so it wasn't a difficult ask. More than anything, Alara was sickened at the fact that even by that evening, there were still people slowly trickling from the levels below, each more haggard than the last. And she knew how many would likely never come out.

Alara refused to move from the main opening deep into Level One as they pulled people out, even as her legs began to shake with exhaustion. Mena hadn't either, each new hand sending a wave of elation and then disappointment across her face as another person was pulled out that wasn't her brother. Runeo was there too, helping others from the rubble, and Alara thought he might be looking for Sol and Dez in the survivors, just as much as she was.

There were a handful of guards that came out, shaken, but alive. Each was taken into temporary custody to be interviewed prior to their official release. Manny had decided on this course of action, wanting to give every guard a second chance. Alara imagined many of them would take it, given that their major had buried them as a means to an end. The ex-guard had also started up a small temporary government made up of a few other former councilguards and a few townspeople to help make decisions about the changes that were inevitable to come.

The sound of her name drew Alara's attention, and she squinted into the crowd. All she saw was a blur of brown and black before a small girl wrapped her arms around Alara's waist and legs, fingers grasping at her tightly as the child sobbed.

"Sol!" she cried, leaning forward and scooping up the child in her arms. "Your mom?" she asked, stomach already sick with dread.

"Alive, thanks to you," Dez said, stumbling out, following her child in wrapping her arms around Alara, though more tentatively. Runeo was there a moment later, joining their tangle of limbs. She didn't even know she was crying until she felt the older woman's fingers brushing across her cheeks.

It was only then that Alara noticed the rags wrapped around the young girl's eyes.

"Can you... can you see?" Alara said.

"Just a little," the girl said. "Mom said it's going to get real bright soon."

"We're taking it slow," Dez said. "But I can't wait for her to be able to see life above ground. To experience the sun."

Alara directed Sol and her mother to one of the healing stations, but was surprised when Dez didn't immediately move. Instead, she lingered, face wrinkled with uncertainty.

"Do you..." she said. "Do you know a Mena?"

Mena's head jerked at the call, eyes finding Dez with some confusion.

"Yes?"

Dez sighed, though whether or not it was from relief or dread, Alara couldn't tell. "This is for you." Still holding Sol at her hip, she reached over and set a small blue earring into Mena's outstretched hand. Alara recognized it immediately as the one Beno had snatched from Level Five. "A man down there. He wanted you to have it."

The bruya was looking down at her hands as if the earring might start talking. Or as if Beno might jump from the mines at any moment. Neither happened.

"He saved my daughter," Dez said, choking on the words. "He died down there saving her."

Mena's head moved up and down, in some version of a nod, and then she crumbled, knees buckling, and a sob tore from her throat as she clutched the earring to her chest. Runeo moved first, scooping up the woman in his arms, not bothering to ask her if she was okay. She wasn't.

And like that, with Mena crying in Runeo's arms, even as his own tears tracked trails of dirt and dust down his face. Alara swallowed her own grief down, focusing instead on the woman and girl that needed her. She helped Dez walk with Sol grasped in her arms. Runeo and Mena followed behind them, and the five of them exited the mines for what she hoped was the last time.

Dez stumbled as they came to the opening that led to the surface. It was near sunset and the sky was the color of the soil, a deep magenta.

"Do you see it, Sol?" Dez said, eyes narrowed against the dim light, even still, and she was trembling where she stood. "The light from the sun?"

It was her turn to have tears flowing silently down her face. Alara wasn't even looking at the sunset. She was too focused watching Dez's and Sol's faces as they felt the touch of the sun on their skin.

CHAPTER 76

QUENTI

The smoke choked Quenti's lungs, bringing her back to day Arbol fell. A time not so long ago, yet somehow an eternity ago.

She grabbed Khuna's hand beside her and squeezed, trying to push the thought from her mind. The funeral pyres outside of town burned so hot and bright that even miles north they could smell the smoke.

Their small group had attended the burnings briefly to honor the dead blameless before marching off north for their own small service.

They lined up in front of the two graves, silent and solemn. Beno's body still hadn't been found in the labyrinth of the mines, but Mena carved him a stone nonetheless, and she carefully moved it to sit next to the mound of dirt where Lena Cruz now rested.

They were all drawn and tired, but Mena looked mind-cleansed, as if any thoughts had been sucked away with the death of her brother. Quenti wasn't even sure she'd heard the woman speak since she'd come back from the mines covered in dirt. Not since Alara had explained what had happened.

It made it all the more startling when she heard the strangled sob leave the woman's throat as she kneeled at her brother's grave. This strong, powerful woman, brought down by her grief. Before Quenti could quite register what Mena was doing, she saw her grab her ear and let out another pained cry. It was as though her entire world had crumbled around her.

Quenti had never had any siblings, but she imagined losing him wouldn't feel much different from losing Khuna. The very thought had her clenching her girlfriend's hand all the tighter.

Runeo moved first from where he stood between Alara and Khuna, hand reaching out to grip Mena's.

"Don't..." he said softly.

"I want—I need to—" Mena said, voice rough from disuse.

"Let me do it then," he said, plucking a small earring from her hand. It was small, not even the size of a marble, an azure blue that matched the earring Mena wore in her right ear. With a gentleness that Quenti didn't think Runeo held, he grasped Mena's left ear and pressed the earring forward with a sharp twist.

Mena didn't so much as wince in pain as the earring pierced her left lobe. Once it was in, she reached up to touch the gem before standing, still emotionless.

"Beno always joked," Mena said, "that he was the careless twin. That it was only a matter of time before I wore these for the both of us. He always said, if he had it his way, he'd never live in a world without me in it."

Mena paused, taking a shaky breath, stoic face wrinkling into another sob. "I take solace in the fact that he'll never have to. May Sol bless his heart and his being." With that, she turned to Runeo, wrapping him in a tight hug.

No one spoke as they slowly filtered away from the small copse of trees, leaving behind the two new graves.

"I almost don't want to leave," Khuna said, looking out over the plaza from the small window in their room. They were back in the inn where they had started, but now, as heroes of the town, they each had their own bed. Khuna and Quenti even had a room to themselves. And what's more, they no longer had to hide.

Quenti had spent her time in Lejon masquerading as a war hero, and now she truly was—one of her own making.

She stared directly east toward where the Ruinedlands were tucked behind the buildings of town. That was where they were going next. It was impossible not to feel a sense of dread at the inevitable.

"At least there won't be fish on this trip," she said, trying to keep her voice light.

"Ugh," Khuna said, collapsing next to Quenti on their bed. "Who knows what there'll be to eat out there."

"Cursed bones and sand?" she said with a grin.

"We may even want fish by the time it's all over."

They laughed. Even with the small trickle of guilt Quenti felt at allowing herself any joy after everything, it felt nice to simply lay next to Khuna and pretend they could live the life they had planned in Arbol.

Mena was still barely holding herself together and had since spent her time twisting her new earring non-stop, eyes distant, thoughts likely on her brother.

Dante, on the other hand, already couldn't shut up about the mission immediately after the service, very clearly desperate to make amends after giving away their plans to Francisco under duress. Though when Alara had pointed out that he could barely stand, even he couldn't argue that they needed to rest longer.

"We still have some time," Khuna said. "It'll be at least a few days until I'm in walking condition, a few more for Alara's face to heal, and at least a week until Dante is in any shape to move at all. The tierren are still trying to understand why the pain in his back hasn't improved." The rest of the group had largely stayed silent about Dante's betrayal, though it was something they'd all likely have to address at some point. None of them knew what he'd gone through while with Francisco, but Quenti wasn't sure she saw it as an excuse.

Quenti hummed, twisting her own body so that she and Khuna were lying face to face on the bed. Her lips danced in a playful smile as she leaned forward, pressing them to Khuna's own.

"I can think of some ways to spend our time." Her lips moved down, ghosting over Khuna's neck and her collarbone. She traced her fingers along the hem of her tunic, pushing it up and away so she could run her hands along Khuna's bare skin. She felt the muscles rippling and moving under her touch, and soft gasps escaped the bruya's lips as Quenti explored. Her stomach turned with acid to feel the new scabs and scars that marred her partner's skin. She had only been allowed glimpses of the girl's back since she'd made it out of the mines, always twisting at awkward angles to stop Quenti from seeing it straight on. She knew from Alara what had happened. But wondered when Khuna would let her see.

She let out a groan as Khuna's fingers slipped under her own tunic, moving against her heated skin. But before they had a chance to do more, the door behind them burst open and Alara stormed in.

"Do you have them?"

Khuna's face was bright red, but Quenti turned to look over her shoulder, eyes hot with annoyance.

"What in Sol's name are you doing?"

"Do you have them?"

"What?" Quenti said, pushing herself away from Khuna, any semblance of intimacy now gone from the room.

"The viajera. The dagger. Please tell me you have them."

"Why would I?"

"They're gone," Alara said, voice starting to shake.

Now Khuna was sitting up, too, body going rigid.

"I'm sure Mena has them or maybe Runeo—he's always digging into things that aren't his business."

Alara shook her head, slumping against the wall and letting herself slowly fall to the floor.

"I already asked. They don't have them. Neither does Dante."

"So—have you asked..." Quenti said, eyebrows furrowed.

Alara's fists clenched and she let out something close to a growl.

"Emaru and Ardo are gone."

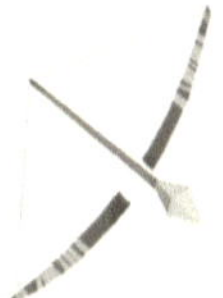

Alara was going to kill him.

Ardo had no doubt about that. The next time she saw him, she'd shove a dagger into his neck before he had a chance to explain.

Or maybe El'dyo would be on his side for once.

"We should stop soon," Senye Emaru said beside him, out of breath. "We don't want to travel here in the dark."

Ardo could only nod. He knew he couldn't even imagine what the mage was feeling, crossing the black sands beneath their feet. To him, the Ruinedlands felt like a place of unease, but for the woman who'd spent weeks trapped in the mines without her magia, he imagined choosing to traverse a land with similar dangers would be near torturous.

Senye Emaru was still pale from her time in the mines, but she had healed for the most part and was moving with determination. Alara's dagger—as Ardo had taken to calling it—was wrapped and slung to her belt, and she was holding the viajera, tracing the small needle as it moved slowly with every step. It wasn't a normal compass, focused on pointing north. Instead, it wavered and moved, but the arrow pointed generally east. It was leading them into the heart of the Ruinedlands.

He looked back behind them, where he could just make out the tips of buildings of Lejon in the distance, peeking out from behind the rainbow dunes they had already crossed over. He sent another prayer to El'dyo that Alara would forgive him.

That she would realize they were fighting for the same side after all.

At least, he hoped they were.

END OF BOOK TWO OF
THE MAGE WAR CHRONICLES

Want a Free Book?

Yes, we're a little crazy. We're offering you a free ebook, on the house!

Journey across the Ruinedlands in the same world as *City of Mages*, to the warring city-states of Anillo and Xaca. Witness Mariela as she tries to reclaim her country from her stepfather—with a little help from a talking firebird and a generations-long enemy, the leader of Anillo.

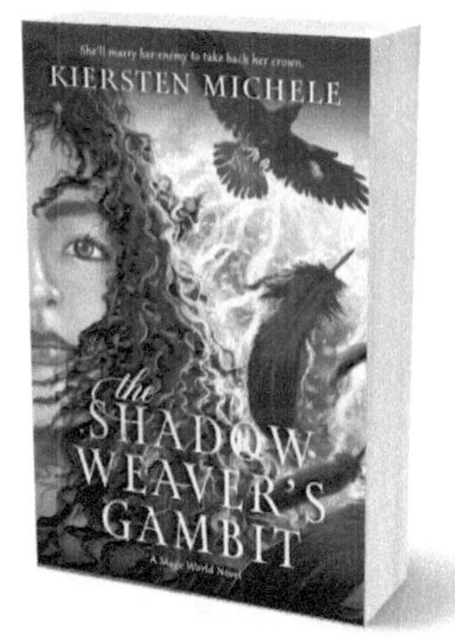

This action-packed Romantasy is perfect for lovers of *Dance of Thieves*, *We Hunt the Flame*, and of course, *City of Mages*.

Pick up your free copy at: https://BookHip.com/CKFMXRQ

THANK YOU, PATRONS!

This book was a couple of years in the making, and in the deepest midsts of drafting, editing, and everything in between, I (A.J. Cerna) had a handful of loyal Patrons at my side. I want to thank each and every one of you for your loyalty and support.

I hope *City of Mages* was worth the wait!

PATRONS

<u>Specter Seeker Tier</u>
J Soderberg

<u>Bruya Tier</u>
Steven Beal

<u>Magite Tier</u>
Bernardo Nuno
Derek Alan Siddoway

Join us on Patreon and get featured in A.J. Cerna's next book:
Patreon.com/magiabooks

About Kiersten Michele

KIERSTEN MICHELE is an author and bookworm who spends her mornings, evenings, weekends, and in-between times reading. She grew up on mysteries, fantasies, historical fictions, and any other story that would take her on an adventure. Her love of reading turned into a love of writing, and she took that love to college and… got a PhD in counseling psychology. Plot twist. But when she's not writing *extremely fascinating* academic articles, she's creating stories to take her on more adventures.

Her books so far consist of *The Shadow Weaver's Gambit* and *The Mage War Chronicles*.

When not tucked into her reading chair, she's out adventuring in the real world, climbing rocks, hiking rocks, and taking way too many photos of rocks.

instagram.com/authorkiersten

youtube.com/@magiareads

ABOUT A.J. CERNA

A.J. CERNA is an author, film-lover, gamer, and all-around story junkie. Like any healthy kid, he grew up imbibing fantasy novels, anime, manga, and movies, and realized at a young age that writing stories was the best way one could spend their time. Eventually, he found his way into film school, where he got his degree in screenwriting. In his time in Hollywood, he pitched animated series around town and worked in the anime dubbing industry in various capacities. He also ran the film site *LRM Online* as editor-in-chief for several years, which allowed him to write about the stories he loves when he wasn't writing stories himself.

His series consist of *Djinn Tamer*, *Champions of MythRune*, *Spectral*, and *The Mage War Chronicles*.

When not reading or writing, he can be found hiking, podcasting, gaming, or checking out the latest craft beer breweries.

Books by A.J. Cerna

THE DJINN TAMER SERIES

Djinn Tamer: Starter (Bronze League Book 1)
Djinn Tamer: Rivals (Bronze League Book 2)
Djinn Tamer: Evolution (Bronze League Book 3)

Champions of MythRune

Spectral

facebook.com/ajcernawriter
x.com/AJCernaWriter
instagram.com/ajcernawriter
youtube.com/@magiareads